Louise Fuller was once a ̶t̶___
pink and always wanted to ___
Princess! Now she enjoys c̶___
aren't pretty push-overs but strong, believable
women. Before writing for Mills & Boon she
studied literature and philosophy at university, and
then worked as a reporter on her local newspaper.
She lives in Tunbridge Wells with her impossibly
handsome husband Patrick and their six children.

Clare Connelly was raised in small-town Australia
among a family of avid readers. She spent much
of her childhood up a tree, Mills & Boon book in
hand. Clare is married to her own real-life hero,
and they live in a bungalow near the sea with their
two children. She is frequently found staring into
space—a surefire sign that she's in the world of
her characters. She has a penchant for French food
and ice-cold champagne, and Mills & Boon novels
continue to be her favourite ever books. Writing for
Modern is a long-held dream. Clare can be contacted
via clareconnelly.com or at her Facebook page.

BOUND & CROWNED

LOUISE FULLER

CLARE CONNELLY

MILLS & BOON

First published in Great Britain 2025
by Mills & Boon, an imprint of HarperCollins*Publishers* Ltd,
1 London Bridge Street, London, SE1 9GF

www.harpercollins.co.uk

HarperCollins*Publishers*, Macken House, 39/40 Mayor Street Upper,
Dublin 1, D01 C9W8, Ireland

Bound & Crowned © 2025 Harlequin Enterprises ULC

Royal Ring of Revenge © 2025 Louise Fuller

Twins for His Majesty © 2025 Clare Connelly

ISBN: 978-0-263-34471-4

07/25

MIX
Paper | Supporting
responsible forestry
FSC™ C007454

This book contains FSC™ certified paper
and other controlled sources to ensure responsible forest management.

For more information visit www.harpercollins.co.uk/green.

Printed and Bound in the UK using 100% Renewable Electricity
at CPI Group (UK) Ltd, Croydon, CR0 4YY

ROYAL RING OF REVENGE

LOUISE FULLER

MILLS & BOON

CHAPTER ONE

BETTY'S FATHER WAS waiting for her in one of the private lounges that offered both afternoon sunlight and unparalleled views of Morroello and its famous brick-built *campanile*. She stopped the requisite three feet away, gave a small, bobbing curtsey and then, stepping closer, brushed first one papery cheek, then the other, with her lips. Theirs was not an affectionate relationship, but convention required that she kiss her father and so that was what she did.

'Papà—'

'Bettina—'

He gestured towards one of the silk-covered armchairs that her mother had chosen during her last redecoration of the palace. The silk was pale peach with tiny embroidered blooms and delicate green foliage to symbolise the national flower of Malaspina, the bergamot. It was exquisite and impractical, a bit like her mother.

'Is everything all right? Are you feeling—?'

'I'm fine.' Her father waved his hand as if he were dismissing a particularly irritating fly. 'Leave us.'

As the uniformed footman retreated from the room, Betty sat down, folding her knees sideways and sitting up straight. Her father was looking at her critically. 'You've caught the sun.'

She felt her cheeks burn then, just as if the sun's rays had touched her there. In addition to her sunny nature and sweet smile, her younger sister, Bella, had been born with the kind of enviable smooth, golden skin that rarely if ever burned. Betty, on the other hand, required the thickest, highest SPF so that she looked as if she had slathered herself in white emulsion paint. At best, a day sitting in the sun would result in a smattering of freckles on her shoulders and along her cheekbones, but more likely her skin would turn a vivid and painful scarlet before peeling to reveal new, even paler skin.

It was one of the downsides of being a redhead.

There were others, the most significant of which was the fact that neither of her parents shared her fiery hair and pale complexion and so there had been questions asked both in private and in public about her paternity. Jokes made in the media at her father's expense, which he hated of course. Which was maybe why he hated her.

Her throat tightened, clamping around her breath so that it was suddenly hard to swallow.

He didn't actually hate her, she thought dully. Hating anything would require an intensity of emotion that was not simpatico with being the Prince of Malaspina, so his frustration and fury were suppressed because her father never forgot, even for a moment, that he was a prince, and the ruler of the principality, a king in all but name.

She could never forget it either, or that she was a princess and the heir apparent to the throne. Since childhood, she had been drilled to appear dutiful and compliant. No whisper of scandal or rumours of even the slightest indiscretion had ever been attached to her.

But it had come at a price.

She glanced over to where her father sat in his wing

armchair, his cufflinks gleaming at his wrists, his cravat loosely knotted beneath his smooth face.

No, he didn't hate her. It was worse than that. He was disappointed by her.

Had been disappointed by her since she emerged from the womb, not the longed-for son but a daughter with the wrong colour hair.

Wrong everything.

'You should be more careful.'

I was careful, she thought. I am always careful. But it was never enough for either of her parents. She was never enough, had disappointed both of them since conception when her mother had been horribly ill during the pregnancy to the point that she'd had to be hospitalised.

Her father shifted in his seat. 'Remember that you don't have your sister's skin.'

How could she not remember? She was reminded of it at least once a day.

No doubt it was just the burn of the wind from driving back to the city with the soft top down, but she wouldn't tell her father that. Despite having agreed to her doing so, he disliked her driving herself. To him it smacked of individuality and any sign of self-expression was a slippery slope as far as he was concerned and could easily lead to the wanton excesses of his father, Frederico, who had abdicated the throne a decade ago following a series of damaging revelations about his private life.

'I know, Papà, but Bella wanted to have a picnic before she went to Switzerland, so we went up to the waterfall.'

'So I understand.' Prince Vittorio nodded. 'It's good to mark these transitions.'

Betty held her father's gaze. Since the operation, he

had been markedly weaker and usually he looked tired in the afternoons, but today he seemed more focused.

'Would you say she seems ready for the next stage of her life?'

'Definitely.' She nodded quickly. It had taken a lot of persuasion, but the Prince had finally, grudgingly, agreed that Bella could take a year abroad in Switzerland, and she knew that Bella would be devastated if their father changed his mind.

'She's grown up a lot in the last year. She is much more aware of her role and she's already thinking about the future of Malaspina.'

That wasn't strictly true. All Bella was really interested in was her twenty-first birthday party. They had discussed the guest list and the entertainment options and, most important of all, Bella's outfit, at length. But her father didn't need to know that.

She'd always had a maternal relationship with her younger sister and since her mother's death, that was even truer. But, remembering her own restrictive adolescence, she had tried to be kinder, more understanding. Which meant that, unlike her, Bella had friends and a social life. She went to parties—with her close protection officers, of course—and she had a strict curfew. But she was having fun as any normal twenty-year-old would, and should.

There was a pause as her father glanced away to the picture-postcard view of his principality and stared at it fixedly as if he suddenly needed to reassure himself that it was still there.

'You asked to see me, Papà…' she prompted. Not asked. She had been summoned, pulled away from the one afternoon off she'd had in months.

He nodded.

'Is it about Bella?' She silently offered up a prayer. *Please don't let him have changed his mind.*

'No. It's about your grandfather.' His mouth tightened. 'He called me this morning.'

She stared at him, her pulse leapfrogging over itself. Ten years ago, the details about Frederico's extramarital affairs had been largely contained by the sympathetic Malaspinian media, but outside the country the Internet had fizzed with kiss-and-tell stories from his mistresses and former staff.

'He called me. To warn me.'

'About what?' Her body stiffened. Surely everything that could have been said or printed about Frederico's affairs was already well documented.

She let her gaze move infinitesimally to the window to where a trio of crescent-shaped swallows were darting joyously through the warm sunlight.

Lucky swallows, she thought, watching them somersault through the sky. They got to leave when things got hard.

Her father turned towards her now, his face composed, but his shoulders were quivering with frustration and suppressed fury. 'That woman of his, the one he married. She's pregnant.'

She blinked. Swallowed. Tried to breathe through her shock.

'That's—' She hesitated, trying to find a word that could do justice to her own stunned reaction and yet not do anything to exacerbate the vein pulsing in her father's forehead. 'That's unfortunate, but what Nonno does is no longer our concern—'

The Prince pursed his lips into a familiar moue of exasperation. 'If you truly believe that then you are either naive or short-sighted. Of course it is our concern. Your grandfather is the Prince Emeritus of Malaspina, and he is having a child. I'm well aware he has no claim on the throne, but it will send shock waves through our country. There will be questions asked. We need to have answers. What we can't do is take anything for granted. Nothing is certain if the people take against you, as you well know from the experience of your mother's family.'

Betty said nothing. Her mother's family had lost their throne ninety years ago and been living in exile ever since. Their banishment had shaped her grandmother's and mother's lives, lacing every day with a bitterness and paranoia that were as exhausting as they were relentless. In fact, that was true of every member of her family except her disgraced grandfather, who had escaped the shroud of despair and was now living freely and happily on the other side of the world.

'I do know, Papà,' she agreed.

'We need to offer a stronger narrative, one that will secure our future. Your future. And as a matter of some urgency. Which is why I asked to see you.'

Her father paused, and for no reason she shivered.

'My future?'

She might as well have asked, 'What future?'

Unlike former widowed princesses in previous generations, she was not required to wear black for an indefinite period, but despite having returned to her official duties just two weeks after her late husband's funeral she hadn't been encouraged to do much more than that.

He nodded. His blue eyes held hers. The Marchetta blue eyes that had been passed down through generations to Bella but bypassed Betty. 'I am aware that you had plans. Plans that had to take second place to the needs of the crown. But I think now would be a good time to revisit those plans.'

'What plans?' Since her mother's death, she had simply stepped into her shoes, taking on her roles as the patron of various charities. It meant she had less time for herself. She stared at him, trying to follow the route he was taking to the end point, the final destination.

'Why, marriage, of course.' Her father frowned.

Something kicked against her ribs so that her body jerked backwards into the upholstery.

Marriage?

No. She tried to say the word out loud, but her mouth wouldn't form the shape of it, but then it had no understanding of how to do so because she had never said no to her father. Even when he had told her that he had found her a husband nine years ago, just a week after she and Vero had broken up. If you could break up from something that had only existed for real inside one person's head.

She had been twenty, the same age as Bella now.

Her eyes flickered to the gold band on her finger.

It was hard to believe she had ever been that young. That woman who had spoken vows in the cathedral in front of a carefully curated congregation felt like someone half remembered from a dream or a novel. Had she been like Bella? She hadn't been as naive as her sister, for sure. By then her heart had been broken, her dreams crushed. She had risked everything for love and for what?

An ambitious young man without scruples. Or a heart.

No wonder her father had been disappointed. Her mother, too. It had been a whole new level of disappointment. And shock, enough to cause the stroke from which her mother never fully recovered. It had all been down-played by the Palace but not forgotten by her. Watching the panic in her mother's eyes as she struggled to speak would stay with her for ever.

That stroke was why she had agreed to marry Alberto. At least being married was one box ticked.

Alberto had been ten years older than her. He had been a loud, boring, humourless man without charm. But he had been a prince. That was all that had mattered to her parents.

And at that point nothing had mattered to her. Most days she had woken up desperate to go back to sleep. If she could have done so she would have stayed asleep for ever. No prince could have woken her with a kiss.

But then she hadn't been in love with a prince.

More importantly, the man she'd loved hadn't been in love with her.

And so she'd married Alberto, who also hadn't loved her despite the fairy-tale hype spun by the Malaspinian media. He had worn a uniform. Trousers with a side stripe, a jacket with gold buttons and an array of medals. And he had been tall. But aside from that he had been entirely average with receding dark hair and that air of superficial courtesy that had been a mask for his stunted intellect and emotional immaturity.

Having a title of equal grandeur had been their only common ground, and after the honeymoon, with its ex-cruciatingly awkward and unsatisfying wedding night, they had settled into a dull equilibrium that had been bearable because Alberto had not expected anything of her. Not wanted anything from her or, rather, anything more from her than her blue blood.

And she hadn't wanted anything from him.

She certainly hadn't wanted him to die. But then his yacht had been caught at sea in a storm and he'd been swept overboard and suddenly she was a widow in her twenties. Overnight she was single.

But not free.

Except, apparently, to remarry.

Lifting her chin, she met her father's blue gaze.

'It's very kind of you to think of me, Papà, but I don't want to marry again.'

'Nonsense. You are a young woman. More importantly, you are a princess. You need to provide an heir, a legitimate heir to the throne of Malaspina, and for that to happen you need to be married.'

It was blindingly obvious that was the case. She had known it when she'd married Alberto. Known it still when she'd buried him. To be relevant, to secure its future, unlike the other monarchies of Europe that had fizzled out, the House of Marchetta needed heirs, but she had simply blocked that fact out.

'And I did marry. I married a man I didn't love who didn't love me.'

'Love!' Her father tutted. 'A monarchy is not sustained by love, Bettina. It is sustained by pragmatism. By treaties and alliances and by an acceptance that the needs of the crown take precedence over the wishes of any one individual. For the House of Marchetta to retain its position, sacrifices have to be made.'

'And I have made them,' she protested, but her voice sounded weak and ineffectual.

'And you will continue to do so. However, in this instance, you will only be required to do what you would have done of your own volition if your mother and I hadn't intervened.'

She could feel the adrenaline pulsing through her body.

There was only one time that she had done anything of her own volition. Only that would mean—

'I don't understand,' she lied, because she did understand. But after so long keeping it separate from her life, she just didn't want to believe it, to accept that this was happening to her, here, now. That her father, her own father, had gone and opened that chest, letting out the past with all its messiness and pain and humiliation.

'I've had an offer for your hand in marriage and, for the good of your family, for your country, you need to accept it.'

She cleared her throat. 'An offer from whom?'

It was a rhetorical question. She already knew the answer but until her father spoke his name out loud it wasn't real.

'Vero Farnese.'

The floor rippled beneath her feet.

Vero with his dark green eyes that were the exact same colour as the pine trees that edged the hills around Malaspina. Vero with his high cheekbones and hard, flawless profile. He might not have stuck around, but he had stayed in her head.

'Why him?' It didn't make any sense. Nine years ago, Vero wouldn't have made the long longlist of potential suitors.

'Because he asked,' her father said tersely. 'And his situation has changed. Improved.'

She wanted to laugh. Because that was something of an understatement. There might be an ocean between them now, but she would have to have been living under a rock on a different planet not to know that Vero's situation had changed, unquestionably and dramatically.

Nine years ago, he had been the son of the family chauffeur living in a cottage on the estate with his parents.

Now his company was a household name. The cars he designed and produced were changing the way people drove. Oh, and he was one of the richest men in the world.

'But we don't need his money.'

Her father tilted his head on one side as he always did when he was displeased with his eldest daughter. 'Don't be childish, Bettina. You know how expensive it has been to settle your grandfather's debts. Signor Farnese is a wealthy man, and he is offering a not insignificant amount of money for your hand.' Her father exhaled as if the scent of non-inherited wealth was offensive to him. 'Naturally, I would prefer someone of royal blood—'

'But he's the son of our former chauffeur. He has no bloodline. Surely you're concerned about that, Papà.'

'He has no pedigree. Or not the sort that matters. He's something of a mongrel—' The Prince smiled coldly. 'But successful monarchies like ours understand the importance not just of maintaining traditions and protocol but of embracing the mood of the times. Marrying a commoner will show that we are open to the changing world. Plus, Signor Farnese has a close connection with the family.'

Close connection.

She felt suddenly sick. Except it hadn't been close, she thought, Vero's deep voice filling her head as she fast-forwarded through their last conversation, out by the garages. It was an appearance of closeness. She wasn't his heart's desire, but simply a means to an end. Only he was her first lover, her first love, and she had got so lost in the intimacy and intensity of sex that it had blurred her senses, made her lose all common sense.

'He grew up in Malaspina, which will play well with the people. And he is here, unlike your grandfather.'

It was one of the things her father did to distance himself from the man who had cast such a long shadow over his life. Not referring to him as his father. Making it Bettina's problem. But right now, she had bigger problems.

Like being married off to a man she hated.

Her father was getting to his feet, using the armrest to propel himself to standing, and she stood too, if only because it gave her more of a chance to flee from this nightmarish conversation.

'We need to get ahead of this story. Otherwise, we will look weak.' He looked suddenly exhausted, and she knew why. Her mother's family, older, grander than the House of Marchetta, had been ousted from their throne, pushed into exile after a series of scandals and allegations of corruption had left them weak and isolated.

Nobody wanted a weak monarch. That was as true now as it had ever been.

She felt her whole body tense. Vero. His name meant true, but he had lied to her, used her, manipulated her, manipulated her trust.

Her fingers tightened into fists. She wouldn't marry him. She couldn't. It would break her, and he had already done that once.

'What makes you think his offer is real?' she said stiffly. 'I mean, why would he want to marry me? Or have you forgotten that nine years ago you sacked his father and evicted his whole family from their home?'

Saying it aloud made her shiver inside. She hadn't seen Vero after that had happened but his anger when she'd ended things had been coldly absolute. So why was he back? Why did he want her?

Leaning forward to press a button on a small marble topped table, her father held her gaze. 'Of course, it's real. What man doesn't want to marry a princess?'

As he walked slowly towards the door that led to his private salon she swayed slightly. She felt sick, but it was just a horrible coincidence. Her father couldn't have known that Vero had asked her almost exactly the same question nine years ago.

It was a question that had haunted her dreams ever since. She could still remember her panic and confusion and then that hot rush of shame as she'd understood that Vero was interested in her title, not her. There was a knock on the other door, the one through which she had entered the room.

Her father turned, his face lined but composed in the afternoon sunlight, and she knew that for him the matter was resolved.

'But if you don't believe me, ask him yourself. Ah, Giuliano—' He turned towards the man in his dark green uniform who had appeared to hover discreetly next to the wall. 'Is the car ready? I should like to leave for Arduino now—'

'But, Papà—'

It was too late. She stared across the sunlit room as the door closed behind him, her heart jumping against her ribs. And then she heard the other door open...

'Your Royal Highness—'

She turned, her legs moving slowly as if it was she, not her father, who was nearly eighty. The footman ducked his chin and stepped back smartly away from the door.

'Signor Vero Farnese.'

And then she felt the air snap to attention, and he was in the room, and she had thought she knew what misery was, but she had to dig her nails into the palm of her hand to redistribute the shattering pain of seeing him again. It was impossible, overwhelming.

He was overwhelming in that dark suit.

Devastating. Powerful. Male.

It was the first time she had seen him in anything other than jeans and a T-shirt. No, that wasn't quite true. She had seen pictures of him online. Pictures that had come up when she'd typed in his name during those occasional moments of self-pity and weakness late at night when the darkness had made her feel as if she were buried alive.

She'd told herself that he would have a stylist now. But the truth was he didn't need a stylist. He never had.

He stopped and gave a small bow and a shiver ran through her, tightening her skin around her bones so that it felt as if she were turning to stone beneath his scrutiny. She felt painfully self-conscious. Was he assessing her, seeing if she had changed for the better? The answer to that question made her so aware of herself that it was hard to breathe, much less appraise him in return.

'Your Royal Highness—'

Had he called her that before?

Maybe, when the grown-ups were there. But never when they were alone. Then he had called her *'dolcezza'*—sweetness.

Her stomach was a snake twisting itself into knots and she put a hand on the back of her father's armchair to steady herself. Behind Vero, the door was closing and nine years, two months, three weeks and five days after he had broken her heart—broken her, truthfully—she was alone again with Vero Farnese.

Had it been a different kind of reunion she might have stepped forward then and embraced him and said something like, *You haven't changed a bit.*

Her blood pulsed sluggishly in her veins. Outside, the noise of the traffic seemed more distant. The curtains that had been fluttering in the light summer breeze stilled. Even the swallows were silent.

Now she looked at him.

But he had changed. The soft-mouthed boy who had ruined her for other men with his kisses had hardened into something almost sculptural. His jawline was smooth like polished marble. A sketch of his body would be all strong lines and aggressive curves, a flagrantly masculine silhouette. Because now he was a man. And though she had probably seen more beautiful, sexier men in the nine years since they last met, she really couldn't remember when.

She couldn't remember much of anything at all. Her brain was just a mush of disconnected thoughts that made no sense. Up until this moment she had been almost proud of how she'd dealt with the past. She would have told herself, told anyone, if they'd bothered to ask, that she was over him.

Now that felt naive, childish even, like something Bella would say.

Somewhere in the palace, a door slammed, and it made her jump, the noise jolting through her body and forcing unexpected tears into her eyes.

Vero's green eyes narrowed onto her face, and she felt suddenly horribly exposed and then furious with herself.

I'm not crying because of you, she wanted to snap at him.

Instead, tamping down her anger and misery in a way

that would have earned one of her mother's rare nods of approval, she said coolly, 'I don't know why you've chosen to come back now after all these years, but you've had your fun, and now you can leave.'

A flood of panic washed over her as he moved then, and it took every ounce of willpower she had not to turn and yank open the windows and hurl herself into the warm Malaspinian sunlight.

'Leave?'

She squared her shoulders as he stopped in front of her, his green eyes cool and narrowed on her face, his gaze so familiar and yet also the gaze of a stranger.

He was quiet for a beat, staring at her as if she were a piece of art he didn't understand, and then he said softly, 'Oh, I'm not going anywhere, Princess Bettina.'

She bit the inside of her cheek as he took another step closer.

'As for the fun…' He paused, his gaze moving slowly down over her body, returning to hover on her quivering mouth. 'That hasn't started yet.'

CHAPTER TWO

IT HAD BEEN a long and uncomfortable flight from New York. There were storms above the Atlantic and the turbulence had left his normally tranquil stewards reaching for the sides of the private jet. But it had been worth it, Vero Farnese thought, to watch that flutter of panic in Betty's grey eyes.

Nine years ago, those eyes had mesmerised him. Looking into them was like walking in that fine mist that sometimes rolled in from the sea near his beach house in Malibu. He had been disorientated, blind and helpless. Willingly so.

Like some supplicant offering himself up as a sacrifice. That was what love did. It made you stupid and vulnerable. Which was why he'd always been so careful, so careful, to keep his distance.

His father had taught him that. Not Tommasino, the man who had raised him as his own, but his birth father, the Duke, who had disowned him before he was even born. The man who had discarded his mother after a short affair and paid for her silence so that his true identity had been known to only four people on the planet. Three now.

That silence had been a heavy burden for his parents to carry, but they had carried it uncomplainingly until he had discovered his birth certificate and demanded answers, and in doing so brought fear into their lives.

Having his birth father in the same headspace as Betty made his shoulders stretch back so far that it felt as if the bones would break.

But then, between them they had broken everything else, so why should his shoulder bones be exempt?

'Is that a threat?'

The warm light caught on her cheekbones, highlighting their sharpness. He wasn't a connoisseur of beauty. Yes, he liked a well-cut suit, and he had a weakness for a raked, low-slung, mid-engine performance car, although he didn't like to classify it as such. But he didn't collect art or decorative 'objects' and his homes were starkly decorated, functional spaces.

And Betty shouldn't be beautiful. Taken separately, her features were unremarkable and yet she had that same mesmeric effect on him as *La Gioconda* had on the millions of people who swarmed to the Louvre in Paris just to see her enigmatic smile.

Only Betty wasn't smiling. Her mouth was pressed together into a line that screamed irritation and it shouldn't have looked attractive, but he found himself noticing that fullness of her upper lip and the pinkness of both lips so that, briefly, he lost track of what they were talking about. That mouth…

He dragged his thoughts back to heel and shrugged.

'I don't know. Are you feeling threatened?'

Her look was excoriating. 'By you?' She shook her head, then frowned, feigning thought. 'A better adjective would be bored.'

She meant every word. Unfortunately, that message hadn't been passed on to her body, he thought, his eyes arrowing in on the pulse jerking in her throat. Her hands were shaking slightly too.

Just as they used to when she ran them over his body.

He sucked in a breath, reeling slightly as his brain unhelpfully offered up an image of Betty naked, straddling him, her graceful fingers tracing the contours of his abdomen.

It had been one of the many confusing, contradictory, compelling things about her. She had always been the first to touch but she was shy about initiating sex, almost as if she needed permission to take what she wanted. He'd had to take things up a notch, licking into her mouth or cupping her face, but once he'd done so it had been as if a switch had flipped, and she'd caught fire like a match striking against a flint.

And he had burned beneath her touch. She had made him feel precious and powerful and necessary.

But, of course, the opposite had been true. He had been disposable and he'd had no power over her. She had simply and briefly given him permission to use her body and in exchange she had wanted to use his.

Gritting his teeth, he blanked out the memory of their naked bodies moving on the sun-soaked bed in his room above the garages, and let his eyes drift over her twitching pulse down to where her nipples were clearly visible against the thin silk of her blouse.

'Oh, I don't think you find me boring, Princess. In fact, I'd lay odds that this is the most stimulation you've had in a long time.'

Her eyes blazed but, probably because she knew that it would only give weight to his claim, she bit back whatever protest was rising in her throat, took a step back from him and walked pointedly across the room to the window.

For a moment or two, he took advantage of that view-point and let his gaze roam over her light curves. Only when he'd had his fill and when it became clear that she was ignoring him, did he say, 'You know pretending I'm not here is not going to change anything. Your father and I have already made the decision—'

Betty turned then, goaded, as he'd known she would be, into acknowledging his presence. 'Yes, the two of you.' There was a flush of colour across her cheekbones and a lost note in her voice that made his breath catch. 'Only it isn't your decision to make, it's mine.'

Wrong, he thought, replaying his conversation with Prince Vittorio.

In any other situation, he would have agreed with her. But truthfully the decision had been made by proxy when her unrepentant scandal magnet of a grandfather had im-pregnated his new wife and looted the Marchetta fam-ily's private accounts to fund his lifestyle.

But he wasn't here to persuade Betty of that fact. Her father could make her see sense.

'So, this part of the palace is where you actually live. I always wondered what it was like.'

The faintest flush, like a drop of cochineal, spread slowly across her cheekbones, and he felt another stab of satisfaction at seeing her so discomfited.

To give himself a little longer to enjoy that sensation, he glanced around the exquisite sitting room. Like most royal residences, the Prince's Palace of Malaspina was mostly given over to state rooms that served as meeting spaces for foreign dignitaries and other guests. These rooms were also open to the public for selected dates during the year when crowds of curious tourists eagerly made their way from the banqueting hall to the throning room, gazing in awe at the gilded mirrors and the grand curving staircase and even grander old masters and the elaborate ceilings with their plaster figurines.

But this was no state room. His green eyes lingered on a portrait of Betty's mother, the late Princess Henrietta.

This particular sitting room was in one of the private apartments that had never been open to the public. Apartments that were reserved for the Marchetta family and the rare, chosen few who were deemed worthy enough to receive an invitation into the inner sanctum.

Which, up until now, hadn't been him, he thought, his jaw tightening.

Nine years ago, when he had been merely the penniless son of the chauffeur, the closest he had got to these particular rooms was standing on the gravel path outside the door to the staff entrance.

'Yes. But only some of the time.'

Coming out of anyone else's mouth, that light, decisive way she spoke would have sounded like flirting. But he knew better. He knew that it was the voice of a princess used to giving instructions to be followed.

He felt anger flare up inside him again.

Anger with her for leading him away from that path he had chosen through the woods. But mostly anger with himself for being led around like some puppy on a leash.

He should have known then that Betty had simply been curious, not committed. It was, after all, a story as old as time. Uptown girl wanting to see how the other half lived. A princess swapping her crown for a baseball cap and sneaking out of the palace to play with the hired help.

Something rose up in his chest as he remembered their 'secret' meetings and the cloak and dagger way they had communicated.

At the time he hadn't questioned it. In part, he'd found it an aphrodisiac. In the same way, the randomness of the encounters had left him in a near-constant state of sexual anticipation, because every moment had been filled with the possibility that she might appear. And even when those feelings had tipped over into frustration, he'd simply accepted that it had been necessary in order for them to have a relationship.

Relationship. The word ripped through him like a blade.

There had been no relationship. For Betty, it had been simply a fling. *Un'avventura*, as their Italian neighbours across the border would say. Other little girls dressed up as princesses, but Betty was a princess and had wanted to drive a getaway car or break out of prison. Instead, she had hooked up with a man who was rough enough around the edges to give her that good-girl-gone-bad feeling.

But it had been just a feeling. A fantasy. He might have thought it was the real thing, but all Betty had wanted was to cosplay *Roman Holiday* for one summer and then go back to her life at the palace and marry her prince.

Which was exactly what she'd done.

He felt Betty's gaze on the side of his face, and he was suddenly close to asking her why she had picked him. And why he hadn't been enough.

It wasn't the first time he'd asked himself that question. That had been when he was fifteen years old. Neither child nor man and, like most teenagers, he had been shedding his skin when he discovered the truth about his father.

His jaw tightened. Father, only in the sense that he had impregnated his mother.

But Vero was illegitimate, and as such he was not just irrelevant but an embarrassment.

The Duca di Monte Giusto had been coldly furious at being confronted by living proof of his infidelity. With two sons already, he'd had no need even for a spare. More importantly he'd felt no compulsion to acknowledge a connection with his bastard on any level. There had been words, and then a moment of temper that he regretted still, and always would, because it had hurt the man who had stepped up to be his father. Tommasino had been arrested, then released, but the threat of prison had hung over him, and left his mother terrified and anxious for the rest of her life.

Vero had been escorted from the estate and warned never to return.

And then a decade later, Betty's father had done more or less the same thing. Or his minions had. Men like Prince Vittorio employed people to do their dirty work.

'In the winter months, we stay here in Morroello but in the summer, we spend most weekends in Arduino.' Her grey gaze was darker now, less like mist, more like storm clouds, and he felt the air around him dip just as it had on the plane.

It was less symbolic than the palace in Morroello but the Castello della Arduino's location in the countryside was a neat decision by the sixth Prince of Malaspina to demonstrate to the largely rural population of the country that the monarch had their ear.

That was the thing about royalty. Nothing was accidental or random. Everything, including marriage, was strategic.

Especially marriage.

It was a lesson he'd taken to heart.

'Of course you do,' he murmured. He had never been there either. During their time together, the Castello had been closed for restoration work. But it wouldn't have made any difference if it hadn't been. There was no reason for the son of the chauffeur to visit the family's holiday retreat. Questions would have been asked and nobody would have liked the answers. He knew that. Moreover, he knew that Betty did too.

Her spine stiffened then, and she tilted back her head and held his gaze and he felt it, that flutter of anticipation that he hadn't felt in so long. Hadn't felt with any woman before or since because her posture was how you knew she was a princess.

That, and her slate-grey eyes. They were things of beauty.

Those eyes locked with his now. 'I don't know if you remember but Morroello can get unbearably hot in July and August—'

'Oh, I remember,' he said softly.

Her pupils flared and he knew why. Knew that she was remembering that summer nine years ago. It had been so hot that the surface of the roads had turned to liquid. But the tar wasn't the only thing that had melted that summer.

His blood thundered in his veins, his body tensing painfully hard as he pictured those afternoons in the rooms above the garage. He could practically smell the motor oil and the leather. And her. Not just the perfume she wore but the scent of her warm, damp skin sinking into his, her breath melting in his mouth, and her hand gripping his arms, fingers biting into the muscle as she came apart on top of him.

A flood of heat surged through him, violent and heady,

and his skin felt suddenly electric, and his voice was hoarse as he replied.

'I remember everything.'

Her chin snapped up and their eyes collided as a quivering silence stretched out to the gilded edges of the room.

'Then you'll know to take the left exit at the Zafferano roundabout to reach the airport,' she said at last. 'I'm sorry you had a wasted trip, Signor Farnese, but there appears to have been some crossed wires.'

She didn't sound sorry. She sounded snippy and cornered, which pleased him almost as much as the pulse jumping in the base of her throat.

'Then let me uncross them for you,' he said calmly, dropping down onto one of the sofas and stretching out his long legs just as if this were his sitting room and he had returned from a day at the office. 'You and I are getting married. As you know, it's a matter of some urgency so it will be a short engagement.'

'It will not be a short engagement,' she snapped.

'You want to marry me now?' He feigned surprise purely for the purpose of watching her cheeks flush with colour. 'I mean, today would be a difficult ask, but if we leave now, we could be in Vegas by sunrise—'

'I'm not going to Vegas to get married. I'm not getting married, full stop.' Her lips parted in a way that made him feel adrift and in those few sharpened seconds, he could have reached out into the space between them and touched her cheek.

'Once was enough.'

She glanced away, the movement making her glorious red hair look molten in the sunlight. But his gaze followed her right hand as she moved to touch the plain gold band on her ring finger and a primitive drum roll of jealousy buzzed across his skin.

Even now, all these years later, he could still remember the shock of reading the news of her engagement. And it had been an entirely justifiable reaction because just one week after she had abruptly ended things with him, she had got engaged to her prince.

It had been more than simply a shock. Way more. Like the ground opening beneath your feet.

Of course, outwardly, he was doing fine. His company, VFA, had gone public on the stock market last year and turned him into the youngest centibillionaire on the planet. Two weeks ago, *Eras* magazine had named him their 'Person of the Year'.

But beneath the surface, he was still scrabbling at the edge of the abyss.

Had she been seeing Alberto at the same time as she was tucking herself in beside him and laying her head on his chest?

It stung to even ask the question. He couldn't contemplate answering it.

What cut the most was that he had been her first. At the time, and against his own will almost, he had liked that fact a little too much. But afterwards, when he'd found out about Alberto, he had felt used. Felt as if she had only got with him so that she could rehearse for the main performance.

He hadn't wanted the man dead, though—not all of the time anyway—and he had been shocked to read about the accident.

And clearly Betty still felt that shock. That loss.

Abruptly he got to his feet.

'Unfortunately, on this occasion, that decision is not

up to you. I know this must be hard for you, Princess, but sometimes in life we have to make compromises.'

'But you can't want this, Vero?'

His name in her mouth knocked the breath out of his chest. Living in the US, he had got used to people pronouncing his name wrong. All their history seemed to be wrapped in those two short syllables.

It made his brain feel grazed.

She hesitated and he heard her try to swallow as if there was something in her slender throat. 'You don't want this. You don't want me. And I certainly don't want you.'

The sunlight was still streaming in through the window, bright and joyfully oblivious of the tension in the room and in the spine of the slim, red-haired woman standing statue-still on the antique rug. Because she was tense, and not just because she wanted him gone.

But because she was lying.

Betty had always wanted him. Out of all the lies and half-truths she had told him and the secrets he had kept from her, that was the one truth that had stayed true and inviolable, truer and more unassailable than any marriage vow.

She hadn't loved him or needed him or respected him, but she had desired him, and with an intensity that had knocked him sideways. It was the reason why he hadn't noticed all the warning signs, that wanting. It had felt so good. Put simply, he'd been flattered, and enough to confuse lust with love.

He wasn't confused now.

Hadn't been confused with any woman since. He wasn't cruel or manipulative, just pragmatic and straight to the point. And thanks to the algorithms of dating apps, it was easy to get straight to the point.

The *sine non qua* of dating was to know what you wanted. Did you want a relationship, or did you just want to meet someone new and have some fun? And by fun, he meant sex.

The simple, no-strings kind. One night or late afternoon or even early morning of pleasure in some anonymous but comfortable hotel. And afterwards, he might hang around long enough to bolt down a cup of coffee and a bagel. No, actually, he had never done that. Prolonged proximity led to intimacy and intimacy tended to negate casualness.

But it was a possibility. Anything was a possibility.

Except falling asleep with someone. That he couldn't do. Sleep was when you were at your most vulnerable. It required a level of trust he simply didn't have, had never had. The only exception was Betty.

She was the one woman he had opened up to. Within reason. Thankfully, he had never told her he loved her.

But he had shared his hopes and dreams and his need for her. That had spilled out during sex when her arms would tighten around him, and her face would go soft and urgent, and he would hear himself babbling a garbled stream of all the things he wanted to do to her and where he needed her to touch him and how beautiful she was.

And again and again, over and over, how much he wanted her.

He still wanted her now, and he knew that there must be something deeply wrong with him for feeling that way. But if there was, then there was something wrong with her too, because whatever she was saying about not wanting him, her body was saying the opposite. Shouting it, in fact, he thought, his eyes grazing her flushed cheekbones and the taut flex of her spine and that slight quiver across her skin as if she was having to hold something in.

She was.

He knew, because he was holding it in too.

'Is that what you told him? Your prince?'

He took a step towards her. 'Did you lie to him like you lied to me?' She blinked—or was it a flinch? But there was no time for him to answer that question because now she was walking towards him, her grey eyes churning and turbulent like a sky filled with nimbostratus clouds.

'You are the liar.' Her voice was shaking now, and, despite himself, he wished it were her body shuddering beneath his. 'And you know nothing about A-Alberto.' She stumbled over the name, emotion resonating in her voice, and now he wished he'd never mentioned the other man. 'You know nothing about him or our relationship. Or me.'

He held her gaze, suddenly furious at having introduced her husband into the conversation. 'Oh, I do know you, Princess Bettina. I was your first—'

'But not my last—'

'Wrong,' he said then, his heart hammering in his chest. 'Your father wants an heir; your family needs one. A legitimate one,' he added, and it cost him to say those words. 'Which will mean having sex with your husband. Me.'

She stepped forward, her hands trembling by her sides and then she was pushing them against his chest.

'I don't want to have sex with you.' Her voice was barely audible as her fingers curled into the lapels of his jacket and, of its own volition, his hand rose to her waist.

'I don't want to have sex with you either,' he said hoarsely, because they were both lying now. And because in the same way that two negatives made a positive, two lies made a truth.

And this, this blistering, gravitational energy between them, was as true now as it had been nine years ago.

For a few seconds, nothing happened and then she was pulling him towards her, closing the distance between them and her mouth was on his—

Her scent enveloped him, and she was leaning into him and in the pull of her desire he felt both peace and pandemonium. And hunger…

A hunger like he had never known.

He could feel it pounding in his veins as his hand splayed against her back and in her open-mouthed kiss. As she licked into his mouth, he lost himself in the taste of her desire and the eager, straining press of her body and the feel of her fingers scrabbling at his shirt. The room was blurring and spinning around them just as if they were in the eye of a storm and he felt dizzy and intoxicated, hurtling towards a pleasure that knew no equal.

With a moan, Betty jerked free of his grip and pushed him away so fast and so urgently that he felt dizzy for a different reason.

'No—' She was stumbling backwards, her irises trembling like a millpond in the rain. Her face looked small and stunned. 'No, I don't want this.'

Didn't want it? The lie grated against his ears. He stared at her, his head spinning. Even now, when he knew who she was, she was still playing games.

He glanced down pointedly at his dishevelled shirt.

'You think?'

'I hate you.'

'I don't care,' he said, and that she was still lying to him, to herself, made his voice rough then, brutal even.

'And I don't care that you don't want to marry me. Because, Princess Bettina, in four weeks' time, you and I are going to be married whether you like it or not.' He stared down steadily into her huge, dazed eyes. 'You know, your father offered me a plot of land out in the hills as part of your dowry, but I'm happy to take that kiss as a down payment.'

She sucked in a breath.

'Get out—'

Her face was flushed with an anger that should have made her look ugly but instead highlighted the luminosity of her skin.

'Don't worry, I'm going.' Without bothering to straighten his shirt, he strolled towards the door. He stopped beside it, his hand resting lightly on the handle, and turned to face her. 'But I believe your father has arranged a dinner to celebrate our engagement, so we'll meet again tomorrow evening, Your Royal Highness. You can be sure of that.'

CHAPTER THREE

BETTY WATCHED THE door close, her breath churning in her chest. The normal steady lub-dub of her heart sounded like a runaway train.

I don't want this.

I don't want this.

Her words echoed inside her head, scraping up scornfully against the tingle of her lips from when she had pressed them against Vero's.

She had pressed her lips against his.

She moaned softly. How had that happened? Like some director of a stage play, she blocked their movements around the room, trying to work out how she and Vero had ended up being close enough for that kiss to happen. It wasn't that hard to do. But it didn't answer the question that needed answering, which was what was wrong with her?

As she remembered how she had leaned in to kiss him, her hands curled into fists. It was bad enough that somewhere inside that beautifully shaped skull of his, he had a detailed memory bank of all her sexual preferences plus a few audio files too, of the noises she'd made. But that had been then, back before she knew the truth about him and his motives.

Back before she knew what lay beneath that curling smile and drowning green gaze.

But she knew now, had known for nine years that Vero Farnese had wanted her for one thing and one thing only.

Her title.

The worst part was that even before her mother had warned her to be on her guard with Vero, she had known that her judgement was flawed. Known it, lived it, and finally learned from it.

But she had wanted him so badly.

She had tried to hold back, to remember who she was and what she was supposed to want and who she needed to be with for the future of Malaspina, but it had burst out of her, the words exploding like pollen from a pine tree in spring. And after she'd told him that she wanted to be more than friends, his face had grown taut and her pulse had gathered inside her, dancing and leaping and staggering as he'd leaned in and kissed her.

She had been so in love. Vero had filled her thoughts awake and asleep and she had wanted him to be her first, her only. She knew now that he hadn't loved her, but he hadn't been going to turn her down out of some heightened sense of honour. Mainly because he didn't have an honourable bone in his body.

Any more than she appeared to have a sense of self-preservation.

Her eyes jerked down and she stared at her bag as if it had suddenly turned into a snake. Her phone was ringing.

Was that him? She didn't want to speak to Vero, not now, not ever. She reached for her bag, breathing out shakily as she saw the name on the screen.

It was Bella.

'Sorry, I forgot you were summoned.' Her sister lowered her voice. 'Are you still with Papà?'

Betty closed her eyes. Bella was not a child but nor was

she fully adult—emotionally anyway—and that conversation she'd just had with her father was not something she could imagine sharing with her sister. Nor did she want to. Let Bella stay young and carefree for as long as possible.

It was the least she could do.

'No, he left a little while ago.'

'What did he want?' Her sister hesitated. 'He hasn't changed his mind about me going to Switzerland, has he?'

'No, of course not.' Betty pressed her hand against the bridge of her nose. It felt as if someone were tightening a vice around her head.

'So, what was it, then? Why did he drag you back?'

'Nothing really. He spoke to Nonno this morning and you know that agitates him.' The truth or a version of it would come out soon enough but she didn't want to risk something slipping out about Vero if she told Bella any more than that. 'Anyway, why are you calling?'

'Because Marcus says he's going to come and visit me in Switzerland. And he thinks he has an idea for getting Balius to stop freaking out over the Liverpools.'

Balius was Bella's favourite horse. She was a talented equestrian and had dreams of competing in international events for Malaspina in the future. Right now, she was taking part in shows mostly in Europe, but Balius was struggling with the water jumps.

'That is good news,' Betty said quickly, grateful for the change of topic.

'And he sent this photo of Nightingale. Isn't she lovely?'

Her phone pinged and she stared down at the photo of a beautiful chestnut mare. Standing beside her was the real reason for Bella's excitement. Marcus was very sweet-looking, and puppyish, very young.

Had she ever been that age? If so, she couldn't remember it.

Truthfully, she felt old. Some days she would look at her reflection and be shocked to see the young woman staring back at her. But then since her mother's death she had been treading water.

No, that was too active, she thought as Bella continued to talk.

For so long now, she had been living like some creature in a tank at the zoo. Without her noticing, her widowhood had gone from weeks to months then years and her routine had barely changed. There had been no dating or even much socialising. Through fear or inertia, she was living vicariously through Bella but, beneath her outward composure, she had been chafing at her life. Wanting to break free. To let go.

Picturing that kiss with Vero, she felt her face heat as if she had dunked it in scalding water. She had certainly got her wish, and in the process she had humiliated herself.

So, was it worth it?

A beat of heat pulsed down her spine and she felt her skin quiver like the ground in the aftermath of an earthquake.

Yes.

No.

Yes.

She licked her lips, remembering the feel of his mouth on hers and that snap of electricity as if he had woken her not from sleep but from something deeper and darker. He had tasted so good, and his hand around her waist had felt better than good. It had felt right.

Curling her fingers, she let her nails bite into the flesh of her palms, welcoming the distracting sting of a different kind of pain, one that couldn't ravage her heart.

It was too late to change what she had done. She was just going to have to chalk it up to shock and abstinence and put it to the back of her mind.

Right now, she needed to focus on the bigger picture, which was this sham of a marriage that her father and Vero had apparently signed off on without so much as a word of consultation with her, the bride.

Her gaze moved jerkily to the rooftops of Morroello and she breathed in deeply, trying to quieten the scamper of her heart. The idea of fighting both her father and Vero made panic slither up inside her and pound against her from the outside all at once. She wasn't sure she could fight the two of them, but she was going to have to because she was not going to marry Vero Farnese.

So, first things first, who else knew about this aside from her father, Vero and herself?

She bit into her lip. Maybe Anselmo, her father's private secretary. But obviously, his silence was a given. Possibly the bishop, but that would all have taken place behind closed doors. Which meant, currently at least, that details about her upcoming nuptials were contained and therefore still negotiable.

She just needed to talk to her father and persuade him that there was another way.

What it was, she didn't know. But what mattered was nipping any talk about this marriage to Vero in the bud.

Ten minutes later she was heading out of Morroello into the Malaspinian countryside. Switching on the air con, she flicked the indicator and overtook a dark grey saloon, taking pleasure in her car's acceleration and the timing of her gear change. And the resentful, indignant expression on the driver's face.

At least there was one man she could outrun and outwit.

These occasional journeys when she was behind the wheel, testing the limits of the car, timing the gear changes and the judicious application of the brakes, were pockets of freedom in a life that was curtailed by a raft of rules, many of which felt as if they had been drafted in the Middle Ages.

Some probably had.

She had always found the palace protocols exhausting, but since Alberto's death it had got so much worse. Now as well as being exhausted, she felt trapped, suffocated by a widowhood that seemed to cast a shadow that stretched further and wider with every passing day so that both the present and the future were just a dark, shapeless cloud.

Only now that cloud had taken the familiar but unwelcome shape of Vero Farnese.

Her fingers tightened around the wheel. It was so typical of her father to simply disappear off to Arduino. No matter that he had tossed a grenade into her life.

But then Prince Vittorio would argue that it wasn't her life. That, as a princess, she didn't have a life, simply a role.

And there was no point in getting angry about that. No point in listing everything she had been denied. For starters, it would be ridiculous and insulting for a princess to whine about a lack of opportunities.

But it still felt as if she had done nothing except be the latest in a long line of Malaspinian princesses, a position she had achieved solely by virtue of her birth. Her academic prowess was just a memory, untested and unchallenged in the real world and, aside from a few months working in the PR department of her father's favourite charity, she had never had a job.

'You are doing something far more important than any job, Bettina. You are performing your duty.' Her shoulders stiffened automatically as her mother's voice echoed inside her head, quiet and glacially cool.

Her mother, both her parents, had been obsessed with duty, and she understood that, for her, that meant being a princess. Being endlessly composed, smiling serenely at every public appearance, listening intently to diplomats and presidents and other regnal heads of state. That she could do, and did, very successfully. Since her mother's death, she had stepped up to be by her father's side. But away from the cameras and the crowds, it felt as if she was still on duty. Always a princess.

Never just Betty.

Except once.

She felt her stomach twist then rise up towards her throat. Only that had been a lie. In postcard-perfect Malaspina there were so many.

But she wasn't going to be part of another one.

Her father was painting beneath one of the huge oak trees that marked the end of the Castello's formal gardens.

Outside, away from the opulence of the palace, he looked smaller and frailer. But she pushed back against the flutter of tenderness as he turned towards her, his face oddly soft in the late afternoon sunlight.

'Bettina. I didn't realise we had a second appointment today.'

'We didn't. We don't, and I'm sorry to interrupt your downtime, Papà.'

Her father winced. He hated modern slang. Although he was more tolerant when Bella used it.

'I hope it is worth the interruption.'

'It is,' she said quickly. 'I met with Vero. And I know

that you want me to marry him and I understand your reasoning, but it's just not a viable option.'

'Viable?' her father repeated. He looked calm and, in the sunlight, his snowy hair looked almost like a halo.

'What happened nine years ago was a whim. A caprice. But we aren't compatible. We never were, and I didn't understand that when you intervened. But you were right, Papà,' she said, hoping that he might be more susceptible to flattery than pleading. 'We can't be in the same room together.'

Picturing that moment when she had pulled Vero closer and kissed him hungrily, she felt her face grow warm.

'I see.' He nodded. 'That is unfortunate and I did wonder whether you would be able to put your ego behind your duty—'

Her eyes were suddenly stinging. 'That's not fair, Papà.' She was irritated, hurt, frustrated, but her words sounded stupid as soon as they left her mouth. They made her sound like some sulky child.

'Fair.' The softness in his face dissolved. 'Fairness is not a criterion in these matters. I am surprised and somewhat disappointed that I still need to explain that to you. And yet, I am not. You have a persistent ability to disappoint me. But if you will not do it, then I cannot make you.'

Was that it? She stared at him in confusion. She had expected Armageddon, or what amounted to Armageddon in her father's world of protocol and restraint. So, an argument. Some kind of extended lecture at the very least, but he had already turned back to his easel.

'Are you agreeing, then? That I'm not going to marry Vero?' she said slowly. When he nodded, she wanted to feel relief and she did, but there was something odd and slippery about the moment that made her heart flutter.

'I do. But,' her father said quietly, his brush hovering over a smudge of green oil paint, 'the situation hasn't changed. Your grandfather is still having a child and that will have repercussions unless we, as a family, can demonstrate to our people that we are fit for purpose.'

He turned then, his eyes reaching hers, their blue irises cool and pragmatic and not at all panicky. In fact, he seemed preternaturally calm, just as if he had a plan B.

A shiver scampered across her skin as her brain frantically tried to catch up.

'I had assumed, naturally, that as my eldest child you would step forward, for the greater good. But fortunately, I have another daughter. And she has a suitor too. And he is both a wealthy and a titled man.'

She felt the ground tremble beneath her feet or maybe it was she who was trembling. She stared down at her shaking hands.

'No.' She hadn't been able to say the word on her own account, but now it rose from her throat explosively. 'No, Papà, Bella is too young to settle down. She has plans, dreams—'

The Prince raised an eyebrow. 'By your own account, she has grown up a lot in the last year and become much more aware of her role. And is already thinking about the future of Malaspina. Your words, Bettina, not mine.'

So that was why he had asked her all those questions? She felt sick and stupid and suddenly full of a fury that she had never felt before.

'She's planning her birthday party, not her marriage. She's not ready—'

Her father was staring at her, a pitiless expression on his face that made her bite the inside of her cheek.

'She is the same age as you were when you married Alberto.'

'That's not the same.'

'How is it not the same? I had an offer for your hand and you agreed to the marriage, now I have an offer for your sister and she will agree to marry too.'

It wasn't the same because she hadn't cared about her life at that point. She had been so wretched and so uncaring about her happiness because after Vero had broken her heart, she hadn't imagined ever being happy again. Nothing had mattered, including who she married.

But Bella was happy. She had friends, a boy she liked and a placement at a university in Geneva. She was so excited about her new life.

'Then let me marry him.'

Her father was shaking his head. 'He wants your sister.'

'I can change his mind. I'll talk to him—'

'Prince Hans von Marburg has some, shall we say, archaic views of marriage. Unlike Alberto or Signor Farnese, he requires a virgin bride.'

She barely registered the censure in her father's remark. Her lungs felt as though they were full of lead. It was impossible to breathe. Alberto had been a decade older than her, but Prince Hans von Marburg was nearly twice as old as Bella.

'She can't marry him. I won't let that happen.'

Her failure to protect her sister once before had led to Bella being taken to hospital in an ambulance. She could not let her be traded into a loveless marriage of convenience.

But how could she stop it? Bella would cry and plead but she knew that her father would not relent. And so Bella would crumble.

She felt almost drunk with despair. Her mind was racing, looking for exits, for some drop-down ladder that could give her a way out. But there was only one way that this could end.

'Your Royal Highness, has it been hard carrying on a courtship without anyone knowing?'

Betty smiled. 'We're very fortunate to have been able to spend time together out of the public eye.'

She was standing next to Vero in the great entrance hall of the Prince's Palace. Dressed in his ceremonial robes, the Lord Chamberlain had just announced their engagement officially to the assembled media.

Hearing her and Vero's names read out had made it shockingly, undeniably real. The one consolation was that, as a result of her agreeing to marry, her father had agreed to let Bella have the option of rejecting any suitors.

One of the court reporters from the Italian TV network Canale 20 held up his hand. 'It must have been a huge decision for you to marry again after losing His Royal Highness Prince Alberto,' he said, making a small, deferential bow in her direction. 'What made you so sure that you were ready to wed now?'

She felt her smile stiffen.

Because I had no choice. Because my father, the Prince, was going to marry off my sister to a man old enough to be her father.

For a moment, Betty imagined what would happen if she told the mass of reporters and photographers and camera crews the truth.

But there was no room for the truth in Malaspina.

'I haven't been able to think about anything else,' she

said slowly. Which was true. She had thought of nothing else for the last twenty-four hours.

Her fingers moved to touch the diamond and 'pigeon's blood' ruby engagement ring that had replaced the band that Alberto had given her on their wedding day. 'It was instant and overwhelming.' Also true.

'So it was love at first sight?'

Yes, she thought, her throat tightening. Nine years ago it was love and longing and need, a physiological need to see him, touch him, be with him as imperative as air or water or sleep. Although she hadn't slept. She had been unable to miss time awake, time with Vero.

She forced herself to smile.

'Not quite. We knew each other already—'

'Did you feel any pressure to remarry, Your Royal Highness?' An American reporter this time. Female, lush and blonde and wearing a smile that wouldn't look out of place on a crocodile.

Her own smile didn't so much as flicker. 'There's always pressure on an heir to the throne to find a partner. I think probably I felt less than most people my age and, in my position, having already been married. But that's one of the reasons that Vero is going back to the States. He wanted to give me the space to make up my mind—'

It was the first time she had spoken his name out loud in public and as the long e and short o reverberated through her body it felt oddly exposing.

That wasn't true. It was something her father had insisted she say to shut down exactly that kind of probing question, so she should have been relieved. But instead, her stomach clenched at the lie.

'But you said yes straight away.' The blonde reporter was gazing dazedly at Vero as if any other option would be an act of madness. Betty gritted her teeth. Have him, she wanted to snap at the woman. You're welcome to him. He might look like a prince but he has no principles, no conscience and no heart.

A British reporter thrust his microphone upwards. 'The House of Marchetta has always followed tradition in their choice of royal consort. Your engagement to Mr Farnese could be seen as a radical step. Some people are saying it amounts to a revolution in royal terms. What are your thoughts on that, Your Highness?'

She felt Vero's hand tighten a fraction around her waist, drawing her closer, and all those hours spent preparing her response to that exact question had all been for nothing as her brain stumbled. Never mind a royal revolution, Vero had turned her life upside down. He made her unstable, made her question everything, question herself.

Blinking, she met the reporter's gaze. 'It would be a unique revolution indeed if it came from inside the palace.'

There was laughter then and she waited for it to die down. 'My family and I are respectful of tradition, but my father Prince Vittorio's reign has been remarkable not just for its stability but its modernity. My marriage to Vero, a Malaspinian citizen, merely reflects that.'

There was another onslaught of questions.

'It will be a short engagement. Is there any reason for that?' The blonde reporter again.

'Might I answer that?' She felt her spine stiffen as Vero leaned forward and she felt the faint trace of his stubble against her jaw. 'I know it feels like this has all happened overnight but Princess Bettina and I grew up in the palace so we had already got to know each other.'

She felt a flicker of annoyance, and something that

even more annoyingly felt like admiration. She had been raised from birth to deal with the press. Even as a shy, self-conscious child, she had been forced not just to attend public engagements but to speak at them.

And yet, out of the two of them, Vero seemed more at ease in front of the cameras than she did. But then the cameras loved him. As did some of the crews, she thought, catching sight of the blonde reporter's rapt face again.

'But you were the son of the chauffeur then.' The American reporter persisted. 'Isn't it a tremendous change to go from playing games with the Princess to marrying her?'

His green eyes rested on Betty's face and she stared almost hypnotised as he reached out to tuck a stray curl behind her ear.

'Less than you think.'

He closed the distance between them and kissed her on the mouth and for a few drugging seconds the world shrank to the feel of his lips on hers and his hand against her waist, and a pleasure that was both dizzyingly immoderate and yet left her wanting more.

There was a sound like popcorn exploding in a pan as about thirty cameras flashed in unison and she could practically feel the combined happiness and relief of the assembled media who had the picture they'd come for.

'I'm sorry, that's all we have time for.' Anselmo stepped forward smoothly as Vero broke the kiss. 'But thank you very much for joining us today.'

'This way, darling,' Vero murmured, taking her hand and leading her back into the private part of the palace and away from the reporters, who were still shouting out questions.

A sleek, dark unmarked car was waiting for them. As

the chauffeur closed the door behind them, she snatched her hand free.

'I really don't see that there's any need for me to come with you to the airport,' she said stiffly as Vero stretched out his long legs and tugged his tie loose. 'It's a private airfield. There won't be any reporters.'

She had thought that first meeting at the palace was awkward and uncomfortable, but the press conference had been a hundred, a thousand, times worse. For the last hour, she had been forced not only to hold Vero's hand but also to look into his eyes as if he alone gave her world meaning, and the whole charade was so frustrating she wanted to snatch the ceremonial staff from the Lord Chamberlain and snap it into splinters.

But, of course, she couldn't do any of those things. Particularly not when there were reporters around.

Gone were the days when the Marchetta family could expect a strict media blackout on sensitive and possibly inflammatory situations. Nowadays news outlets paid lip-readers to scan famous couples' mouths as they chatted in private. They employed experts to 'read' their body language and then made up headlines to suit their interpretations of a glance or a frown.

If only she could just tune Vero out somehow.

But there was something vital and shimmering and intensely physical about his presence. It didn't help that he had a body that was more suited to a professional athlete, a tennis player maybe or a swimmer, rather than the typical slack-faced, slightly out of shape businessmen who made up his peers.

'We are supposed to be madly in love and I am not going to be back in the country for another three weeks so obviously you would want to say goodbye to me.'

Tilting up her chin, she glowered at him. 'If only it were goodbye.'

'Careful, *dolcezza*,' he said softly. His gaze encompassed the chauffeur and the close protection officer sitting in the passenger seat. 'You and your father wouldn't want any rumours about the perfection of our upcoming marriage reaching the media.'

She held his gaze. 'Are you suggesting that a trusted member of my staff would leak our private conversation?'

He didn't quite roll his eyes. Vero had never done that even as a teenager. Unlike most of the boys his age, including the ones with titles, he hadn't hidden his shyness or inexperience with girls by goofing around. On the contrary, there had been something restrained about his responses.

Her pulse dipped like a plane hitting turbulence. Not all his responses, she thought, picturing how he had used to shake when they had been together but not alone. As if having to hold himself back.

She felt her pulse crash-land. Because he had been holding something back. The truth of his motives. He had admitted them and then gone on to speak to her in a way that nobody had ever spoken to her. Not even her father at his worst. There had been a hostility and a savage precision to his words so that afterwards she'd felt as if she'd been filleted, and every blistering syllable had been accompanied by that blistering green gaze.

That gaze zeroed in on her now. Still cold, still green but less withering and more incredulous.

'I thought the palace was a closed world. I didn't realise it was a different planet. Yes, I am suggesting that, for the obvious reason that it's exactly what has been happening. Or are all those stories about Frisky Frederico just figments of some overactive reporter's imagination?'

* * *

She hated that.

Watching Betty's face stiffen, Vero felt a nip of satisfaction. She hated not just that there were skeletons in her wardrobe but that they were bursting out through the doors and onto smartphone screens all over the world.

But he had to stop with the point scoring. It was childish and more importantly it was counterproductive. Mostly it left him feeling more churned up than if he'd left it alone. That was the best-case scenario.

The worst was something he still regretted now.

He hadn't gone to confront his birth father with the intention of letting things get so out of hand. In the main it had been curiosity but a part of him had been excited. His father was a duke! And discovering that Tommasino was not his 'real' father had answered so many of the questions he'd had. But it had thrown up even more.

He had been a typical teenager, spilling over with hormones and contradictions. He'd wanted to be heard but left alone. He'd loved his parents but he felt as though they came from another planet. And then he'd found out the truth by accident.

He'd been curious, nothing more, when he'd stumbled across his birth certificate. But his curiosity had turned to shock and disbelief when he'd seen the name of his father. It had taken several minutes for his brain to accept what his eyes had been seeing. An hour at least before he had been able to confront his mother, and the man who both was and wasn't his father.

They had argued. But only when he'd said he wanted to meet the man who had fathered him, then given him up. His mother had wept and pleaded, and he had shouted. Only Tommasino had stayed calm.

He should have listened to them. He should have waited. But he hadn't been willing or capable of waiting.

Had he expected to be welcomed like some prodigal son? No. He wasn't that naive, but he had assumed that the Duke would at least be curious about the son he had never met.

He'd been wrong.

The Duke had been quietly appalled at the sudden appearance of his bastard son, but after the initial shock had worn off it had been clear that he was completely and unapologetically uninterested in forming any kind of bond, and certainly not with some impulsive, scruffy teenager who hadn't even known how to address him correctly. To him, Vero was simply a reminder he didn't want of an affair he'd rather forget.

Feeling the Duke evaluate him and find him unworthy of the complications he would bring to his life had hurt, and he had lashed out because he had been a teenager. His father had not simply disowned him to his face, but revealed that he had paid Tommasino to marry his mother and adopt Vero as his own.

The message was clear: stay away, you're not wanted here.

But he was no longer some powerless teenage boy. He was a man now, a man who was about to marry a princess. As the Duca d'Arduino, he would be equal to his father, and then, in a year's time, following protocol he would be Prince Vero of Malaspina, and the man who'd had him removed from his home would have to, not just acknowledge him, but bow to him too.

The car was slowing. Ahead of them, his private jet sat on the runway, white and streamlined like a gull at rest.

'You shouldn't believe everything you read in the papers.' Her voice was taut and quivering like an overstrung bow, but he was distracted by the way it made that bee-stung mouth of hers tremble.

'And you shouldn't act the fool. It doesn't suit you.'

Her chin jerked up but he was already reaching her hand and uncurling her fingers, half guiding, half pulling her from the car.

'There might be a privacy screen, but your driver and bodyguard have got eyes and who knows? Either one of them might have a gambling addiction. Or a huge mortgage that they've fallen behind on. Or a grandfather with multiple mistresses who need paying off to keep quiet,' he said as they walked swiftly towards the jet.

Her eyes flashed and he felt her hand tense with frustration. But then it must be hard for a natural-born liar like her to hear the truth spoken out loud.

'That's how it works. One tempting offer and the next thing you know our conversation will be a headline.'

He watched as she shook hands with the air stewards and the pilot and co-pilot, bestowing each of them with one of those smiles that she was so famous for. The smile that was as exquisite as a Golconda Diamond. The kind of smile that was only natural to a princess who'd grown up basking in the love and approval of everyone around her and was certain of her place in the world.

She was still smiling as the crew retreated but her eyes were wary and distant.

'Not everyone is as self-serving as you.'

'Or they don't like to admit it. They like to see themselves as better than other people.'

Her lip curled at one corner.

'Probably because, in your case, they are.'

She tried to pull her fingers free then, but he simply

tightened his grip, daring her to make a scene, knowing she wouldn't. That wasn't Her Most Serene Royal Highness Princess Bettina's way. She preferred to dazzle her victim then lead him to the edge of the cliff and shove him off.

He leaned forward, tilting his head to one side so that, to anyone watching, it would look as if he were about to kiss her.

'You know, I think you really believe that crown you wear on state occasions is proof that you exist on some moral high ground. And maybe those sycophantic supplicants that surround you at the palace and your adoring subjects believe that too. But you and I both know that no amount of regalia can change the fact that you are a spoiled, self-serving little snob.'

Harsh, he told himself, watching her eyes widen with shock, but fair. Which was more than she had been to him.

Now he kissed her, although it was less a kiss and more a whisper of contact, enough to breathe in her scent and watch her pupils flare. But not so much that he wouldn't be able to sleep. Because someone had to put an end to his body's incoherent and humbling response to her.

He had to put an end to it, otherwise he would run the risk of letting those thoughts that took over his mind turn him into her eager servant just as they had nine years ago.

That wasn't who he was any more. This time, he was in charge.

'I'll see you at the dress rehearsal,' he murmured and then, before she could respond, he let go of her hand and walked swiftly up the stairs and into the jet.

CHAPTER FOUR

'WOULD YOU MIND tipping your head back a fraction, Your Highness?'

Betty's eyes flickered up to meet those of Daniel, the make-up artist who was staring down at her assessingly. 'I'm going to add in a tiny dab of bronzer just here, and here for a snatched effect,' he murmured. 'Bring out those beautiful cheekbones.'

Smiling minutely, Betty tilted her chin up slightly. Daniel was part of her inner circle. He had been doing her make-up since she was a gauche, self-conscious teen-ager and had helped her evolve from youthful ingénue to the refined, understated look she preferred.

Now, he took a step backwards and smiled. 'Perfect. Now we can move on to your eyes.'

At her first wedding, she'd had little if any input. Her mother had basically made all the decisions and she hadn't cared enough to get involved. This time, her father had taken on that role, reminding her with the precision of a Swiss clock marking the hour that her people were expecting the perfect princess.

She had agreed to everything.

But she needed to be able to look at her reflection and see something of herself today of all days. So, her hair would be in a slightly undone chignon and although her dress was long sleeved with a high neckline, there was a lace-edged cut-out veiled in tulle on the back. As for her make-up, it was determinedly lo-fi. There would be no contouring or ombre or strobing or draping. Just a fluffy lash, a hint of peach blush on the cheek and a swipe of coral-pink balm on the lip. Oh, and freckles.

Her freckles proudly on display.

'Are we okay for time?'

Unlike other brides, a royal bride was never late. But a part of her, the part not bound by duty and protocol, longed to drag her heels. Or better still to stop time so that the hour of her wedding simply never arrived.

'Yes, Your Highness. We have plenty of time.' Taking a step back, Daniel nodded approvingly. 'Your skin is just gorgeous, by the way.'

Betty smiled back at him and her gaze moved involuntarily to the mirror. Was it gorgeous? She always felt so pale and washed out but today her skin did look luminous.

Hopefully it would be enough to convince the world that she was marrying Vero for love and not because she had been blackmailed into doing so.

The idea that anyone should suspect made her suddenly feel as though she might throw up.

She'd already imagined it happening so many times. At night she would dream that she was standing at the altar and the bishop would ask if there was any known impediment to the marriage taking place and each night a different faceless member of the congregation had got to their feet and she would wake in darkness, her body shaking with panic.

It would be fine, she told herself firmly. Judging by the cards and gifts that had been delivered to the palace, the population of Malaspina were united in their joy and the media outlets were similarly enthused by the prospect of a royal wedding.

Of course, it helped that Vero was one of their own.

Her pulse twitched. And that he looked the part.

Of their own accord, her eyes darted to the magazine lying open on the bed. It was one of the special supplements that had been produced for the wedding. Bella seemed to have all of them so they were all over the palace and every single one had the same photo from the engagement announcement on the front cover.

That kiss.

It had been over in the time it took to press a shutter button. Over before it had started and yet even now just thinking about it, she felt singed inside. And it felt wrong that Vero could make her feel like that. He had lied to her. Led her on. Taken her love and made it feel cheap and ridiculous.

So why did she still get lost in the press of his mouth against hers? It was like being an alcoholic. It didn't matter that she hadn't touched a drop in nine years, one sip, or, in Vero's case, one kiss, was all it took to make her spiral out of control.

'I have something for you.'

Betty glanced away from the mirror to where her sister was leaning forward, her blue eyes shining with excitement.

'Close your eyes. She can, can't she?' Bella looked up at Daniel's assistant, who had been applying tiny individual lashes to Betty's natural ones.

'Of course, Your Highness.'

Smiling at her sister, Betty closed her eyes.

'Okay, you can open them.'

As Betty stared down at the earrings in her hand, Bella

leaned forward. 'I know Papà has given you the Valletti necklace and Vero will probably have something special for you too, but I wanted to give you something just from me. Do you remember when I got them?'

'Of course.' She nodded. It had been the first time her sister had competed, and it had taken hours of pleading to get her father to agree. But it had been worth it. Bella had come first and, as well as a trophy, she had won these earrings.

Betty swallowed. Her eyes were burning. 'They're lovely, and it's so sweet of you to give them to me, but they're yours. You won them.'

Her sister frowned. 'Only because you persuaded Papà to let me compete. I was so happy that day. So when you wear them, I want you to remember that. I want you to remember all the things you do for me and for Papà and everyone else, because you never do. You never put yourself first.'

Until that moment, she had held it together, channelling her panic and fear and anger into efficiency, but now she floundered.

A memory of footsteps pounding down corridors and of her mother's tear-streaked face. Up until that moment she had never understood what the phrase wringing one's hands meant. But watching her mother's fingers clench and unclench in trembling spasms, that had changed her for ever. That day, that one, selfish moment when she had put her ego, her vanity, her pathetic need to be liked above everything, including her sister's life, would live with her for ever. Even now, just hearing her own voice telling Bella that she could have cake, made her squirm with shame and remorse.

'It won't be different, will it? You being married, I mean?' Bella's blue eyes were suddenly bright.

She shook her head. 'Nothing is going to change. Now, help me put these earrings on.'

But life with Vero Farnese was going to change everything.

It was twenty-eight days since she had last seen him.

They had spoken on the phone, short formal conversations that had left her feeling weak and unbalanced. And Vero had sent her flowers every day, which she had dutifully distributed to local hospitals. She had acted surprised, but the flowers had been her idea.

What was surprising was that Vero had requested a 'real' royal wedding. Given that, for her, this was her second marriage and, for both of them, it was purely a marriage of convenience, she had expected Vero to want something small, private, perfunctory.

Only it turned out that wasn't what he wanted. In fact, almost everything he wanted was the opposite of what she'd expected.

But should she be surprised? Vero had always defied classification. He had grown up in the grounds of a palace but was the son of the chauffeur. His dark hair might be classically Italian but there were those outlier green eyes.

So the wedding venue was not the Lady Chapel at the Palazzo Vanvitelli, the smaller palace used by her grandmother up until her death, but the cathedral. And instead of a minimalist guest list, more than a thousand dignitaries, royals and celebrities would be filling the pews of the Basilica di San Paolo.

She got the feeling from her father's tight-lipped expression whenever the list was discussed that last part hadn't been a request. She didn't know how to feel about that. A part of her would have liked to have witnessed that showdown, but mostly it made her feel nervous.

Even more nervous, because it wasn't as if she'd been feeling relaxed about her upcoming wedding day.

Or the wedding night?

She shivered inside. That too, but that was just part of the general panicky swell that rose up and threatened to swamp her whenever she thought about the post-wedding period of her life. Unlike everyone else, aside from her father and Vero, she was under no illusions that there would be any kind of 'happy ever' attached to their after. Truthfully, she hadn't quite worked out what their version of 'after' would look like. Obviously, it would involve children, an heir and a spare.

First, though, she had to get pregnant.

'Betty? Is everything okay?'

Her sister's voice cut across her train of thought and she reached out and took Bella's hand.

'Everything's fine. And you don't need to worry. I'll always be your big sister.'

And big sisters looked after little sisters even if that meant dancing with the devil. A green-eyed devil without scruples or a heart.

Better that than sacrifice Bella to a loveless marriage with a man twice her age.

Because it was too late for Betty. She had loved and lost, although you couldn't lose what you never had in the first place, could you? And Vero had never loved her.

But then she didn't deserve to be loved anyway because Bella was wrong. She had put herself first and, on each occasion, she had ended up hurting her family.

Selfishly, brutally, stupidly, that one time when she should have looked after her little sister, she had been more interested in looking cool in front of her friends and a boy who had fled from the room when Bella had started to clutch at her throat. But being the focus of positive attention had been such a novelty and so exhilarating that she would have done anything for it not to end. And everyone always preferred Bella. Since her sister's birth, that had been drummed into her and so she had needed her sister to leave. Which was why, despite knowing that Bella's allergies were dangerous, she had let her sister eat the cake.

And then there was Vero. She had wanted him blindly and without thought for the consequences or his motivation in pursuing her. Flattered by his focus, she had let her ego and libido stifle her mother's warnings.

Maybe if she had listened then her mother would never have had that first stroke and then the others wouldn't have followed.

Her fingers tightened around her sister's as the bells of the cathedral rang out the hour. It was time to change into her dress.

Twenty minutes later, Elsa Venturini, the woman who had designed the wedding dress, straightened up from where she had been flicking the fabric of Betty's skirt.

'Would you like to see yourself, Your Royal Highness?' she said quietly.

Betty nodded. 'Yes, but does it—? Do I—?'

'Yes.'

Everyone spoke at once and Bella pressed her hand against her mouth. 'Oh, Bibi, you look so beautiful. Just like a princess should.'

Betty turned slowly towards the mirror and stared at her reflection, her pulse beating erratically. The dress was undeniably lovely. A simple column of pure white satin with a lace-edged cut-out on the back accompanied by a cathedral-length veil but, even without it covering her face, the woman in the mirror didn't look like her and yet she wasn't a stranger either. She was an idealised version of herself.

The perfect, Most Serene Royal Highness Princess Bettina.

And that was who everyone wanted her to be today.

Particularly the groom.

The carriage to the church was Vero's one concession to her father. The streets were crammed with people craning over the barriers, peering over the heads of the uniformed guards of the Palace, to catch a glimpse of their monarch and their princess. There were Malaspinian flags everywhere and she focused on the fluttering pennants as she waved.

Beside her, her father seemed calm. Thanks to her mother's strictly reinforced mantras about the need never to reveal her emotion, she knew that she looked calm too. But as the Prince helped her out of the carriage, she felt anything but serene.

Run.

The word reverberated inside her like a drum roll or an alarm bell. And in her mind's eye she could see herself picking up the skirt of her dress, then kicking off her shoes and running, head down, like a sprinter.

But then her father held out his arm and she slipped her hand underneath and they climbed the steps to the cathedral.

'Ready?'

No, she thought. Not that it mattered. The Prince's question was rhetorical. There would be no backing down.

She met his eyes and nodded, trying to ignore the

feelings of inevitability closing around her like high-sided walls.

As they stepped through the arched doorway into the nave, her heart was lurching against her ribs so heavily that when the guests turned towards her for a moment, she thought it was because they could hear it beating. But, of course, they just wanted to see what she was wearing.

Some of the faces would be familiar. But today they were just blurred ovals. She felt a rush of panic, and then her eyes fixed on Bella's small, heart-shaped face and she remembered why she was there, and that sense of purpose calmed her. Now she could see people. A prime minister here. An actor there. Several footballers and their gazelle-like wives. Some distant relations, the older ones dripping with jewels, their younger counterparts taking furtive glances at their phones, and, dotted in between, a few business colleagues of Vero.

Conspicuous by his absence was her grandfather. Behind the scenes, there had been a stand-off with Vittorio refusing to allow Frederico to bring his young bride, but then Nonno had tripped and fractured his ankle and, horrified at the idea of being photographed in a wheelchair, he had decided not to attend on the grounds of mobility.

Also absent was anyone from Vero's family.

He had no siblings; his mother had died the year before and his father was too ill to travel. That fact had emerged at the engagement dinner. Vero had offered no further information and when she had started to suggest that they wait for Tommasino to recover, he had shut her down. He hadn't raised his voice. It had stayed low and cool but he had changed the subject shortly afterwards.

'Smile, Bettina,' her father murmured softly but his eyes were sharp. 'Our people want to see you smile.'

He was right. Former royal brides like her mother and grandmother had been instructed to look serious on their wedding day. Royal weddings were not like ordinary weddings. The bride was not simply taking a husband, often she was forming an alliance. In other words, they had been doing their duty and smiling had therefore been inappropriate.

But times had changed, and today the crowds who came to cheer the bride and groom wanted to believe in the magic, to believe in the happy ever after.

Which meant she needed to smile, but her mouth wouldn't make the right shape. It was as if all the energy in her body were being diverted into her legs, forcing her on to where the tall dark-haired man was standing by the altar.

Alberto had not bothered to turn round. But as she got closer, Vero turned, and she felt her legs waver beneath her and static filled her head and as the green of his irises met her gaze, she had to stop herself from looking away.

Because that was what hurt the most. To have to look into his eyes and not see them soften. Which was beyond stupid given that she knew now that he had been simply playing the part of a man in love. Playing her, so that for a few sweet months she had believed that there might be another way for her to live.

Her throat clenched around the lump forming there.

Growing up, she had never been one of those little girls who fantasised about her wedding day. But nine years ago, she had dreamed about this moment, and with the light slicing through the stained-glass windows she let herself slide back into the time before everything changed when she still believed that Vero loved her for herself.

Believed that their wedding would be the day when the whole world would bear witness to their love.

She had let him inside her head and under her skin. Let him get closer than anyone ever had, before or since, even Bella. And she had so wanted it to be real that she had ignored the glaringly obvious truth. That, like so many other poor little rich girls, it was her money and wealth and, in her case, the glitter of her crown, that were the real draw.

It was almost unbearable to compare the naivety of her hopes with the reality of this charade.

And it was a charade, she thought as his green eyes fixed on her face, his features moulded into one of those classification-defying expressions that had fascinated her once but now made her want to weep or rage.

He was astonishingly, unreasonably beautiful. Every woman's fantasy of a bridegroom.

It wasn't just his height or that lean, muscular body or even that absurdly beautiful, sculpted face. He had a kind of gravitational pull that was based on something less tangible than limbs and muscles and bone structure. Not power or wealth. He'd had neither when they'd first met but he'd still had it then. A magnetism that was outside science and science fiction. Nameless. Captivating. *Dangerous.*

Prince Vittorio released her hand and stepped back to take his seat and suddenly it was just her and Vero. Alone. In a cathedral filled with over a thousand guests and choristers and musicians and members of the Malaspinian armed forces.

It hurt to look at him, to imagine what might have been, only she couldn't let him know that was what she was thinking and so she trained her gaze on his face.

The service went like clockwork in that it was smooth flowing and, unlike her first wedding, she managed to say her vows without so much as a stammer even though her throat was alarmingly dry.

Marrying Alberto, she had been in a daze, as if she were sleepwalking.

With Vero, everything felt crisp and sharp-edged. The vows slipped from her tongue like rubies and pearls in that Russian fairy tale Bella loved so much, even though they should have been serpents because every word was a lie.

There was only one moment off-script.

When he slid the ring onto her finger, her hand twitched and his eyes snapped to hers and there was something in how he stared down at her that made her feel as if she were a kite caught in a gust of wind, dragged upwards, soaring higher and higher.

Exactly sixty-two minutes later she was walking back out of the church, her fingers no longer resting on her father's arm but interlinked with Vero's as if he were leading her onto a dance floor, his grip both possessive and suggestive. And much as she wanted to, she could think of no way to extricate her hand without drawing attention to it. Of course she had to hold his hand, he was her husband.

Her legs did that wavering thing again. She felt dizzy and precarious, as if she were standing on a windowsill.

For so long there had been a place inside her, a gap, an emptiness, a Vero-shaped hole in her life, and now he was here, and not just here. He was her husband.

'Aren't you forgetting something?'

They had paused at the top of the steps to the cheers of the crowd, and her smile froze to her face, the train of her thoughts cut in two by his quiet but authoritative voice.

He was smiling too and even though she knew he was faking it she felt as if every cell in her body were turning towards him and opening like sunflowers at dawn.

'I don't think so.' Mentally, she ticked off all the bullet points in the day's schedule.

'That ceremony was for the bishop and your father. For your people, the fairy tale starts now.'

'Starts how?'

For a moment, he didn't reply. He just stared at her, his green gaze flickering over her face too fast to read the emotion, but she felt every flicker of his eyes stir something inside her and she wanted to look away but he kept looking at her, just looking and looking and all the time there was that hungry undercurrent of restlessness and restraint.

'With a kiss.' And then he leaned in, his irises a deep, drowning green, and fitted his mouth to hers.

It wasn't like that kiss at the palace. That had been an almost involuntary eruption of hunger, a blistering loss of control. This was all about control. *His.* He was kissing her to make a point, to show the world that they were man and wife.

Her man. His wife.

She jerked her head back and he stared down at her, his mouth curving at the corners as he led her down the steps to the carriage as the sound of the crowd's cheers engulfed them.

'You look beautiful.'

It took her a moment to register the compliment because none of the warm afternoon sunlight was threaded through his voice. Instead, it sounded cool with an undertone of something like anger. As if he regretted having spoken. He certainly didn't sound happy about it.

'It's a beautiful dress.'

His pupils flared. 'Yes, it is. But I'm not talking about the dress.' She felt his fingers loosen almost as if he was going to let go of her hand and then, abruptly, they tightened, and she heard his breath catch.

'I'm talking about you. You're beautiful.'

It sounded even less like a compliment and more like an accusation.

'You don't need to tell me that. We're married now so there's no reason to lie. Or rather, there's no reason to add to all the lies we're already telling today.'

His face didn't change but she felt the flex of his muscles as he helped her into the carriage. After the scale of the cathedral, the interior of the carriage felt tiny and Vero seemed to fill it, taking up both space and air as the door closed behind him so that all her senses felt crowded.

As it started to move, he shifted back against the velvet cushions. He looked relaxed but, like a jaguar dozing in a tree, she knew that he wasn't.

'You seem confused, *dolcezza*,' he said slowly. 'That was a real wedding. We made vows in front of a whole cathedral full of witnesses. It's legal and binding, and I meant every word I said. But then I suppose I shouldn't be surprised that you didn't. I mean, you've spent most of your life tossing out lies like some tourist throwing loose change into the Trevi Fountain. Why should your subjects be treated any differently?'

'I don't lie to my subjects.'

'Right, so all those people waving their little flags know that your grandfather has been skimming money from the Marchetta bank accounts to fund his lifestyle?'

She hated him then for being right, for being there in the carriage and for having this power over her. For being willing to wield that power and for that hot, hard light in his eyes.

'And they won't ever know now, will they?' he said softly. 'Thanks to me.'

'Don't make out you're some kind of hero,' she snapped. 'You're getting something out of this too.'

'And you hate that. Hate that my money puts us on an equal footing.'

'You wish.'

He held her eyes for a beat, his mouth a hard line, then he turned towards the window, and as he waved at the crowd, she heard the cheers magnify.

'What a pity that you didn't have a better offer. Another prince waiting in the wings for you.'

'He wasn't waiting in the wings.'

His words stung, again stupidly because he was the bad guy here. He had lied and manipulated her and yet even at the time getting engaged to Alberto had felt wrong for reasons she could neither name nor articulate.

But she hadn't had the energy to argue with her father, not after Vero's deception and her mother's stroke, and so she had agreed to the engagement.

He shrugged. 'If you say so.'

Smarmy bastard, she thought, and his head snapped towards her as if she had spoken aloud.

'I do say so,' she said, her fingers tightening around her bouquet. 'Not that you care what I say or think or feel. You've made that perfectly clear already.'

'Well, opposites attract and let's face it, Princess, nobody could accuse you of being transparent.' He shook his head. 'Your whole life is a performance. Nothing about it is real. Everything is edited and managed and polished to such a shine that everyone is dazzled, but the heart of it is hollow and empty of anything profound or true.'

Her heart stumbled then beat loudly in her chest. Only one person had ever spoken to her like this. The same person who was speaking to her now.

'Then you should fit right in,' she spat at him, goaded now but instantly regretting her words because they made her sound weak and wounded and she couldn't bear for him to know how badly he had hurt her. How much it was hurting to have to be here with him now.

Except he didn't, Vero thought later as he sat at the wedding breakfast, surrounded by a thousand strangers and beside a woman who despised him. He didn't fit here in this world.

That fact had been made painfully clear to him when he was fifteen years old. He might share his father's blood, but he would never be in his life. He was an embarrassment, something to be swept aside, denied, disowned.

But not today.

His eyes narrowed over the assembled guests to the iron-grey head at the far end of the ballroom. In an ideal world, Tommasino and Vero's mother would be here with him on the top table and he hated that they couldn't be.

Either way, having the Duke there was non-negotiable.

That was his revenge. Forcing his birth father to witness the son he had abandoned marrying a princess and publicly having to acknowledge that shift in status. That was why he had demanded a wedding of this scale and why his birth father was currently sitting at the outer edge of the room furthest away from the guests of honour.

The wedding breakfast was being served in the great

ballroom, the world-famous Stanza delle Luci. Like most of the guests, he found himself admiring the delicate, embellished plasterwork on the ceiling, the colossal, mirrored doors and the thirty legendary, glittering chandeliers.

Unlike most of the guests, he had seen it before, nearly a decade earlier. He and Betty had misjudged the time one day and the only way for him to get back to meet his father had been to go via the palace. Betty had distracted the footmen so that he could sneak in through a side door.

His body tensed as he remembered the flush of colour in her cheeks. The way her eyes had been wide with panic and excitement and the tight grip of her fingers. Ducking into doorways and under staircases as she'd led him from room to room.

She had pulled him through another door into the ballroom and they had both stopped and stared up at the towering ceiling, and then she had suddenly started to spin on the spot, her head thrown back, her arms outstretched.

Watching her spin, he didn't think he had seen anything so beautiful.

They had spent so much time together, leaning over the engines of various cars, her beautiful clothes covered up by his overalls. And he'd kept telling himself it was all in his head. Those looks. That way her eyes would move shyly but frequently to meet his. All those times they would finish each other's sentences.

But then she had stumbled, and he had stepped forward and steadied her and suddenly she had been in his arms, and she'd been kissing him, and he had realised that all that stuff he'd been thinking was in her head too.

And then he had been spinning as well, and he could taste her panic and her excitement and something that he'd thought was love.

Did she remember that day?

He glanced over at the woman sitting beside him, her head tilted to catch something the bishop was saying.

Perhaps. But not in the way he did. Perhaps not at all. And he wanted to reach over in front of all these strangers and pull her against him and take that voluptuous bow of a mouth of hers and keep on taking until she relinquished herself to her need for him. The need that made them equal.

The breakfast seemed to last an eternity. There were five courses then toasts, speeches and now it was time for the first dance between the Prince and his daughter.

A hush had fallen on the ballroom and then the musicians began to play a beautiful waltz.

He watched, his blood pounding in his skull as her father spun Betty in a circle, his patrician features breaking into a smile as the crowd broke into polite applause. It had been hard enough sitting so close to Betty and feeling the distance between them. But now it felt as if he were watching her through glass, almost as if she were inside a snow globe, and her beauty and remoteness were a punch to his stomach, a reminder that he was still an outsider, an intruder to be removed.

He didn't realise he was moving until he stopped in front of the Prince. 'Excuse me, Your Royal Highness.' He bowed minutely. 'May I cut in? I'd like to dance with my wife.'

He could tell from the way the Prince's eyes bulged slightly that he had broken with protocol, but he didn't care.

Betty's eyes widened as he held out his hand, but she took it calmly.

There was a smattering of applause as he pulled her

closer and now, as if some invisible signal had happened, other couples joined them on the dance floor.

'What are you doing?' she murmured against his cheek.

'Dancing with my wife.'

The chandeliers in the vast ballroom might be the most photographed in the world but nothing could compete with Betty. She looked luminous in that beautiful shimmering dress, pure and remote like a bride in a storybook, but he felt her hand twitch against his as his fingers splayed against her back, and he was suddenly grateful for the lack of direct skin-to-skin contact.

His palm flexed against her back. She felt temptingly good, warm and soft where he was hard, and he had forgotten how good she smelled. Enticingly good, to the point that he couldn't stop himself from leaning and breathing in the scent of her perfume and, beneath that, her skin.

'*Scusi...*'

Still lost in her scent, he barely glanced up as one of the spinning couples encroached on their space.

The woman bobbed a curtsey, and the man bowed. 'My apologies, Your Royal Highness—'

Vero felt his breath turn to air. He'd played this moment inside his head so many times and in every variation he had been ready for his father, ready to meet his gaze and watch his discomfort, to savour the disorientation. But now, as the Duke glanced past his shoulder, purposely avoiding acknowledging him in any way, he was the one feeling disorientated, dizzy, ripped open.

Ashamed.

And he hated that feeling. Hated that, despite his knowing everything the Duke had done to deny his existence and conceal the connection between them, it was still there inside him. That longing for acceptance.

It was a few seconds at most and then they were moving again, turning in slow circles, Vero's feet moving automatically. He could feel Betty's eyes on his face, and not just her eyes. It felt as if the eyes of everyone in the room were looking at him, as if everything, the tables, the chandeliers, the floral arrangements, were watching him, judging him—

Abruptly, he pulled away. 'I think that's enough dancing for one night.' Ignoring Betty's confusion, he tightened his grip on her hand. 'It's time to leave.'

CHAPTER FIVE

THE DRIVE TO the Marchetta royal residence in Milan took less than thirty minutes. But for Vero it felt as endless as the walk back to a locker room after losing the match.

The housekeeper was waiting for them in the entrance hall and, in an ideal world, the one he had pictured at this point in time, her bobbing curtsey and effusive congratulations would have chimed with his private, triumphant celebrations at having finally got his revenge.

But he didn't feel like performing a victory lap. Why would he?

He thought back to the moment in the ballroom when the Duke cut him. The floor had felt as if it were made of glass. Or quicksand. He had felt like an imposter, an intruder. As if everyone were looking at him and he'd felt their attention as a thief would feel a security spotlight.

Maybe because she hadn't enjoyed being dragged away from her wedding party, Betty had given him the cold shoulder in the limousine, but now she stepped forward, smiling warmly, and, watching her mouth curve upwards, Vero felt a nip of something that was almost like jealousy.

'Thank you, Elena. And thank you for your beautiful gift. I—we love it, don't we, Vero?'

He nodded, noting the correction. Was it normal for

a bride to forget she was married on her wedding day? '*We* do,' he said, although, truthfully, he hadn't paid that much attention to the gifts they'd received.

As was usual among engaged royal couples, they had sent their guests a list of charities they wished to support and encouraged them to donate. But there were exceptions. Members of the household staff like Elena, and close friends and family, were permitted to give presents.

But he was only really interested in what Prince Vittorio had given him. Or, more accurately, bestowed upon him. As Betty's husband, he was now to be known as the Duca d'Arduino. And when she took the throne, he would be His Royal Highness Prince Vero.

It had been agreed as part of the wedding negotiations. His marriage to Betty would provide heirs for the House of Marchetta and in exchange he would have a title, one that equalled and would ultimately rank higher than the Duke's.

It was what he had been working towards for years.

At first, it wasn't a conscious ambition, just a vague, nameless need to show the people who had looked down on him and tossed him aside as if he were a scratch card without a prize that they had been wrong.

He wasn't worthless or inferior or disposable. He couldn't be discarded and ignored any more. And he would not prove it in some equally vague, nameless way. He wanted to rub their faces in it.

Meeting Frederico by chance in Cairo had crystallised those shapeless thoughts into a plan. And the plan had worked. Except it hadn't. He had been visible yet unacknowledged.

As if to prove that point, Elena stepped forward to address Betty, ignoring him completely.

'Would you like any refreshments, Your Royal Highness?'

Vero felt a sudden, strong urge for a glass of whisky. Or better still a bottle, although that probably wasn't the best idea. Undoubtedly their early exit from the celebrations would be greeted with approval, but the groom necking a bottle of spirits on his wedding night didn't have quite the same optics.

Betty was midway through shaking her head, and then she glanced over at him, and he knew that she had forgotten that 'you' was now plural.

He felt his throat tighten with the old anger, the anger that he'd worked so hard to contain.

'No, thank you, Elena. I think we might go up.'

The Marchetta residence was modest in comparison to the Prince's Palace. It was only the royal coat of arms with its crown and sceptre and pelican with outstretched wings on the external gates that gave any indication it was a royal residence. Its location in Milan had been another strategic decision, this time by the tenth Prince of Malaspina, to demonstrate the country's close links with its neighbour.

And to offer a handy bolt-hole in case of any revolution, although that was not widely publicised. There would be worse places to sit out a revolution, he thought, his gaze grazing the opulent red wall coverings and the striking painted ceiling as they made their way upstairs. But then his eyes moved of their own accord to the back of Betty's dress.

He licked the back of his teeth.

It had fascinated him all day. The front was modest and high cut but turn her around and there it was. That cut-out. Just a lace-edged oval. Simple, tasteful. But looking at it made him feel like a voyeur.

Tilting his chin, he inched back his head.

There was no bare flesh on display. Nothing so overt for Princess Bettina on her wedding day. Her pale skin was veiled but again that only served to pique a man's curiosity.

His curiosity, and his alone. Because as far as Betty was concerned, there would be no other men.

As for those buttons. His gaze ticked down her spine. Stopping as they did just above the curve of her buttocks, they seemed designed solely for the purpose of tantalising and distracting.

And, more pragmatically, to make it a Herculean challenge to access the tempting body underneath, he thought sourly as the housekeeper led them through a doorway. Not that those buttons were necessary. On the rare occasions they had been alone today, there had been a cool but tangible forcefield of resentment around Betty that made it clear that any intrusion into her private space would result in ice burn or frostbite.

Vero stared around the huge, beautiful bedroom, his blood thudding jerkily in his veins.

'Is there anything I can do for you, Your Highness?' The housekeeper again.

'No, no, thank you, Elena.' Betty smiled. 'I think we have everything we need.' She was tired, he could hear it in her voice. Tired of posing and pretending to be a happy, blushing bride. And she wanted the housekeeper gone so that she could relax. 'Why don't you go and join your family and watch the fireworks?'

'Yes, why don't you do that, Elena?' He slipped his arm around Betty's waist, shifting his weight so that she had to grab his arm to stop herself overbalancing. 'No need to hang around. We'll be fine on our own, won't we, *cara*?'

He could feel Betty's heart beating against his ribs, but she smiled, and she kept smiling right up until the moment when the door closed behind Elena.

Instantly, she jerked free of his grip and stepped backwards, her grey eyes swirling like storm clouds.

'Do you mind?'

'I don't. And you shouldn't either. If you want this marriage to be in any way believable, you need to get into character. We're newly-weds, remember?'

'And when we're in public, we will act like newly-weds. But right now, we're alone.' Her voice was quiet and calm but that grey glare could have given a tornado-building supercell a run for its money. 'So there's no reason for us to touch one another.'

'How about kissing?' he said softly. 'Is there a reason for that?'

A flush, pale like the underside of a rose petal, seeped along the curve of her cheekbones.

'If you're talking about the kiss on the cathedral steps—'

'I wasn't.' He tilted his head, the better to see her reaction. 'I was thinking back to how you kissed me that first day at the palace.'

'That was—'

'What?' He held her gaze. 'A mistake? A muscle memory.' He watched her eyes widen. 'Do tell, Princess. I'm longing to hear you tie yourself up in knots trying to explain that away.' Better still, he could tie Betty up in knots. Splay her out on that big bed and take his sweet time licking every inch of her.

'Don't call me that. And I don't need to explain anything,' she said coolly. 'Because it meant nothing. In fact, until you mentioned it, I'd forgotten all about it.'

'Liar.'

She took a step towards him, her hands curling into fists by her sides, her eyes dizzyingly close to his, and he wondered whether it was some twisted cosmic joke that she could stand there and lie so emphatically to his face and yet look so innocent and vulnerable in that dress.

'Only because you made me stand up and lie in front of all those people.'

And nine years ago, she had made a fool of him, so maybe they were all square.

No, he thought, not yet.

'And you did it so beautifully, so convincingly. But then look at all those lies your grandfather told, and all the lies your father told and is undoubtedly still telling to cover up those original lies. It's in your blood, isn't it, Your Royal Highness?'

She glared at him, all storm-cloud eyes and that mouth of hers forming a shape that made hunger spark sharply inside him, and for a moment he wanted to cross the room and press an open-mouthed kiss on her mouth and keep kissing until she had no breath left to fight her need for him.

'Your opinions might carry more weight if they weren't simply some regurgitated nonsense you've read online,' she said crisply, her grey eyes beautiful, bored. 'But as you've never met my grandfather, I'd rather you kept them to yourself.'

He felt a pang almost of sympathy. She had no idea that he had met Frederico or that the old man had encouraged him to pursue Betty. As he watched her throat quiver, it was on the tip of his tongue to tell her the truth. But he wasn't ready to share the contents of that conversation in Cairo just yet.

'The same goes for the rest of you. Keep your hands, your mouth, your everything to yourself—'

'And that's your plan, is it, for how we're going to make this work?'

'At least I have a plan. And there is no we.' She still sounded bored but there was a hoarseness there too that made his chest pull tight.

'You might want to tell your mouth that,' he said softly, mainly to watch her lips part in outrage. 'It seems to have trouble keeping its distance from my mouth.'

She gifted him one of those glacial stares she seemed to reserve for him alone and stalked across the room to the dressing table.

Staring after her, Vero felt his chest tighten.

Betty was wrong. He did have a plan.

It had felt like fate meeting Prince Frederico at the casino in Cairo. He had been on a business trip in the region and his hosts had suggested a visit to neighbouring Egypt to play roulette. He wasn't a big gambler, but he had hit a jackpot of sorts when he had sat down at the baccarat table and his neighbour had turned out to be Betty's grandfather.

He'd never met the Prince, but he'd heard the rumours and, after two hours listening to the old man talk, he could understand why Frederico was there with him instead of sitting on the Malaspinian throne. He was funny, charming, garrulous and indiscreet. In short, everything that made him great company also made him an unsuitable monarch.

After several more whiskies Frederico's tongue had been well and truly loosened and his blue eyes had misted over as he had let slip that he was having a baby with his new, much younger wife.

By the end of the evening, her grandfather had been rambling and repetitive, his charm diminished by alcohol and age, but two things were clear. The old man had no intention of challenging the line of inheritance, but he knew that the pregnancy would send his pompous, pedantic son into a tailspin.

Vero glanced over at Betty, replaying what happened next.

It had been simple enough to set everything in motion.

He'd encouraged the old prince to call his son once the pregnancy was established and then he'd waited. And that had been the hardest part. Judging how much time to let pass before approaching Vittorio. After that, everything had just fallen into place.

And then it had all fallen apart in the ballroom.

Not that anyone would have realised. Betty wasn't the only one who could present a perfect shopfront to the world.

'If you're going to keep this up, this will be a very long ten days,' he said mildly.

'We might be married, Vero, but that doesn't mean that we can just carry on where we left off.'

He shrugged. 'Why not? It's not that different from before. As I recall we had a "no touching" rule in play nine years ago.'

Her beautiful lips pressed into a thin line but there was a huskiness to her voice that was like a match striking kindling.

'That was different. There was no touching in public. This time, there's going to be no touching in private.'

'That's very confusing. What if I get confused? I'm only the son of a chauffeur.'

She sighed. 'You're not confused, you're contrarian.' Her hair was coming loose from where it knotted into some kind of bun at the base of her neck. If only he could pull out those pins, loosen it some more. He'd never been that attracted to redheads, but as usual Betty was his rule-bending exception.

'Not at all. I'll agree to anything and everything you want, just like I always did. But maybe I need to jog your memory.'

The temperature in the room seemed to shift up several degrees.

'Stop looking at me like that,' she said then.

'Like what?'

He knew how he was looking at her, but he wasn't going to let her get off that easily. He watched her face, saw the sideshow of emotions and felt a pang of disappointment as they were replaced by her go-to expression. That serene mask that covered all eventualities from greeting local dignitaries to opening a sports centre. And giving the brush-off to her ex-lover.

Of course, nine years ago he had viewed that mill-pond composure differently. Back then, it had fascinated him. That she could be so poised and serene in public and then, once they were alone, she would shed her inhibitions with her clothes, becoming decisive, unbound, going from zero to wanton and slowing, much less stopping, had been a concept, not a possibility.

And he loved that switch flicking. Even just thinking about it now made his brain stumble and his skin twitch.

'It's been a very long day. It's time to go to b-bed.'

Her sentence fizzled out as she stuttered around the

word bed, and something swelled low in his throat and his head began flooding with memories of when she had stammered out words on other occasions and for different reasons.

'I agree,' he said slowly.

Her pupils flared then, and her eyes narrowed infinitesimally, and he hated that she could do that. That she could build barriers between them on a dime. But then he was making her angry. Which was a different kind of barrier.

'I'm looking forward to it.' Slipping off his jacket, he tossed it onto a small armchair. Holding her gaze, he tugged his tie loose and then the top button of his shirt.

'I'm glad,' she snapped. 'Your bed is through that door. You have your own room.'

'Separate beds? Separate rooms?' He raised an eyebrow. 'And how exactly are you planning on explaining that to Elena and the rest of the staff?' It might be customary among the upper classes, and particularly royalty, for couples to sleep in separate rooms, but even he knew that didn't apply to the wedding night.

'I'm a princess. I don't explain myself to anyone. And as you very well know, I don't share a bedroom.'

'What, even with your husband?'

'You're not my husband. You're just a man who I've been coerced into marrying.'

That stung, more than he wanted to admit. 'Yes, by your father. Who wants an heir. I'm sorry to burst your bubble, Princess, but this isn't *Dumbo*. A stork isn't going to fly by and drop one at the Prince's Palace in nine months' time.'

He tapped the back of the chair. 'Not even a royal pelican can do that.'

'Enough.' Her voice was high and thin sounding, as if she were facing down a storm, the storm he could see in her eyes.

'Enough of what?'

Her irises were huge and limpid. 'Everything. This. You. Today. Being tugged around on strings like some puppet. And you making out it's all a bit of a joke because you don't care that we've just lied to the whole world. To each other.'

'Betty—'

'Just go, please.'

For a moment he held her gaze and then he took a vacillating step backwards, ducking instinctively as she snatched up a delicate figurine from the dressing table and hurled it across the room.

There was a splintering sound as it hit the wall behind him. 'I said get out.'

'With pleasure,' he said and in that moment he meant it. He spun round and stalked towards the connecting door, his fingers gripping the handle as he yanked it open with unnecessary force.

Later, he would wonder why he turned back to look at her. Was it the need to face her down? To have the final word? If there were any words waiting, he forgot them instantly.

Betty had turned and was fumbling with the buttons at the nape of her neck. They were tiny, the kind fastened with looping elastic.

His hand tightened around the handle, his anger unspooling as he watched her tug ineffectually at the loops. Her head was twisted over her shoulder, and she was glancing at the reflection of her back in the mirror, her fingertips straining for the satin-covered buttons. But even if she managed to undo the ones closest, her arm wasn't going to reach others.

Not my problem, he told himself, watching her struggle. But if someone didn't help her, she was going to have to sleep in that dress.

He swore silently.

'Why don't you call Elena?'

She stiffened, but she didn't look over at him as she replied. 'I can manage.'

She couldn't. That much was obvious, but he knew she wouldn't call her housekeeper. She wouldn't call anyone, and not because it would mean having to explain herself. If anyone found her here alone, fighting to get undressed, no explanation would be required.

And all it would take would be one careless word or casual remark…

He let go of the handle and strode across the room towards her.

'Here. Let me—'

She pushed his hand away. 'I don't need any help, especially not—'

'Mine.' He finished the sentence for her. 'But unless you're going to call someone else, then it's my help you're getting. Otherwise, your maid is going to find you in your wedding dress tomorrow morning, which probably isn't going to scream true love and happy ever after.'

Vero was right, Betty thought. But the idea of him unbuttoning her dress made the air around her snap against her skin like a lightning current striking the ground.

In the past, he had loved to watch her undress and she had loved how he had looked at her, his face stilling, growing blunt with a hunger that had matched hers. A hunger that had enveloped her and left her shaking inside. The first time it had happened had been the most erotic moment in her life and he hadn't even touched her. It was the first time she had felt power of any kind and she had slowed down, taking her time, revelling in her power over him until he had lost patience.

Her skin felt hot and tight as she remembered that moment when his control had snapped and the green of his irises had locked onto hers like a big cat, and then he had reached for her, his hands moving with swift, urgent precision.

She felt tears sting her eyes and it would be so easy to let them fall and ease the frantic, spiky static inside her chest. But if she started crying, she might never stop, and the thought filled her with such panic that she couldn't speak or even shake her head.

'Just let me help, Betty. I'm not going to jump you. I may be a lot of things you don't like but I would never do that,' Vero said then and there was an uneven note to his voice that made her chin jerk up.

'I know.' The chemistry between them had sometimes been wordless but he had always waited for that touch of her hand. 'I know that.'

It was ironic really. Princesses, in Malaspina anyway, were required to look modest on their wedding day. That was why she had worn a dress with long sleeves and such a high neckline. Only it was that very same neckline that made it impossible for her to undo the buttons herself and forced her to seek help to undress.

As if he could sense her softening, Vero took a step closer.

'Then let me help. Please.' There was still tension in his voice but that 'please' grazed her skin. He looked heartbreakingly handsome and her imperfectly repaired heart lurched against her ribs as his complex, compelling features regrouped. Now he gestured towards her dress. 'It'll take a couple of seconds.'

It didn't. The buttons were tiny and the satin covering them made it hard for him to get a purchase. She could feel the intensity of his concentration as his fingers moved over her back and she tried not to let herself drift into his gravitational field. But it was hard when he was so close, and she could feel the brush of his biceps as he wrestled with the buttons.

'How many of these damned things are there?'

'There's one hundred and sixty down the back and twenty-nine on each sleeve. They don't all need to be undone,' she added as he raised an eyebrow.

'I thought car engines were fiddly. This is harder than changing a timing chain.'

'Do you still play around with engines?'

His hand stilled against her back and her eyes moved to his reflected face. 'I wouldn't call it playing and, yes, I do. I have a couple of cars I'm rebuilding at the moment.'

Their eyes locked in the mirror. Was he remembering those afternoons in the cool of the garage? She couldn't answer that question. Instead, she stared up at him and he stared back down at her until she couldn't bear it any longer, and maybe he couldn't either because he suddenly jerked his gaze away as if it hurt to look at her.

'Let me just do a couple more.'

He shifted position and, in the mirror, she watched the bands of muscle across his stomach and shoulders flex against the thin material. It should have reduced the impact, seeing them second-hand, but it made her feel like a voyeur. Except she didn't just want to watch. She wanted to touch, to caress, to trace her fingers over his smooth, contoured skin. She wanted to kiss. To lick.

Her pulse twitched at the thought.

'Try now.'

She tried, pulling the bodice forward, but there was still not enough room. 'One more maybe?' she said, shaking her head.

He undid another button and without warning the dress slipped over her shoulders and she clutched it closer.

'Sorry—' His eyes were very green on hers.

'That's okay. Thank you,' she muttered.

He stared at her in silence, nodded and then took a step backwards.

He was leaving. Her stomach cramped, the tension of the last four weeks, and of the wedding and the guilt of lying to the world and the shame of being powerless and unheard, all of it was pushed out by a nameless, slippery panic. Hot and ungovernable, it rose inside her.

He was leaving.

'No.' Her hand closed around his wrist and he stopped. Everything stopped. Time stilled and they stood frozen, each absorbed in the other, rapt, transfixed, spellbound.

'No?' His voice was hoarse. He sounded dazed, disorientated.

'Don't go.'

He didn't kiss her. Instead, he kept staring at her, his stare and that shimmering thread of heat and possibility and punch-in-the-gut hunger pulsing through the silence, and then he reached out and wrapped his hand around her waist, pulling her closer.

And now he kissed her, and she tasted his need and frustration and something that might have been relief.

His fingers were moving now, pulling at her arms, unpeeling the sleeves from her body, and she felt the dress start to slip over her breasts.

The bodice had a built-in bra, and she shuddered as it grazed her nipples and suddenly she was bare from the waist up. She felt his breath hitch against her mouth and then his hands were cupping her breasts and she moaned softly as the tips hardened and she started to shake inside.

'I want you.'

It felt good to tell the truth, finally. To say what she wanted. What she needed. To be herself and not be ashamed.

'And I want you.' Her skin tightened, and every muscle in her body tensed as he leaned in and kissed her again, his hand pushing at the mass of fabric around her waist until it spilled onto the floor around her feet.

He stumbled back, his pupils flaring, and then he swore loudly.

She was naked now except for a tiny pair of panties, some stockings and her beautiful satin shoes.

His eyes were sharp with a hunger that left her in no doubt that he liked what he saw. She made as if to slip off one of her shoes but his hand caught her wrist.

'No...' He breathed out shakily. 'Keep them on. And the stockings.'

Her body twitched with need as he stared down at her and kept staring and staring and then he started to kiss her, hard, open-mouthed kisses that made heat blister up inside her pelvis. She moaned against his mouth, and he sat down on the stool and lifted her onto his lap, his hands sliding up to cup her breasts.

She shuddered against him, her nipples hardening beneath his thumbs, and then she reached for the zip of his trousers, and he groaned, his breath hot against her cheek as she freed him, her fingers moving over the smooth, swollen head of his erection, and now their breath hitched at the same time and then he was grabbing her hand and pressing down on himself as if he was trying to restrain himself.

But she didn't want him restrained.

She wanted him out of control. Ungoverned. Undone.

'Touch me,' she said hoarsely.

He grunted as she took his hand and pressed it against the damp silk between her thighs, shivering with need as he pushed the fabric to one side and slid first one then two fingers into her slick heat.

Now his eyes changed as she knew they would and he tugged her panties away from her body and lifted her up, and she reached down to guide him in.

He breathed in sharply, she did too, as he pushed in a couple of inches. Because she had forgotten what he felt like. The breadth of him and how hard and solid he was. Her hands gripped his shoulders and then she pushed herself down onto the length of him and his face stiffened and she moved against him, arching her back to offer her breasts.

She jerked forward as he sucked first one, then the other nipple into his mouth and she was grinding against him, her muscles tightening inside, trembling with impatience as she rubbed herself against his flexing body, chasing the heat and the friction. Her legs began to shake and then everything broke apart and she cried out as he drove upwards, thrusting inside her again and again and again as they both found their pleasure.

After, they sat panting, his body hot against hers and slick with sweat. Her body felt loose and tight all at once and it all felt so familiar and right.

She blinked, her eyes fixed on where the wedding dress lay on the carpet. It looked like a rose that had been knocked off mid-bloom by a summer storm or a chrysalis shed by a caterpillar as it became a butterfly. But she wasn't a rose or a butterfly in this man's eyes. She never had been.

To him, she was a means to an end.

And she had just had sex with him. Sweaty, urgent, breathless sex. And she had done it voluntarily, eagerly, as if she didn't know who he was or what he had done.

She stared at his chest, the line of his stomach, the iliac crests, the six-pack—or was it an eight-pack? Either way, he had a beautiful body. And just looking at him made her want to start touching him again, to curve her hand around the still hard length of him. To lose herself in the grip of his hands on her body and the weight of his body on hers and hurtle into that shuddering, unbound pleasure again and again and again.

Her chest heaved, and she sat up.

'What is it?' He shifted back, his eyes tracking down over the curve of her bottom as she got to her feet. 'What are you doing?'

He watched as she plucked a couple of tissues from a box on top of the dressing table and began wiping her thighs and then she walked swiftly to the dressing room and took one of the robes hanging on the rail.

'It's time to go,' she said as she came back into the room.

'Go,' he repeated softly. His eyes narrowed. 'We're not leaving until tomorrow.'

'For the honeymoon, yes,' she agreed. 'But I'm not talking about that. I'm talking about you needing to go to your room.'

'But I don't need to.'

'It's not about what you need. It's about what I want,' she said, using a tone that could have come straight out of her mother's mouth.

He scanned her face slowly. 'Wasn't that what just happened?' His green eyes felt like searchlights.

'Yes. Obviously, I wanted that, and now I would like you to leave.'

'This isn't some one-night stand. We're married.'

'I don't need reminding of that,' she snapped.

'You think? Maybe I'm wrong—unlike you, I've not been married before—but I was given to believe that married couples don't do the walk of shame after they have sex, even if it is only a few steps into the next room. And in case you've forgotten, this is our wedding night.'

She took a deep breath and took a step back.

'Why are you making this into such a big deal? We had sex. I'm sorry if you were expecting more but that's not going to happen. And nor are we spending the night together, so you need to leave.'

His eyes were dark and glossy like a jungle cat's and his muscles were bunching at his shoulders. 'You're unbelievable.' He gave a short, humourless bark of a laugh. 'You think I came back for this. For you. I didn't. But I'll take what just happened if it's on offer.'

She stared at him, mute with a shock that she knew was showing on her face, the hurt too.

'Get out,' she said finally.

'Why? You going to throw something else at me?'

He held her gaze, his face still as the air in the room quivered like lava. And it felt as if she were playing not with fire but an active volcano. Not that Vero would ever harm her physically. But there were other ways to cause pain.

'Fine, if you won't leave, then I will.'

His eyes narrowed and he made a grab for her as she turned away in one smooth movement. But his limbs were still loose and languid with post-coital endorphins, and she reached the door and slammed it, turning the key in the lock.

'Betty—' He swore loudly and the door trembled as he slammed his hand against it. Then again and again.

But it would hold. The doors were not just fire resistant, they were bulletproof, and the locks had a break time of three hours. Walking swiftly across the room, she locked the door out into the corridor. That too would hold.

Unlike her willpower apparently.

As Vero kept shouting her name, she curled up on the sofa, shaking slightly. She had made a mistake. A big one. But unlike tonight, there was no handy connecting door that she could bolt through to escape what she'd done. She was married.

And the scandal of divorce meant that couldn't change. But right now, she couldn't do this. Couldn't pretend and lie. She needed space. She needed somewhere to get her thoughts straight otherwise she was not going to survive this marriage.

She needed somewhere safe to hide. Somewhere Vero wouldn't look.

And she knew just the place.

Getting to her feet, she opened the wardrobe. Bella used this room so there were clothes neatly folded on the shelves and she put on a pair of jeans and a T-shirt, snatched up a baseball cap that her sister had brought back from their last trip to New York and then she sat down and waited.

Vero had stopped calling her name, but she waited another hour before she approached the door into the hallway. Her heart was pounding in her throat. She had no idea what she would do if he was waiting for her outside the room. But there was no one there and, clutching some of Bella's trainers, she ran lightly down the stairs.

There was a thin line of light along the horizon as she slipped into the garage and let herself into one of the cars. The key was on the charging tray and she started the engine, grateful that it was an electric vehicle.

Her heart thudded erratically as she waited for the security gates to lift, her gaze darting back to the door, expecting Vero's furious form to fly through it any moment. But then the gates were open and she accelerated up the ramp and out through the main gates onto the street, and freedom.

CHAPTER SIX

THE MORNING SUNLIGHT didn't so much wake Vero as nudge him out of a stupor. Reaching for his watch, he glanced at the face as he slid it onto his wrist. It was early: five-thirty. It felt earlier. Felt as if he hadn't slept at all, but he had. He knew that because he kept jerking awake from dreams where he was reaching out to grab Betty's arm only for her to slip through his fingers.

He sat up, his gaze pulling instantly to the connecting door between the two rooms as he remembered how he had hammered on it in the early hours of the morning shouting like a man possessed.

It had been a short-lived and unsuccessful siege—

The doors were security doors. He would need a battering ram to break through them and it was humiliating enough having to carry the memory of pleading with his new wife to open the door to him on his wedding night. He didn't need it to be accompanied by a soundtrack of police sirens.

It was definitely not his finest hour.

But then he'd still been coming down from his orgasm, and hers.

He felt his pulse twitch, picturing Betty's face, hearing that choking gasp she'd made as she'd contracted around him, and his own pleasure spiking and spilling out of him as they had shuddered against one another.

His fingers bit into the mattress.

He would be lying if he said that he hadn't wanted it to happen. Betty was his ex and there couldn't be many men who hadn't thought about sex with an ex. Only she wasn't his ex any more. She was his wife and truthfully, since that kiss at the palace, taking her mouth again, taking her, had been playing on repeat inside his head. Several times a day some version of that kiss and a myriad X-rated what-happened-nexts would pop into his head, usually at some completely inappropriate moment like during a meeting with his shareholders or when he was on a factory tour.

So yes, he had thought about it. But since the press conference to announce their engagement, they had only met once in the cathedral for the dress rehearsal, and she had been cool and composed.

And that hadn't changed at the ceremony or at the wedding breakfast afterwards or even when they'd arrived here, and they had finally been alone. If anything, she'd felt even more out of reach. Despite the fact that she was wearing his ring.

He had wanted to punish her for that. To get under her skin in the same way that she managed so effortlessly to get under his.

And it had worked. They had argued and he'd had the satisfaction of watching her hurl priceless porcelain across the room.

Only then she had got stuck in her dress, and he should have left her to it. After all, it was her own fault. She had dismissed Elena and the rest of the household staff. She had dismissed him.

But then he had caught a glimpse of her face, and the

panicky fumbling of her fingers, and he hadn't been able to leave.

And then everything had happened so fast. One minute he was unbuttoning her and trying not to let his gaze wander to the cut-out panel on the back of her dress and that tantalising glimpse of skin, and then it was done, and he was stepping backwards.

Which was when she'd reached out and touched his arm.

Because it was still there. That need. That blistering hunger that he'd never felt for any woman before or since. And there had been many 'befores' and 'sinces'. But Betty was different. Unique. Compelling.

Irresistible.

He breathed out unsteadily. Should he have stopped it? Probably. But he hadn't wanted to. He hadn't been able to tear his eyes from hers, much less wrest his hand from her body. He had been spellbound, dazed and lightheaded, drowning in heat and hunger, and her.

And hell, they were on their honeymoon.

Picturing Betty's face when she'd gripped his wrist, he felt his body harden, his erection pressing painfully against the zip of his trousers. She had looked fierce, almost as if he was something essential to her, like water or oxygen.

The sex had felt like that too. Urgent. Necessary. Imperative, and it was fast. A dam breaking. And then it was over. Only he could remember thinking that couldn't be it. That things had only just got started. That it was simply a pause, a moment of reprieve to catch their breath before he got to do all the things he wanted to do to her.

His skin had still been twitching with pleasure, one hand curved around her waist, the other moving over her, dipping to where they were still joined. And then she had batted his fingers away and was pulling back, walking away to the dressing room.

Because she was done.

He gritted his teeth. *Done.*

His eyes snagged, magpie-like, on the glittering diamond necklace that she'd left behind, discarded casually as only a princess with a vault of jewels could do. Really, he shouldn't have been shocked by the ease with which she could walk away.

But it had been like a punch to the head. Actually, it had felt as if she were swarming him against the ropes, punching over and over.

And after complaining that it was hard to lie to the world, she had lied to his face. Telling him it had meant nothing to her. That if he'd come back for sex, then he'd made a huge mistake.

So yeah, it had stung. Knowing that, knowing she had just used him for sex.

Used him for sex? He swore. Yeah, because he hadn't wanted sex, wanted her?

The only possible answer to that question made his body tense so painfully that he jerked forward and rolled out of bed in one swift movement. He had been too furious and thwarted last night to get undressed but now, gazing down at his crumpled suit trousers and creased shirt, he felt a different frustration, the kind that had nothing to do with sex.

Because he shouldn't have said what he had.

'You think I came back for this. For you. I didn't. But I'll take what just happened if it's on offer.'

The words reverberated inside his head, growing louder and uglier with every repetition.

He'd picked a fight with Betty because the Duke had snubbed him.

The tightness in his chest seemed to be spreading through his limbs.

He'd known the Duke would be there. Had specifically requested a large-scale wedding in order to guarantee his biological father's presence. And yet bumping into him on the dance floor like that had knocked him off balance not just literally but metaphorically. Probably because he was already on edge after watching Betty being spun round by her father and all the memories that had provoked—

So many lies in one room.

Too many.

And they were, all of them, still lying now. He thought back to the moment when his father's eyes had met his. The Duke had bowed to Betty but when he'd greeted Vero, the slight tilt of his head could have been directed at one of the standing candelabras.

And he'd hated how that made him feel. Hated that it even had the power to make him feel anything. It was humiliating. He felt humiliated and diminished, and also guilty that Tommasino wasn't there, and it had been easy to blame Betty and the pragmatic, focused way she had been trying to clean herself with tissues.

As if he were something to be wiped away.

It was all such a mess, and someone needed to sort it. He needed to sort it. Not with an apology, never that. More a reset.

This marriage might be fake but there was no point in pretending that the history between them hadn't happened. But he was prepared to put it behind him and if he could do that then she could too, and then she could stop fighting what she so obviously wanted. What they both wanted.

He tucked his shirt into his trousers. His feet were

bare, and he needed a shave but that could wait. First, he would talk to Betty, make it clear how this was going to work from now on. He spotted the necklace, and picked it up. It would serve as a peace offering.

He tapped on the interconnecting door. There was no response and when he tried the handle it was still locked so he made his way to the other door...

It was ajar.

He pushed it open. The room was empty.

His heart beat irregularly against his ribs as he checked the bathroom but that too was empty. He glanced back at the bed, his breath congealing in his throat. The bed didn't even look as if it had been slept in.

The walls shuddered in and out of focus as he stared around the silent room and then he turned and walked swiftly back through the door and towards the stairs. The villa was silent and there was no evidence of any staff on site although he could see the uniformed security guards standing stiffly at their posts. Shoving the necklace into his pocket, he strode from room to room, moving quietly but with purpose, but there was no sign of Betty.

Finally, he found himself in the underground garage. His eyes moved over the three bays. There were cars parked in two of them.

He felt his stomach lurch in his throat as he gazed at the third bay. It was empty, and he knew why.

Betty had taken the car. And he'd lay odds that she wasn't coming back.

'Excuse me, Your Highness.'

Betty glanced up as one of the maids darted forward to clear away her plate and then she smiled. It was her first real smile in weeks. Leaning back, she gazed up at the silvery foliage and breathed in deeply. And it was all thanks to Ponza.

She was having a late breakfast-cum-lunch out on the terrace behind the Villa Giglio. She had arrived in the early hours of the morning and, stepping off the speedboat, she had felt relief and gratitude. Here she was not at risk of making a fool of herself.

It might only be for a couple of days—she would have to join Vero in the Caribbean eventually—but in the meantime, she could get her head straight, formulate some ground rules for how their marriage would work.

It was what she should have done the moment she'd agreed to marry him, but she had been sleepwalking towards the wedding. Going through the motions. Thinking was beyond her.

But she could think here.

Situated roughly midway between Naples and Rome, Ponza was little more than a dot in the Tyrrhenian Sea, small enough that if you were looking at a map you might think it a stray spot of ink.

It was the largest of the Pontine islands, an archipelago that made her think of the breadcrumbs dropped by Hansel and Gretel to find their way back home. Which was ironic because when Odysseus stopped on Ponza on his way back from Troy he ended up staying a year, seduced by the sorceress Circe and her magical potions.

But for her Ponza was more than just a stopping place. The Prince's Palace might be her official home but the Villa Giglio on the island of Ponza was where she had always felt at home. Home was where the heart was and for all his faults her grandfather had the biggest heart of anyone she knew.

Tilting her head back, she gazed up at the olive tree,

watching the branches move in the sea breeze. Here, she and Bella had been free to play like normal children. They had not been on display. Not been critiqued and judged and, in her case, found wanting. They had climbed trees and swum in the sea and played hide and seek in the orchards.

And now it was hers. Bella had been given the apartment in Paris, but the Villa Giglio belonged to Betty. It was the perfect bolt-hole. Situated at the southern tip of the island, it had a jetty and a private beach, which was so surrounded by rocks that it was practically a lagoon. And because her grandfather had charmed the island's residents, they were sympathetic to Betty's need for privacy and so she was never bothered in the street. Not that she went out much.

The joy of Villa Giglio was that it was truly the only place in the world where she got to be herself. Not a princess. Not the heir to the throne. Not the wife of a man who didn't like her, much less love her.

Just Betty.

Here, the sun was always shining, the sky was blue, and she could breathe. It was addictive and intoxicating.

'Excuse me, Your Highness.' This time it was the housekeeper, Mariangela. 'I wondered if you might prefer to have a later lunch today?'

Mariangela hadn't so much as blinked when Betty had arrived on her own at a quarter past one in the morning and this was, she knew, the closest the housekeeper would get to referring to the matter. Mariangela had worked for her grandfather and embodied discretion and old-school loyalty.

'You know, I might skip lunch. I'll dine earlier this evening. Have there been any messages for me, Mariangela?'

she added after a moment, casually as if the thought had just occurred to her. Or that was what she was aiming for, but she could feel the heat rising up over her face just as if she were sitting in direct sunlight rather than beneath the canopy of leaves.

'No, Your Highness.'

Which meant that her father didn't know what had happened.

But Vero did. He must do by now.

Her stomach somersaulted. Stupid, she told herself. Because Vero couldn't have made it any clearer last night that she meant nothing to him. Although he was happy to have sex if it was on offer.

On offer.

Now her cheeks felt as though they were on fire.

She remembered the shiver that had zigzagged through her body as Vero had gripped her waist and kissed her. It had been a rough kiss, a kiss of hunger and release.

No words had been spoken. But none had been needed.

He knew what she wanted. Knew her body as a migrating bird knew the ley lines of the earth. He had mapped every inch of her skin with his fingers and tongue. And she had done the same with him.

It had felt like coming home, and danger all at once.

Her eyes tracked upwards, following a sweep of cirro-cumulus clouds in the otherwise empty blue sky.

Except there was nothing homely about Vero. He might look every inch the urbane business titan, but he was dangerous.

Not violent or abusive. Never that.

But he made her reckless. Made her forget that her judgement was flawed. But that was the trouble with sex. When it felt right, as it did with Vero, it did something to your brain. Took the brakes off. And when that happened there was collateral damage.

Which was why she was here, in Ponza, not halfway across the Atlantic Ocean in Vero's private jet en route to her honeymoon at his villa on Turks and Caicos.

She wondered what he was telling people.

But that was a Vero problem.

This whole wedding had been cooked up between him and her father. If at any point either one of them had asked for her opinion she would have told them that she didn't want time alone on an island with the man who had broken her heart and who was currently in the process of pressing on the imperfectly repaired cracks.

But nobody had asked her opinion or required any input on her part. So, Vero could deal with any fallout, and she was going to spend a couple of days here doing absolutely nothing for anyone but herself.

She spent the rest of the morning doing precisely that, starting off in a hammock strung between two olive trees and then wandering through the orchard down to where the estate jutted out into the Tyrrhenian, letting her gaze drift out across the shimmering aquamarine water to where it became a thin dark line at the sky's edge. There was so much blue. It was like drowning but without the struggle. Right now, that seemed like a win.

But it was time to get back. She walked slowly through the orchard, stopping here and there to test the ripeness of the fruit. Every step was done at her pace. She was pleasing herself and it felt wonderful.

Her body stiffened reflexively, and she squinted through her sunglasses. Someone was walking towards her. No doubt it was one of the staff. She raised her hand and waved as the dark, indistinct shape grew sharper.

And then her hand froze in mid-air and the tenacious, exuberant beauty of the day collided with reality and shock washed through her in waves.

No.

Not him. It couldn't be him. Not here. She couldn't take it in, couldn't understand how he could be here in Ponza. Slowly she slid off her glasses, half hoping that they were distorting her vision in some way.

They weren't.

And even though she didn't want to, she found herself marvelling at the way he moved. There was both an elegance and a fluidity to it, like a dancer. Only there was also a sense of purpose in the rippling muscle and, even from a distance, she could feel the incredible focus of his green-eyed gaze.

Less dancer, she thought, her pulse skittering forward like a startled rabbit. More panther.

Was this how Circe had felt seeing Odysseus approach?

Vero stopped in front of her.

The sun was on her face so it was hard to see his expression but then he shifted to block out the light and her heart beat out a drum roll of panic and irritation, and something she didn't want to acknowledge, much less feel. Because he looked good.

Her breath snatched and she felt the leaves blur around her into a mass of swirling silver that matched the fog in her brain.

By good she meant every kind of right.

There was no mirror to hand, but she knew that her face was probably flushed and possibly sweaty from the heat of the sun and she could feel a slight stickiness around her mouth from where she had been eating figs straight from the tree.

But aside from a graze of dark stubble, Vero looked exactly as he had in the cathedral although his clothes, as befitted a man on his honeymoon, were less formal. Gone was the dark, tailored suit and made-to-measure shirt. Instead, he was wearing cream chinos and a green polo that was a shade darker than his irises and clung to his body as if he'd been shrink-wrapped.

Her eyes slid over him jerkily, snagging on the stripe of muscles bisecting his torso.

She felt it beat through her blood then. Anger. Hot and furious because what gave him the right to do this? To turn up looking so distractingly enticing. To turn up at all.

This was *her* home. She had the deeds. She paid the household bills out of her pocket. But it was more than just a home. It was her sanctuary.

A safe space where she could be herself or at least try and find out who that was after so long just simply being what was required of her. And this marriage had made her feel even less solid and sure of herself.

All she had wanted was time alone. Time to regroup, to bolster herself against this life she hadn't chosen. He couldn't even give her that, she thought, resentment twisting her stomach.

But she was ready for him.

'How did you find me?'

'Your father.' His eyes rested on her face. He sounded calm, but his eyes told a different story. 'Not intentionally. He doesn't know you're here. He let slip something at the wedding. It was lucky I remembered. Your staff were not helpful at all.'

'It's called loyalty, Vero. It's not a concept you understand.'

He stared at her in silence, regrouping maybe or more

likely just making her wait for his reply. Tilting up her chin, she glared at him.

'What are you doing here?'

'I think that's my line, Your Highness?' he said softly, but the smile that accompanied his words was hard and dangerous.

He stared at her in silence for a long, level moment as if he was considering his response.

'You left something at the house,' he said finally. Her muscles tensed as he reached into his pocket and as he pulled out his hand, she saw a flash of diamonds.

She lifted a hand to her throat. 'My necklace.'

'That too.' He held her gaze. 'But I was actually talking about me. You do realise we are supposed to be on our way to Turks and Caicos?'

She tilted back her head. 'I do.'

'I do?' Pausing, his smile hardened into a frown. 'I do. That sounds familiar?' He shook his head now, doing mock confusion. 'Oh, yeah, I remember. I said it yesterday in the cathedral when we got married. You said it too.' His smile vanished and she saw the anger in his eyes flare and, beneath it, the smouldering, wounded male pride.

'Although that appears to have slipped your mind, unless you have some other, compelling reason for leaving me to go on our honeymoon alone?'

'Let me see.' Now it was her turn to feign confusion. 'How about not wanting to spend any more time alone with you than I have to? Does that count?'

His eyes narrowed. 'Don't play games with me, Betty.'

'You think this is a game?' She held his gaze. 'Games are for pleasure. I'm just doing my duty.'

'Is that what you think you're doing here?' She felt a jolt of heat as he took a step towards her. 'And what about your father? Do you think he'd agree with your interpretation? Perhaps we should surprise him? Give him a call, find out?'

There was no need, she thought, trying not to picture her father's cool, disdainful expression. He wouldn't be surprised. Whatever she did, his response was always the same. The only variable was the extent of his disappointment and how long it lasted.

What was a surprise was the sharp, tangible pain she felt knowing Vero would betray her to her father.

'Be my guest.' She took a step backwards, turning on her heel. 'You can have a nice little chat with him because right now I'm not ready to talk with you, which is—'

What happened next was such a shock that by the time she had processed it Vero had caught her arm, stopping her mid-flight, the impetus spinning her round, and was already scooping her into his arms.

She fought his grip, pitting her strength against his until they reached the villa and then she stilled, seething with fury as he strode through the house, past Mariangela and one of the open-mouthed maids, and up the stairs to her room.

He dumped her on the bed without ceremony and she flew to her feet, her hands curling into fists. It was a long way from being the perfect princess, but she didn't care.

'How dare you?'

They were inches apart, their breath staccato, and his eyes were the darkest they had ever been, and she could feel them pulling her under, feel herself flowing towards him—

She slammed her hands against his chest.

'How dare you humiliate me like that?'

'Oh, I dare, Princess.' He caught her wrists, holding

her at arm's length, his grip tight enough that she couldn't break free. 'I'm not some footman you can ignore. I'm your husband. And frankly you don't get to talk about humiliation, not after that stunt you pulled.'

'You got off lightly.' She sounded breathless now, as if she were running, not fighting, and for a moment she wished she were.

The tendons in his hands were taut with the effort of holding her still. Or holding himself back. 'You walked out on me. On our wedding night. Just skipped off into the sunset alone, without so much as a word—'

She stared at him, stung and stunned not just by his words but by his evident belief that they were justified.

'And you plotted this whole marriage behind my back,' she said after a moment.

He ignored her. 'You left me to come up with some explanation for why my wife had vanished into thin air.'

Her arms were tiring now and she let them go limp, and after a breath he let go of her.

'I'm sure you thought of something. Telling bare-faced lies is your forte.'

His irises blazed, glittering like gemstones against the black of his pupils, but she held her ground. 'I don't see why you care. Our marriage isn't real, ergo this honeymoon isn't real either.' He hadn't even proposed, she realised, a lump filling her throat. He had given her a ring but had simply handed her the box and let her slide it onto her finger.

For a moment neither of them spoke and she knew that the silence filling the room must be taut and uncomfortable, but her pulse was so loud in her ears that she couldn't hear anything. Breathing in, she stared past his shoulder at the square of limpid blue sea through the window, trying to calm herself. If only she were Circe, she could give him a potion and he would be hers to command, and she could command him to leave.

Would she though? She hated that the question, the need to even ask it, made her heart beat in her throat.

'We have to have a honeymoon,' he said brusquely after a moment. 'Surely you can see that.'

'I do. I did. I just—'

All she had wanted was a couple of days to clear her head but why should she explain herself? Besides, any explanation would expose her to that glittering green gaze and reveal just how badly he had hurt her.

'Then you also know that it has to look real. Making that happen will be better for everyone.'

Her stomach knotted. Better for everyone was what people said when something went their way. But nothing could ever be better for everyone.

'Better for you, you mean,' she said bitterly. And for her father too. But it was bad enough that Vero didn't care about her feelings. He didn't need to know that Prince Vittorio had no qualms about sacrificing his daughter to a man he had previously despised.

Vero shrugged. 'Better for Malaspina too. And the House of Marchetta. Which is why you're marrying me, isn't it?'

She could feel Vero's gaze on her face, cool and intent as though, if he stared hard enough, he could see her thoughts passing through her head. She forced her eyes up to meet his.

'Why else would I ever marry a man like you?'

'Why indeed?' There was no emotion in his voice. 'Perhaps if you're struggling it might help to focus on your responsibilities,' he said then. 'You need heirs.'

It didn't help to be reminded. What was more, she didn't need to be reminded. Her responsibilities were with her constantly. And theoretically she understood, had always understood, that she had to sacrifice her wishes and the paths she wanted to follow, to deny what she needed, in order to ensure the security of her family and the prosperity of her country and its people.

But increasingly it had felt like a crushing weight smothering her.

The only times she felt free and able to breathe were here on Ponza, only now Vero had taken that from her too.

'I don't need you to give me advice, particularly not when it comes to my responsibilities,' she snapped.

'So, what do you need?' His gaze was suddenly intent so that the air between them seemed to soften treacherously, and she bit the inside of her mouth hard enough that it hurt, hurt enough to make her snap straight into a forward-weighted stance like a boxer squaring up her opponent.

Because whatever her body might be telling her, that was what he was.

'For you to leave.'

'You know that's not going to happen. I'm not going anywhere, and if you try to run away again, I'll let the press know that we're here, and then your little bolt-hole will be crawling with paparazzi.'

She flinched. 'You wouldn't do that.' Unlike its more cosmopolitan, better-known neighbour Capri, Ponza remained happily under the radar.

He looked at her for one long, excruciating moment. 'Try me,' he said coolly and the calmness in his voice knocked the breath from her chest.

When her father had threatened to marry Bella to the Duke, she had told herself that marriage to Vero was worth it to save her sister from the fate she had suffered at the same age. It had felt like the right sacrifice.

But now…

'You're a monster.'

His unyielding mouth was a hard line, his expression flat and unforgiving. 'You didn't think that last night.'

Heat burned in her cheeks and she turned her head. She didn't want to look at him. Didn't want to have anything to do with him.

'I wasn't thinking last night, I was—'

Wanting. Needing. Craving.

His gaze sharpened into a point of such intensity that it seemed to puncture her skin and leave her open and exposed. Why else would it feel as if he could read her mind?

She cleared her throat. 'It was a lot—the day, all the people, the expectations. I was tense and—'

Her heart hammered against her ribs as his pupils fattened. 'Yeah, sex is good for that,' he said slowly. 'Our sex anyway.' He seemed taken aback by that admission, or maybe by the fact that he had made it unprompted.

Our sex. *Our. Sex.*

She stared at him sideswiped, unhinged, feeling his words fizz against her skin like pulses of electricity, and she hated her brain for not policing her synapses better. Hated her body for being so susceptible to the idea of 'our' and 'sex' when it came to Vero, and she knew that she couldn't survive this marriage, couldn't survive him unless she drew a line, here, now.

Lifting her chin, she shook her head. 'Having sex like we did last night is a complication we don't need.'

Her heart beat erratically as his eyes found hers. 'On

the contrary. I would say it's non-negotiable. How else are you planning on producing an heir?'

'You're not listening to me,' she said as evenly as she could. 'I didn't say we wouldn't have sex. We just won't have it randomly—'

He frowned. 'Randomly?'

The tension in his voice was suffusing the air so that it crackled against her skin. But this gravitational pull between them had to be managed. Once upon a time she might have dreamed of marriage freeing her from her suffocating life at the palace, but this marriage to Vero made her feel breathless all the time.

Her throat worked around her breath now as she pictured him, his hand tightening in her hair as he was overwhelmed by his shuddering orgasm.

She needed to break this spell. What she needed was a protocol, a ruling that would permit no exceptions. That was how she'd been raised. It was what she knew.

It was not lost on her, the irony of her wanting what she had chafed against for so long, but she needed to do something to expel Vero from her head.

'You know, spontaneously. For pleasure.' She was speaking quickly now, wanting to get the words out. 'I've downloaded an app so I can work out when I'm ovulating and maximise the chances of getting pregnant, and that's when we'll have sex. Then, and only then.'

CHAPTER SEVEN

VERO DIDN'T REPLY, didn't so much as blink, but abruptly the temperature in the room plummeted as if their argument had triggered a hyper-localised disaster-movie-style flash-freeze.

'Let me get this right. You downloaded an app so you can work out when you're ovulating and that's when we'll have sex. Just then, and only then,' he repeated, tilting his head back as if he was considering her words.

'Yeah, that's not going to happen.' His voice was quiet and unwavering but there was a hoarseness to it that made her take a steadying breath.

'It is exactly what's going to happen,' she said, trying her hardest to ignore the panic fluttering against her ribs. 'Surely you weren't expecting us to be lovers.'

His gaze snapped to her face and she felt it like a flame licking her skin. As if he were actually touching her. His open mouth hot against her throat. His hand tightening against her waist as she came apart uncontrollably around him…

'You're my wife, so weirdly I was expecting a conversation, not some royal decree that I present myself in your bedroom when summoned, solely for the purpose of breeding.'

'Funny, I never had you down for being melodramatic.'

'And I never had you down for being delusional.'

She had been delusional once. Nine years ago, when Vero had returned after a three-month internship in America, and the green-eyed boy she knew had disappeared. In his place was a man who made the air shimmer brighter than the sun.

He was dazzling, and like a moth she had allowed herself to be fascinated by the light. She had let him get close. Let herself believe that he had seen the woman beneath the crown and liked her, loved her.

Stupid, she thought. Deluded.

But not any more. It was humiliating to admit it, but this was something she couldn't lie about, at least not to herself, and the truth was that she was vulnerable where Vero was concerned. Too susceptible to that catch-and-trap green gaze of his. Just signing off on a sexual relationship with him without adding in some checks and measures would be an act of self-harm comparable to voluntarily wading through lava.

But she needed heirs, which was why there had to be rules.

'Hard to be delusional over something so transparently transactional. Which is what this marriage is. There's a trade-off. You get your title.' She couldn't keep the bitterness out of her voice, but she forced herself to keep speaking. 'I get an heir. So, we need to have sex. Only I would rather that there be less of it, and that it serves a specific function.'

'Can you hear the words coming out of your mouth?' He stared at her incredulously. 'Have you forgotten what happened last night in Milan?'

She tried to swallow but couldn't. Of course she hadn't forgotten. Every feverish kiss, the feel of his hand between her thighs, his other hand tightening in her hair, it was all there inside her head, pressing forward. And she was like the little Dutch boy with her finger in the dam wall, trying to hold it all back.

But what if by holding back she was making things worse? Vero was like a virus in her blood. Perhaps what she needed was to sweat him out. For a moment she imagined how it would feel to give in to her need for him. Imagined the varied and many acts it would take to work him out of her system and the serenity that would follow.

What if? What if?

The question echoed inside her head, and she felt a stab of irritation at her indecisiveness. But then her judgement had been proven to be flawed before and with such appalling consequences.

'What happened in Milan is exactly why there needs to be rules—'

'And you expect me to believe that's what you want?'

'It is what I want,' she said quickly, but then she shivered and his mouth, that indecently seductive mouth of his, curled into a shape that was part sneer, part snarl.

'Hasn't there been enough lies?' His voice vibrated with a complex dissonance of the raw and the restrained. 'Can't you just be honest about wanting this?'

Honest? She wanted to scream. Throw more things at his beautiful face. Instead, she said crisply, 'Thanks to you I can't be honest about anything. You breed lies and now you've turned my life into one too.'

'Then we're even.'

Her stomach lurched and she opened her mouth to protest but he was already speaking.

'You might be able to fool everyone else with that butter-wouldn't-melt-in-your-mouth smile, but I know you,

Betty, and you've wanted me ever since I walked back into your father's palace. You wanted me at the airfield and on the steps of the cathedral and you want me now—'

Her heart was racing, and she felt a shiver rake through her almost as if his hands were moving over her body and she were rushing towards that splintering rush of pleasure.

It would be so easy to surrender...

She shrugged. 'I know this must be hard for you, Vero, but sometimes in life, we have to make compromises.'

If he recognised his words, he gave no sign.

'I'm not agreeing to this.' His voice was cool and measured again but his eyes were a dark, glittering green like the lightning that accompanied the ash clouds above a volcanic eruption.

Tough, she thought, her own eyes narrowing in on his beautiful, symmetrical face. The resolve she'd felt earlier, the need to make a stand, hardened inside her like quenched steel because it wasn't a coincidence that she had swapped living with one single-minded, ruthless man who wanted things entirely his way, for life with another. The only difference was that this was married life.

But this wasn't simply about her father or Vero. It was about her, and she was done with being the perfect princess. Done with letting men jerk her strings to make her dance until her body ached and her feet were blistered and all the while smiling through the pain. Done with being weak.

'You mean like I didn't agree to this marriage. Yet here we are, married.'

His jaw twitched. 'Except, you did agree, Princess Bettina.'

Yes, she had agreed because the alternative was to

sacrifice her baby sister to a loveless marriage of convenience and the stifling, early widowhood that would inevitably follow. 'I was given no choice,' she said tightly.

No choice.

Vero almost laughed. What did Betty know about having no choice?

She had never been evicted from her home or sacked from her job and been powerless to do anything about it. She didn't understand how it felt to offer love and be rejected, be deemed unworthy, because she was a princess who was loved unconditionally by thousands of her subjects. She didn't know what it felt like to have been written out of one's own history, excised from a bloodline, spurned and scorned from birth.

From before birth, he thought, his breath suddenly jagged edged. It still stung just as it had all those years ago, not just discovering that his whole life was a lie but the efforts his biological father had made to distance himself from his bastard child. And was still making.

Remembering how the Duke's eyes had shuttered on the dance floor, he felt so angry that when he spoke he made no effort to soften his tone.

'Do you know how unbelievably spoiled you sound?'

Her eyes jerked to his face, the pupils widening just as if he'd slapped her, but he didn't care. 'Choice is a luxury. It's earned, not inherited. But what do you know about earning anything? Never mind a silver spoon, your entire life was gilt-wrapped and handed to you at birth. Nothing has ever been out of reach. People go out of their way to try and make you happy. And they worship you. Do you know how rare that is? How fortunate you are?'

Taking her lack of response for assent, he continued.

'Then what exactly have you done with all those opportunities and all that favour and adoration, Princess Bettina?'

There was a short, ugly silence.

Betty was staring at him, only she didn't look like herself. That luminosity beneath her skin had vanished as if a candle had been snuffed out and seeing her like that blew out the flame of his anger.

She shook her head slowly. 'You know nothing about my life. You know nothing about me. And I know nothing about you. But I think that's probably for the best given that the more I get to know you, the less I like.'

He wanted to pull her close then and kiss her until she melted into him, and he could prove inarguably that he knew her better than she knew herself. But she looked so brittle he was scared that if he touched her, she might break into a thousand pieces.

Instead, he turned and walked back out of her room and through the house and out into the sunshine that seemed overtly, mockingly cheerful in comparison to the dull ache inside his chest.

The perfect dive was a blend of poise, power and precision. There was no time to blink or breathe as you plummeted into the water.

Stretching out his hand, Vero gazed down into the clear, rippling water. He'd dived off cliffs before but not with this level of emotion churning inside him. It was risky but right now he needed that rush of adrenaline to swamp his anger and frustration with Betty, and himself.

He was supposed to be pulling the strings but instead he'd finally been shipwrecked after days on stormy seas.

Releasing the rock he was holding, he watched it fall,

tracking its path, his brain filling with equations for velocity and distance as he watched its descent, calculating how long it would take to hit the surface and how long it would therefore take him.

Sometimes you had to let things go.

He bent his knees and pushed off, soaring forward, his arms up and over his head, his elbows pressed against his ears, thumbs locked together.

As he hit the water, his world went blue and then he pushed up towards the light, breaking the surface tension and breathing in sharply.

But Betty wasn't one of those things you let go.

He swam then, needed to swim to counteract the tension and the rush of adrenaline that thought produced, cutting through the waves, momentarily lulled by the freedom of movement and the easy rhythm of his body. Finally, he pulled himself onto the spray-soaked rock, smoothing his wet hair back against the contours of his skull.

His arm was bleeding. He must have scraped it on a rock. But the blood was nowhere near as shocking as that conversation with Betty in her bedroom. That had blown his mind.

Afterwards, maybe an hour later, they had eaten dinner together and by then her emotions had defused and she had recovered her poise. Which was a relief, at first. He hadn't liked seeing her so shaken and he'd felt uncomfortably out of his depth.

But it also needled him that she could contain her feelings like that. Conceal herself from him. And he kept remembering what she said about his not knowing her and he hated that, despite his having married her, she could still defy him, still stay out of reach and opaque.

That wasn't part of the plan.

Exiting the water, he pulled on a T-shirt and some flip-flops and made his way back up to the villa.

Then again, what worked on paper often stalled and stumbled when confronted by the limitations of reality. Over a decade working in the automotive industry had taught him that.

But his marriage to Betty had been deceptively simple to arrange.

There had been no real negotiations. Vittorio had not just offered him the title of duke; he had insisted on it. But then money was a great emollient, and the Prince needed money. Not that he'd shared that fact with Vero, but then Vero hadn't revealed that Frederico had already blabbed to him about the Marchetta finances, so they were equal.

His mouth twisted. Equal. It was all he'd ever wanted to be, and he'd got lost in the feeling and stupidly assumed that everything else, and by everything else he meant Betty, would fall into line.

That now seemed both ludicrous and naive.

His eyes moved over the terrace. The loungers were empty but there was an indent in one of the cushions and Betty's book lay open on it, its pages fluttering open in the breeze as if it had been discarded in a hurry.

Which no doubt it had the moment she heard him approaching.

He felt his jaw tighten. It was a game they were playing. A cross between catch me if you can and hide and seek and he was pretty sure her staff were in on it. He could see no other explanation for why his wife was always one step ahead of him. And why, when she finally emerged from the shadows, they were never alone.

It was driving him insane. All of it.

Not only had his father looked through him as if he

were a servant, but his wife had also reduced his status to that of a stallion brought in to cover a mare and was currently avoiding his company so successfully that he was starting to wonder if she led a parallel life as an intelligence agent.

But he hadn't become the CEO of one of the biggest global automotive businesses on the planet by chance.

Nobody at the top had got there without stamping on a few fingers. It came with the territory. They knew right from wrong but engaged in immoral or sometimes illegal behaviour anyway. Sabotaging or intimidating their rivals, using their wealth and influence to get their own way.

But, as his mother used to say, *'Si prendono più mosche col miele che con l'aceto.'* Honey caught more flies than vinegar.

It was time to go back to the drawing board. He wasn't going to be kept standing at stud for weeks at a time until Betty decided it was time for him to service her. He wanted what they'd had nine years ago, what they'd had in Milan, and so, he was sure, did Betty. They just needed some time alone without a phalanx of her staff chaperoning her and then it would happen. He felt a surge of desire. She would reach for him, and he pictured her hand touching his face, his chest, his—

His eyes narrowed. Mariangela had appeared on the terrace.

Raising his hand in greeting, he strolled towards the housekeeper, a smile melting onto his face.

'*Ciao*, Mariangela—'

'Your Grace.' Smiling politely, she bobbed a curtsey.

'It's a beautiful day, isn't it?'

'We are blessed.' She nodded. 'Is there something I can help you with, Your Grace?'

To the right of the housekeeper, Vero could see the indent in the cushion and his body tensed, painfully.

He nodded. 'As a matter of fact, there is…'

Watching her staff clear the plates away from the table, Betty sat stiff-backed in her chair, her mind a whirlpool of confusion and resentment.

She had taken a stand, finally, and arguably too late because Vero was still her husband. But she had done it. She had pushed back against the juggernaut that was Vero Farnese and given him a taste of what it felt like to be powerless. And it felt good.

Less than she'd expected, but it was something to have wiped that complacent expression off Vero's handsome face.

Afterwards they'd dined together. A truly uncomfortable experience but she hadn't let on and, more importantly, she had made sure that they were never alone. Actually, that wasn't true. She hadn't said anything to Mariangela or any of the staff, but then she hadn't needed to. As her grandfather always used to say, what marked out a good housekeeper was that rare mix of intuition and anticipation of what was required.

Which was how she had managed to avoid being alone with Vero.

Until this evening. And she was still trying to work out what had changed, and how she had ended up eating a romantic supper out on the terrace with a pink and yellow ombre sunset as a backdrop.

Mariangela glided forward as the final piece of cutlery was whisked away. 'Would you like some coffee, Your—?'

She cut across the housekeeper's question. 'No, that won't—'

'Yes, please, Mariangela.' Vero spoke at the same time, leaning across the table to wrap his hand around Betty's. 'We'll take it in the lounge...unless, of course, you're ready to go up, *cara*?'

She gave him a glacial smile. 'Not at all. I feel wide awake, as it happens.'

'Perhaps we should skip the coffee, then,' he said, feigning concern.

'Aren't you sweet to worry about me?' She gave him a smile that didn't reach her eyes. 'But there's really no need. I don't get affected by caffeine.'

It was like a dance. Except that not only did she have to follow her partner's lead, she was also having to redirect him and all without making it so that they ended up colliding with one another.

Her pulse twitched.

Dancing was hard enough but there were rules about where you could touch and the distance between you. Whereas a collision...

She wasn't talking about a physical collision, but her brain went there anyway, which was both predictable and proof that she was right to create a framework for their relationship, the sex part anyway. She needed distance from Vero. Not just the spatial kind but inside her head where the boundaries were less defined and he was always so close.

Too close. He needed to be contained.

Was that possible?

Her gaze moved briefly to his beautiful, sculpted face. He had been furious earlier but maybe now he'd had time to cool off, he could be reasonable.

Reasonable? Her heart, which had been beating steadily until then, began to race as she got to her feet.

* * *

Vero wasn't sure how she did it but Betty managed to extricate her hand from his, rise like Cleopatra from her palanquin and was following Mariangela back into the villa before he'd even got to his feet. Once again, he found himself having to chase after her.

And despite his irritation, he found himself admiring her poise. It came so naturally to her, but he had learned the hard way that emotions were better kept in check.

For a moment, he was back in his birth father's palatial villa watching a police officer cuff Tommasino, the wild, choking anger that had propelled him there swamped now by the slippery panic building in his chest. That day had taught him a lot about the world, and the man who had fathered him and the man who was his father in every way except genetically. But most of all it had taught him that emotions were dangerous and so he had learned how to manage them.

In a world where he was helpless and silenced, exercising a rigid control over his feelings was a power of sorts.

And that ability to stay focused, to not get distracted by his emotions or other people's, had been the best business lesson of all. That it overlapped into his private life had never been a problem.

Until now.

Vero's eyes moved to Betty's face. The mask was back in place. Only a slight smokiness to her eyes and that pulse beating somewhat erratically against the smooth skin of her throat suggested that she might be a fraction less composed than she appeared.

He watched, torn between irritation and amusement as she skirted past the sofas and armchairs to feign interest in the view of the sunset through the French doors. It was a beautiful view, he conceded, dropping down onto a pale green velvet-covered sofa.

But he had a better one. His eyes moved over her light curves and he felt his body respond with humbling predictability.

It was like being held hostage.

His one consolation was that she felt the same way. She had to feel the same way.

He pulled his gaze away from Betty's silhouette and stared around the room.

The Prince's Palace and the Marchetta residence in Milan were one of a kind. High-ceilinged, opulent, ostentatious, with their layers of gilt and marble and bronze, but the Villa Giglio had an entirely different vibe. Comfort was key. Furniture was fit for purpose and rather than being smothered in oversized portraits of illustrious ancestors, the cream-coloured walls were bare aside from a striking canvas of a woman.

'Who's the artist?'

Betty turned now as he'd hoped she would, her grey eyes tracking across the room to the painting. 'Marie Laurencin.'

'Interesting choice.' His eyes narrowed on the woman gazing back at him from the canvas. 'Yours?'

He watched her walk towards the painting and stop in front of it.

'My grandfather's originally, but I always loved it.'

Watching her talk, he realised that it was the first time she hadn't been on high alert since he'd walked into the sitting room at the Prince's Palace. And he found himself relaxing too and not just because he was able to watch that mouth of hers without needing a justification. That seriousness and her obvious sincerity mesmerised him now just as they had nine years ago.

Tricked him, he corrected himself, and the memory of his stupidity, then and now, made his own voice rough as he gestured to the painting. 'It suits the room.'

She turned back to face him, and he took the opportunity to let his gaze roam over her small, high breasts and the slight uptilt of her chin.

'I'm guessing it's not to your taste.' Her response was accompanied by one of those grey-eyed stares and a silence swelling with quivering bow-flexing tension.

Vero stared assessingly at the woman in the painting. Despite the pastel colour palette and demure clothing, there was something arresting about her eyes, something provocative. She might be presented as soft, submissive even, but beneath the composure there was fire.

Without warning, his brain switched focus from the painted woman with the taunting gaze to the real-life woman standing across the room and he found himself remembering Betty's fire, and the way she had melted into him, her mouth seeking his to kiss him hungrily with those bee-stung lips of hers...

For a few undulating moments he forgot how to speak. 'You guessed wrongly,' he said after a moment, getting to his feet and walking towards her. 'I like it a lot. There's something subversive there.'

'Yes, that's right.'

She glanced up at him sharply, her eyes widening with shock and recognition, and it was so intoxicating to be the focus of her attention in a good way that the world tilted momentarily on its axis.

'You have to lift the veil but it's there,' he said softly.

Her pupils flared and her lips did something complicated as if she was about to speak then forgot what she was going to say and his brain blanked as he felt her silence inside his bones, and, more critically, low in his groin.

'What happened to your arm?'

He glanced down. 'It's just a scratch. I was diving off the cliffs and I must have scraped it against a rock. It looks worse than it is.'

'You could have been hurt—'

'Would you care if I was?'

'How can you ask that, Vero?'

His name in her mouth made him lose the ability to breathe, to think, to form a sentence. All he could do was stare and his need for her was so intense, he had to take a breath before he could speak and when he did, his voice shook slightly.

'You know it's indecent how badly I want you. And how many hours I spend thinking about you and what I want to do to you and what I want you to do to me.'

It had been a somewhat circuitous route, but they had got there in the end, and he felt a jolt of triumph and relief because she had finally admitted her desire and now anything was possible. He leaned forward.

'What are you doing?' Her palms flattened against his chest and she pushed him backwards, the slip-sliding intimacy of moments earlier dissolving into her frown and his plunging disappointment.

It had to be addressed. He needed it to be addressed.

'Why are you fighting this?' he said then and he hated the hoarseness in his voice. Hated it almost as much as he hated the shutters that dropped like guillotines across her eyes. 'Fighting yourself. I know you want it, want me—'

'But that's why it can't happen. Why I have to walk away—'

He stared at her in confusion. He wasn't into being bound or gagged or humiliated. Nor, despite what Betty had said, was he a contrarian. If a woman wasn't interested, he walked away. Or that was what he told himself.

But there was only one woman who had rejected him, and he hadn't walked, he'd been pushed away, only instead of staying away he'd come back for more. Back for her.

And even now when he knew enough to leave well alone, he was still here. And he didn't know what to do with that need to stay. All he knew was that he couldn't fight her and himself at once.

'You're not making any sense.'

'Because you don't understand. You're like everyone else; you see a princess with a crown. Her Most Serene Royal Highness Princess Bettina.' There was a tremor in her voice that shook in time to her hands.

'So, make me understand.'

'I make bad decisions. Stupid choices, the wrong choices and I don't trust myself to make the right ones…'

She didn't finish the sentence. She couldn't. Her hand was pressed over her mouth.

His anger had long since dissolved, but there were other feelings filling the space it had left. Guilt, shock and remorse. He reached out to touch her, but she stumbled backwards.

'No, I don't want you to touch me, I don't want you—'

She wanted him gone, just as she had back in Milan. But this was different. In Milan, she had been angry with him and herself for giving into their desire.

Now there was an ache in her voice. She looked pale, younger, as young as if the last ten years had never happened, and he knew that she was hurt and scared by the pain she was feeling and like an injured animal she wanted to curl up in a ball and hide.

From him.

His chest felt as if it had been ripped open. For so long he had imagined this moment. Imagined seeing Betty crushed, deposed from her throne of complacency and calm. But seeing her in so much distress was unbearable.

'I know.' It hurt more than it should to admit that, but right now his pride was a long way down his list of priorities. 'But I can't leave you like this, so you'll have to make do with me until someone better comes along.'

She burst into tears then and this time when he reached out, she let him pull her close and he held her against him, tight enough that she felt held but not so tight that she couldn't breathe through her tears.

Finally, she let out a shivering breath and, trying not to tense his body, he waited for her to push him away but she just kept leaning into him and, closing his eyes, he brushed his mouth against her hair, breathing in her scent.

Finally, he felt her move and he had to force himself to let go as she inched backwards.

'Do you want me to get Mariangela?'

She shook her head. She still looked pale and gently he pushed her back onto one of the sofas and sat down beside her. 'Here.' He reached into his trousers and pulled out a handkerchief. 'It's clean, I promise.'

He watched her wipe her face. Her lashes were clotted together, and she was still fragile, he realised. But whatever was going on inside her head, it was a burden she needed to shed.

'So what makes you think you can't trust yourself?'

Her head bent low and she didn't reply, and for a moment or two he thought she wasn't going to. But then she took a shaky breath and said, 'I don't think, I know I can't.'

She sounded stubborn, childish almost, but he sensed that she had been carrying this around with her since childhood. And the tension in her spine suggested she had never told this story to anyone.

'For what reason?'

'Because I killed my mother, and I nearly killed my sister.'

He almost laughed. Whatever he'd been expecting her to say it wasn't that. But then it was so ludicrous. Only looking at her face, he saw that she believed every word.

'That seems unlikely.'

She was shaking her head. 'I told you, I make bad decisions, selfish decisions that end badly. That's why my mother warned me about getting involved with you.'

He frowned. Her mother had warned her? 'I never met your mother.'

'It was the concept of you. For her you were a threat. A scandal in waiting. Her family lost their throne because there were so many scandals and their people got tired of them. It was her biggest fear that would happen in Malaspina. I knew that. I've always known it, and I ignored her. I knew she was worried, but I didn't care. But I didn't realise how much it must have affected her until she had the stroke. And then she kept having them.'

He could hear the guilt in her voice. The regret. Could hear and understand it. He'd had nearly two decades to pick at the guilt and regret and recriminations he felt for getting Tommasino arrested and forgiving himself was still a work in progress.

'You couldn't have known,' he said gently, taking her hand. 'And I doubt your mother would have stopped worrying even if you were the perfect princess.' Reaching out, he tucked a loose strand of hair behind her ear. 'Mothers worry. Mine did, for sure. Even when I towered over her.'

She was shaking her head.

'But I did know about Bella. I knew from when she was little that she had a peanut allergy. And I still let her eat the cake.' The pain in her voice tore through him. Tears were sliding down her face. 'We had to call an ambulance. She could have died. And it was my fault.'

His hand tightened around hers.

'And it must have been terrifying. But you were a kid too and you made a mistake.'

Her mouth was trembling.

'It wasn't a mistake. It was a choice. My parents had some people over for lunch and they brought their children. I wanted to be cool and popular, and everyone was making a fuss of Bella, and I knew if I let her have some cake that she'd go away and for once I'd be the one everyone liked best.'

She pressed her hand against her face again, only not to hold back her tears this time. There was a look of panic in her eyes, as if she had shared something without quite meaning to. Something she was ashamed of revealing.

He stared down at her uncertainly. She looked stricken and he hated seeing her like that. 'You can't think you were responsible. I know you do—' he corrected himself because she so obviously did '—but nobody else would ever think that.'

'But they did.' Her mouth was trembling. 'They thought it and said it.'

'Then I hope your parents had them banished from Malaspina,' he said fiercely.

'No, that didn't happen.' She gave him a small, sad smile that made something inside him crack open. 'Mainly because they were the ones thinking and saying it.'

Vero stared at her in shock. Surely that couldn't be true. But then he thought back to his conversations with the Prince. There had been a chill to the older man's voice when he'd referred to his daughter and the marriage he was setting up for her without her knowledge. At the time he had assumed that Vittorio disliked having to deal directly with someone like Vero. Now though he realised that he had misread the old man and that his haughtiness masked an indifference to his daughter's needs and wishes. That, to him, she was simply an asset to be exploited.

And he had participated in that exploitation.

'They were wrong to do that,' he said, choosing his words carefully. 'But people lash out when they're upset. That isn't what they feel deep down. They know who you are.'

She glanced away and he stared at her profile, the beautiful curve of her cheekbones and the delicate jaw, and he was searching for words when she started speaking.

'Yes, a disappointment.' She breathed out shakily. 'I always have been. My mother's pregnancy with me was difficult. She was horribly ill, and the labour was awful, and of course I wasn't a boy. Even worse, I had the wrong colour hair and freckles, so my father had to endure loads of speculation about that. And I was such a shy and anxious child. Then Bella came along, and they were so different with her. So proud and happy. You know, if Nonno hadn't turned everything upside down I sometimes wonder if they would have asked me to step aside. I tried so hard, I even—' She broke off, frowning.

'Even what?'

'It doesn't matter. None of it matters. Nothing I did, or do, is ever enough.'

Enough. The word scraped across his skin, but he ignored the pain.

'Listen to me, Betty. Whatever you did wrong, however you messed up, that doesn't make you a bad person or a disappointment. You didn't know your mother was ill. As for Bella, you love her and she loves you. But more importantly you take care of her. You look out for her.'

He pulled her against him, wrapping his arms around her, holding her close.

'Everyone messes up. That's how we learn. And young people mess up the most because their brains are wired differently. It's a medically proven fact that they act on impulse and have less ability to self-regulate.' He met her gaze. 'Automotive billionaires have the same problem.'

It was a weak attempt to make her smile and she didn't, but her eyes were soft like smoke. 'Why are you trying to make me feel better? You hate me.'

Had he said that? It felt like a long time ago if he had ever felt it. Stroking her hair, he shook his head. 'I don't hate you. I thought I did. I thought I wanted to punish you. I thought a lot of things apparently.'

He watched her frown, trying to make sense of that last remark, but she was so tired and at that moment a clock chimed the hour and, taking the opportunity to change the subject, he reached out and stroked her face. 'It's late. You need some sleep.'

She let him lead her upstairs like a child, and he waited

outside the bathroom as she brushed her teeth and got changed.

'Shall I turn the lamp off?' he asked as she climbed into bed.

She nodded but as she slid down under the sheet, he could feel her reluctance to lose the light. 'Or I could stay for a bit. Until you fall asleep and then I could switch it off,' he said, only realising as he spoke how much he wanted her to agree. How much he wanted to stay, and his dread of having to be separate from her.

'I can't ask you to do that.' She let out a shaky breath.

'You didn't. I offered.'

He sat on the edge of the bed, and after a moment, she reached out and took his hand. 'I do care about you.'

Seconds later she was asleep.

Breathing out unsteadily, he stared down at her, his chest tight, feeling exhausted and relieved. But mostly confused.

Because he had started the evening intending to make Betty admit the truth about her desire for him, to have sex with him not solely for purposes of procreation but pleasure. Only suddenly, even more than he wanted that, he wanted her to trust him. To trust herself. If he could do that then maybe the two of them could...

Could what?

The answer to that question kept him sitting on her bed until, exasperated by the complexity of his feelings, he let go of Betty's hand and went to sit on the sofa, where it stayed unanswered because he found that he had another, more pressing question.

Surely her first husband was the one person who liked her best. Why then hadn't she told Alberto what she had just told him?

CHAPTER EIGHT

BETTY WOKE UP with a start.

She had been dreaming. Of Vero. They were in her grandfather's little green sports car, driving in the hills behind Morroello. There were no landmarks, but she recognised the road, and she was driving, and Vero was smiling that megawatt smile that made her bones soften and her breath turn to air.

And then the road took a sudden, unexpected turn to the right and suddenly they were heading towards a cliff edge and Vero was undoing his seat belt and getting to his feet and for a moment he stood there, poised and calm, and then he was gone, and the car was tipping forward and she was falling, falling—

Breathing out shakily, she pulled the sheet around her.

Last night she had opened up to Vero in a way that she had never done with anyone.

Bella knew, and her nanny had known, but behaved as if she hadn't. Outside that, it was only Nonno who had, somewhat surprisingly, guessed at her parents' cruelty and manipulation. But was that surprising? For all his careless, rakish ways, her grandfather was astute and observant. A people person, unlike her parents.

Their disappointment in her was painful enough to live with in private. Discussing it with other people would simply add to the shame. Worst-case scenario, they might even take her parents' point of view. After all, the facts were clear and undeniable. That in her desperation for approval she had put both her mother's and sister's health at risk.

It was why she had worked so hard to be the perfect princess. That fear of exposure and the potential for yet more humiliation and pain.

And yet she had chosen to confide in Vero. She still didn't know why she had opened up to him. It made no sense. He hated her. Saw only the bad in her. And not in some abstract way. He was back in her life because he'd wanted to punish her for what she had said to him all those years ago, for how she had made him feel and for what her father had done to his family.

Rolling onto her side, she stared across the room to where Vero lay sprawled on the sofa, still dressed, his feet hanging over the arm, his head wedged uncomfortably up against one of the large, embroidered cushions.

She stared at his sculpted face, her heart skipping forward.

Last night she had not just let her mask slip but smashed it to pieces. She had shown him her scars, letting him see the frailest, ugliest part of herself. She had been his to hurt.

But he hadn't hurt her. Despite having motive, means and opportunity he had listened and comforted and cared enough that it felt like love.

No, she thought firmly. Not again.

Because what did she know about love? The romantic kind anyway.

Her parents' marriage had been a masterclass of pragmatism on both sides. There was understanding and affection of sorts. And she had recreated that with Alberto.

Minus the understanding and affection.

With Vero she had thought she was in love. Thought he was in love with her, but in truth their relationship had largely been a sexual one. A sexual awakening for her, and perhaps for him too, she thought, remembering those afternoons on his bed, his hands trembling, white-knuckled against the sheets, as she took him in her mouth.

But as she'd since found out, you didn't need to love someone or trust them or even respect them to have good sex.

At the time though, in her naivety, she had conflated sex with love and lust with that consummation of a need that went beyond the physicality of bodies and breath. And she had been a willing participant. Eager, in fact. And she could admit now that if Vero hadn't said what he had, she would have given up everything for him. Because it was better to have someone pretend to be in love with you than nobody loving you for real.

And now?

She tensed as Vero shifted in his sleep, rearranging his limbs and rolling onto his side so that if his eyes had been open, they would have been looking straight at one another.

He had done more than look. Last night, he had seen past the facade, seen who she really was, and he hadn't moved away, hadn't pushed her away. He had held her and stroked her hair and made space for her between his arms.

Which was kind and compassionate, and compassion was a form of love. But it was the kind you might offer to children and injured animals. In short, it was simply part of a universal humanity that made people bond and look out for each other.

And her best chance of making this marriage 'work' was to remember that, and not get distracted by the way his eyes seemed to soak her up.

The following morning, she woke late, later than she had done in years.

Someone had opened the shutters a fraction, just enough to let in the cooler, morning air. Even before she glanced at the clock, she could tell from the intensity of the light that dawn was a distant memory. For a moment, she stared at the view through the window, taking pleasure in the strip of blue sky and sea, and then everything from the night before rolled over her like a wave and she sat up.

Vero.

But aside from the cushions sitting plumply at either end, the sofa was empty. She felt his absence sting her skin, but had she really expected him to wait for her to wake up?

Unsurprisingly, given that it was nearly half past ten, there was no sign of Vero at the breakfast table, and, stemming her disappointment, she nibbled a pastry and drank some black coffee before wandering oh-so-casually through the sitting room and onto the terrace.

But Vero wasn't there either. Nor was he by the pool or in the orchard or on the beach. Back at the house, she dithered about asking Mariangela but just as she was crunching her way across the gravel, she noticed that the door to the garage was ajar.

Pushing it wider, she stepped inside, her pulse skipping a beat as she breathed in the familiar scent of warm leather and oil. It took a minute for her eyes to adjust to the gloom. Her grandfather's pistachio-coloured convertible was sitting where it always did. Glancing at it, she stiffened. Usually it was covered, but someone had taken the soft top off.

'This is one dope whip, Princess.'

She felt a jolt of heat as Vero stepped out of the shadows, moving in that loose-limbed way of his that made her skin tingle and, gazing into the half-light, she almost lost her balance.

He was wearing a black T-shirt that stretched endlessly across his shoulders and slouchy blue jeans and with his dark hair falling in front of his eyes and the light striping across his face it was like tumbling back in time.

'Two questions. One, when were you going to tell me that there was a 1955 Alfa Romeo Giulietta Spider on the premises?' he said, walking slowly alongside the car, his fingers trailing, almost caressing the glossy paintwork. 'Secondly, why is that big, ugly behemoth out on the drive instead of this little beauty?'

'By "big, ugly behemoth", I take it you mean the limo?' She met his gaze. 'That's my official car. My father prefers me to use that for security reasons.'

He held her eyes for a split second. 'What a waste. So who drives it? Please tell me it's not Mariangela. I saw her trying to put some roasting tins in the oven yesterday and I'm not going to lie, she has no spatial awareness.'

There was a moment of silence as their eyes met. Quickly, in case she saw pity there, she gave him a small, tight smile and said, 'Thank you for yesterday. For mopping me up and listening. I'm sorry for burdening you with all that.'

He smiled, one of those curling, 'raised by loving parents and never had to question his own worth' smiles that made her breath feel hot in her throat. 'That's what a husband is supposed to do, isn't it?'

Yes, it was.

But Alberto had shown no interest in the inner workings of her mind. He had shared her parents' attitude that an aristocratic marriage worked best as a union whose purpose was to cement an alliance or shared wealth.

She took a steadying breath. It was uncomfortable thinking about Alberto when Vero was standing so close. Like a betrayal. Only not of Alberto but of Vero. It was the same feeling she'd had when her father had told her that he had found a suitor for her just a week after she and Vero had broken up.

It had felt wrong then. It still felt wrong now. But there was a way to make it right.

'There's something I need to tell you. I wanted to tell you before, right after it happened, but obviously that wasn't possible.

'I wanted you to know that Alberto wasn't waiting in the wings. And I wasn't waiting for a prince. I know what it must have looked like, but I never met Alberto until the day our engagement was announced.'

Vero's deep green eyes didn't so much as blink, but she could feel him processing her words.

'Why did you marry him so soon after we split, then?'

'After you, after we— My mother thought I needed to be settled. And my parents wanted the match.'

'Did they force you?'

She hadn't needed forcing. She had been numb. Uncaring. But then her parents had known that.

'My mother had had the first stroke and my father blamed me. It felt like the least I could do. And everyone wanted it to happen.'

'And what did you want?'

You, she thought. And she had admitted so much already, but that was too much.

'I wanted to please them. And they were worried somebody would find out I'd slept with you, and Alberto didn't care that I wasn't a virgin. That's why it all happened so quickly.'

'And then he died.'

'Yes.' She breathed out shakily. 'But I didn't want him to die. I might not have loved Alberto, but I never wanted that.'

He pulled her closer. 'Of course not.' His face creased. 'I thought you wanted to marry him. If I'd known that you had no choice… I just wish I'd been there to stand up for you.'

'I thought you wanted to punish me,' she said slowly. 'Not take on my father.'

'I did but I've ended up punishing myself instead.'

She stared up at Vero in confusion, but he was looking back at the car. 'You never said who gets to drive it.'

'No one at the moment. It can't be driven. The cam belt is busted. I ordered a new one but it's such a long time since I looked at an engine and I was nervous about handing her over to just anyone. How did you get in here?' she added, glancing over at the door. 'Wasn't it locked?'

'Yes, Nancy Drew, it was. But I'm on good terms with the owner. Or I think I could be,' he said then. 'If she'd give me a chance. Or it might even be a second chance.'

He took another step forward and stopped in front of her.

Her breath hitched. She knew that it was risky to stand that close to him. Knew too that it was the leather and oil smell acting like catnip on her senses but any input from her frontal lobe had got lost somewhere between the sweet, eager look on his face and the snatch of her breath.

'And what would you do with this second chance?' she said slowly.

In the soft sunlight filtering in through the half-open door, his skin was smooth and even and his green eyes were serious and steady.

'Look, I know all of this is fake. But I think we've been focusing so much on what's fake, we've forgotten what's real. So why don't we just forget about the wedding and the honeymoon and have some fun being plain old Betty and Vero? Do you think we could do that? Would you like to do that?'

Her heart, which had been beating steadily until then, began to race. It was the first time that Vero had asked for her opinion, her assent, since he'd walked into the Prince's Palace all those weeks ago.

The first time she could remember anyone asking for her opinion or assent in probably her whole life.

Maybe it was that fact or perhaps it was how he was looking at her as if nothing else existed in the world, but she found herself nodding. 'How would that work?'

A tension she hadn't realised was there seemed to ease from his shoulders and jaw and she watched mesmerised as the sunlight licked a path along the curve of his cheekbone.

'I had my yacht brought to the island this morning.'

He had? She stared at him dazedly.

'It was only a short hop from Capri.' The shrug that accompanied that statement transformed him from the son of the chauffeur into an automotive billionaire whose every wish became reality with the sending of a text.

'She's moored at the jetty. I thought we could take her out and go do some diving. You can snorkel, can't you?'

She nodded again. 'I haven't done it in a while.'

'But you enjoy it?'

She almost nodded again but caught herself at the last moment. 'Yes.'

'Then let's go do it.'

Was that it? She'd asked herself the same question when her father had agreed to her not marrying Vero. But then she'd felt as if she were standing on a trapdoor that was going to suddenly open beneath her feet.

This felt different. Easy. Effortless. Just as it used to, and she stared up at him dizzily. They were standing close enough that she could have reached out and touched those miraculous cheekbones and it was impossible not to focus on their closeness.

Clearing her throat, she said quickly, 'I'll go and tell Mariangela.'

An hour later she was swimming through the clear, cool water of the Tyrrhenian Sea.

Gianluca, the yacht's captain, had dropped anchor near the Cala Gaetano, a secluded crescent-shaped cove where the water was closer to green than blue.

The beach itself was covered in stones but the reason for stopping lay beneath the waves several metres from the shore, as Betty discovered when she submerged her head and shoulders. Instantly all sounds were muted and the sun and the sky were forgotten. It was like being in another, hidden world. There was so much to see that wasn't visible from the surface. Octopus and crabs and tiny, dancing seahorses. And it was easy to forget all those land-based expectations that normally followed her like a shadow.

'We'll have to wait a bit before we go back in,' Vero said as they sat down for lunch. 'I wouldn't want you to get cramps.'

She nodded. 'I'm happy to wait.'

Not just happy to wait, she thought with a jolt. Just happy, and lighter, as if a burden had been lifted. But then it had. Talking to Vero, unpicking her past with him, unpicking their past, had been uncomfortable but holding everything in had been breaking her from the inside out.

She hadn't planned on telling him anything. Quite the opposite in fact. It was humbling enough to admit that her parents viewed her primarily as a puppet on a string. Revealing that out loud, and to the man who had shared their opinion, would be an act of deliberate and unnecessary self-harm. Like rubbing salt into a wound.

Her eyes moved to his face, to the impossible symmetry of his features.

But Vero had been not salt, but a salve. He had listened, and offered not pity but comfort. He had made her realise that the House of Marchetta was a house of mirrors, each one reflecting a different, distorting view. Looking into his green eyes, she had seen herself as he saw her, not as a disappointment or an idealised, perfect princess, but as Betty.

'Or we could go looking for dolphins.' Vero had looked up from his food and was gazing at her across the table. 'Gianluca says he saw a school off Santo Stefano.'

'I'd love that,' she said truthfully, and then because she wanted to, and because now it was easy to do so, she added, 'And maybe tomorrow we could go and see the cathedral cliffs at Palmarola.'

It wasn't storming the barricades, but it felt undeniably good to say what *she* wanted to do.

'Sounds like a plan.' Vero held her gaze. 'Maybe we should renew our wedding vows while we're there. Just the two of us.'

His words oscillated between them in the bright sunshine. But that was all they were, she reminded herself. Just words that happened to be spoken by an intensely beautiful man who was also the only man she'd ever loved.

The dolphins didn't disappoint. She had seen them before when she had gone out with Alberto as part of the official engagement photo shoot but, in truth, she could hardly remember their marriage, much less one isolated day.

Vero's deceit and his absence had undone her, turned her world dark and she had been alone in the darkness. Who could she have talked to about her broken heart? Not her parents. Not Bella, who had still been a child. And not her husband.

And then first her mother, then Alberto, had died. One after the other, and there had been more pain and guilt and regret. In the everlasting, formless grey of her life, she had learned to live through Bella and all the colours of her younger sister's hopes and dreams.

But today she was here, on a yacht, breathing in fresh sea air, feeling restless and hopeful and planning for tomorrow. And it was because of Vero.

She glanced over to where he was leaning against the rail. 'Thank you for today.'

'My pleasure.'

The word pressed inside her head like a stone inside a boot.

They had touched so many times yesterday and today in a completely non-sexual way but now she felt almost shy around him. And he was being careful too. At one point she had lost her balance and he'd caught her arm to steady her and she had felt his touch like a current of electricity. But then he'd immediately let go when she'd found her footing. As if he'd burned his fingers.

Or was scared of what he might do if he didn't let go.

'Do you want to go and get changed?' His eyes lingered on hers, then shifted away to the rippling blue water. He looked as if he wanted to dive in. To her, not the water.

They hadn't talked about sex since that explosive conversation in her bedroom but there was no need. It was always there. Blooming and charging the air around them like a heat shimmer above the roads that criss-crossed the Malaspinian countryside, changing the way they looked at one another and how they breathed and moved.

She glanced down at herself. She was wearing one of Vero's shirts over a bikini. 'It's fine. I'll change when we get back to the villa.'

'You could. If we were going back to the villa.'

'Are we not?'

Shaking his head, he took a step closer then and she felt the usual current of heat snake between them as he reached out and caught her lightly by the wrists, and his voice was low and a little scratchy as he said, 'We will later. But first, you and I are going to have some fun in Rome.'

Betty had been to Rome multiple times. Most recently she had accompanied her father to a dinner with various European trade delegations. But she had never been solely for fun.

But then she hardly went anywhere solely for fun. The odd day out with Bella, the occasional weekend in Ponza. And she had never been anywhere with Vero.

Their relationship had been a series of covert encounters, some little more than feverish embraces.

Now she was sitting in a taxi, holding Vero's hand as the driver manoeuvred through Rome's traffic.

'We could have gone back to the villa. I have a wardrobe of dresses and event wear.'

'Princess Bettina goes to events. You're Betty, remember? And Betty doesn't wear formal gowns and tiaras. So, first things first, you're going to choose something to wear tonight and then we're going to go to my apartment to get changed.'

'You have an apartment?'

'*Sì.*' He nodded. 'I use it when I'm in the area.'

'In the area? Are you talking about Italy or Europe?'

His mouth curved up fractionally and as usual she forgot to breathe when he smiled.

'Italy. I have another apartment in Paris and a house in London. I travel a lot and I'm not a fan of hotels. Too little control. Too many interruptions,' he added obliquely. 'Here's fine,' he said, switching to Italian as he caught the driver's eye.

'Okay, the rule is, there are no rules,' he said as he helped Betty out of the taxi. Leaning in, he kissed her softly on the mouth. 'Pick anything. But promise me that it's what the real Betty would choose.'

That was a promise worth making, he thought two hours later as Betty walked into the huge, open-plan sitting room in his apartment wearing faded jeans and—

His breath punched in his throat.

That was some top.

His eyes moved hungrily to the oscillating cowl of fabric that almost reached her waist. Or more accurately to the occasional glimpse of smooth, bare skin it offered whenever she moved.

It was casual and punch-in-the-gut sexy, and she looked completely different from the poised, demure princess known to the world. And yet to him, she had never looked more like herself.

Breathing out unevenly, he felt his gaze move to her hair.

Naturally it fell into soft waves, which Betty almost always contained and controlled and smoothed into a bun. But now it hung loose, the mass of autumn-coloured curls tumbling past her shoulders and fanning out riotously around her face, part Pre-Raphaelite, part flower child.

In the past when she was with him, she hardly ever wore it down.

Except in bed.

He sucked in a breath, remembering the weight of it in his hands and how he could twist it into a kind of rope.

'Hi,' she said quietly.

His head was spinning.

If this was the real Betty, then he wanted to do more than say 'hi'. A whole lot more. Tamping down the pornographic slideshow in his head, he walked over and stopped in front of her.

'You look—you look incredible.'

She was nervous, he could tell. 'Do you think?'

What he thought was that he would be spending the evening staring down his rivals like some primate marking his territory. What he thought was that he had a whole day planned and she had just made it a thousand times harder for him to stick to that plan. But this wasn't about him.

It was about Betty.

It was about giving her the freedom and fun her life had lacked.

His chest felt tight. He was still stunned by what she had told him.

Hearing her talk about how her parents had treated her made him want to smash things with his bare hands. It seemed impossible. How could it not? Betty was a princess. To the rest of the world, she lived a charmed, cosseted life behind the palace walls. But behind those walls she had been manipulated and gaslit, been judged and found wanting by the very people who should have been protecting and praising her.

Including him.

He hated himself for that. It was bad enough that he hadn't seen or chosen to see what was happening in front of him. Instead, he had made assumptions. Seen her serenity as evidence of a power she didn't have.

But worse still, he had been complicit. Her parents might have manipulated her into her first marriage, but he had played a part in forcing her into the second.

'Can a goddess be too much?' he said, pulling her closer so that he could have counted all her beautiful freckles if she'd asked him to.

She smiled. 'I'm a princess not a goddess.'

'You are definitely a goddess, *dolcezza*. Right. Let's go. *Andiamo*.'

And, grabbing her hand, he towed her towards the lift before he did something stupid like sliding his hands under that shimmering, shifting top.

CHAPTER NINE

THEY ATE AT Il Pellicano, a trattoria that served unpretentious Roman dishes to in-the-know locals rather than tourists. It was busy and buzzing and they ate at the counter, pausing to talk and occasionally offer each other a mouthful of their food.

Which was something he'd never done before and wouldn't do again with Betty, not in public anyway, he thought, his pulse stumbling as he watched her lips close around the mouthful of the risotto he'd ordered.

After dinner, they walked through the streets, holding hands. It was strange. Handholding was such an innocuous gesture and yet it felt radical to feel her fingers clasping his in full view of everyone. Not that everyone was looking at them.

Some people looked.

As he'd predicted, Betty was the subject of a lot of, admittedly furtive, male gazes but nobody did anything more than glance.

'Do you think anyone has recognised us?'

Hearing the anxiety in her voice, he shook his head. 'How could they? Nobody knows Betty and Vero here.'

She tried to smile but there were two little frown lines on her forehead and he pressed his thumb against them to smooth them flat. 'Nobody is looking for us so they won't see us. Even if they do look, you don't look like Princess Bettina and I'm just some anonymous guy nobody cares about.'

'You're not anonymous. People all over the world drive your cars. You're a household name. And people do care about you. Your family, your friends, your staff.' She hesitated. 'I care about you, remember?'

They had reached the nightclub, but he barely noticed, he was too lost in the simplicity and truth of her words.

'I care about you too.'

They stared at one another, silent and unmoving like rocks in a river as people surged round them. 'Are we going in?' Betty said finally.

He nodded. 'Yeah, let's do that.'

The club was rammed.

'Can we do shots?' she asked as they reached the bar.

Frankly, he already felt somewhat intoxicated by her nearness and that oscillating tease of a drop but this was Betty's night.

'Here.' He handed her the shot glass. Betty drank hers and then took his hand and turned towards the dance floor.

'You want to dance now?'

Beneath the strobe lights, her eyes were darker than shadows. 'I've wanted to dance with you for ever.'

'We danced at the wedding.'

'Not like that. Not some waltz with everyone watching. I want to dance like we did at the palace that time.'

The expression on her face was so soft, so open, he forgot to speak. 'I want that too,' he said after a moment, and he let her lead him onto the dance floor.

This was a different kind of dancing from the wedding waltz. For starters the dance floor was full of people pressed up close to one another and nobody was looking at anyone. A lot of them had their eyes shut and were just weaving to the bassline. The room radiated heat and sweat and freedom.

And he felt freer than he'd ever felt. As free as Betty looked, turning in the circle of his arms, her own arms reaching above her head. Free to look at her openly, to lean in and breathe in her scent and let it settle in his brain. Free to touch her waist, to press his hand against the warm damp skin of her back.

'Are you having fun?'

Her eyes rested on his face and she nodded and then she looped her arms around his neck.

'Yes.' She laughed against his mouth and kissed him and the floor tilted sideways. Or maybe that was him because everyone else kept dancing. And he told himself to get a grip but that only made his hand press her closer.

She moaned softly and the sound made him feel light-headed and powerful and enslaved. Was that what she wanted? It was what he wanted. But not here. With an effort of will, he broke the kiss.

There was an empty booth at the edge of the dance floor and he shouldered his way through the sticky mass of dancers. 'Do you want another drink?'

'I could get them.'

He hesitated. 'I don't know if that's the best idea.'

'It's what Betty would do.'

His eyes jerked up to that bee-stung mouth like a compass needle finding its magnetic north. He wanted to beg her forgiveness. He wanted to lick into her mouth and between her thighs until she was begging him to do anything he wanted.

He watched her make her way to the bar. Watched the barman's eyes widen appreciatively. His own eyes narrowed but Betty was already returning, only without the drinks. She was no longer smiling. Instead, she looked tense and anxious.

'What is it? What happened? Did the barman say something to you?'

'No.' She glanced over her shoulder. 'I just saw Edoardo and Cicciu. I don't think they recognised me—'

'Who are they?'

'Their father is the Duca di Monte Giusto. He's a friend of my father. He and his wife came to the wedding. You probably don't remember them.'

Vero felt as though his chest were being pushed through a shredder. He knew his face must be showing his shock and that it must be obvious to Betty. Any minute now she would notice and ask him what was wrong.

'How well do you know them?'

He had spoken more harshly than he'd intended and she glanced up at him, her eyes widening. 'Well enough.' She bit into her lip. 'I think we should go.'

By 'go' she meant run.

'Why should we leave because of them?' They were his family. His half-brothers. It made his head spin even just thinking that sentence inside his head. Not only the sudden, shocking truth of it but the fact that to them it wasn't a truth. To them, he was just a random man in a nightclub. That even if they met and he was introduced, there would be no nod of recognition. He had no doubt whatsoever that the Duke would have kept his existence a secret from them and suddenly he was fifteen again, and feeling an anger that seemed to lift him off his feet and smack him to the ground because Betty was doing exactly what his father had done, what her father had done. She couldn't deny his existence or evict him, but she wanted to sweep him away.

And he had given her the power to do so.

She blinked. 'Because if they see us then they'll make a scene.'

'I thought you wanted to be yourself.'

'I do…'

Someone who wasn't so attuned to Betty's every breath might have missed the infinitesimal flinch that accompanied her response, but Vero saw it, and heard the slight hitch to her breath that accompanied it.

He was being unfair, cruel even, expecting Betty to face her fear when he couldn't even say his out loud, but adrenaline was soaring through his body. He could taste it in his mouth, and he hated that it came from fear and shame. Hated that he could use so many words to not say what needed to be said.

'Then why are you running and hiding? Your father isn't here. I am. But that doesn't count for anything, does it, Betty? Because you never forget, not even for one night, that you're a princess.'

'Why are you being like this? What are you doing?'

He had got to his feet. 'You wanted to go. So, let's go.'

The journey back to the villa was silent. He couldn't find the right words, any words in fact, that could explain why he had acted as he had. And maybe Betty too was lost for words.

Lost to him.

As they walked back into the villa, she stopped and turned to him.

'I know you're upset that I wanted to leave. But that can't be the only reason.'

'Oh, because it couldn't be you. So, I guess it has to be me. So why don't you just say what you're thinking, which is that I'm the problem?'

'That's not what I'm thinking. I just think there must be something else, only I don't know what it is. And I can't help you if—'

'Help me.' He felt his jaw clench. 'You've never helped me. In fact, you made things worse. You saw who I was and made me believe that I was good enough. And just for a short time, you wanted what I wanted. But you couldn't do it, could you? You couldn't follow through. Just like tonight, you bottled it.'

He could see her shock, her pain, but he had smashed everything to pieces, so many pieces and he didn't know how to fix what he'd done and so he stood and watched her turn and walk up the stairs, and then a moment later, he heard the soft click of her bedroom door, and he turned too.

Closing the door, Betty felt her legs give way and, breathing out unevenly, she slid down to the floor. She felt sick, winded, shivery with shock. Vero was like a stranger. An angry, green-eyed stranger. And she felt as if she were living in a nightmare, only there was no way out because she was already awake.

And it hurt, hearing the hostility in his voice and seeing that distance in his eyes as if he didn't know her. As if she hadn't spent the last twenty-four hours peeling away her armour.

Her legs were shaking now and she hugged them against her chest, trying to hold them steady.

She had been so happy earlier, happy to be herself and to be with Vero.

Only something had happened.

She pictured Vero's face at the club. He had been anxious about her, concerned, and that had been so sweet of him, only then she had told him who she'd seen at the bar and he had flipped. But that didn't make any sense. He'd never even met Edoardo and Cicciu.

Perhaps he just hated dancing. After all, it was the second time he'd virtually dragged her away from a dance floor.

She had a sudden, sharp memory of the moment when Vero had bumped into the Duca di Monte Giusto. There had been no acknowledgement there, which was odd in itself, particularly as it had felt as if something had passed between the two men.

Then suddenly they had been leaving. At the time it had all happened so quickly, and she had been furious with Vero, mainly because she had known that once they left the party, they would be alone together.

Now, though, she could remember more, remember how he had been tense in exactly the same way. Like a sail stretched taut in a running wind.

And he was taut now. Angry too, almost like someone in shock.

Her legs had stopped shaking and she got unsteadily to her feet. She kicked off her towering heels and considered finding her flip-flops but then she turned and opened the door because when someone needed your help, every second counted. And Vero needed her help.

She walked swiftly downstairs, moving through the villa. There was no sign of him anywhere, but she knew where he was almost as if he'd left a trail of pebbles for her.

The garage door was open. Slipping inside, she stopped, her bare feet pressing into the cool concrete floor.

Nonno's car sat in a shaft of moonlight looking exactly as it had yesterday. Except that Vero was sitting behind the wheel.

His head was lowered, and he didn't look up as she

approached, not even when she opened the door and sat down in the passenger seat.

They sat in silence for what felt like a long time, but she waited because she knew how hard it was to admit something painful to oneself. To admit it to someone else was like consciously turning a car round and driving straight into a hurricane. It required a different level of courage and steadiness and only the driver could choose when to turn the steering wheel and press down hard on the accelerator pedal.

'When I was fifteen,' he said then, 'my dad lost his job. He was working at a garage, repairing cars, and the owner sold the site to a developer, and we had to move house. We couldn't afford to pay anyone to help so me and my dad did all the moving with some help from the neighbours. My mum had this chest of drawers that she had by her bed and somehow it got put in my room.'

Now he lifted his head.

'I wasn't prying. I had to take the drawers out so that I could lift it. That's when I found the envelope. It had my name on it. That's why I opened it.'

She felt oddly calm even though her heart was racing. 'What was in it?'

His face, his beautiful, fine features were as unreadable as bronze and she was trying to think of something eloquent that might unlock him when he said, 'My birth certificate. It was tough at home. There was never that much money. My mum was only eighteen when she had me and I blamed my dad for not being more careful. For a long time, I gave him a hard time. Except it turned out he wasn't to blame because he's not my dad, biologically anyway.'

'The Duke,' she said softly.

He turned, his green eyes jagged looking like bits of broken glass. 'You knew?'

'No.' She shook her head. 'Not until I went upstairs a moment ago. And I didn't know. I just remembered when we were dancing—'

Vero's mouth twisted. 'Yeah, he wasn't pleased to see me. But then he wasn't pleased the first time we met either.'

'He asked to meet you?'

He shook his head and there was something in that small movement that tore her up inside.

'I had a temper then. He has one too. It's probably the one thing he's ever given me. When I found the birth certificate, I had a huge row with my mum and then I went over to his house. I thought—I don't know what I thought,' he admitted after a moment.

Young people act on impulse, she thought.

'I guess I thought he might be curious about me. Curious to meet his own flesh and blood. But he wasn't curious. He was furious. He thought I was looking for money...' His voice slowed as the sentence fizzled out.

'So, he'd had an affair with your mum. But he must have had the boys by then.'

Vero nodded. 'She was their au pair.'

Betty was stunned. Horrified. 'Did anyone know?'

Vero shrugged. 'I don't think so. It wasn't serious, for him anyway. But he was rich, and he bought her nice things, and he told her that he loved her. And then she told him she was pregnant, and he ended it. He sacked her. She never saw him again. He never got in touch. He didn't even know that I was a boy. He washed his hands of her and me.'

Betty felt sick. No wonder Vero had been so angry with her. The Duke had got rid of his mother to punish her for getting pregnant, and then history had basically repeated itself when her father had sacked Tommasino, knowing instinctively that would be the most effective way to punish Vero.

'What did you say to him?'

'I was pretty out of shape. I shouted at him and then this maid came into the room and said my dad was there and the Duke said that Tommasino had been paid already. That he'd signed a legally binding contract to marry my mum and take me on and that there would be no more money.'

'He paid Tommasino to do that?'

'It probably felt like a lot at the time because neither of them had any money, but it wasn't. That was hard. Finding out how little I was worth. But also, I felt so guilty. You know, I'd been giving my dad grief for years for getting my mum pregnant and he never rose to it.' His voice sounded taut as if he was having to keep control. 'He never put me right. He took it because he wanted to protect me.'

'He's a good man,' Betty said quietly. 'And so are you.' Reaching out, she touched Vero's hand.

'No, I'm not. I lost my temper and then the Duke did too, and my dad tried to calm things and somehow the Duke got knocked down and he cut his hand and then he called some mate of his at the police and they came and cuffed my dad. And that's when the Duke told me that he would let Tommasino off but that it would go on his record and if I bothered him again then my dad would be arrested again.'

He looked devastated. 'So, I'm not a good man. My mum was petrified the whole time that I wouldn't be able to keep away. And my dad had this threat hanging over him. Because of me.'

'No, not because of you. Because of a situation over which you had no control. You can't blame yourself, Vero. You were fifteen years old.'

'Maybe, but I can blame myself for this. Your father is partly to blame but I am too. I forced you into this marriage. I just wanted to prove to the Duke that he was wrong. That I wasn't disposable, that I was worthy. And I knew if I married you that I would have a title because your father would insist on it and then I would be equal to him, and he'd have to acknowledge me.'

She could hear the pain of his teenage self pushing through the words and the newer pain layered on top.

'I know. I knew that nine years ago.'

There was a shifting silence.

'What do you mean?' He frowned. 'I didn't want you for your title nine years ago.'

Now she frowned. 'But you told me that's what you wanted. We talked about getting serious and—'

'And I said, "Are we talking about marriage?"' Vero held her gaze. 'And you said, "What would you say if I was?"'

'And you said, "Yes, obviously. Who doesn't want to marry a princess?"' she said, the words as crushing now as they had been then.

He nodded, his throat working through a swallow, and she felt his fingers curl around hers. 'Because I thought you were joking, and then you said you were. You said that you wouldn't marry the son of a chauffeur. That you were a princess, and you would marry a prince. And then you did.'

She could feel her pulse beating heavily. Vero was staring at her. They were a foot apart, close enough that she could see the truth in his eyes, touch it almost.

'I only said that to hurt you because you hurt me.' She pressed her hand against her forehead. 'I kept hearing what my mother said about you. That I shouldn't get too close to you. That I was being naive, and then you said that thing about princesses—'

And she had panicked. Pain and anger had followed but in that moment all she'd felt was a swirling fear. Because she'd known what it meant. Known that it had to end.

So that was what she had done. Only it hadn't needed to end.

She felt a terrible sadness then at the pointlessness of it all. 'I hurt you for no reason.'

'We both hurt each other.' In the moonlight, his eyes on hers were wide and unflinching. 'But I'm the one who came back to hurt you some more.'

'You were angry—'

'Don't do that.' His anger was abrupt and intense. 'Don't minimise your feelings at the expense of mine or anyone else's. You matter, Betty. And I made you unhappy.'

'I know, but I made you unhappy too, and admitting it doesn't change that. And it doesn't make me weak. It makes me honest, and I want us to be honest.'

He took a fast breath. 'I want that too.'

'Good.' She felt that shared desire for something other than sex press softly around her. 'That's good because everything bad that's happened to us happened because of lies and I don't want to lie any more. So yes, you made me unhappy, but today you made me happy. Happier than I've ever been.'

He was staring at her, scanning her face, and there was a fine tremor in his voice as he said, 'Do you mean that?'

How could she not be happy? She was in love. Hopelessly and completely in love. And it was as terrifying as it was beautiful. And she wanted to tell him the truth; it was what she said she'd wanted. But he was vulnerable right now, and love had failed him in the past. Maybe it would be better to give him some breathing space.

She nodded. 'It's a low bar, but yes.' She was still trying to smile when he pulled her closer, wrapping his arms around her, and she felt his heart slow to a steady, hypnotic rhythm.

'I wanted to hurt you too. That's why I said that thing about not having sex unless I was ovulating. But I didn't mean it. Or maybe I did at the time, but I don't mean it now.'

She felt every cell in his body tense. Even the air stilled and the silence around them felt loaded.

He shifted against her, inching back just far enough that their eyes were level, and then he reached out and ran his finger down the side of her face. It was the lightest of touches, a whisper of a caress but she felt it ripple through her like an electromagnetic pulse.

He stared at her for one long, swelling moment.

'Are you saying…?'

'Yes,' she said hoarsely.

The kiss that came after was hot and slow and sweet and inexorable. As he parted her lips, she moaned against his mouth, her body softening, stirring.

They'd had sex in the garage in the past but never in any of the cars so it felt both familiar and new.

'Are you sure?'

She pressed her hand against his already hard erection, and he grunted low in his throat as he shifted the seat as far back as it would go and lifted her over the gearstick and onto his lap.

'Help me undress,' she whispered.

Vero breathed out unevenly, her words acting like gasoline on a bonfire. He tugged at the buttons of her jeans and then pulled them down her thighs and over her bare feet, taking her panties with them. Sliding his hand between her legs, he felt how wet she was, and his breath swelled in his throat.

She moaned as he slid his fingers inside her, and then he reached under that top, that maddening tease of a top, and found her breasts.

Her nipples were hard, and she made that sound he liked as he pinched them gently, then a little harder, watching her eyes grow glassy with a need that matched his own.

'I want to touch you,' she said hoarsely and he watched mesmerised as she unbuttoned his trousers and then her hand was closing around the hard, smooth length of him and, gripping her waist, he breathed out, breathed in the feeling of her thumb and fingers circling him, slipping back and forth until he had to dig his heels into the footwell of the car to stop himself lifting up his pelvis and ending things too quickly.

Batting her hands away, he lifted her up. He cupped her bottom in his hands and leaned her back against the steering wheel, moulding her pliant flesh with his fingers before dipping his face between her thighs.

He loved this. Loved the taste of her and the way her breath hitched when he licked her. She was already close and then her thighs tightened around his head, and she let out a small, hoarse cry. Then she arched against his mouth, and he felt her body contracting and expanding in long, expansive shudders as he felt her pleasure everywhere.

'Can you go behind me?' she murmured as he lowered her back into his lap and, nodding wordlessly, he helped her lean over the seat and then positioned himself behind her naked bottom, bracing himself against the frame of the door, his pulse accelerating as she tilted her pelvis up slightly and he pushed inside her, moving slowly at first then deepening his thrusts until he could feel her pressed up tight against him.

He'd been going to hold back but then he felt her fingers slide up his thigh to cradle him in her hand and suddenly everything, his breath, his body, his hunger, was beyond his ability to control, and he was in freefall. And then his orgasm tore through him, and he wrapped his arms around her stomach and ground into her until his body shook.

Vero woke to find Betty curled against him, her arm flung across his chest, her breath warm against his throat. Shifting slightly, he eased backwards just enough that he could watch her sleep. They had made it upstairs to Betty's bedroom and he had stripped her first and then himself. Yes, having sex in the car had been unbound and exhilarating, but the bed had more scope for his and her imaginations.

He had let her take charge. Let her guide him to where she wanted to be touched and stroked and licked and held, keeping himself in check. Over and over and over again until it got too intense, and she pushed his head or his hand away.

And then he waited, his thumbs grazing her nipples, his tongue tracing circles on her skin until she reached for him again.

He still couldn't get his head around it. But it had happened. The world was rearranging itself so that he no longer had to fantasise about having Betty in his arms or splayed out under his surging body. He didn't have to conjure up memories of her sweet, serious face on his pillow. Or wake in the morning and have to discover that her presence was simply a dream.

Now he could reach out as his eyes opened and know that she would be there beside him. Heat surged through him. And she wanted to be there. Wanted him there with her and inside her and that was the biggest turn-on of all.

But it was more than sex.

There were her shy smiles and that intent way she would look at a part of his body before touching it and the way she had pointed to things under the water, her grey eyes wide with excitement. He had loved that moment of her wanting to share something other than her body.

He loved everything about her.

He loved her.

He took a breath, trying to get his bearings. But he felt as if he were a rowing boat without oars. He had loved Betty nine years ago but in the intervening years his love had felt like a weakness.

Now, though, the magnitude of what he was feeling was impossible to deny or contain. It was like lava pushing up, cracking him apart.

He felt Betty shift beside him, and he watched her eyelashes flutter, his blood stirring.

'*Buongiorno,*' he said softly.

She opened her eyes then, and arched her back in a stretch and he pressed his hand lightly against her flat stomach. His heart beat loudly as she lowered her spine back down to the mattress and gazed up at him. Her grey eyes were soft and peaceful like the sky after a storm and he felt peaceful too.

'You look like a fairy-tale princess.'

'I do have some experience in that area,' she said, her hands moving to touch his face as if she found him as fascinating as he found her. 'The princess part, not the fairy tale.'

'That's something to work on, then.'

For a moment there was nothing but the sound of the sea and her shimmering grey gaze and then he leaned in and kissed her, a hot, open-mouthed kiss, and she arched upwards again.

An hour later, Betty made her way downstairs. As she caught sight of her reflection in the huge hall mirror her feet stuttered on the marble tiles. Her hair looked wild, and her eyes were huge and limpid. She looked undone. And she was, and she couldn't be happier about it.

But she told herself to be careful because she looked like a woman in love.

Mariangela beamed at her when she walked into the kitchen, and she got the distinct impression that her housekeeper knew exactly what she was thinking and feeling.

'His Grace the Duke is out in the garage, Your Highness. He said that you needed to sleep because you'd had a restless night. But he asked that you go and find him when you came down.'

'Did he?' Cheeks burning, she made her way out to the garage.

Vero was leaning over the Giulietta's engine. He turned as she walked in, and she felt her stomach flip over. There was a smudge of oil on his cheek and a smile was tugging at his mouth.

'There you are. Did you get some more rest? I told Mariangela not to wake you.'

'Yes, because I'd had a restless night. Restless!'

He grinned. 'She's Italian and a woman and she dotes on you. She wants you to have your happy ever after.'

'And that's you, is it?'

He pulled her against him and the smell of oil, and his warm skin, made her feel untethered from the ground. 'I intend to make you very happy.'

'You do make me happy,' she said, and she could have told him then that she loved him, but she would be acting on impulse and that scared her.

'And I'm about to make you happier.' Letting go of her waist, he flicked the stand and let the bonnet drop. 'I just finished changing the cam belt, so this baby is good to go.'

He held up the keys.

'Can I drive?'

He tossed them to her, then pulled open the door on the driver's side and took a step back. 'Of course, Your Highness.'

Aside from a few longish driveways and some farm tracks, there was only one road on Ponza. It bisected the island never more than a mile from the coastline. As well as only one road, there were few cars on the island. Visitors hired scooters or microcars or used the public minibuses, so it felt as if they had gone back in time to a golden age of motoring.

'Having fun?'

Betty turned to where Vero was sitting beside her. The wind was whipping her hair in every direction and she knew her face must be flushed but she'd never felt more beautiful than when he looked at her.

He made her feel more than beautiful. Even a week ago, being seen in public like this would have felt like a revolutionary act, but she felt sure of herself and of her judgement in a way that had eluded her for so long. She could feel the change in her body too. After she and

Vero split, she had felt stiff and wooden and trapped inside her skin.

But on the dance floor in Rome and moving through the clear water at Cala Gaetana and in bed with Vero, it felt as if she had woken from some hibernation. Her body no longer felt stifled and weak but strong and sure of itself.

What was more, Vero clearly liked what he saw. She could feel his gaze now and its steady intensity made her feel as if she were free falling. And he did more than look. Ever since they had gone snorkelling, he kept reaching for her, touching her face, her hair, leaning in to nip her throat or lick a path to her mouth.

And she was the same. It was as if the sea were reclaiming the land, and everything were free flowing. Remembering just how free they had been, she pressed her thighs together around the heat building there.

She felt Vero's gaze on the side of her face. Turning, she bit her lip.

'Are you really that keen to see the north of the island? We could just turn around and go back to the villa.'

'You read my mind,' he said hoarsely.

Back at the villa, they pulled off each other's clothes and then Vero nudged her into the bathroom and under the shower, spinning her around, barely waiting for her hands to press against the wet tiles before he was pushing into her, his breath shuddering against her cheek as she pressed back to meet his thrusts.

Afterwards, they made it back to the bed and he buried his face between her thighs and mapped her sensitive spots with his tongue until she jerked against his mouth, surging forward like the waves toppling against the shoreline.

They finally made it downstairs just after two for a late lunch. Vero leaned forward and speared a piece of burrata from his plate. 'Do you still want to see the cliffs?'

Putting down her cutlery, she nodded. 'But I just need to call Bella first. She's seen a horse she wants to buy and I don't want her to rush into anything.'

He smiled, one of those easy, tugging smiles that she wanted to reach out and touch.

'That's fine. I'll go and tell Gianluca our plans.' He leaned in and kissed her softly on the mouth. 'Send your sister my love.'

It was just a figure of speech, Betty thought as he strolled out of the room, but she felt hope ripple through her all the same, like a field of wheat in a summer breeze. And instead of picking up her phone, she opened her laptop. She wanted to see her sister's face.

She frowned as a melodic tune filled the room. Someone was video-calling her.

Had Bella read her mind? But it wasn't her sister. It was her grandfather.

'Nonno—how lovely. I wasn't expecting to hear from you. Is everything all right?'

Her grandfather's lined face filled the screen. He was still a handsome man and, for all his faults, she loved him for his warmth and his enthusiasm for life and living, and for his unconditional love of her.

'I'm fine.' He waved his hand dismissively at the camera. 'Don't you worry about me. I'm just sorry I was such a clumsy fool. I so wanted to be at your wedding, but my unplanned absence was no doubt an enormous relief to your father. Probably put an actual smile on his face rather than one of those smug simpers he favours, which will improve the official photos no end.'

She laughed. 'Well, Bella and I were sorry you weren't there. Vero was too. He's so looking forward to meeting you.'

'Looking forward to it?' her grandfather repeated, his confusion adding more lines to his face. 'But we've already met. In Cairo, remember? Played a good hand at baccarat. Generous with the whisky and subbed me when I got into a spot of bother.'

Betty stared at the screen, feeling a chill spill over her face and something else, something shivery and nameless rising up from her stomach.

'I forgot, Nonno.' She smiled, but it was hard to make her lips move. Her jawbone felt as though it were wired shut. 'I've been so busy. Remind me when you met.'

'It would be a couple of months ago now. Maybe a little longer. Obviously, I knew your man had money because he was playing at the private tables. I just didn't realise how much. And then it turned out he was from Malaspina. Worked for your father. I'm a gambling man but what were the chances of that? Of him sitting down next to me?'

Probably higher than her grandfather imagined, she thought, trying to focus on breathing and smiling. But then he didn't know Vero Farnese as she did.

'And you got on?'

Her grandfather nodded. 'I liked him. He's got brains and drive. We had a good chat. I told him about the baby, and he said he was looking to get married. I said that when I told your father Nina was having a baby, he'd be in a tailspin looking for husbands for you or your sister, and then I suddenly thought, why not him? And here you are, happily married.'

He leaned in towards the screen now, his blue eyes

narrowing. 'I heard von Marburg was interested in your sister, but I knew you wouldn't let her be bartered off to that old bore. I told Farnese, Betty would do anything to stop that happening.'

She stared at the screen, letting him ramble on, barely taking in a word, until finally he hung up, after promising to send her a necklace of his mother's as a wedding present.

Her head hurt. Everything hurt. Except her heart. That was numb. As if a chip of ice had pierced it and frozen it solid. And as the numbness spread, she found she couldn't move, so that she was still staring at the now blank screen when Vero walked in, the beautiful muscles of his stomach and legs moving in unison.

'You're done. That was quick. I was thinking I would have to stage an intervention. Was she okay?'

Was she okay? Was Vero really asking her that? The shocking hypocrisy and deceit of his question jerked her explosively to her feet, scraping back the chair.

'Don't do that. Don't pretend you care.'

'I do care.' He leaned back on his heels, his forehead creasing in confusion, his green eyes scanning her face. 'Why are you upset? Has something happened?'

She laughed, and then stopped because she knew if she kept laughing, she would cry and she didn't want to cry any more tears for this man. 'Yes, it has. I did it again. I made a fool of myself. I let you get under my skin and inside my head. I let myself believe you again. Trust you again. Care for you again. I laid myself bare. And all the time, you were lying.'

'I'm not lying.'

'We said we'd be honest. That we'd tell the truth.'

His hands clamped around her wrists. 'And I was, I am.'

'So why didn't you tell me you'd met my grandfather? He just called me, full of praise for you and excited to tell me about your meeting in Cairo.'

In the pause before he answered, she allowed herself to hope, to pray, to pretend, but then she saw his face and she realised that he had never stopped pretending. She just hadn't realised until now.

Vero stared at Betty, his bones heavy, his breath blistering his lungs. Around him, the walls of the room were starting to sway as if he were standing on a high, narrow ledge. It was making him feel dizzy and vertiginous and he wanted to step back. But Betty was blocking his way.

Stupid. Stupid. Stupid.

The word echoed around his head in time to the thundering of his heart. He should have told her. There had been multiple times when he could have done so. But it was never the right time. First it was too soon, then it was too hard.

And now they were here and he had no reasonable explanation except cowardice and the aforementioned stupidity.

'I was going to.'

Her eyes, Betty's beautiful eyes, flared not with anger but pain and he hated himself then, more than he had ever hated anyone.

'But you didn't. You lied.'

'I didn't—'

'By omission.' She cut across him, her disdain as terrible as the pain in her eyes. 'And why would you do that? Unless you had something to hide?'

She breathed out unsteadily. 'And you did, didn't you, Vero? Because Nonno told you everything. My dear, careless, gullible grandfather told you everything. And it would have been so easy. How you must have laughed. You plied him with drink, and you covered his debts, and you let him talk. He told you about the baby. And what my father would do when he found out. And then he told you that Hans von Marburg wanted to marry Bella and that I would do anything to stop that happening. And he was right.'

Vero was shaking his head. The skin across his cheek-bones was stretched taut. 'I don't understand—'

'Then let me explain. I told my father I didn't want to marry you and he said that was fine because he had two daughters, and that if I didn't marry you Bella would have to marry Hans von Marburg.'

He felt sick to his stomach.

'I didn't know—'

'So Hans wasn't mentioned in that conversation you had with my grandfather?'

There was a beat of silence before he answered and then slowly, stiffly, he nodded. 'He was, but—' He broke off as her hand flew up to cover her mouth.

'Betty, I'm sorry.'

Her eyes were filled with shock and disbelief.

'She's twenty years old.'

'I know. But I didn't know that your father would do that.'

'Nonno told you that I'd do anything to stop that happening. Why did you think I married you?'

His eyes flared. 'The same reason you do everything. To please your father. To earn his approval and protect the House of Marchetta. That's all you've ever cared about.'

'And you only care about yourself. You're ruthless and selfish. Self-serving.'

'Yes, maybe in the beginning I was all those things. I wanted to punish you and my father—'

'And I understood that. But you were also ready for Bella to be punished too.' There was a sheen of tears in her eyes. 'You need to leave.'

'I can't. I can't leave because I love you, Betty.'

There was a shake to his voice, and an hour earlier those three words would have made her heart sing and her life complete. But it was just another lie designed to manipulate her. She felt suddenly, incredibly tired.

'You do that so well. I can see why you've been so successful. You make it sound so true and you can keep lying to yourself if you want but what you're talking about is lust.'

'I'm not lying to you or myself. I do love you. And I think you love me. So let's work this through.' He yanked a chair out from the table. 'Let's sit down and talk. Look, I know I messed up but I was a different person then. You were different too. But we changed, we grew together, not apart. That's the truth. Our truth. You have to believe me, Betty. Believe in me, in us. That's all I want. I don't care about the title. I don't want to be your prince. I want to be your husband—'

He was looking at her as if she were standing on a window ledge and he were reaching out with his hand. And it would be so easy to just lean forward and take it, and let herself be drawn back in.

But then it would get so much more difficult, and painful, even more painful than this.

She nodded slowly.

'You're right. I am a different person. For so long, I tried to be the perfect princess. To make my parents love me. But I'm done with that. Because perfect isn't just the enemy of good, it's the enemy of happy too, and I want to be happy. I want a divorce.'

For a split second, she saw something flare then fade in his eyes and the pain of it almost robbed her of the power of speech, but she had to do this. She couldn't take his hand, couldn't take a chance.

'But you can keep your title so you can be happy too. That's all you ever wanted anyway.'

'I haven't been wearing a condom. You could be pregnant.' His voice was so devoid of emotion it took her a moment to take in what he had said.

'And this is what you want to bring your child into? A life of lies and deceit. I don't understand you, Vero. I thought that was what you hated.'

He stared at her in silence and then his mouth pulled into the saddest smile she had ever seen. 'I did hate it. And you're right, our child deserves better than that. You deserve better. You deserve a man you can trust and love. A man who doesn't make you pretend. A man who you're proud to call your husband. Don't let anyone ever tell you differently. Whatever it takes, don't settle for anything less.'

There was a strange, shifting light in his eyes, and his breathing wasn't quite steady. For a moment she thought he was going to say something else and then he turned and strode out of the room without a backward glance.

Anxiety and panic ripped through her and for a frantic moment, Betty was tempted to run after him. But there was no point. Her judgement was flawed. That was the only truth and, sitting down on the chair that Vero had pulled out moments earlier, she started to weep.

CHAPTER TEN

WALKING BACK THROUGH the villa and out onto the terrace, Vero felt as if everyone were watching him. Although the opposite was true. Mariangela had smiled stiffly then glanced away and Bianca, one of the maids, had actually reversed back into the kitchen through the doorway.

He doubted they had heard much. Betty's pain and his guilt for causing that pain had directed his anger and despair inwards so that he had barely raised his voice. And Betty had got quieter and quieter as if her voice wanted to shrink back inside her. In the same way she had wrapped her arms around her waist to hold herself close.

He had hated that, hated that she was so closed off to him. Even more so than when she had been on the other side of the world.

Then he'd had his anger to warm him, to give him purpose, to drive his days. Now he couldn't think of how he was going to live the rest of his life without her.

He had reached the steps leading down to the jetty, and for a moment, he stopped at the top.

But he was going to have to find a way because Betty didn't want him. She wanted a divorce.

The word and its implications made his breath stutter, his feet too, so that he almost lost his balance and had to reach for the handrail to steady himself.

A life without Betty. A life without her warm, eager body straddling him. A life without that smile, not the public princess smile but the one that made her grey eyes turn silver and dance like raindrops on the surface of a lake. A life without her face tilted up expectantly towards his as they talked and laughed.

It tore into him then and the need to see her again was like the dragging, inexorable pull of the moon on the tide, and he wanted to turn back.

He would tell her that she couldn't have a divorce. That he wouldn't agree. He would make her sit down, make her listen, make her agree to what he wanted.

And then what?

Wasn't that what he'd already done? And it had crushed her, he thought, picturing her small, trembling body and the way she was trying to hold it all in, hold herself together, not trying to be the perfect princess but a woman trying not to break.

No, he couldn't go back. He couldn't force her to stay with him. It would crush her, hurt her again and even more than he'd already hurt her.

There was an ache in his chest that came from not knowing when, if, he would see her again. But he let himself feel the pain. If he loved her, and he did with every breath and bone in his body, then he had to leave. He had to accept her choice.

He stepped up onto the yacht. Gianluca glanced up from where he was talking to one of the crew.

'We're leaving,' he said to him quietly. 'I'll be in my cabin.'

Gianluca nodded, then hesitated. '*Sì*, Signor Farnese… I mean, Your Grace. But which course shall I set?'

Vero shrugged. 'I don't care. Just sail for the horizon.'

It didn't matter where he went because he would be going without Betty, and anywhere would be nowhere without her.

Thirty minutes had passed since Vero had left but Betty could still feel his presence in the room. And probably she always would. He had left scars and watching him walk through that door was the hardest thing she had ever done. But it was for the best.

Her hand moved to press her stomach. Best for everyone. Even Vero.

He didn't love her.

In their entire time together, he had never once mentioned love until today. Need, in its most primal sense. But that wasn't love. It was lust and she had thought briefly that it might be enough for them. That urgent, sweet, encompassing, humbling hunger they felt for one another.

'*Scusi*, Your Highness?'

Betty glanced up. Mariangela was standing in the doorway with a tray. 'Yes? Sorry, did I order some tea?'

'No, Your Highness. But His Royal Highness Prince Frederico always took tea when he needed to calm his mind.'

'I remember.' Betty cleared her throat. Nonno had picked up the habit during one of his early love affairs in London. 'That's very kind of you, Mariangela.'

The housekeeper smiled. 'Just ring the bell if you need anything, Your Highness.'

But she wouldn't need to, Betty thought as she picked up the teapot and poured out a cup. Mariangela always knew what was needed before any bell was rung. If only she had the same sixth sense. Maybe none of this would have happened.

Or maybe it would. There was something there with Vero, something that transcended time and distance. A tiny shimmering thread that had refused to break for all those years. It had straddled the globe, criss-crossing America and the Middle East and Europe and it should have snapped or snarled into knots like the necklaces that Bella used to bring to her to untangle when she was little.

Only what should have weakened or damaged it had made it stronger.

It had stayed strong and straight and true, surviving their anger and distrust and the high-pressure spectacle of a royal wedding. And they had both fought it. Furiously. But in the middle of all that fury and frustration they had met in the middle.

They had talked and listened. They hadn't sat in judgement or walked away. She thought back to Vero sleeping on the sofa in her bedroom, his big body contorted against the cushions.

He had stayed there all night. And then he had magicked up his yacht and taken her out on the ocean, sensing, knowing, that the freedom and the fluidity of the water were what she'd needed most.

But that wasn't all he had done. Afterwards, he had surprised her by taking her to Rome and they had spent the rest of the day being Betty and Vero. Shopping, eating, dancing, like any normal couple in love.

And then, they had made love.

Her chest felt as if it were about to burst open. Because it wasn't just sex for Vero. He loved her. And she could spend the rest of her life doubting that, doubting herself, but she knew she was right.

It took her seven minutes to run, no, sprint, to the jetty. But as she reached the top of the steps, her legs slowed.

The yacht was gone. Vero was gone.

She felt a knot in her throat. She was too late. And she had lost him again. She had no idea where to look or how to find him.

But there had to be a way. Her brain scrambled through the possibilities. There was one. It would mean asking Mariangela for help.

She turned and stopped. Mariangela was walking down the steps. Smiling, she held out her phone. 'I hope you don't mind, Your Highness, but I took the liberty of calling my cousin.'

Reaching for the whisky bottle, Vero unscrewed the cap and sloshed a finger-width into a glass. He was taking his time, letting the alcohol seep slowly through his blood rather than drinking it straight from the bottle as he had the last time Betty and he had broken up. But this time he needed to keep feeling the pain, her pain, otherwise he knew he'd be tempted to order Gianluca to turn the yacht around.

So he was drinking just enough to take the edge off, and hopefully he would be far enough into the ocean by the time the bottle was empty, and Betty would have spoken to her father and there would be another reason to add to the list of things that would keep them apart for ever.

There was a knock on the cabin door and he ran his hand over his face.

'I told you I don't care where we go,' he shouted, without getting up from his desk.

The door inched open and one of the crew stepped into the crack, looking nervous. 'I'm sorry to bother you, Your Grace—'

'Don't call me that.'

'Yes, Your— I mean, Signor Farnese. It's not about the course, sir. The captain has asked that you come on deck.'

'I'm sure I'm not needed.'

'Unfortunately, you are. The coastguard has pulled us over and they want to speak to the owner.'

Vero shut his eyes briefly. The last thing he needed right now was to have to deal with some officious jobsworth, but the Guardia Costiera were essentially the police at sea.

As he stepped out on deck, the sunlight made him blink so that for a moment he only saw the men in their dark uniforms.

'I'm Vero Farnese. What seems to be the problem?'

The coastguard cleared his throat. 'There is no problem, Your Grace.'

He frowned. 'Then might I ask what you're doing on my boat?'

And then he saw her.

Her.

He almost lost his footing and suddenly it was a struggle to stop the air leaking from his lungs.

She was standing slightly to one side, her hand resting on the rail as it had done only days ago when he had leaned in to kiss her throat. But she couldn't be real. He stared at the woman in the striped sundress in confusion. He must be hallucinating. But he had only drunk one glass of whisky.

And then she stepped forward and he knew instantly that he wasn't dreaming. Knew from the way every nerve ending in his body tightened and the sense of loss stabbing beneath his ribs. And because of that hair. Nobody had hair like Betty. Right now, it was tied loosely with a scarf, and he would have given every share in his company to reach out and touch those rippling auburn curls.

'I asked these gentlemen if they might give me a lift and they very kindly agreed to drop me off,' she said into the shifting silence on deck, in that quiet, clear way of hers that made his stomach perform a low, swooping loop. Just as if the coastguard were her chauffeur and she were going to a garden party.

'You did?'

Just seeing her again made him feel tender and bruised inside.

She nodded, then turned towards the assembled men in their uniforms 'I think I can take it from here. But thank you very much for your help.'

Vero watched the coastguards return to their boat. There was a sudden, loud rasping sound as the engine started that faded as the boat accelerated across the water and all that remained then was the slap of the waves against the yacht's hull. It wasn't just the coastguards who had disappeared, he realised a moment later. His crew had vanished too.

Now it was just him and Betty and all the things he wanted to give to her and needed back, but which she was incapable of reciprocating.

'What are you doing here, Betty?' he said finally.

'I realised after you left that I had left some important things unsaid. About the future.'

The tiny fluttering shoot of hope that he had been ignoring at the margins of his brain withered and died. So she just wanted to talk about the divorce.

'Of course. What is it that you want to say?'

'That I'm sorry—'

He stared at her in appalled silence. The last few days she had grown in confidence and now he had set her back, crushed her again.

'You don't need to apologise to me, I should be the one apologising to you.'

'And you did. But I wouldn't accept it.'

She sounded vulnerable, but then he realised that she was showing him her vulnerability as proof of her trust.

'I didn't want to. I was angry and upset so I did what you did. I lashed out. I hurt the person I love, because I know you love me, Vero, and I love you, and I didn't say it before, and that's what I'm sorry for. For not being honest. But you were right. I do love you. I've only ever loved you.'

'And I've only ever loved you.' Reaching out, he pulled her into his arms.

Betty leaned into him, breathing out unsteadily.

'That's why I came after you. You told me not to settle for anything less than a man I can trust and love. A man who wouldn't make me pretend, who I was proud to call my husband. And I am proud of you, Vero, so very proud and happy to be your wife.'

Her face was soft and open, and he felt her love for him in his bones.

'I can't believe you got the coastguard to pick you up.'

'I didn't know how to find you but then Mariangela called her cousin for me. He's a coastguard down by Naples and he knew who to call. They patrol all the time, so they came to the jetty to pick me up.'

'What did you say to them?'

She screwed up her face. 'I told them we'd had an argument. And that I'd said some things I didn't mean. And that my husband had said some things he did mean. But that we loved each other and that I needed their help so that we could find our way back to each other.'

He stared at her incredulously. 'You do realise this is going to be all over the Internet by tonight.'

'Why do you think I wore this dress?'

He laughed then. 'Your father is going to lose his mind.'

'He'll get over it. But I would never get over losing you.'

His arm tightened around her. 'I meant what I said. I don't care about the title.'

She kissed him softly on the mouth. 'I don't care about it either. It doesn't matter at all because you're a prince among men to me, and more importantly you're the love of my life.'

'I love you, Betty,' he said, leaning in and kissing her slowly, and then, scooping her into his arms, he carried her across the deck and down the companionway to his cabin and to their future.

* * * * *

Did you fall head over heels for
Royal Ring of Revenge*?*
Then you're certain to love these
other dazzling stories
from Louise Fuller!

One Forbidden Night in Paradise
Undone in the Billionaire's Castle
Reclaimed with a Ring
Boss's Plus-One Demand
Nine-Month Contract

Available now!

TWINS FOR
HIS MAJESTY

CLARE CONNELLY

MILLS & BOON

PROLOGUE

AT NINE YEARS OLD, Crown Prince Octavio de la Rosa knew certain things for sure. He knew that he was destined to one day rule the prosperous island kingdom of Castilona, that he was being groomed for this purpose every day of his life, and he knew that his mother was the most beautiful, perfect creature on Earth, whom he loved more than anything. He also knew that he hated it when his parents travelled.

'It's only two nights, dearest.' Queen Eleanora crouched down, effortlessly graceful despite the formal evening gown she wore. 'And when we come back, you can show us how much you've learned.'

Octavio pulled a face. Part of his education included mastering the piano. His mother, a gifted musician, had insisted. And though he was naturally talented, he didn't enjoy lessons, nor practising, and saw the only silver lining to his parents' absences as the reprieve it gave him from learning.

'I mean it, Tavi. No slacking off.' She winked at him though, before tousling his hair as she stood.

Octavio nodded, transferring his attention to his father, King Miguel, who was fiddling with one of the diamond cuff-links he wore. 'Be a good boy, won't you?' he said, already distracted by the evening ahead. 'And call if you need anything.'

He nodded, hating the rush of emotion flooding his chest.

'Okay, bye.' He tried to sound casual and relaxed.

But his mother saw. She understood. She reached down and squeezed his hand in hers. 'Two nights, my love. Don't forget…' She trailed off, waiting for Octavio to finish the sentence.

'We'll always share the stars.' He repeated the words he'd learned by rote when he was very young and would weep whenever his mother had to leave the country. She had taught him to look out at the stars and know that she was doing the same, that they would always be connected by the heavens.

The phrase did make him feel calmer. He watched as his parents walked out of the elegant gallery, his father's arm wrapped around his mother's waist, their heads bent close together as they began to converse privately, a bubble forming around them indicating how happy and in love they were.

Octavio watched them until they were out of sight, and he would always be glad for that, because that was the very last time he saw his parents. Within days, they would be dead, and his life altered for ever. Soon, Prince Octavio de la Rosa would be utterly, completely alone.

CHAPTER ONE

Nineteen years later

FROM THESE PARTICULAR windows in the prestigious Clínica San Carlos, King Octavio de la Rosa had an unimpeded view of his palace. The place that defined who he was in life—a king of this prosperous Mediterranean island country. He stared across at the palace now, the sky a jet-black. Even the stars were blanked out by low cloud cover, giving the impression the heavens were utterly bereft of light, the darkness almost bleak enough to match his mood.

Grief flooded him. Grief, for his uncle Rodrigo had just died and with him, the last touchstone to his life *before*. Before his parents had been killed and he'd been orphaned, before his life had been turned upside down. He felt it deeply, but there was also a dark anger, so intense it burned through him, alongside frustration, despair and a cloying sense of being truly alone in the world.

In reality, he wasn't.

He was rarely alone—as the King, that wasn't possible. But Rodrigo was different. Rodrigo had been a last link to his parents. The man his mother had always joked she might have married if she'd met him first had died, and Octavio had been powerless to save him. Maybe if he'd known about Rodrigo's ill health sooner?

A noise startled Octavio out of his reverie. He glanced

up, on autopilot, to see one of the hospital's cleaners stepping into the luxurious suite he'd been appointed since arriving at the facility. He'd seen her before and noticed her. Even in his state of grief, he couldn't fail to notice her. She was beautiful, but it was more than that. She was graceful, like a ballerina, and there was a wistfulness in her gestures that couldn't help but convey itself.

The *clínica* was the last word in medical excellence, but it also shared some hallmarks with a five-star hotel—there were several suites such as this made available for guests of patients. For Octavio, the biggest and best had been reserved, allowing him to spend days at a time sitting vigil by his uncle's bedside.

Not that it had made a difference.

His stomach churned, impotent fury at his inability to help Rodrigo a slick of regret deep in his chest.

The woman busied herself clearing rubbish, keeping her head bent, evidently trained as his palace staff was, to exist without being seen.

It had never bothered him before. He'd been surrounded by staff all his life and had learned to live with the constant intrusion, but now, something about her self-effacing attempt to fade into the background was galling to him.

He attributed the sensation to his grief, to the shock of having sat at his uncle's bed not one hour earlier as the machines began to beep in that awful way, a flatline appearing on the equipment.

Soon he'd return to the palace, but he needed a little longer to process his loss.

To work out what he'd do next.

His uncle had died, but it had been preventable. The truth was, one uncle had all but killed the other, and Octavio had to work out how to deal with that.

The woman was lifting glasses now, stacking them on

a tray, her fingers so delicate, even when they were capable. He stared unashamedly, as one might watch a performance. Her uniform was dark blue, a dress that fell to her knees and cinched in at the waist, with buttons up to her throat. Her neck was elegant, swan-like, the alabaster colour of her skin revealed by the way her long blonde hair had been swept up into a ponytail. If she wore make-up, it was minimal. Her face was clear, her eyes wide set and a striking shade of green. As if his ruminating on their colour had somehow conveyed itself to the woman, she glanced across at him then, her cheeks flushing pink when their eyes connected. Her lips parted on a quick exhalation of breath, and she looked away once more, turning her back on him.

Frustration, anger, irritation grew.

Suddenly, he didn't want her to fade into the background. He didn't want her to clear his plates and glasses and act as though she wasn't there.

'What is your name?' His voice was gruff from disuse. Even as the hospital director, an efficient, impressive woman named Lola Garcia, had gently explained the procedures from this point onwards, he'd barely spoken a word.

The woman's shoulders squared as she turned back to face him, and there was a caution in her features that should have served as a warning. He wasn't himself. He wasn't remotely like himself. Famed for his control—a control that had been etched from the fires of his life—he was disciplined at all times.

Only, he didn't feel disciplined right now.

His veins were coursing with emotions he couldn't control, with a need for something he couldn't explain.

And this woman was in the firing line.

'I asked for your name.'

She blinked quickly, her lips, full and pink, quirking

down a little in one corner. 'Phoebe.' Her voice was soft, like her hair.

'Phoebe what?'

'Phoebe, Your Majesty.' She grimaced in apology.

The dark emotions in his gut twisted. He didn't want to be 'Your Majesty' in that moment. How different might his life have been had he not been born royal? If his parents hadn't been travelling on behalf of the kingdom, if his uncle Mauricio hadn't desperately sought the power of the throne? How different might it all have been?

'I meant to ask for your full name.'

'Oh, right.' Her tongue darted out, licking her lower lip. His veins pulsed with unexpected and not entirely unwelcome heat. 'Phoebe James.' Her words were lightly accented. Where was she from? What brought her to Castilona? In a fog of grief, he fixated on this woman, on the distraction she might provide.

'Take a seat.' He gestured to the chairs opposite, aware that he had no right to ask it of her, aware that she might feel pressured to agree because of who he was. He softened the request by muttering, 'If you have time.'

She hesitated and he immediately regretted adding the second statement. However, a moment later, she glided towards the armchair, pressing her hand into the back of it. She didn't sit, but she moved closer to him. He caught a hint of her fragrance, vanilla and strawberries, reminding him of summer fields.

'Did you need something, sir?'

Did he?

Yes. But what?

He knew only that he didn't want her to leave. Perhaps he was hiding from reality, avoiding his return to the palace as long as possible. Whatever the reason, it changed nothing. He was here and so was she.

'My uncle just died.'

Her eyes widened and her skin paled. 'I'm so sorry. I should leave. I didn't know, or I would never have intruded on your privacy at this time. My condolences, Your Majesty.'

She spoke quickly, the words tripping over themselves, and her sympathy was so obviously genuine that it pulled at something deep in his chest. If he allowed it, her words could weaken him, could erode his outer shell to reveal the grief and desolation deep at his core. He straightened, infusing his spine with steel, showing strength even when he didn't feel it, as was his way. As had been expected of him since his parents had died.

'It was expected.'

She hesitated, not leaving, not moving, just standing there like a deer in headlights. Then she exhaled quickly, so he was conscious of the way her body moved with the action of breathing, her breasts shifting beneath the dark blue dress.

'That doesn't make it any easier, in my experience.'

'Do you have experience with this?' Or did she mean working at the *clínica*? She must see such loss all the time. Except that wasn't what she'd meant, he was sure of it. Her teeth pressed into her lower lip, and her eyes turned a stormy green, like the ocean far, far out in its deepest parts.

'Yes, sir. And I don't think you can ever really prepare for the loss of someone you love. Nor do I think you ever fully recover.'

Fascinating. He knew her words were true—he lived them every day. There was an emptiness at his core that had been created on the day of his parents' death, an emptiness he had no hope of filling. Then again, perhaps that had as much to do with what happened to him after his parents' death as their actual loss itself. Whatever the reason, he'd spent his adult life avoiding anything like emotional dependency. Soon he would marry the Princess his parents had chosen for him, but that was an arranged marriage, without any kind of personal connection—it was a step he would take for the good of the country. He had no interest in exposing himself to any kind of loss ever again: he would be a far more effective ruler that way.

'Anyway…' Her voice trailed off a little. His eyes slammed back to her, a frown etched on his face. He reached for his tie and unfastened it, removing it completely before flicking open the button at his throat to reveal the column of his neck. Her eyes dropped betrayingly to the gesture; her cheeks flushed pink again. 'I should leave.'

'Stay.' There was command in his tone now and he didn't care. If she'd wanted to go, she would have done so by now. Ordinarily, he wouldn't have cared, because Octavio was not a man who needed anyone else in his life, even temporarily. But tonight, grief had weakened him, temporarily, and to himself he admitted that this woman choosing to remain with him carried more weight than he welcomed.

'Why?'

It was a whispered plea, a request for truth, and so he spoke the truth that was at his core in that moment.

'Because I don't want to be alone right now.'

She hesitated. 'Is there someone I can call for you?'

No one. He was alone. His gut churned. It was how he wanted it, how it had to be, and yet the creeping sense of isolation spread through him, turning his veins to ice. Of course, there was always Xiomara, the cousin with whom he was close, but even his relationship with her was complicated, and at times tainted by the fact that her father had been, in Octavio's eyes, responsible for their uncle Rodrigo's death. He wouldn't put Xiomara in the position of coming here, now.

'No.'

A soft sigh. 'Can I do something for you, sir? Would you like a tea? Coffee? Something stronger?'

His lips twisted. 'The latter.'

'Of course, Your Majesty.'

'Don't do that.'

She blinked, surprised. And no wonder. He was acting out of character yet he couldn't stop himself.

'Just—call me Octavio.'

'I'm sorry, sir, I really can't.'

'Why not?'

'My job—it's against protocol.'

A wry grimace tilted his lips. 'Who is going to know?'

'Well,' she prevaricated. 'No one, I suppose. But I—'

He waited for her to elaborate. 'I am asking you to treat me like a man, not a king. When I leave here and return there—' he nodded towards the palace, glistening like a beacon, calling to him '—I will be Your Majesty again. But now, I am just a man who is grieving his uncle.' Grieving his parents, his family, all of it. 'Treat me like a man.'

She moved towards the kitchen and removed a glass from the cabinet. He stood, striding across to her. 'Join me.'

Again, those eyes changed colour, to almost an emerald green. Fascinating. Her lashes were long and dark, curling and soft.

'Do you mind if I make an observation?'

One single brow lifted.

'You do not act like any man I've ever met. Treating you like one would be…difficult.'

'In what ways do I differ?'

'Seriously?' A small laugh escaped then but she stifled it, glancing at him with that frustratingly deferential expression of apology.

'Yes, I am serious.'

'Well…' She looked around, lost for words. 'You're… just very regal.'

'What does that mean?'

'It means that you're clearly used to giving commands and to having them obeyed.'

'Is that a bad thing?'

'Not at all. But it's not a "normal guy" thing.'

'I only became King two weeks ago,' he pointed out.

'But you were raised to be King, weren't you?'

He was raised to be King, yes. Raised by a man who hated him, raised by a man who hired a succession of nannies to do the actual caregiving—though he used that term loosely. The only prerequisite for his nannies' hiring, from what Octavio could tell, was that they be ice-cold, and cruel to boot.

He dipped his head forward.

'And when you walk out of this hospital, you'll return to the palace, where everyone will refer to you as "Your Majesty"?'

'And I will act as though I am not feeling this,' he said, pressing to his chest, indicating his grief. 'Because that is what is expected of me there.'

'But here, with me, you can be honest,' she murmured, eyes wide, as if articulating that thought gave it more power.

'Yes.'

'Okay.' She hesitated. 'Octavio.'

His name on her lips was different; she imbued the syllables with the softness that was inherent to her, taking a name that was, by its nature and design, a symbol of strength and making it somehow more human. Just as he wished to be.

But it was more than just a softening of his name, it was the forging of a connection. She addressed him like a man and he felt it—not normal, exactly, but powerfully aware of something between them that was transcending his rank, his title, even his grief. Or perhaps it was because of his grief? Perhaps in such moments, where awareness of death was at a peak, people were wired to seek expressions of life. He wanted to feel alive, and there was something about Phoebe that caused his blood to hum.

'Tell me about your uncle,' she invited, pouring a Scotch and sliding it across to him. He ignored the drink.

He thought of Rodrigo and his insides tightened uncomfortably. 'Before last week, I had not seen him in a long time.'

'He was exiled?' she murmured, and he was surprised. The history was well-known—though legitimacy had been given to Mauricio's actions, few understood that it was sheer self-interest that had governed his choices.

'Shortly after my parents died, yes.'

Her expression softened. 'Were you close?'

Memories blurred at the edges of his mind. Rodrigo catching him in his arms and tossing him into the air, his eyes crinkling with laughter, the way he played piano and sang along and played cards until far too late. The sense of safety and security he had, in those days, taken for granted—and never known again since. 'At one time, yes.' His voice was gruff. He cleared his throat. 'It was a long time ago.'

'Does that matter?'

His eyes met hers, burned through them. 'No.'

'How come you didn't see him, after he was exiled?'

'Until I was eighteen, I had very little autonomy. And after that, I didn't have the resources required to find him.'

'He disappeared?'

'He took the exile hard, apparently. I have learned a lot since my coronation. His life was far from a bed of roses.'

'In what way?' she asked, coming around from the

kitchen and standing close to him. So close he caught a hint of her perfume again, and this time when his gut rolled, he understood the feeling. Desire. Physical need. While he was an expert at maintaining relationships that were emotionally contained, he was still a red-blooded man with physical needs, and he indulged those needs as and when required.

'When he was exiled, he was cut off from his assets as well. He had some cash, but it wasn't enough to start a new life. He scraped by, but it was difficult for him.'

'And then he got sick?'

'He had AIDS,' Octavio murmured. 'And didn't realise. Medication now is so effective, he could have been treated, he could have lived a long life, but he didn't know and he didn't get help. So by the time I became King and launched a search for him, the disease had progressed and nothing could be done.'

'I'm so sorry,' she whispered. 'I still don't understand why he was exiled?'

Octavio's lips curled into a derisive smirk. 'That would require an explanation into the darker side of human nature and I'm not sure either of us want to go there tonight.'

She tilted her head a little, as if digesting his words. 'You don't want to talk about it?'

'There's no point. It's ancient history—nothing can be done now to right that wrong.'

'But you do think his exile was wrong?'

'Oh, I know it was.'

'And you couldn't do anything?'

'My uncle—my other uncle—had all the power of a king until I ascended the throne. It was his will, his way.'

'But we're talking about his younger brother?'

'Yes.'

'I don't understand. Why would he want him sent away? They're siblings.'

'Do you have a brother or sister?'

She shook her head. 'I always wished for one, but I was an only child.'

His expression shifted. 'As am I.'

'No spare to your heir?'

'No.' He didn't elaborate; it wasn't necessary. There was no need to go into the fact his parents tried for years after his birth, without success, to conceive another baby. Even as a young boy, he'd come to understand the vulnerability of his position. He'd always known that he would have to marry and have children—a reality he grappled with even now, because he would have preferred a solitary existence. An arranged marriage, though, offered some reassurance.

'Did you want a brother or sister?'

He'd never been asked that before. Then again, this was probably the most real conversation he'd had in a long time with anyone other than his cousin Xiomara.

'Not as a boy, but once my parents died, I wished for someone who understood what I was going through.'

'What about your other uncle?'

He bristled visibly. 'No.'

'Why not?'

'We weren't close.'

'Weren't? Aren't?'

'Both.'

'Because of the darker side of human nature?' she prompted.

His eyes scanned her face, studying her. She was different. Unusual. Though she'd insisted on using his title initially, she didn't seem at all nervous around him. She wasn't speaking to him with the exaggerated deference he was accustomed to, and he liked that.

'Yes.'

She expelled a small sigh. 'Would you like me to go?'

He frowned. 'Why do you say that?'

'You've clammed up.'

'I didn't mean to.'

'It's okay if you don't want to talk. I mean, if you'd rather be alone.'

He would always rather be alone. Except now, when his heart was splintering from the loss of his uncle and he wanted the distraction of *this*. A beautiful, warm, vibrant woman, keeping his mind occupied.

'I don't want to be alone.'

Her lips parted.

'I just don't want to talk about my family.'

Her smile was wry. 'I understand the feeling.'

He didn't push her. 'Have you worked here long?'

She shook her head. 'Just a couple of weeks. So you could say we both changed jobs around the same time,' she quipped.

He was surprised to feel a smile flash across his face.

'What did you do before this?'

She swallowed, and something crossed her features that made him wonder about more than just her vocation. He wondered about *her*. Her life, her history, what brought someone from a foreign country to Castilona, to work in a hospital as a cleaner.

'I was a receptionist at a school,' she murmured, but her voice was strangled, her features tight. 'Back in New Zealand.'

'Touchy subject?'

She grimaced. 'Not really.'

But he saw through her. 'Phoebe?'

'Okay, a little.'

'What brings you to Castilona?'

She hesitated a moment. 'My birth father is from here.'

He waited for her to continue.

'I never knew him. He was on holiday in New Zealand when he met my mum. He never knew about me and she didn't know anything more than his name. She put him on my birth certificate but had no way of contacting him. All I know is that he may be here, somewhere.'

'And you want to find him?'

She nodded. 'I was raised to speak the language. My mum even tried to cook some of the more traditional meals. It was important to her that I have access to this side of my heritage even though I never met my father.'

'She must be happy you've travelled here then?'

'She passed away a few years ago.' Her voice was carefully controlled, but he could feel the emotion coming off her in waves, and his own grief was so close to the surface that he did something he wouldn't usually contemplate. He stepped closer and lifted a hand to her cheek. As soon as his fingertips connected with her skin, he realised he'd been wanting to do this from the moment he'd first laid eyes on her. She had reminded him of gossamer silk, and in the back of his mind he'd wondered if she'd feel so soft to touch. She did. Her skin was flawless and as he allowed his fingers to glide lower, she closed her eyes and let out a shuddering breath.

'Octavio,' she murmured, and now his name was soft with a plea, as though she were floating and asking him to catch her, to bring her back to Earth.

Only his body was driving him now, making him want to forget his grief, to live in the most vibrant of ways, to exist purely for feeling. His fingers shifted towards her mouth, so he could smooth his thumb across her lower lip. She let out a soft moan.

'This isn't a good idea,' she groaned, but her eyes met his and they were awash with the same sense of out-of-body need that was vibrating inside of him.

'Do you want me to stop?'

She lifted a hand to his chest, curling her fingers in his shirt as she stared up at him, totally bewildered. 'I didn't say that.'

His smile now was tight, his gut rolling with a visceral need. 'Do you want me to start?'

Her throat shifted as she swallowed. 'I—want—' Her teeth pressed into her lower lip and her eyes dropped to his mouth, lingering there so long he began to feel his skin tingle.

'Would you like me to kiss you, *querida*?'

Anguish flashed in her gaze, and surrender, too. She nodded slowly. 'Yeah, I think I'd like that.'

He didn't need to be asked twice, but caution was ingrained in Octavio. It came innately to him, and his position as heir presumptive and now King meant he had always focused on ensuring discretion with his private life. He wasn't an ordinary man, no matter what he wished.

'You understand I will leave for the palace tomorrow?'

She nodded softly.

'That my role will require me to disappear from your life?'

Her eyes narrowed. It was hardly the stuff of romance, but he knew from experience that it was better to be upfront about what he could offer.

'I know that.'

'It's only fair to be honest,' he explained.

'I agree.'

'I would appreciate it if you kept our interaction private.'

'But I have so many tabloids on my speed dial,' she responded archly. 'And I'm just itching to be known as a king's one-night stand.'

'Point taken. I'm sorry. I'm not myself tonight.'

Her features softened, sympathy gleaning in her eyes.

'That's understandable.' She lifted up onto the tips of her toes. 'Kiss me, Your Majesty.'

'Now who's being bossy?'

'Is that a complaint?'

His response was to crush her mouth with his own, his body rejoicing in the instant contact and connection and yes, vitality. He was alive. His blood rushed through his body, strength gathered in his muscles, and kissing her made every cell in his body reverberate with brilliant awareness. Best of all, death and loss and grief were nowhere now—there was only this.

CHAPTER TWO

DAWN STIRRED ACROSS the kingdom, like the breathing of fresh life into the night, a whisper and a kiss, light and gentle. Darkness turned to silver and then to mauve, before a hint of gold glimmered across the city, drawing Phoebe's eyes to the palace, which she glimpsed through the window.

What had seemed so natural and easy the night before now slammed into her with a growing sense of awe.

What had she done?

And *why*?

Phoebe had *never* had a one-night stand before in her life. In fact, she'd only been with one other man, whom she believed herself to be engaged to—little had she known, he was actually already married. But to Phoebe, it had been real, and she'd thought herself in love, and their intimacy had been a natural progression of that.

Last night with King Octavio had been something else entirely. Something wild and passionate, something quite feral, as if they were simply animals, unable to keep their hands off each other. Maybe it had started out as something else. Comfort? Sharing grief? An understanding of life's cruellest losses? But within minutes it had escalated. They'd torn clothes from one another, tangled arms and legs, lips meshed, bodies fused by a desperate, aching need that had refused to abate. The first time they were together had been wild and manic, but there'd been no answering calm afterwards. No sense of satiation. It had simply morphed into a different type of need, this time, a compulsion to explore slowly, to almost torment one another by holding back until they were once more at fever pitch. He'd kissed her all over, his mouth ravaging her breasts, her nipples, the sensitive skin just beneath her ear, her everywhere. She pressed the palm of her hand to her lips to contain a moan.

Dawn was breaking and she was *at work*. She needed to get out of the *clínica*, go home, freshen up and then get back to work, all without anyone knowing how she'd spent the small hours of the morning. Her heart was in her throat as she contemplated how exactly to handle the etiquette of the situation.

Last night, they'd agreed it was a one-night thing, and she'd been fine with that. She was still fine with it. Only, having known the mind-blowing pleasure that had been sex with Octavio, she was experiencing just a hint of remorse at the idea of leaving without one more kiss, one more everything…

But she had a shift starting in a few hours, which left just enough time to get home, shower, eat something and return. As quietly as she could, she crept from the bed, easing one leg out first and then the other, watching him the whole time, waiting to see if he would stir, half hoping he would even as she did her best to be quiet.

He didn't.

The combination of yesterday's grief and last night's activities must have worn him out, because she'd have put money on him ordinarily being an early riser. There was an intensity to him that made her think he was the kind of man who wouldn't want to waste a moment of the day.

Her clothes were in the lounge room, where they'd been flung the night before. She pulled them on quickly, tidied her hair, pinched her cheeks, then paused only to check her reflection in the mirror.

Phew.

She looked completely normal. There was no outward way to deduce how she'd spent last night.

Her handbag was still in the locker room, she realised with a groan, and she'd need it to get into her place. A slight complication, but she'd just have to try not to be seen by anyone who knew her well enough to be familiar with her shifts.

She crept out of the suite, shutting the door behind her as softly as possible, then moving quickly down the plush, carpeted corridor, head bent the whole way.

By some miracle, she managed it. Not only to retrieve her handbag, but also to slip out of the staff doors of the *clínica* without running into anyone she knew. She barely breathed until she'd boarded the bus that would take her within a few blocks of the apartment she was renting temporarily.

As she showered and dressed, her mind kept flashing back to last night. To the way he'd been with her. The way he'd kissed her and touched her as though she were the most perfect, rare, beautiful object in the world.

What a gift, to be able to make a woman feel like that. She'd never known anything like it.

She probably never would again.

She dismissed the thought. She wasn't thinking about men or relationships right now. God knew, she'd been so badly burned by Christopher, she wasn't sure she'd ever trust anyone ever again. She couldn't so much as think of her ex without a horrible, all-consuming sense of shame. That she'd been 'the other woman', while he'd been married, got his wife pregnant, seen his first child born, and his second, all the while stringing Phoebe along, treating her like a first-rate idiot. And she had been an idiot, utterly and completely.

He'd been such an accomplished liar, though, it wasn't really that she was stupid. Just that she'd been alone and lonely and wanted to feel loved, and he'd offered her so much of that.

Memories of Christopher were just the antidote she needed to the swoony feelings Octavio had invoked. All men were bastards, she thought with satisfaction, as she dressed in her other uniform and prepared to return to work.

His first waking thought that day had been born of desire. He'd reached for Phoebe automatically, his arm stretching across the bed, his fingers seeking, wanting, needing, only to connect with the empty sheets. A cursory glance at the suite had shown him to be alone, and his instant reaction had been a visceral sense of disappointment before he'd told himself he should be relieved.

Despite his clarity the night before, there'd been a part of him that had worried she might want more than he was offering, that she might get the wrong idea. She was a cleaner in a hospital and he was royalty—was it possible she harboured some kind of romantic Cinderella notion?

Evidently not.

She'd disappeared, leaving no note, no number, nothing.

Until now. Standing in the foyer of the clinic, he listened as the director spoke gently.

'As there are no complicating factors, your uncle's body will be released as soon as you convey your wishes as to the funeral preparations. If you should wish for any further medical information, please—'

At that moment, there was a loud crash. One of his security agents had knocked an enormous vase of flowers to the tiled floor, leaving a cascade of water and stems in disarray.

'I'm so sorry, Your Majesty. Please excuse me a moment.'

Dr Garcia moved quickly, her heels clacking over the floor, and it was then that he saw her.

Phoebe James.

Phoebe James, who loved to be kissed just above her hip bone. Phoebe James, who had loved being on top last night, her body arching as she took him deep inside, her breasts so perfect and full, he hadn't been able to stop staring at them. Phoebe James, who'd run her hands all over him and moaned his name at the top of her lungs.

Phoebe James, with huge green eyes that were very determinedly *not* looking at him now, no matter how much he willed it.

Phoebe James, who was being instructed by her boss to clean up the mess his guard had just made.

Oh, for Christ's sake.

It was her job as a cleaner to clean things, but the sight of her scuttling across the tiles and scooping down, picking up the stems first and then moving on to the broken glass had him wanting to shout something. To force her to stop. The broken vase shouldn't be her responsibility. And he definitely shouldn't care this much, he admitted to himself. Not for some woman he'd just met and would never see again. But there was something about her that fired all his protective instincts to life.

So, when Lola, the director, returned to continue their conversation, he directly addressed the broken vase. 'That should not be your cleaner's responsibility. My guard knocked it—he will take care of it.'

'It's fine, Your Majesty. These things happen.'

Impotence grew inside of him. But how could he argue the point further without revealing something more? He had been worried about his own privacy the night before, but now he considered Phoebe's job. She had been such a stickler for convention initially; she hadn't even wanted to use his first name.

He listened as Lola continued to outline the protocols from here, but his eyes kept straying to Phoebe, and he was sure she knew he was watching, because her cheeks began to glow pink. At one point, a piece of glass cut her finger and he had to bite back a curse.

It was too much.

He strode across the tiles, uncaring for what Lola might think, and crouched beside Phoebe. Up close, memories of last night throbbed in his gut and spread through his whole body, so when he spoke his voice was raw with hunger. 'Let me help you.'

Startled, she looked at him, her lips parting. It was a mistake.

A huge mistake.

He couldn't help but stare at them, and the memories came thick and fast now. What would she say if he pulled her into his arms and kissed her until she was moaning against him, as she had the night before, begging for him to take her? He tamped down on that very real temptation. It would obviously be one of the stupidest things he could do, and Octavio was not stupid. Nor was he controlled by his libido. Generally.

'You're bleeding.'

'Go away.'

'You're hurt.'

'It's nothing, *please*.'

'Phoebe—'

'Don't,' she hissed, her eyes flashing past him, to the hospital director and whomever was watching. 'Please don't,' she whispered, plastering a bright smile on her face. 'This is my job.'

But he hated that.

His whole body was flush with emotions he couldn't process and didn't want to analyse. He continued to pick up pieces of glass.

'Your Majesty, you must stop,' she whispered. 'People will notice. People will talk.'

'Who gives a damn?'

'I do,' she promised. 'And you do, too. You've just forgotten it because of yesterday.'

Yesterday—his uncle's death. Not last night, with her. He shook his head once, to demur, but her features were so cold, her look so laced with warning. 'Please leave me alone,' she whispered.

He hated it.

He felt those words deep in the core of his being, and he couldn't say why but he knew that they mattered. He stood slowly, hands thrust into hips, looking down on her working, wishing it weren't this way. Wishing they were back in his bed, where they were thoroughly equals, wondering if he could move heaven and earth to make it so.

'Please go,' she whispered again, without looking up at him.

He turned on his heel and strode back to the clinic director, but Phoebe James was burned into his brain.

'The funeral was beautiful.' Octavio glanced at his cousin Xiomara without really seeing her. The funeral *had* been beautiful, Xiomara was right. Private, small and in accordance with royal traditions. Rodrigo had been brought home and laid to rest in the family crypt, reunited with his brother and parents.

'It was a good funeral, yes,' Octavio agreed.

Xiomara's smile was wistful. 'Thank you for letting my father attend.'

'I was surprised he wanted to.'

'I suppose time…' Her voice trailed off into nothing and she sighed. 'I can't defend it. You know that. But today was nice. You did well, Tavi.' She walked across and placed a kiss on Octavio's cheek. 'Do you need anything?'

Did he need anything? Hell, yes, he needed something. He needed the same thing he'd needed the night Rodrigo had died. The same thing he'd been craving every night since—or rather, someone. A craving he'd been fighting, because it was so out of his realm of experience, so overwhelming in a way he resented and instinctively shied away from.

He'd thought of calling Phoebe though, even when he knew it would be a mistake. But even if he'd wanted to, how could he? Apart from the fact he was now King, his every move tracked and speculated upon, he'd been manically busy dealing with the aftereffects of Rodrigo's death.

Funerals, though, were an end-point, a line in the sand, and now the background hum of noise that was his need for Phoebe had exploded into a full-blown absorption.

He wanted her in a way that was driving him to the point of distraction and then well beyond it. She had flooded him with something that night, something he'd become addicted to, even when he knew addiction was bad. Only, it would be problematic if he wasn't in control. If he let things really overtake him. But what if he could see her again whilst maintaining his usual vice-like grip on his emotions and strength?

Just once more. One more night.

Was there anything wrong with that? Octavio knew he wanted her more than he'd ever wanted another woman, but so long as he put a very clear end-point on this thing, what harm could come of it?

She had been discreet. There had been nothing in the papers about their tryst, no speculation online. He could trust her, just as he'd somehow known he could, even then. There'd been something about Phoebe's manner that had set her apart.

Or was it just that he'd wanted comfort and she'd been there, and for once in his life he hadn't worried about the consequences? It wasn't like Octavio to display such ambivalence. He trusted his instincts at all times—they'd served him well. And his instincts were pushing him, hard and fast, towards Phoebe and the comfort she could offer, and the pleasure they could share, just for one more night…

For a long time, Phoebe had held to a policy of ignoring calls from random numbers. They were always spammy sales calls, or lately would-be scammers, and she hated the interruptions. But she'd been making enquiries to find her father and was waiting on a return call from an investigator in the north of the country. So when her phone began to buzz and the screen showed *Number Withheld*, she swiped it to answer on the first ring. 'Phoebe James,' she said, stepping to the side of the footpath on which she'd been jogging, so she could concentrate.

Silence. A spam call, after all?

'Hello?'

More silence. She was about to hang up when a voice— deep, gruff, husky and immediately recognisable—came down the phone line. 'Phoebe, how are you?'

She almost dropped the phone in shock.

'Octavio!' His name was a breath from her lips. Out of nowhere, images of him, her, them flooded her mind. She gripped the railing that ran alongside the footpath. 'I— didn't expect to hear from you. How did you get my number?'

'Are you free right now?'

Her heart sped up. Her pulse throbbed. Her insides

squirmed. Every part of her began to tremble and shake. She shook her head, even when she knew she would go to him, go wherever he asked her.

'Phoebe?'

'I can be,' she admitted. As if she had anything else to do! She knew no one in the country, apart from a few acquaintances at work.

'I'm going to give you an address. Take a cab there, and then my driver will bring you the rest of the way.'

It took ten minutes to drive across town in the taxi she hailed, and by the time she arrived, a sleek black sedan with darkly tinted windows was waiting, a man in a suit standing near the rear door. She waited until the taxi driver had left before moving towards the car and taking a seat, and she fidgeted her fingers the whole way. The car drove through the winding streets that were so Castilonian she couldn't help but sigh at their obvious beauty. Old terracotta houses with wrought iron balconies, roof tiles and thick, green bushes which, in the light of day, would show shocks of colour. Red, purple, white geraniums and lavender, fragrant and stunning. The Mediterranean country was charmingly old-fashioned, and she felt a connection to it deep in her bones.

After around ten minutes, the car paused outside an old-fashioned-looking townhouse that had been adapted at some point to include an under-cover garage. The door lifted and the car drove into it. Phoebe's heart sped up as she briefly contemplated the potential risks of her decision to come here. She'd been so overwhelmed to hear his voice, so overwhelmed by a rush of need, but also concern, because the whole country had been talking about the funeral for his uncle and how that must be affecting the King. In the back of her mind, she'd worried for him all day, because she'd seen firsthand how Rodrigo's death had upset Octavio.

But here he was, standing in the garage, dressed in suit trousers and a white shirt with the sleeves pushed up to his elbows. She stared at him from behind the tinted car window, greedily soaking up the image of him, only belatedly realising that she was wearing exercise gear and no make-up and wishing she'd somehow managed to squeeze in a quick trip back to her apartment to freshen up a little.

The door was opened by the driver, and then Octavio stepped forward, not smiling, his features set in a mask of intensity that took her breath away.

He held out a hand to help her from the car. As she put hers in his, she was conscious of her unpainted nails, cut short so they were easy to maintain, but then a spark travelled as if by magic from his fingers to hers, and all the way up her arm towards the very centre of her torso. She throttled a small gasp, low in her throat.

'I'm glad you came.'

She stood, so close to him she could feel his warmth. Her body tingled. 'How are you?'

He nodded once—what did that mean?—then put his hand on her lower back to guide her out of the garage, through a doorway and into a small entrance foyer that led to a set of polished timber stairs.

She walked ahead of him, up the stairs and into a stunning open plan living area with a whole wall of glass that overlooked a garden. Though it was night, the garden itself had beautiful lighting, showing the advanced trees and a water feature right in the middle.

'What is this place?'

'I lived here, before I became King. In many ways, I consider it to be my real home.'

She looked around with renewed interest. It was modern and sleek, a space that oozed elegance but not much warmth. She ran a hand over an end table, then turned her attention to Octavio. 'How did you get my number?' She'd asked him that on the phone, but he hadn't answered, and she wanted to know.

'It wasn't difficult.'

'I've only been in the country a short while, and I don't really know anyone...'

'But your employer has your details on file.'

She gasped. 'Tell me you didn't ask the *clínica* for my number?' Her heart sped up. She couldn't believe she'd got away unscathed after that night. She'd been waiting for the axe to drop, for someone to reveal that they'd seen her, but so far, nothing.

'No, *querida*. When my uncle was admitted and I announced that I would be spending time at the hospital, my head of security was given details of all employees so he could vet them.' Her jaw dropped. 'It was a necessary precaution.'

'Wow.' She pressed her fingertips to her temple. 'Okay, next question. Why did you call?'

His eyes traced her face for so long that she could *feel* heat on her skin, as if he was touching her. 'I needed to see you.'

Her stomach dropped to her toes. 'Did you?'

He nodded slowly, frowning a little, as if not sure what to say next. 'I needed you.'

Because of the funeral. Because he was grieving again, and she'd been such a successful answer to that last time. But did she care why he needed her? Hadn't she been craving him, too? That night hadn't been enough—she wanted more. Just one more night? Would that cure her of this obsession?

'Phoebe, nothing's changed. Who I am, what I can offer...but I'm asking you to spend tonight with me.'

He was asking her. And he was being honest with her. Christopher had used her, he'd manipulated her, he'd broken her trust again and again. He'd made a fool of her, because he'd always been lying. The whole time they were together had been a falsehood. Octavio was being honest with her, and he was asking her what she wanted. This was her choice; she could do what she wanted, on her terms.

And she knew what she wanted.

'Yes,' she said, simply, walking towards him with a sense of purpose she had no interest in doubting. 'I'll spend tonight with you.'

CHAPTER THREE

THE NEXT MORNING he reached for her, just as he had the other morning, only this time, his fingertips glanced across soft, smooth flesh, her body warm and close. He didn't know what time it was. Light was filtering through the windows of his bedroom, but it was still a pale, golden light, promising the freshness of a just burgeoning day.

She shifted in her sleep, rolling to face him, her eyes shut, her lashes long against her creamy skin. Her lips curved into a smile. He closed the distance between them, kissing her slowly, softly, savouring this moment of waking her, his naked body pressed to hers, so she responded immediately. Her arm snaked around his middle, her mouth moved beneath his, and deep in her throat she moaned, a husky sound filled with need.

He moved his body over hers, delighting in the feel of her nakedness beneath him, of her responsiveness to his touch, delighting in his power over her. As he moved his hands, he was invoking a powerful, age-old spell, stirring her body to fever pitch with every brush of his fingers, every movement of his mouth. She was soft and supple, her skin lifting in goose bumps with his touch, her body reacting with warmth and need. His kisses dragged across her flesh, padding the goose bumps with his lips, his tongue, tracing her lines. He worshipped her sex with his mouth, his strong hands on her thighs, holding her apart for him, so he had total access to her most private, sensitive core.

She bucked against his mouth, her body beaded in fine perspiration, her moans louder and faster now, so he grinned as he pulled away from her purely to grab a condom and then returned, his own need an insatiable beast controlling him completely.

He nudged her legs apart and thrust into her hard, deep, her muscles squeezing him tight, her whole body reacting to his presence, her cries filling the room with that partic-ular note of fervent need. His own cries were low but no less infused with desperation; he was buried inside of her, but it wasn't enough. He moved faster, kissed her harder, his tongue an unconscious echo of his movements, his hair-roughened chest brushing against her hardened nipples. Her hands ran down his back, cupped his buttocks, held him where she needed him, and then she was screaming his name as her whole body began to tremble and the muscles that were surrounding him began to tighten almost unbear-ably, making restraint impossible. He came almost as she did, losing himself to this overwhelming sensation of plea-sure, his body throbbing with satiation, his release intense.

He collapsed on top of her, burying his face in the crook of her neck, feeling every deep, rasping breath she took, hearing it inside his own body. This had started as a distrac-tion, as a need to forget, but it was now just simply *need*. He contemplated rolling away from Phoebe and then ending this. He thought about not seeing her again, and he knew he wouldn't do it. He didn't want to.

There was something about her that made his body sing, and he wasn't ready to give it up yet. Even when it was the right thing to do. While his betrothal had never been for-malised, it was very much expected by both royal house-holds. His parents' wishes, and her parents' wishes, were in alignment, and Octavio had always known he would honour his parents' choice for him.

But his marriage was still some time off. It would take at least a year to finalise arrangements and prepare the ceremony. Until then, he was a free agent. Free to do what he wanted, but not if that proved harmful to Phoebe.

He pushed up onto his elbow so he could see her more clearly. Her beautiful face was flushed pink, her eyes wide as she stared at him.

'Good morning,' she murmured, running her fingers through her hair.

He shifted his hips a little, revelling in the way she bit into her lip. Sensations were still flooding his body, and he was sure she was also feeling the aftereffects of their coming together.

He wanted more of her; but how much more? And for how long? It wasn't fair to use Phoebe to fill a gap in his life while it suited him, then discard her when he was ready to marry. Besides, he had no idea what she wanted.

Everything between them was incredibly simple and organic—it just felt easy. At the same time, it was also impossibly hard. He had been born to serve his country; that was his duty. It was something he'd always known, but after the death of his parents it had crystallised in his mind as the primary purpose in his life. He had focused on that every single day after their deaths, when his uncle had made his life a misery, and his nannies had delighted in punishing him and isolating him, he'd thought of his country and the kind of King he would be, how he could make his parents proud. It was the sole focus of his life.

He wasn't interested in relationships—not relationships that might take that focus and split it. Particularly not now he was finally in the box seat and had been crowned King. He needed to work hard to undo the damage Mauricio had wrought, and then he needed to marry the Princess his parents had chosen and create enough heirs that the line of succession would be safe for ever. These were his priorities. Not losing time and energy to a woman. Not even a woman as tempting as Phoebe. In fact, she was so tempting that she reminded him how important it was to walk away from her—to remind them both that this was meaningless and unimportant, because nothing mattered to him like his role as King did.

A heaviness sat in his chest as he mentally closed the door on temptation. He wanted Phoebe, but he couldn't have her, and he'd known that right from the start of this thing.

'I'll have my driver take you home.'

Even to his own ears, his voice was cold; no wonder she flinched a little. The light that had seemed to glitter in her eyes was instantly extinguished. Her lips parted on a soft sound of breath escaping. He could see her physically wrangling with his meaning, trying to interpret it differently, and watching the shift in her emotions was something he didn't enjoy. He wanted to apologise. To explain. To help her understand that she was wonderful but he was limited, so limited, in what he could offer and even what he could want. But for some reason, he couldn't properly grasp how to vocalise any of those feelings. He couldn't even properly shape the explanations in his own mind, so how could he offer them to her?

With growing frustration and a sense that he'd bitten off more than he could chew, Octavio pulled away from her, the separation almost a physical pain. He turned his back, strode across the room, stepping into his bathroom and closing the door. Only then did he expel the breath he'd been holding.

He made it five weeks. Five weeks without weakening and calling Phoebe. Five weeks without getting his driver to take him to her place, so Octavio could knock on the door and apologise for the ice-cold way he'd ended things that morning. Five weeks in which sleep had been made almost impossible because of the nature of his dreams and the strength of his wants. Five weeks in which he'd pushed himself to work long days in the hope he would be tired enough to get her from his mind and actually find some kind of relief.

For things to go back to normal.

But nothing was normal. In the space of a couple of months, he'd turned twenty-eight, ascended the throne, witnessed his beloved uncle's death and got to grips with the parlous state his other uncle had left the country in. And met Phoebe.

Phoebe, who was beautiful and fascinating but in no way suitable to be anything more than a secret fling. A cleaner from New Zealand was not exactly the kind of woman his parliament and advisors would expect him to date, let alone do anything more serious with.

In any event, a relationship with Phoebe was a moot point. His betrothal loomed, which meant he shouldn't have been thinking about Phoebe at all.

Never mind that he had known for a long time he wasn't interested in a relationship that had the ability to monopolise his mind and worse, his heart. Not that his heart was involved in his calculations. He'd slept with Phoebe, that was all. He hardly knew her beyond that. It didn't matter that there was something about her that was different from the women he'd been with in the past; she was unsuitable for any part in his life. And even if she had been serious, when he was with her a part of him, a deep, important part, had turned into a bright red flag, warning him to be careful.

So couldn't he see her *and* still be careful? Couldn't he create parameters that would keep them *both* safe from the sort of vulnerabilities he sought to avoid?

The thought kept rolling around and around in his mind though, and eventually, he found it impossible to ignore.

Maybe there was one way in which he could see Phoebe, in some capacity, if she were willing. Just maybe he could make something work with her, just for a while. Just maybe he could have his cake and eat it, too…

Phoebe could not have been more shocked if a Martian had been on the other side of the door. 'What are you doing here?'

'His Majesty asked me to speak to you.'

She stared at Octavio's driver, anger blooming as though it hadn't been five long weeks since he'd all but dismissed her. He hadn't gone so far as to thank her for services rendered, but he might as well have. That was exactly how he'd made her feel. Cheap, and used.

'Yeah, well, I have no interest in anything His Bloody Majesty might have to say.' She went to slam the door in the driver's face but his foot caught the door before it latched.

'I'm afraid I can't take no for an answer.'

'That's your problem,' she snapped. 'You can take it or leave it, but my answer is still no.'

This time, when she slammed the door, he didn't stop it.

She should have known better than to believe that would be the end of it. Only two minutes later, with hands still trembling from outrage, in the midst of making a mug of peppermint tea, the doorbell rang once more. *Damned persistent driver*, she thought with chagrin, making her way into the small foyer and wrenching it inwards.

Only to find Octavio staring back at her, all unmistakable royal importance and unfairly perfect good looks.

'What are you doing here?'

'You left me no choice.'

'We always have a choice,' she replied, gripping the door.

'Mind if I come in?'

She cast a glance over her shoulder, aware that her place was as tidy as usual, but still hating the thought of Octavio seeing where she was living. It was only temporary, a place to stay whilst she searched for her father, but it was still a reflection of her. It was intimate. Exposing.

Only in that brief moment, rather than waiting for an answer, he swept past her, brushing his body to hers by virtue of the cramped entrance area, so her pulse went haywire.

She stood there, staring at him, door still open, so Octavio made a noise of impatience, reached over and unpeeled her fingers. Just his touch sent a thousand little fireworks into her veins. She jumped back from him, holding on to her anger as though it were an anchor she desperately needed.

'What do you want?' Before he could answer, she clicked her fingers in the air, and when she spoke her voice was heavy with sarcasm. 'Oh, let me guess. A quick roll in the hay? What's gone wrong in your life today that you need me to fix, Your Majesty? A problem with the budget? A servant? Did you come here to sleep with me so you could forget something else?'

His features were locked in a mask of steel, giving nothing away, and she was glad. If he'd looked even slightly chastened or apologetic, she might have softened her anger a little. Instead, he stared back at her with a look of cynicism and *nothing*.

Nothing.

He'd come here and he was looking at her as though it was the last place he wanted to be.

Damn him.

'What do you want?' she demanded, her tone as withering as she could make it. In the back of her mind, she wondered if he'd ever been spoken to like that. She couldn't help it though. His quick change of heart and immediate dismissal of her once she had performed her purpose had resonated so perfectly with the feelings she'd suffered on that awful day when the penny had finally dropped and she'd realised how utterly and completely Christopher had been using her. Octavio hadn't done anything nearly as bad as Christopher, but Phoebe had a big, open wound that Octavio had unknowingly and deeply plunged a knife into.

'Is there some place we can talk?'

She gestured to the small foyer as if to say *here*, only it was *small* and he was *big* and there was a sudden dearth of space that made it hard for Phoebe to think. With an angry expulsion of breath, she whirled away from him and practically stomped into the living room.

Small, but neat as a pin, it was light-filled and perfectly adequate for the six months or so Phoebe intended to stay in Castilona. After that, she expected her savings to have run out, and if she hadn't managed to find her father in that time, she'd go home and work out how to get on with her life. At least she would have succeeded in putting some space and distance between herself and the disastrous breakup with Christopher.

'Okay, talk,' she said, then added with faux deference, 'Your Majesty.'

She was used to seeing Octavio smile, but this time, when his lips shifted into a general approximation of that expression, there was no humour in his face. Rather, it was a look of cynicism, or even mockery.

'You're angry with me.'

She crossed her arms. 'Do you blame me?'

'Why are you angry?' he prompted.

She stared at him as if he'd just asked what feet were used for. 'I would imagine it's pretty obvious.'

'Humour me.'

'Why?'

'Because I'd like to understand what I'm dealing with before I start.'

'Start what?'

'What I came here for.'

'Are you being deliberately cryptic?'

'I asked you first.'

'What are you, eight?'

He didn't answer. Those dark, mesmerising eyes of his just bore into her, and as the seconds ticked by, the force of his look and the caustic silence surrounding them eroded her strength. She lifted one shoulder in a gesture of conversational surrender. 'You were rude.'

One thick, dark brow arched upwards.

'I knew what you wanted from me, and why, but I still never expected you to make me feel so disposable. I thought you were...*nice*.' It was a very insipid way to explain what she'd thought of him. She'd *liked* him. She'd thought he was *nice*, yes, but also kind and funny and decent. In short, she'd been fooled, just like with Christopher. Would she never learn?

'You are not disposable,' he said, but the words were tinged with something like anger. 'If you were, I would not be here now.'

'Why are you here?'

'To explain.'

'There's no point. It's over. Ancient history. I don't even think about it any more.'

Another quirk of his brow and this time, his quick half-smile was definitely, unmistakably mocking. 'Don't you?'

'No.' She doubled down on the slight exaggeration. She thought about it, him, what they'd done from time to time. As in, at least several times a day. Most days, even more often than that. 'It's old news.'

'Prove it,' he growled, taking a step towards her.

Her throat felt thick suddenly, her bones liquid. 'How?'

He pressed a finger to her chin. 'Show me I'm old news. Don't react when I kiss you, Phoebe, and I'll believe you.'

She opened her mouth to protest but he took the opportunity to drop his mouth to hers and kiss her. Oh, she could have pulled away, kneed him in the groin, shoved at his chest, elbowed him in the ribs. When she looked back, she realised he'd deliberately hesitated a few seconds—between laying down the gauntlet and making good his threat, he'd given her time to respond, to push him away. But she hadn't.

Because even when she knew her body would show her to be a liar, she didn't—couldn't—care. She just wanted him to kiss her.

She did her best not to respond as his mouth separated hers and his tongue invaded every single one of her senses. She tried to think cold, practical thoughts as his fingers tangled in the hair at the back of her head. She willed her body to stay completely still, as if frozen, as he pushed himself forward, his large frame easily engulfing her smaller one. And for several long seconds, she managed. She stayed almost limp against him, refused to kiss him back, refused to show that her heart was beginning to pound dangerously fast and her pulse was thready.

But then his knee caught a little between her legs, and the moan that escaped her was impossible to resist. It was like opening the floodgates. All the desire she'd felt and had no place for in the last five weeks suddenly went from gas to flame, and her whole body was alight with passionate wants. They stirred in her belly and spread throughout, so not only was she kissing him back, her hands were roaming his body, separating his shirt from his trousers and lifting it so she could touch the warm flesh of his bare back.

'I hate you.' She groaned against him, though she wasn't sure if that was true. She hated Christopher, and how he'd made her feel, and she hated that Octavio had unwittingly found that old emotional injury and reinflamed it, proving that she wasn't anywhere near healed yet. Maybe she never would be.

'But you want me,' he said, moving his kiss to her throat, flicking the pulse point there with his tongue, which he clearly knew drove her wild. 'And that's the most important thing.'

'Is it?' She tilted her head back to give him better access.

'Oh, absolutely, *querida*. It's all that matters.' And then he was cupping her breasts and the last vestiges of thought dispersed so she was just a quivering mass, his to do with what he would. And he understood that moment of surrender. It was as though she were a book and he could read her just perfectly. He pushed her shirt over her head, growling when he realised she wore no bra, but not hesitating before taking one of her nipples into his mouth and rolling it mercilessly, until she was incandescent. He moved a hand down her belly, finding the fastening to her jeans and pushing it open so that he could slide his hand into her underpants and brush her sex. She whimpered; he moved his mouth to absorb the sound, kissing her while his other hand turned its attention to her breast, squeezing the nipple that was already oversensitive.

'Please,' she groaned. 'God, please.'

His response was a gruff sound of surrender and then he was stripping them both of their clothes with an efficiency Phoebe couldn't have managed, given how badly her hands were shaking. Naked, he lifted her easily, wrapping her legs around his waist, so his arousal was nestled between the cheeks of her bottom. She rolled her hips, silently inviting, needing, desperately hungry for him. He made a deep sound of understanding and strode through the apartment, his lips seeking hers as he walked.

'Where?' he grunted.

She pointed to her bedroom door. Octavio shouldered it open and dropped her to the bed, his eyes firing to hers as he ripped open a condom she hadn't even realised he'd brought with them. Then again, in his position, he couldn't exactly take chances, and God knew she didn't want to run that risk either.

He unfurled it over his length and then he was moving over her, pushing inside of her, and she cried out at the sheer relief her body felt to have him filling her once more. The world seemed to stop spinning and every noise silenced, so there was only the solid racing of their hearts.

'Octavio...' She said his name long and slow, like a prayer that had been answered, and then she said nothing else, because he moved in such a way that made her body come alive and rendered her mouth mute—save for the little moans of ecstasy that escaped without her knowledge.

CHAPTER FOUR

WHEN THE DUST settled and her breathing returned to normal—though pleasure was still a fog wrapping around her body—sanity began to return, and Phoebe was nervous.

Nervous because she'd let this happen again, even after the way he'd been, last time. Nervous because he might treat her like that again, and if he did, what did that mean for her decision-making?

She'd come here to find her father, but also to grieve and move forward from the Christopher debacle. She needed to heal, to find peace and to reassure herself that she was capable of exercising some solid judgement with men. But wasn't this falling into the same trap? Being so blinded by desire that she couldn't think straight?

Well, if he thought he could just come to her apartment for sex and then leave again, he had another think coming. She wasn't going to lie there, waiting for him to make her feel worthless. If anyone was going to get up and leave, it would be her.

Despite the fact that her bones were heavy and her muscles like liquid, thanks to the pleasure he'd lavished on her, and despite the fact she liked how it felt to lie right there, cradled to his side, she quickly jerked away, turning her back on him before standing and going to her chest of drawers. She pulled out a summery dress and yanked it over her head, not worrying about underwear, before turning to face him. 'Do you need anything else?' She crossed her arms over her chest, ignoring the look of wry amusement on his face.

How dare he?

'We still have a conversation to get through.'

Pink bloomed in her cheeks. 'I can't see that we have anything to talk about.'

'Really? Would you like another demonstration?'

She bit down into her lower lip and refrained—just—from telling him that maybe she would. 'That doesn't mean anything.'

He sat up a little straighter, the sheet draped over his lap. Her sheet. Would she ever wash it again? She banished the errant thought, narrowing her gaze.

'Doesn't it?'

'No.'

'I'm glad to hear you say that.' He nodded slowly, as if that had been exactly what he wanted to hear. 'How would you feel about coming to a sort of arrangement?'

Lights danced on the edge of her field of vision. 'What do you mean, an arrangement?'

'Obviously, this works.' He ran his hand over the bed beside him. 'I like being with you, Phoebe. In fact, in all sincerity, I have been able to think of very little but you for the last five weeks.' She smothered a small gasp—but barely. 'Which, as I'm sure you can imagine, is not particularly convenient, given my responsibilities.'

She ignored the flush of pleasure his confession wrought. But it meant a lot to know that he'd been as afflicted by desires and memories as she had been. Careful to keep her expression neutral, she fidgeted one hand behind her back. 'So? Where are you going with this?'

'A long time ago, my parents entered into a sort of contract with King Stanos and Queen Margerite. It's more an agreement of intent, rather than legally binding. However, my plan has always been to honour it.'

'What kind of contract?' She wasn't following—perhaps because the sheer force of her pleasure not two minutes ago had robbed her brain of most of its blood.

'A marriage contract. They have a daughter—Sasha. She's three years younger than I am. It was always their intention that we would marry.'

Phoebe stood very, very still but inside, her heart was turning to ice faster than she could handle. He kept talking, evidently oblivious to the pain he was inflicting.

'They felt—as I feel now—that a royal marriage would be best. To secure our family's position on the throne.'

Octavio wasn't Christopher, but echoes of the moment she'd met Christopher's wife and had needed to act as though everything was perfectly fine made her whole world spin wildly out of control. The hand that had been fidgeting behind her back flattened so she could press it to the wall for much-needed support.

'Why are you telling me this?'

'Because if you're going to agree to my proposal, I need to be perfectly clear about the boundaries of what I'm offering.'

She blinked quickly. 'What proposal?'

But there was a sinking feeling in her stomach that showed she already understood. Still, she waited, with breath held, needing to hear him say the words and confirm her worst fears.

'I want you to be my lover, *querida*. I want to see you for as long as we feel like this, for as long as it works, and for as long as I am able.'

She flinched. 'You mean until you're married?'

'Until the engagement is formalised,' he corrected. 'Anything beyond that would not be right.'

She made a scoffing sound, half laughter, half deranged disbelief. 'No, of course. Whereas this is all perfectly above board.'

He studied her, as if trying to read her every thought. She hated that. She hated him. She hated what he was making her feel—worthless and cheap, all over again. She ground her teeth, glaring back. 'And what would be in it for me?' she demanded. 'You get sex whenever you want it. What do I get?'

'The same thing. No one could know about it—this would be between you and me.'

'Why?'

'It's for the best.'

'Because I'm a cleaner?'

'You would be hounded by the press, and to what end? This could only last another six months or so, at the most.'

'So you're telling me the fact I work as a cleaner at a hospital has no bearing on how you'd feel being seen with me?'

'I don't care what you do for a living, Phoebe.'

'Sure you don't,' she scoffed.

'But other people would,' he conceded after a beat. 'That is not why I would need this kept secret. I don't care what people say, but my uncle—who until recently was on the throne—has worked hard to undermine me, even before I was crowned. I would prefer to avoid scandal.'

'And I'm a scandal.'

'Potentially. So we could go between the house of mine we used the other night and your apartment. I also have homes around the world—we could travel together, when our schedules allowed.'

Just like a real high-class mistress, she thought with a wave of nausea.

Outwardly, she made another scoffing noise. 'You've really thought all this through, haven't you?'

'I've had five long weeks to come up with a plan.'

'And this was the best you could do?'

'Well, what do you suggest?' he demanded. 'What other option is there?'

'That we go back to Plan A and never see one another again.' Her voice was shrill now, control on her emotions almost non-existent. She needed him to leave before she reached for the crystal vase beneath the window and hurled it at him.

'I do not believe that's viable.'

'Nor is this.'

'Why not?'

'Because I won't be treated like some kind of...of... whore!' she spat, slicing her hand through the air. 'I won't become your mistress. No way.'

'You would be my lover,' he corrected gently, standing now, uncaring for his magnificent nudity as he strode towards her. 'Here, and at my apartment, we would be equals. Two people who can spend time together, make love whenever they want, until this madness passes.'

She flinched. 'And then you ride off into the sunset and marry Princess Whatever-Her-Name-Is?'

'Sasha,' he supplied gently. 'And yes.'

'And what about me, Octavio?'

'You move on with your life, too. This would be our arrangement, Phoebe. *Our* arrangement. I am not dictating terms to you, I am asking you to be a party to a deal that enables us to keep seeing one another.'

It was all so reasonable and sensible, but Phoebe didn't feel either of those things. She felt sickened by his suggestion and she felt mad. Mad up to the eyeballs! She wanted to scream at the insult he was wrapping around her, and somehow expecting her to be almost relieved about. 'It's not enough,' she spat. 'I don't want what you're offering.'

'I can't offer more.'

'Then I don't want you.'

'But you do, and we both know it,' he said, with a hint of regret, because they were both trapped, in a sense, by this desire. 'The question is, do you want me enough to accept this deal?' He gently caught her chin with his finger and angled her face up to his. 'I really hope the answer is yes.'

Tears threatened to form on her lashes. She blinked quickly, squaring her shoulders. 'It's not. Now please, get the hell out of my apartment and don't ever contact me again.' And with her last thread of strength, she pulled away from him and stalked out of her bedroom.

He knew he should have left straight away, but he was reeling. He had come here with no expectation that she would refuse him. In the back of his mind, he'd seen the arrangement as a *fait accompli*. He'd been almost unforgivably rude the last time they'd seen one another, but their chemistry was such, he'd fully expected it to overcome any obstacle. More than that, the parameters he'd put in place surely made the whole concept of this safe and easy and even fun. At least, that's how he viewed it. The perfect non-relationship relationship.

Instead, every word he'd said after they'd finished making love had seemed to rile her more and more. But he hadn't been wrong about her feelings for him—on a physical level, she was as invested in this as he was. So why was she fighting him?

'Listen, Phoebe.' He followed after her, hands raised in a placating gesture. 'This doesn't have to be a big deal. Let's leave it a week and then touch base. If you're available, you can come to my place for dinner. We can talk more.'

Perfect. Casual. Easy. As though he didn't care one way or another—he just wished that were true.

The jut of her chin was laced with defiance; she might as well have sky-written *No way.*

'Just think about it,' he said, because he wasn't ready for this conversation to be over, and he didn't think she was either. Once her initial reaction faded, she'd calm down, think this through and realise that he was offering them a way to be together that was easy, uncomplicated and had the potential to be endlessly satisfying—for as long as possible.

Phoebe waited until he'd left before giving into the nausea that had gripped her from the moment he'd made his hurtful proposition. He couldn't have known how badly he was wounding her, but Phoebe had—unwittingly—been a mistress before. For years she'd been falling in love with someone else's husband, and she wasn't about to make the same mistake twice. Okay, he wasn't offering love. It was even worse. He just wanted to sleep with her, all the while formalising his engagement to some far-away princess. Not bloody likely!

Indignation flared in her belly, but so too did a wave of nausea she'd struggled to contain while they were arguing. Now he was gone, she bolted for the bathroom and kneeled over the toilet, shuddering with each violent expulsion, vomiting until her brow was beaded with sweat and her face flushed pink.

If only it were so easy to push Octavio from her mind…

Six weeks had passed since that afternoon at Phoebe's, and over the course of that time, Octavio had come to accept that she'd been serious in her refusal. She might have wanted him with the same intensity as he did her, but she was clearly determined not to fall in with his convenient arrangement.

And maybe that was for the best. Because he'd presumed they were in the same place, and wanted the same things—no strings—but her reaction had indicated otherwise, and emotional complications were the last thing Octavio wanted. So it was fine that she'd turned him down.

Just fine.

Except when it wasn't, which was most nights. And often in the days, when his mind wandered and he remembered the smoothness of her skin or the softness of her lips or how tightly her muscles squeezed his length, how good she made him feel.

His pride had been wounded, he accepted. That was why he was so focused on this. It wasn't really about Phoebe, or his need for her, so much as the fact she'd turned him down—and so easily. As though he meant nothing.

So maybe it wasn't just his pride, but rather an old, familiar, awful sense of cold-hearted rejection. A feeling he'd had so often in his childhood he thought he'd inured himself to its effects, but if that were true, then being turned down by Phoebe wouldn't have bothered him as much as it did. He knew the best defence to that feeling was to wall it up, ignore it. And certainly never show anyone how you were feeling.

So when he walked into the Clínica San Carlos for an appointment with director Lola Garcia, he was frustrated to realise his eyes were constantly sweeping the corridors as if seeking her out. Did she even still work here? And what kind of a weak-minded idiot did it make him that he still couldn't get her out of his head?

If only she'd agreed to his suggestion, he'd have probably got her out of his system by now. Or at least be partway there.

But Phoebe James was burned into his blood, and he halfway hated her for that, because it made a mockery of his determination to never need anyone. Even if that need was purely physical, it was still an exertion of power over him that he resented bitterly.

'Your Majesty.' Lola dipped her head in a gesture of deference. Beside her, the hospital's head of security kept a watchful eye on the entrance to Lola's office. His attention was superfluous. Octavio was accompanied by his usual security detail, and he knew the hospital had a state-of-the-art system in place. There was no threat to him here.

Then again, hadn't his parents thought the same thing?

When was someone in his position ever truly safe?

'Dr Garcia,' he responded, itching to continue prowling the hallway until he saw Phoebe. Just a glimpse, to prove he was over his stupid infatuation. Octavio had worked hard to conquer his obsession with Phoebe, and he wanted proof that he'd been successful. He was not about to let one woman he happened to share insane chemistry with weaken his ability to rule. No, he was focused on the future now, and on the engagement that was becoming inevitable. 'Thank you for seeing me.'

'Of course, Your Majesty. Anytime.' She took a seat behind her desk. 'Is there something in particular I can help you with?'

'Actually, I'd like to help you.' He crossed one ankle over his knee and braced an elbow on his thigh, staring directly at her. 'I appreciate the care your staff took of my late uncle. His passing was a tragedy, but the loss was made a little less difficult by your hospital's professionalism and care.'

Lola looked genuinely moved.

'I would like to make a large donation to the hospital— a personal donation, you understand—and I would like the donation to be in his name. In fact, I would greatly appreciate the naming of a wing after him.'

Lola's jaw dropped and he knew why. Even hospitals as lavish as this struggled with funding. Providing top-notch healthcare was expensive and in order to attract the best staff in the business, you had to pay well and have exceptional facilities. All of which cost a bomb.

'I'm talking about a substantial sum, you understand.' He reached into his shirt pocket and retrieved the cheque he'd had drawn from his personal wealth, handing it over to the director.

'Your Majesty.' Lola's voice was barely a whisper. 'That's very generous of you.'

'You do good work here, Dr Garcia. It's my privilege to make this donation, in my uncle's name.'

'I don't know what to say.' Her fingers were shaking a little, but she didn't relinquish the cheque.

'There is nothing to say—please, keep me apprised of how you decide to honour Rodrigo.'

'Of course. Sir, would you like to have a tour of the hospital facilities? I know you have been here, but in circumstances that might have prevented you from seeing everything we do. Once you've witnessed the wards, you might have ideas on how you'd like to see the donation used.'

'You are best placed to know how to spend the money in a way that will benefit the hospital. But,' he said, pleased that his voice sounded completely normal, 'I would welcome a chance to look around.'

Lola stood and handed the cheque to her chief of security. 'Don't lose that.'

'No, ma'am.'

They stepped into the corridor, and Octavio's own security entourage followed behind. The tour lasted some thirty minutes and though he spotted several other cleaners wearing the same fitted navy blue uniform as Phoebe, they were not her.

Right at the end, as he was preparing to say farewell to Lola Garcia, he thought, for a moment, that he'd finally glimpsed her. The hair was the same, and the tone of skin, but this woman had a different figure. Larger breasts, perhaps even a slightly rounded stomach, indicating pregnancy.

And Phoebe wasn't pregnant. Or at least, she hadn't been, the last time he'd seen her.

Unless…

Even before the thought could fully form, she angled her body away from the wall, showing not just the fact that yes, her stomach was indeed rounded in that way of pregnancy, but also a face that was burned into his brain, eyes that were as familiar to him as his own. He stared across at her and noted the exact moment she glanced up and saw him. He recognised the colour being sucked from her face, the parting of her lips, the panic in her features. And he recognised, even before it happened, that her knees were about to buckle.

'She's fainting,' he said to no one in particular, breaking into a jog and reaching Phoebe just as her legs gave way and she began to fall to the ground. He caught her, but only just, enabling him to ease her slowly down and save her head from cracking against the marble tiles.

'Oh, my goodness.' Lola Garcia was right behind him. 'Enrique, get a nurse.'

'I'm okay.' Phoebe had momentarily fainted, but she'd also recovered quickly. Her skin was regaining a hint of colour and her eyes were focused on Octavio, as if trying to work out if he was really there or not.

'It's you.'

'I'm sorry, Your Majesty,' Lola murmured with concern. 'She's obviously still not with it.'

'She seems with it enough to me,' he responded, his brain not able to put two and two together and get four, even when the number was flashing in front of him in neon.

Phoebe was pregnant.

But not too far along. Her belly was only noticeably rounded because she was so naturally slim. And only because he knew her body inch by inch and would have noticed even the smallest of differences.

'I'm okay,' Phoebe repeated, pushing away a little now, trying to stand. He watched as she sat up first, then went to bend her knees, but it was evident that she was still too woozy. Besides, Lola wasn't having a bar of it.

'You'll have to be checked out and signed off by a doctor. It's a workplace health and safety issue, you see.'

'I only fainted. It's nothing,' Phoebe said, not daring to look at Octavio.

'Yes, well, we can't be too careful, particularly not in your condition.'

Phoebe's face scrunched up, and Octavio realised she'd been holding on to some kind of fool's hope that he hadn't realised she was pregnant.

'Director Garcia is right,' Octavio said, his voice so darkly menacing he didn't recognise it. 'A pregnant woman cannot be too careful.'

Phoebe's eyes jerked to his and he saw the panic in their depths and he was glad. Almost as glad as he was livid. Phoebe James had seriously crossed a line and he was going to make sure she knew it.

CHAPTER FIVE

PHOEBE WAS REELING. Her mind was spinning and it wouldn't stop. On top of the shock of seeing Octavio for the first time in six weeks, and knowing he had *seen her*, was the news the doctor had delivered after her fainting episode.

In an exercise in 'above and beyond' care, they'd done an ultrasound to check on her pregnancy. Phoebe hadn't had one yet, and she was close enough to twelve weeks for it to be time. She'd been grateful when they'd suggested it—one less thing for her to take care of.

But as the room filled with a cacophony of beats, and the doctor had turned to her, beaming, he'd said, 'Well, well, aren't you clever? It's twins!' Phoebe had almost fainted again.

Twins.

Twins.

She'd just been getting her head around the fact that she was going to be a single mother to *one* baby—a task she knew from experience to be one of the hardest in the world. But a single mother to *two* children? She felt hot and cold.

So when she emerged from the *clínica* a little while later and saw Octavio's driver waiting for her, she wanted to refuse to go anywhere with him. But even though she was in shock, she knew there was no chance Octavio would let this matter drop. In a total fog, she slid into the back seat

of the car, her mind racing as the sleek limousine slipped
through the streets of the city. She didn't notice the beauty
of the place, the beaches she loved, the Mediterranean buildings all rendered in shades of orange and cream, the paved
paths and laundry strung from window to window. She noticed nothing, *nada*.

Her whole body was in a state of suspended animation.

'There's paparazzi waiting,' the driver said with a tone
of apology as the car slowed.

Phoebe looked around, belatedly realising they were not
at the townhouse she'd expected to be taken to, but rather
approaching Octavio's palace. Her breath hitched in her
throat at the sight of this place, which was so utterly beautiful it almost hurt.

The ornate wrought iron gates with their gold spikes and
large coat of arms swung inwards. On either side of their
car, several guards stood in military uniform, their large
guns displayed proudly at their front. Gravel crunched beneath the tyres as the car rolled forward, towards the front
of the palace, where a large golden fountain was spurting
water. There were several archways in the façade of the
palace, and they drove through one to the right of the impressive main entrance, into a courtyard that had another
fountain, more guards and a lot of perfectly maintained
greenery in pots.

A quick glance showed all the things Phoebe might have
expected—pale stone walls, columns, domed roofs, arched
windows, small balconies, abundant flowers growing in
pots. It was just as exquisite inside the palace walls as outside. The car drew to a stop by a set of six shallow steps
that led to a double set of extra tall doors. When the driver
opened her door, she found it took a moment for her legs to
cooperate, but she forced herself to step out of the vehicle,
even when her palms were sweaty.

'This way, ma'am.'

The driver gestured for her to precede him, and as she walked up the stairs, one hand on the cool metal railing, the doors swung inwards, held that way by two maids in old-fashioned uniforms.

'Thank you.' She smiled tightly, her heart rabbiting in her chest.

Twins.

Her knees knocked.

The guards' vision remained focused straight ahead, almost as if she hadn't spoken. The inside of the palace was overwhelming, but Phoebe barely noticed any of the details. She was conscious of snatches—burgundy carpet, high ceilings, dark wood panelling, enormous flower arrangements that were as fragrant as they were over the top, but her pulse was rushing through her body and her stomach felt so huge and visible, and she knew that in a matter of moments she'd have to explain all of this to Octavio when she was still unpacking it herself.

It was a conversation she'd thought she would have one day, down the track, when she was safely on the other side of the world and he'd married and produced an heir with his perfect princess bride.

And Sasha *was* perfect.

Phoebe had tortured herself by searching the other woman online and had wanted to poke out her eyes afterwards.

They walked through the entrance and down a gallery lined with the kind of art that would have been at home in the Louvre, turned left, so she had a view of the courtyard through one set of windows and the ocean the other, and then, at a set of wide timber doors, the driver paused. A woman stood outside, wearing a suit. They held a low, hushed conversation, and then the woman nodded, knocked once on the doors and stepped inside.

Phoebe exhaled slowly, her body trembling. She trained her attention on the view of the ocean, imagining herself on one of the boats bobbing far out to sea, rather than here, about to have one of the most important conversations of her life.

'Miss James? His Majesty will see you now.'

Phoebe's heart was pounding so hard it hurt. She nodded once, aware that her face must have been incredibly pale. She surreptitiously lifted one hand and pinched her cheeks before she began to walk towards the doors and then, through them.

And she froze.

Because if Octavio had wanted to choose a venue for this conversation that would throw off her ability to concentrate, that would overwhelm her with his power and importance in this country, he'd succeeded completely. She'd expected an office or a sitting room or a *room* of some sorts, not a palace within a palace, but that's exactly what she was looking at. The floors in here were pure white marble, the walls at least twice as high as in the corridor, the chandeliers hanging from the ceiling were crystal, and the walls had intermittent panels that she suspected were actual gold. The windows were enormous, and because the room was at the corner of the palace, the views were stunning in all directions. The furniture was old and beautiful, and in here there were many, many potted plants, all fragrant and glossy green.

And in the centre of the enormous room stood King Octavio, dressed in a black suit, with eyes that were even darker.

The door shut behind Phoebe, and his obsidian gaze seemed to intensify. 'You're pregnant.'

The words were laced with accusation. What could she say? 'Yes.'

'The baby is mine?'

Babies. Babies.

She thought about denying it—panic made her cling to that choice. Wouldn't that be the easiest way out? After all, how could he know she hadn't been sleeping with a whole host of men at around the same time?

'If you deny it,' he forewarned grimly, 'I will arrange a paternity test.'

She gasped. 'I—wasn't going to deny it.'

'Liar,' he said, but softly, as if he was goading her.

She closed her eyes, feeling at a complete disadvantage. Feeling weak, too, and exhausted after the shocking news she'd received that day. 'Can I sit down?'

She blinked over at him to see his eyes narrow, and a muscle jerk in his jaw. He wanted to deny her that. To punish her. He was furious. She could read it all in his face. But he gestured towards a bank of plush sofas, covered in a gold and lavender fabric. 'Go ahead.'

She walked a little unsteadily to an armchair and sat on the very edge of the seat. Hardly a relaxed pose but at least she knew her legs weren't going to give way again.

'I hardly know what to say to you,' he muttered, tone scathing. 'It's true, we barely knew each other, but I thought, I believed—though perhaps it was wishful thinking—that you were a decent person with some kind of moral compass. And yet, now I learn that you were intending to have my baby and what? Never tell me?'

Her jaw dropped at his rendering of events. 'That's oversimplifying things,' she said, fidgeting with her fingers. 'I couldn't tell you.'

'Why not?'

'Putting aside the practical reasons—like I had no way of contacting you and you're not exactly an easy person to reach out to—you were abundantly clear about where your life is headed and what you need from it. You're getting married to a princess, you're going to have perfect royal babies. I'm a cleaner you're ashamed to be seen with. Hello…? What was I going to do? Ruin your life by telling you that somehow we conceived on a night when neither of us ever planned to see the other again?'

He ground his jaw. 'The first night?'

'Yes.' The scan today had confirmed the dates as well.

He grimaced. 'The day of Rodrigo's death.'

She'd thought of that, too. She nodded once.

'So what was your plan?' He returned to his questioning, his voice cold.

'I barely had a plan.'

'You chose not to tell me about the baby,' he pointed out.

Babies, she wanted to scream.

'So then what?'

'I—I'm going to go home. To New Zealand,' she whispered.

His face was carefully blanked of emotion but something stirred in the depths of his eyes. 'I see. And then what?'

'Then I'd take care of… I'd…never bother you again. You're free to keep going with your life, just as it's been planned out for you.'

'Were you ever going to tell me about the baby?'

'Of course I was,' she said. 'I've spent my whole life not knowing who my father is, there's no way I'd inflict that on another soul.'

He took several steps closer, then thrust his hands onto his hips. It drew her attention to his taut physique. She had to look away again quickly.

'When were you going to tell me?'

'Eventually.'

'I don't believe you.'

She bit into her lower lip, then stopped when his eyes dropped to the gesture.

'When you were married,' she whispered. 'And had a baby—a royal heir.'

He let out a slow breath, dragged one hand through his hair and then cursed. 'You're serious?'

'It seemed best for everyone.'

'Best for our baby not to know me?'

She flinched. She hadn't expected him to feel that way.

'That is my child,' he gestured towards her, 'and that child is a Prince or Princess of Castilona. Their place is here.'

Her skin paled. It was everything she'd been most afraid of—that he would take her baby and raise him or her with his perfect princess wife. But now there were *two* babies to consider. She dropped her head a moment, sucking in air.

'Our babies' place is with me,' she struggled to say.

Silence crackled in the room. She waited on tenterhooks for him to say *Yes, of course*. To say *anything* that would calm her anxiety. But he held the silence, simply staring at her until her stomach was in too many loops to function.

'When did you find out?'

She closed her eyes on a wave of feeling. 'Does that matter now?'

'When?' His response was taut, flattened by stress.

What was there to gain from obfuscating? 'A couple of days after the last time…'

He swore again. 'That's *six weeks* ago.'

Yes. Six long, lonely weeks. She ignored the traitorous thought.

'And you didn't once think it would be appropriate for me to know I had helped to conceive a child?'

'I've explained that. After the way you spelled out your

life's plans, how could I think you'd want to know about this? It would ruin everything for you.'

'That was not your decision to make.'

'Given that I was the only one who knew about the pregnancy, it was precisely my decision. And I did it *for you*. For your life, for your future, your family's position in the country, for all the things you made so abundantly clear mattered most to you. Why should a meaningless fling lead to a lifetime of consequences for you?'

'But it should for you?'

She floundered.

'I—am not royal,' she said after a beat. 'I am not betrothed to some prince. I'm a free agent, and while being a single mum is definitely not what I had planned for my life, it's not like I have other plans that this is getting in the way of.' Her voice cracked a little, because she was so close to admitting how off the rails her life had become. The breakdown of her relationship with Christopher had shaken her off-track, and then not being able to find her father had made it all so much worse. She felt completely alone in life, and now she wasn't. Her hand curved over her belly, connecting with the little lives in there.

'Are you telling me this decision was purely altruistic? That no part of your choice came down to the fact you were insulted by my proposal that day?'

'That was not a proposal, it was a proposition, and it was disgusting. But as angry as I was with you, that didn't guide my decision-making.'

'I don't believe you.'

'That's your prerogative. It doesn't matter. None of this matters.'

'It matters a hell of a lot to me. You should have told me.'

She swallowed past a lump in her throat. 'Well, would you like me to tell you something now, Octavio?' She felt her sanity slipping. She felt the shock of that day all mounting up inside of her, forming a wall that was hard and cold yet cracking all over. 'News that will really give you something to shout about?'

His nostrils flared. She knew she should stop, take a breath, try to calm down but her blood was firing at the unfairness of all this. How dared *he* be angry with *her*? 'The hospital director insisted on me getting a full checkup today.' She stood then, needing to feel at more of a level with him. 'I had my first scan.'

Something shifted in his expression. Emotion. Feeling.

'I should have been there.'

'Oh, yes, of course. Because that would have caused no scandal whatsoever.' She rolled her eyes in a childish gesture that felt wonderful in that moment.

'And?' he demanded, voice like ice.

'And what?'

'The baby is fine?'

'Oh, the baby is fine. In fact, both babies are fine,' she snapped, almost maniacally now. 'It's twins,' she added, and then she sobbed, lifting a hand to her mouth to stop the torrent of emotion from pouring out in a large wail.

Silence cracked around them but she barely noticed. She was shaking now, processing the truth of the scan, the reality that lay before her.

'Well, then.' His voice was low and silky, as though she hadn't just told him they were going to have *two babies* in a matter of months. 'That makes our decision even easier.'

'What decision?' she asked, whirling around to face him. Did he think she was going to have an abortion? Her skin paled and she looked for something to grab hold of, landing on the edge of a large bronze pot.

'There is no way on earth you are leaving the country

whilst pregnant with my children, so forget about returning to New Zealand.'

She flinched. She hadn't expected that.

'Nor will my children be born under a cloud of illegitimacy.'

Her heart almost stopped beating; his words made no sense. 'I—don't—what are you saying?'

'That you must marry me—and quickly.'

His words were issued so calmly, with a matter-of-factness that almost seemed to present them as a *fait accompli*, implying she had no say in the matter, that there was no room to negotiate. But of course that wasn't the case. Of course she could choose what she wanted.

'I won't marry you.' She was pleased to have spoken so emphatically.

'That is no longer a choice for either of us.'

'Don't be absurd. Last time I checked, I had free will…'

'But you are pregnant with my twins, and I am the King.'

In the back of her mind, Phoebe wondered how many shocks she could endure in one day. 'So? You might be a king but you cannot force me to marry you.'

'That is true, but there is no court in this land that would award you parental rights over me.'

She gasped.

'Are you saying you'd actually fight me for our babies?'

His nostrils flared. 'That is the very last thing I would want to do.'

'But you'd do it.'

'If you refuse to be reasonable.'

Her eyes swept shut. 'Are you hearing yourself? What you're suggesting is the definition of unreasonable.'

'It's the definition of necessary,' he corrected. 'I know it is far from what either of us wants, Phoebe. I know that.

But from the moment you conceived our twins, any other path was closed to us.'

She shook her head, wanting with all her heart for that not to be true.

'I can't marry you,' she groaned, dropping her head into her palm. 'I can't.'

'Why not?'

'Because we're not—we don't know each other. We don't love each other. I don't even *like* you. Scratch that, I loathe you. What kind of marriage would that be?'

'A perfect one, in my book.'

Her jaw dropped.

'Loathing me is not ideal, but I have never sought a typical marriage. My role as King is everything to me—my marriage was always going to be about an heir. That is what I need most right now, and here you are, almost halfway to giving me not one but *two*.'

'Not giving you two,' she snapped. 'Giving birth to them.'

'Unimportant semantics.'

'Not to me.'

'Our marriage can be whatever you wish,' he continued in the same vein, as though she had no say in this. 'You would have some official duties but on the whole you could carve out a role for yourself that was as visible or not as you choose.'

'Gosh, how accommodating you're being,' she muttered sarcastically. 'You're a paragon of reason.'

He expelled a rough breath. 'What do you want me to say, Phoebe?'

'I don't want you to say anything. I don't want *anything* from you.' Her nostrils flared. 'Six weeks ago you walked out of my apartment and as far as I was concerned, I never wanted to see you again.'

'So this pregnancy changed nothing for you?'

'The pregnancy changes everything for me,' she contradicted sharply. 'But none of that concerns you.'

'How are you erasing me from our babies' life?'

'You erased yourself,' she reminded him. 'You made it abundantly clear how unsuitable I was to be anything more than your secret, shameful mistress.'

'So like I said, this was about punishing me? Because you were offended by the pragmatic and realistic nature of my proposal?'

She stared at him. 'Are you listening to me? You wanted to hide me away back then and now you're saying we should get married. How would that work? You said no one would accept me as your mistress. But they will accept me as your wife?'

'It won't be straightforward,' he said, voice steady. 'You are not who I am expected to marry.'

She stood up then, anger coursing through her veins, and she was so relieved to feel it, because it was easier to manage than anxiety and nervousness. 'You really are a gigantic horse's ass.'

'That,' he enunciated clearly, 'is precisely the kind of thing you will be expected *not* to say when you are Queen.'

The world tilted. Everything went hazy.

She stared at him, aghast.

Queen.

Not just his wife, but Queen of Castilona. She pressed a hand to her stomach, moving towards one of the windows that framed a view over the city and towards the ocean. She stared at the glittering water, made to look almost magical by the way the sun bounced off its surface. This was an ancient and storied kingdom. Its royal family was one of the oldest surviving in the world. There was so much history here, so much tradition. And he was asking her to be a part of that. To be Queen.

She had never sought the limelight though. If anything, Phoebe was shy, and the thought of living her life so publicly sent a chill through her spine. But what did that matter? Octavio was right. Their babies would be princes or princesses of this kingdom, if he chose to acknowledge them as such. That would mean their lives would be public, their role in the line of succession ensuring they were always persons of interest to the public. There was no way Phoebe could let that happen without her being there to protect them. If Octavio was determined to do this, then Phoebe had to be a part of the deal.

But...

Surely she could change his mind?

'This doesn't make sense,' she said with a small shake of her head. 'You're meant to be marrying a princess, and I'm meant to be going home in a few months.'

'This is your home now.'

Something tugged at her heart. Hadn't she felt that way the moment she'd landed? Hadn't the air and the sea and history and architecture weaved in and out of her DNA, reminding her of something she'd never even known? The first time she'd gone to the beach and the water had washed over her bare feet, she'd felt almost as if she were being baptised. It had been remarkable—inexplicable. But that was a connection to her father's homeland; it didn't matter right now.

She glanced at him and then looked away again quickly, when just the sight of him made her pulse tremble.

'What about Sasha?' There was no sense pretending she didn't remember the other woman's name.

'She'll be surprised,' he conceded. 'But not disappointed.'

'You sound convinced of that.'

'We are not a couple.'

Phoebe nodded slowly. 'Still, it might prove embarrassing to her.'

'Unfortunately, that's unavoidable. We were not officially engaged, however. It's only rumours, and they can easily be countered.'

Phoebe's lips pulled to the side. 'This is a lot,' she said, rubbing her temple gingerly. 'I think we should both go and think about this overnight.'

'You may go and think, but it will change nothing for me.'

Her jaw dropped in the face of his absolute certainty, but at least he was offering her a reprieve. She thought longingly of the apartment she'd rented, and the space it would afford her to come to grips with this development.

'Okay.' She lifted one shoulder. 'We can talk tomorrow.'

'Fine. My aide will take you to my apartment.'

Her eyes widened. 'Your apartment?'

'So you can think.'

'I…can think at my place.'

'Impossible.'

'What?'

'You live here now.'

Her jaw dropped at his heavy-handed presumptuousness. 'Octavio, perhaps you're forgetting that I am my own person with an ability to make my own choices in life?'

'I'm not forgetting that.'

'Then stop acting like a bull in a china shop. I'm going back to my apartment where I can think *clearly*.'

'Your apartment is now empty.'

Her heart twisted. 'What?' The whisper was barely audible.

'My security guards have brought your things here. Or rather, they're in the process of bringing them.'

She glared at him, utterly infuriated. 'You had no right to do that.'

'You're going to marry me, and soon. The sooner the better, in terms of your acceptance by the people of Castilona.'

'I'm not going to marry you,' she shouted, her heart racing at the very thought.

'Then you're going to stay here until the babies are born. After that, you may do what you want. It would make things a hell of a lot easier for me, and our children, if you would at least marry me before then, though. Castilonian succession laws are somewhat outdated, you see.'

The colour faded from her skin. She could feel it seeping from her, like tea might stain a mug of boiled water. 'Stop doing that.'

He arched a brow.

'I'm going to be wherever my babies are.'

'Our babies are heirs to the throne of Castilona. They're going to be here.' He enunciated every word of that last sentence with perfect gravity.

Her heart sank to her toes. His proposal seemed almost inevitable, and she hated that. She hated *him* for that. But she also felt something else—something a little like relief. Even though she was furious with Octavio, what he was offering was the kind of safety net she couldn't have imagined, at least materially.

All of Phoebe's life, she'd watched her mother struggle and worry and fret. Money had always been tight, and Phoebe had known her mother had wanted, so badly, to give Phoebe more than she could. She'd wanted her little girl to have so much more, but they'd never been able to afford anything, and in the end, Phoebe had left school at sixteen to get a job, to help pay the rent. When her mother had died, Phoebe had been just seventeen, and everything had fallen apart. No wonder Christopher had been able to draw her into his web so easily. She'd been so alone and so intensely vulnerable, floundering with no idea where she was going in life. He'd come along and swept her up, all handsome and charismatic, and she'd believed his act: hook, line and sinker.

At least Octavio wasn't lying to her. He wasn't trying to charm her into this marriage. Heck, he could have kissed her and got her to agree to just about any damned thing he wanted. But he was laying it all out—what he needed, what he would do if she didn't agree, and what she'd get in exchange.

Yet it still felt like a pathway lined with danger for Phoebe. After all, he held all the cards in this scenario, and she held none. 'I need to think,' she muttered, barely looking at him.

'Then go and think. We'll discuss it further over dinner.'

A shiver ran the length of her spine, because that wasn't an invitation.

'Fine.' She stalked towards him now, her back ramrod straight. 'I hope you know what a bastard you're being.'

He glared back at her, his eyes like coal. 'As opposed to you, who decided to hide this pregnancy from me?'

Her lips parted on a swell of outrage but tears sparkled in her eyes because he had a point. She didn't have any interest in seeing things his way, but if she had wanted to, she could understand how angry he must have been at her. 'Oh, go to hell,' she snapped, stalking from the room and wishing she never had to see him again.

Go to hell? Go to hell? Did she have any idea that he had been plunged into that very state this afternoon?

Seeing her again had been instantly terrifying, because his body had rejoiced on a cellular level, and in that very instant, he'd had to admit to himself how woefully inadequate his attempts had been to forget her, to tell himself she meant nothing to him.

Even if it was just a physical thing, he was still attracted to her in a way that had a horrifying power to fell him to his knees. He accepted then that he could never see her again. He would run a mile over steaming hot coals before he'd open the door to anyone with that power over him.

And a millisecond later, he'd seen that she was pregnant, and a rush of comprehension had dawned on him, like a single bomb at first and then a whole series of them, detonating one after the other as the future he had carefully mapped out and made his peace with was blown to smithereens.

The only future he now saw included Phoebe: the one person he suspected he should never, ever be in the same room with again.

CHAPTER SIX

THE CITY GLITTERED beneath them, an impressive panorama of ancient buildings with golden lights making it look like something from a fairy tale. The moon, full, round and shiny, was high in the sky, bathing them in a lustrous light. The terrace of his apartment in the palace overlooked a private rose garden, and the flowers were heavy with blooms, filling the air with a sweet fragrance. Or perhaps that was the night-flowering jasmine vine that scrambled up the side of the palace and across the stone balustrades? The table had been set for two, decorated with candles and flowers, like some kind of romantic restaurant. Romance, though, was the last thing on either of their minds.

Phoebe had changed into a pair of jeans and a tee-shirt—as Octavio had unceremoniously announced, all her worldly possessions had indeed been invasively handled by his staff and brought to the palace shortly after she'd returned. Though it hadn't been the fault of any of his security team, she couldn't help but glare at them as they carried her goods into the luxurious suite and began to unpack. 'I can do that myself!' she'd exclaimed with heat in her cheeks.

How could she ever get used to living like this? Phoebe wasn't someone who wanted another person to do her bidding. She wasn't comfortable with the idea of being waited on. She'd taken care of herself—and then her mother—for as long as she could remember.

Dinner was no different. The moment she sat down, a servant appeared to place a napkin across her lap, and another poured sparkling water into her glass, while a third explained the meal to them. Octavio barely batted an eyelid, showing how ordinary this was for him. Though she doubted he'd shared a meal with a pregnant ex-lover at the palace before.

He gestured to the food. 'What would you like?'

Her eyes dropped to the dishes. They all looked excellent, but her stomach was too twisty to think of eating. She glanced at the line of servants across the terrace. 'I thought you wanted to talk,' she said between clenched teeth, her lips forced into an approximation of a smile for the benefit of their audience.

He arched a brow in silent enquiry, so she blinked sideways more obviously, indicating the staff.

'Ah.' Octavio nodded once, then turned to the uniformed group. 'Leave us.'

Two simple words and they began to file away in a perfectly formed line.

'Better?'

Her lips pulled to the side. 'Marginally, but that's not saying much.'

He didn't respond. 'Tell me, how did your thinking go?'

She swallowed past a lump in her throat, reached for her drink and took a sip. 'I don't want to marry you.'

His eyes flashed to hers, so she lifted a hand to forestall anything he might say.

'But I understand why you feel it's necessary.'

He was silent.

Phoebe looped a finger around a clump of hair, twisting it over her shoulder as she searched for the right words. 'I don't want to do this alone.' She bit into her lip. 'I mean, I don't particularly want to do it with you either, but I have to admit, there's something appealing about knowing I'll have support. Even if it's just this.' She gestured to the palace. 'I mean, not having to worry about paying rent and buying food and getting a job when the babies are still young…'

'You would never have to worry about any of these things,' he confirmed slowly.

She massaged her lip with her teeth. 'My mother was alone. Money was always tight. It's hard. I've seen it, I've lived it. I know it's not exactly the best reason to agree to marry someone, but at the same time, it's not the worst reason. You can offer our babies something I never could. I don't think it would be right to turn my back on that.'

He sat back in his chair, watching her without speaking.

'And if you weren't the King, I'd fight you on the necessity of marriage. Lots of people raise kids together and don't get married. We could work out a way to do exactly that.'

'For me, that is not possible.'

'I just said I understand that,' she replied sharply.

He took a sip of his water.

'So, let's talk about it.' Her voice was tentative, thoughtful.

'Aren't we doing precisely that?'

She shook her head. 'I mean our wedding, our marriage. Talk to me about how it would all work.'

'The wedding is not something you need to think about. The palace would organise everything. You only need to show up, repeat the right lines, sign on the dotted line and it's done.'

Her heart turned cold. 'Wow. That's every little girl's dream right there.'

'Did you dream of a big white wedding, Phoebe?' he asked, and the question lacked the acerbity she'd become used to from him.

'I—' Once upon a time she had. Her eyes flitted sideways. 'Is it possible that my personal life isn't going to end up in the tabloids?'

'Not even remotely possible, no.'

'So you might as well hear it from me. I was engaged.'

Surprise flashed across his features. 'That's not ideal, but we can cope.'

'Okay, for starters, that's incredibly hypocritical, given that up until a couple of hours ago you were also planning to marry someone else. And secondly...it gets worse.'

He made a noise that might have been a garbled half-laugh and might have been a groan. 'Of course it does. Go on.'

'My fiancé was married to someone else.' Her voice was so calm, so cold, even though she was telling him something that had shattered her into a billion tiny pieces. 'They had two babies during the three years we were together. I had no idea, obviously.'

He swore softly under his breath, his eyes scanning hers, and for a moment—the briefest of moments—he was human again, not some angry royal automaton trying to manoeuvre her into a cold marriage of convenience.

'You really didn't know?'

She stared at him, aghast. 'Do you honestly need to ask that?'

'I don't know. I don't know you. I thought I did, but this—' He gestured to her stomach.

She angled her face away, frustration coursing through her. 'How dare you?'

'I'll take that as a no.'

'I had absolutely no idea. I thought he loved me. I was planning the damned wedding.' She shivered. 'I thought I'd found my Prince Charming, and my life was finally, finally going to work out. I was wrong.' Another shiver.

She didn't see the emotions that flitted across his face, nor the way a hand tightened into a fist in his lap.

'How did you find out?'

'That doesn't matter. It's not likely to come out.'

'Does anyone else know?'

'Well, my ex, for one.'

'He's not likely to reveal this to anyone. Who else?'

'I don't know. I didn't tell anyone the reason we broke up, but I told people we were engaged. So that's probably going to get out there, and after that, it's not hard to unpick the rest of it. God, I should probably tell him this first, so he has time to prepare his wife.'

'You are seriously thinking of how to mitigate that bastard's inconvenience after what he did to you?'

'Not for his sake, but for his wife's. She was just as innocent as I was.'

He swore. 'Ignore them. They don't matter to you. If his wife wakes up and realises what he's like, then he will have to deal with it, and she'll be better off.'

Phoebe's stomach swirled.

'What else?' His voice was gruff.

'What do you mean?'

'Is there anything else I should know? Anything that will hit the papers and read like a scandal?'

'Anything else that makes me a liability, you mean?' she enquired sharply, and then sighed. 'This is so far from what you imagined, isn't it?'

'Yes.'

Her heart dropped. 'I bet you wish we'd never met.'

She'd said the words flippantly, but the longer the silence stretched between them, the more she realised she needed him to contradict her. She needed him to reassure her.

And he did, finally, but not as Phoebe wanted. 'I'll never wish that. For a long time, the order of succession has plagued me, and now this. Within months, two legitimate heirs will be born. Believe it or not, apart from having to sort out some logistics, this is good news for me.'

It was nothing to do with Phoebe and it was nothing to do with their babies as people, it was all about the power-brokering and importance of an heir to the King.

'Great,' she said, the word dripping with sarcasm. 'Well, that's pretty much the only scandal in my life. Everything else has been squeaky clean. But you were right that day... I'm definitely not someone who's been groomed in any way whatsoever to become a queen.'

'We can take care of that. You'll undertake lessons here—in protocol, history, languages, politics. By the time the babies arrive, you'll be every bit as regal as if you were born a princess.'

Her heart was heavy with hurt.

She wasn't good enough for him. He wasn't the kind of man to take her, just as she was. He wanted to change her, to improve her, to make her more suitable for him and this role. She'd been a cleaner and he'd used her for sex, he'd propositioned her for more sex, and now he was trying to turn a sow's ear into a silk purse. He was expecting her to play a part, to sell this. At least, that's what it felt like to Phoebe.

She tried not to show how offended she was, but she knew her eyes were likely awash with pain. If he saw it, he didn't say anything to ease the feeling.

'I have two press releases to show you.'

She went very still. Octavio pulled a couple of pieces of paper from his pocket and slid them across the table. Phoebe picked them up and read the first one:

While I understand the temptation to create rumours around long-standing friendships, I am now reiterating the fact that His Majesty Octavio de la Rosa and I are nothing but friends, brought together by our parents' closeness. In fact, I would like to be the first to congratulate him on his impending marriage. I have never seen him so happy, and I wish him and Miss James all the very best.

'From Sasha,' he explained needlessly.
Phoebe flicked to the second statement.

His Royal Highness King Octavio de la Rosa is delighted to announce his engagement to Miss Phoebe James. Their relationship has been conducted in private, and earlier this week the decision was made to marry.

They are also delighted to announce that they are expecting twins, due late in the Autumn.

The couple asks that their privacy be respected at this joyous time.

She stared at the words until they made sense. There was just enough there to make it seem plausible that this was a love match—that their twins had been conceived and their relationship was one of several months rather than three nights—before the truth about her pregnancy came out, as surely it would.

She pushed the papers back towards him, nausea rising in her belly.

'When would these go out?'

'Our social media channels would push them at the same time—tomorrow afternoon. That gives us a chance to have an official portrait taken first.'

She groaned. 'An official portrait?'

'Without it, the press will be clamouring for whatever they can get their hands on. That could be anything from anyone. Let's remove as much of that as possible and simply provide an image.'

Phoebe's gut rolled. 'This is really happening, isn't it?'

'Apparently.'

'You sound about as thrilled as I feel,' she whispered, tears sparkling on her lashes. After several beats of silence, she shook her head forlornly and said, 'God, what a mess.'

He didn't answer her. He couldn't. He sure as hell couldn't contradict her. This was a royal mess and of their making. He wanted to be gentle with her, to sympathise with her predicament, but whenever a tendency like that came to him, he quashed it.

She had known about this pregnancy for six damned weeks. Six weeks in which she'd contemplated telling him and dismissed the idea. For his sake. Six weeks in which she'd made the cold, calculated decision that he wouldn't be a part of his babies' lives, until it suited her. Weeks and weeks in which she'd decided, every day, that she would deny their babies their birthright and run far away from him.

How dared she?

How dared she think she had any right to do that? And after her own childhood and the absence of her father! Sure, she had said she planned to tell Octavio at some point, but he had only her word for that. What if she'd gone back to New Zealand, met someone else and decided it was just easier to raise the babies with them?

Every iteration made him seethe, and worse was the fact this had all come about by happenstance. If he hadn't gone to the hospital today, he would probably never have seen her again. And he couldn't live with that possibility. It wasn't about Phoebe, but the twins she carried, the babies that he had every right to know and raise as his own children, to raise as his heirs.

He wouldn't forgive her for what she'd almost taken from him, and he doubted he'd ever trust her.

But even when he felt like that, he still hated seeing her suffer. He hated knowing he was the cause of her pain, and he hated knowing that they would never recover from this. He could never forgive her for planning to keep the babies a secret from him, and she would never forgive him for strong-arming her into this marriage.

Their chemistry was as palpable as ever. Desire was whipping him, practically forcing him to reach for her, to obliterate her anxiety the only way he knew how: kiss by kiss by kiss…

'You seriously mean for us to share a room?' Her voice was unnaturally high-pitched, but she couldn't quell it.

'You're expecting me to believe that's a problem?'

'Yes, it's a problem! God, Octavio, we're not a couple!' She lowered her voice to a whisper, even though they were alone. 'We don't like each other, we're sure as hell not sleeping together.'

He arched a dark brow and her irritation grew.

'You can't expect me to find you attractive after the day we've had?'

His laugh was soft and throaty. 'Careful, *querida.* You know how I like to react when you bait me with obvious lies.'

Her jaw dropped. 'I am *not* lying, you…you…' But she floundered, trying to find the perfect way to describe him. 'I am so mad at you.'

'Be that as it may, tomorrow our engagement will be announced to the world. You had better get used to the fact this marriage is happening.'

'This marriage is happening for the sake of the twins, nothing more,' she hissed. 'Behind closed doors, I'd prefer to forget you exist.'

His smirk made her fingers itch to slap him, and she'd never done that in her life. He stepped closer, but didn't touch her—and it was only then that she realised how badly she wanted him to touch her, regardless of what she was saying. Damn her body for its treacherous reactions to him!

'Let me know how you go with that, won't you?'

'You are unbelievably arrogant.'

'Not arrogant,' he corrected, the humour slipping from his tone. 'Honest. I am furious with you, Phoebe. Angrier, perhaps, than I've ever been with another person, and that's saying something. But I still want you. I'm not afraid of accepting that reality—when you're ready to do the same, I'll be here.'

She glared at him, her nostrils flaring as she expelled an angry breath. 'I guess that leaves me to go find a guest room,' she threw at him, before turning and stomping down the corridor of his incredibly luxurious apartment.

'Stop.' His voice arrested her in her tracks. 'There is no guest room.'

She whirled around to face him. 'What?'

'This is my apartment. I have a study, a gym and a bedroom. Why would I want a guest room?'

She floundered. 'Then in the palace…'

'Yes, there are many bedrooms in the palace, but that's not appropriate.'

Her jaw dropped.

'We are pretending to be in a whirlwind love affair, so madly passionate that we became engaged only months after meeting. I cannot have the veracity of that questioned.'

'Questioned by whom?'

His expression darkened. 'By anyone who would seek to challenge me.'

'Challenge you?' Her brows knit together. 'What do you mean?'

'You take the bedroom. If you're so determined that you can't control yourself around me, I'll take the couch.'

Two pink dots appeared on her cheeks. 'That's *not* what I meant.'

'Of course it is. You don't want us to sleep together, fine. But that's no reason not to share a bed. The bed—by the way—is huge. Easily large enough for us to each take a side. But you know that the minute we're lying down and within arm's reach, something will happen, because we both still want one another. I'm the only one who's game to admit it though. So take the bed, I'll take the couch, and when you accept the reality of our situation, let me know.'

She wanted to fight him. She wanted to scratch him and push him and shout at him, but in the end, she was getting what she wanted. She wasn't even going to feel sorry for him, having to curl his huge frame onto a sofa for the night.

'Okay.' She smiled with exaggerated sweetness. 'Goodnight then, Your Majesty.'

'Sweet dreams…'

CHAPTER SEVEN

LEAVE IT TO Octavio to get the last word in. Sweet dreams, indeed. Not only had she *not* slept remotely well, she'd also been tortured all night. By dreams and memories, by thoughts of their future, by the bed in which she tried to sleep, by the lingering fragrance of him, by the weird temptation to go padding out into the lounge area and watch him sleep. It was all so unsettling, so destabilising, so she awoke in a terrible mood with every intention of giving him a piece of her mind.

Only to find the apartment empty.

He'd left a note on the marble kitchen benchtop.

P—
I had a meeting.
I'll see you at the photoshoot. Try to smile.
O

She screwed the note up and threw it onto the floor before remembering his strange remark the night before about the necessity of fooling everyone into believing this was real. He'd implied his rule was at stake, and whatever she might think of him personally, she didn't want to cause him any problems there. She retrieved the note, tore it into a dozen pieces, then dropped them into the bin.

Phoebe had managed to eat a piece of dry toast and drink

a cup of weak tea when a knock sounded at the door to the apartment and one of the staff members she vaguely remembered from the day before stepped inside.

'Madam, the stylist is here.'

'Stylist?' Phoebe gawked, aware that she looked absolutely awful. Her hair was straggly and her face was pale and wan. Her eyes were sunken, courtesy of a lack of sleep, and she was dressed in an oversized tee-shirt that she liked to sleep in.

'Her name is Marie Domingo. May I send her in?'

'I—' But what could she say? The photoshoot loomed large, and Phoebe was nowhere near prepared for that. It was actually kind of thoughtful of Octavio to have arranged this. 'Yes, okay. Why not?'

A moment later, an elegant woman strode into the room—tall and slim with jet-black hair and darker eyes. 'Madam.' She dipped her head. 'I'm honoured to have been asked to work with you.'

Phoebe grimaced. 'Well, don't count your chickens. I need a lot of work.'

'Nonsense.' Marie waved a heavily bangled hand through the air. 'You are beautiful, just unprepared. This will be easy to deal with.' Phoebe went to stand but Marie shook her head. 'Stay, stay, finish up. It will take us a while to set up, anyway.'

Us? Phoebe thought, bewildered.

'Us' turned out to be a team of about six people. Hairstylists, manicurists and two people whom Phoebe gathered were required to carry various outfits around for Phoebe to inspect, to take her measurements, squeeze her feet into shoes and ferry whatever food or drink anyone required. It was a whirlwind three hours, in which Phoebe was outfitted, had her face made up, her hair washed, trimmed and styled, her nails painted, and when all of that was done, she spent thirty minutes with Marie looking at bridal dresses.

'A Castilonian designer is preferable, but it's a matter of finding who can arrange a gown within a week. It cannot be off-the-rack, it must be sensational, as befits this fairy-tale romance. Are you happy to leave it with me?'

Phoebe stared at her, totally shocked into silence. 'I… yes, of course.'

'Excellent.' Marie consulted her elegant gold wristwatch. 'I've taken up too much of your time.'

'That's fine. It's not like I have anything else scheduled.'

'Actually—' Marie tapped the side of her phone efficiently '—someone from protocol has been waiting to meet with you. We'll leave you to it.'

'Someone from protocol' happened to be an incredibly intimidating man in his sixties who seemed to carry an encyclopaedic knowledge of Castilona, the royal family, the rituals, histories, priorities and requirements. He spent an hour going through what he deemed to be the most vital—mainly surrounding her etiquette whilst engaging in public duties. 'This is only a photoshoot,' he said with a wave of his hand. 'There'll only be a few people in attendance, so it's a good opportunity to practise.'

By then, Phoebe was feeling woozy with everything she would have to convey. Her walk, her expressions, how to hold her hands and position her feet and legs—it was all so much to hold in her mind, she felt like she might explode.

It was a relief when the time for the photoshoot finally approached and a staff member could lead her from the apartment, through the palace, out of a side door and down a wide set of stone steps that led to an elegant courtyard overgrown with vines. Dressed in a loose silk blouse with puffy sleeves, and a pair of slim trousers, her belly was barely noticeable, though her breasts felt enormous.

She looked around and saw a photographer was already set up, surrounded by a few assistants who were busy managing the set up and checking lighting levels. Phoebe stared at them, her heart in her throat. She was so engrossed in their activity that she missed the moment Octavio strode out from an entrance to their left, fixing one of his cuff-links in place.

She missed the way his eyes landed on her and stayed there, heavy on her frame, as if he couldn't possibly look away. She missed the way admiration softened his features a moment, parting his lips, and she missed the way he fought to regain his equilibrium. She saw only cynicism on his features when he approached her and she realised he was there.

Phoebe shivered at the expression.

'Ready?' he asked, one brow lifted.

'As I'll ever be.'

'It's a photoshoot, not a form of torture.'

'It's what the photoshoot represents.'

'And what's that?'

'The beginning of the lie.'

'I thought you'd be more than comfortable with lying by now? After all, six weeks of keeping your pregnancy from me should have made you practised in deceit.'

She wanted to shove him.

Before she could respond, he reached into his pocket. 'Here, put this on.'

She glanced down at his hand expecting—strangely enough—something like a microphone. Instead, he held a small black velvet box. Phoebe made no attempt to take it, so a moment later, Octavio impatiently opened the box and turned it around for her to see. Inside was a beautiful ring, a large solitaire diamond in the middle of a circlet of black diamonds.

'It's...so lovely,' she said honestly, and frustratingly, tears sparkled on her lashes. 'God, I'm going to ruin my make-up.'

He was quiet, his lips pushed together. She reached for the ring, her fingers shaking a little.

'I don't trust myself not to drop it,' she murmured.

With a sound of something like impatience, Octavio removed the ring and took hold of her hand. The moment their flesh connected she felt it—the same thousand little sparks from their first meeting flew through her arm and exploded into a cacophony of fireworks inside her body.

'It was my mother's, and my grandmother's before her.'

'Oh.' Her heart twisted. It shouldn't have made a difference, but somehow it did. Just imagining herself wearing something that was so personally significant felt wrong, given what they meant to each other. 'Are you sure?'

'Yes.'

'But it's obviously very special to you—'

'And my wife, therefore, should have it.'

'But I'm not really—'

'From now on, for all intents and purposes, you are.' He compressed his lips, glanced across at the photographers then back to Phoebe. He drew her closer, close enough that only she could hear his raspy whisper. 'Stop acting like a deer in headlights and remember that in a week's time, you'll be Queen.'

The stylist Marie had also said something about getting a dress in a week but it hadn't quite penetrated the fog of Phoebe's brain. Now she blinked up at Octavio, eyes wide with surprise. 'A *week*?'

'The sooner the better,' he agreed.

'A week.' Phoebe struggled to draw in breath. She pressed a hand to her belly, heart pounding. She could do this. She *had* to do this. She'd agreed, for the sake of their baby, and Octavio's role as King required a certain amount of play-acting. If he wanted her to go out there and sell herself as the doting, loved up Queen-to-be, so be it. He was right—the time for 'deer in the headlights' was over. 'All right. I'm ready.'

His surprise was obvious, his eyes scanning her face as if looking for vestiges of doubt, but there were none. Phoebe had been terrified a moment ago but now, she was ready. She could do this—she had to.

When he'd first seen Phoebe, he'd been mesmerised by her grace. He remembered thinking that she moved as if she were in a ballet. It turned out, she acted like it, too. He was almost rendered speechless by the way she captivated the photographers, charming them with her casual yet intelligent conversation, moving with fluid grace and beauty, smiling in a way that seemed to channel every star in the heavens.

'We'll always share the stars, my darling.'

He pushed his mother's voice from his mind, not wanting to think about her then. Not wanting to wonder if she'd have approved of the way he'd manoeuvred this marriage or not—because he suspected she wouldn't have.

'Your Majesty, we thought we'd try a photograph of the pair of you standing by the trees here. The pink of the oleander will pick up Miss James's complexion so nicely.'

He glanced across at his bride-to-be and saw what they were saying—her cheeks were sweetly pink, her lips, too. 'Fine.' He sounded gruff and impatient—now who needed help playing a part?

As if to remind him, Phoebe reached down and took his hand. But what might have appeared to be a normal thing for a couple to do was actually a tight squeeze from his fiancée, to prompt him into behaving.

Something twisted in his gut. Frustration. Annoyance. *Need.*

Sleeping on the sofa had been almost unbearable. He'd

craved her for more than a month and a half, but he'd put up with it. He hadn't even known for sure that she was still in Castilona. But now she was in his palace, in his apartment, just one room away, and he wanted her with a ferocity that almost felled him. Yet he'd stayed on the sofa, hadn't pushed his cause, and he wouldn't. If they were together again, it would be because she asked him. He wasn't going to throw himself at her—he wasn't going to debase himself by risking rejection. Not from Phoebe. He'd known enough rejection in his life, and he'd survived it, but somewhere deep inside he understood that if Phoebe kept pushing him away it would be worse somehow.

In front of the trees, he stood as stiff as a board. Little wonder the renowned portrait photographer frowned. 'Could you try a different pose? Just relax. Pretend we're not here,' she invited with a wry smile.

Phoebe turned around and her own frown echoed the photographer's. 'You look miserable,' she murmured.

'I'm not.'

'Then why do you look as though you're about to walk on a bed of nails?'

He flashed her a look and felt a weird tug on his lips. A half-smile.

'Better,' she said, tilting her head, 'but not quite good enough.'

She stood on tiptoes, whispering into his ear so only he could hear. 'I am pregnant with your children and in less than six months you'll have your heirs. Surely that's enough to make you smile for a few photos? Remember, this was your idea.' But she tilted her head after she'd spoken and a form of madness overtook him, so instead of just saying he agreed, he angled his own face and caught her mouth with his, kissing her even though he hadn't meant to and she hadn't expected it.

Kissing her even though she wore lipstick and they weren't alone. Kissing her as if he had every right, as if they were a real couple, as if it was the only path for his salvation. Kissing her even when he'd vowed to himself moments earlier that he wouldn't keep putting himself in a position to be rejected by Phoebe.

He didn't want to be rejected by her.

He pulled away and managed to control his reactions to her, to his body's sharp physical need for her, assuming a mask of control. 'I remember what we're doing, Phoebe—pretending to be a couple in love. Let's just get this over with.' He saw her frown and hated himself as soon as he'd said the words; he saw the hurt in her eyes and wanted to punch something.

He was so angry with her for keeping the pregnancy from him, for what had almost happened. If he hadn't seen her in the hospital, quite by chance, he would never have known about these babies, and that was a reality he could never accept.

And yet she was here and had agreed to marry him. It wasn't fair to continually punish her for a decision she'd made, according to herself, out of a desire to do what was right by him.

He opened his mouth to apologise, but she was already stepping back from him. 'I just need to check my make-up,' she said with a wave of her hand, gliding away from him as though he were a bomb set to detonate.

In the end, the photos they got were excellent. Only Phoebe could see beyond the poses they'd chosen to imitate a happy couple to the lines of tension around Octavio's eyes or the slightly too static line of her own smile. The announcements had predictably set off a feeding frenzy. Octavio had been wrong—sharing a couple of images and a press release hadn't come close to assuaging the interest in their romance. Some staff at the hospital evidently decided it would be more profitable to become royal informants rather than continue working their jobs and had breached *clínica* regulations by professing to be Phoebe's dearest confidants and having all sorts of inside details on the relationship.

Of course, that was false. There had been no relationship, and what she and Octavio had shared had been kept completely private by Phoebe. She'd had no interest in discussing her personal life with anyone. She'd still been reeling from the breakup with Christopher and had learned not to trust anyone with anything.

Phoebe had left school at sixteen, when her mother had become sick and couldn't work. She hadn't really kept in touch with any of those friends and yet a couple of them were also cashing in on their tenuous links to Europe's new soon-to-be queen. Old school photos surfaced on the internet, as well as silly anecdotes about her teen years. 'I always knew she was destined for something amazing. Phoebe's the kind of person who could do anything she wanted in life. She'll make a wonderful queen.' That quote had been from her high school English teacher, and it made her smile. Of all the people who'd been interviewed about Phoebe, Mrs Warwick was the one who had actually known her. She'd pushed her to stay in school.

'You're too bright to walk away from this, Phoebe. You have such potential.'

There were trolls, too. Everyone had opinions on Phoebe, and apparently, she didn't live up to what they saw as Octavio's match. The comments, whether good or bad, were infuriating. She was tempted to throw her phone into the lake that sat perfectly in the south gardens of the palace.

By the fourth day, the palace's PR machine was approaching her about doing an interview.

'The world wants to know about you. If we don't give them the information, they'll fill the void.'

Phoebe wasn't interested in that.

On the fifth day she received a message, out of the blue, from Christopher. It was so unexpected she clicked into it without taking the time to prepare and read his words with a wave of nausea:

Phoebe, we need to talk. Call me. X

She flicked out of the message, with warm cheeks and a sense that she'd done something wrong.

The palace continued to gently question her about doing an interview. She broached the subject with Octavio two nights before their wedding. 'If you want to do an interview, then do one.'

Hardly helpful.

Nor was it helpful that he continued to sleep on the sofa, that he hadn't even suggested joining her in bed since that first night.

To be fair, he was doing exactly what she'd asked him to do, but Phoebe's whole body was screaming for him now, and in the maelstrom of all this, she could only think how comforting it would be to have *him*. To at least have that touchstone to cling to, when everything else felt so wildly out of control. Not that sex with him was *in* control, but it was predictably wild, and reassuringly passionate. It made Phoebe feel alive and in the moment. It made it impossible to think about anything else, to worry, to stress. It was just…good.

But Octavio was acting as though she barely existed. He was in the apartment sparingly, the palace was too huge to run into him, and she gathered he was busy with government matters, meaning Phoebe was left to do her lessons with the private tutors that had been arranged for her, in peace.

Too much peace.

Too much time to scroll her phone and read the comments and articles and predictions and feel like her tummy had been hollowed out.

The worst were the ones that were true. Comments like:

It's obviously just because of the babies. No way would sexy King O marry someone like her except for the pregnancy.

On the morning of the wedding, Phoebe got through the extensive preparations by separating herself from her body. She stood in the middle of the suite as a team of stylists set to work on her hair, skin, make-up, nails, feet. Everything. She extended her arms when they asked her to, pursed her lips, angled her head, whatever they needed she did, and when it was time to slip into the stunning designer gown Marie had arranged for her, she was careful and neat and very still as they fastened the dozens of buttons that ran down the back.

In the fuss of preparations, when Phoebe was ready, the door opened and a beautiful woman with hourglass curves and shiny honey-brown hair sashayed confidently towards Phoebe. She had a kind of beauty that was rare, and unfair to other women. Her skin was soft and supple, youthful, her eyes were stunning in shape and colour, her lips a full, curving line, painted a dramatic red. But she also seemed to glow with kindness. 'Can we have a moment?'

Phoebe knew who she was immediately. This woman had the same innate confidence as her royal cousin—this must be Xiomara, whom she'd heard Octavio speak of a couple of times.

'I'm glad I finally get to meet you,' Xiomara said, when they were alone. 'My cousin is very protective of you.'

'Is he?'

'Oh, yeah. He's been keeping you locked up so you had time to get ready for the wedding. I told him I'd be better at helping you than anyone else, but he disagreed.' Xiomara rolled her eyes. 'You know how insufferable he can be.'

'Oh, I sure do,' Phoebe agreed, liking the other woman immediately.

Xiomara grinned, then studied the bride. 'You look beautiful, by the way.'

'It's all their work.' She gestured towards the closed door. 'I'm just the canvas.'

'Don't be so self-deprecating.'

Phoebe opened her mouth.

'No, I mean it. *Don't*. There's a pack of wolves out there, and they'll eat you alive if you give them the slightest chance. You have to appear confident even when you don't feel it, okay?'

'You're right, you would have been way better at preparing me. What else?'

'Bet you wish you could have some champagne right now, huh?'

Phoebe laughed. 'Actually, I wish I could have a shot of something stronger, but I'm not even drinking water because I don't want to have to pee again.'

Xiomara grimaced. 'Right. So let's run through the day.'

Xiomara was thorough and so confident that it couldn't help but rub off on Phoebe, and they spent thirty minutes discussing the wedding, the dinner afterwards and the people she should avoid.

'You'll have to meet my father, but take my advice and don't get stuck with him for long. I'll try to manage that for you. The King and he…they don't see eye to eye at all.'

Phoebe nodded.

'One last thing.' Xiomara reached into the small designer clutch she carried. 'Tavi asked me to give you this.'

Tavi. Her heart twisted. What a sweet nickname for a man who seemed far too intimidating to ever have such a thing.

'What is it?'

'No idea, sorry. I'm just the messenger.' She handed over a small velvet pouch. 'Would you like me to leave you in privacy?'

'No, that's fine. It's probably just something… I don't know.' Her fingers trembled a little as she opened the pouch and removed a fine platinum chain on which a locket was suspended. It was dainty, oval shaped and with diamonds inlaid. She ran a finger over them. 'It's beautiful.'

'A locket? What's inside? Don't tell me he's put a picture of himself in there,' Xiomara said on a soft laugh.

Phoebe separated one side of the locket from the other, hinging it open, and her breath caught in her throat while her heart rammed into her ribs.

'It's my mum,' she whispered, staring at the picture of her mother smiling back at her.

'Oh, God. That's actually really sweet.' Xiomara's arm came around Phoebe's waist, squeezing her. 'She's beautiful.'

'Yeah, she was.' Phoebe blinked back tears. 'I can't cry. My mascara will run.'

'He should definitely have given you that himself,' Xiomara said with a shake of her head.

'It's just so thoughtful of him,' Phoebe said unevenly, her mind spinning. Had he understood how badly she was missing her mother? Not just today, but ever since learning of her pregnancy and feeling so alone on that journey?

A knock sounded at the door. Xiomara looked at Phoebe. 'You ready?'

Phoebe nodded, but tears still sparkled on her lashes.

'Come in,' Xiomara called, then turned back to Phoebe. 'Would you like to wear it?'

'Of course.' She nodded quickly. 'Would you mind helping me?'

Xiomara clasped the necklace in place and Phoebe glanced at the mirror. It was perfect.

Marie entered the room with two guards, one of whom carried a velvet cushion with a diamond tiara on it. Of course there'd been mention of a tiara but stupidly Phoebe had envisaged something small and, well, cheap, something almost for show. But this was quite obviously from a royal vault of some kind, and it was most definitely not small, nor cheap.

'This tiara was commissioned for the King's great-grandmother,' Marie explained. 'It has one hundred and eighty carats of diamonds, a mix of pear and marquise cut, and is set in platinum. It's very, very special and we all think it will look perfect on you. Do you like it?'

Phoebe's jaw dropped. 'Did you say one hundred and eighty carats?'

'Don't think about it,' Xiomara advised quickly. 'Trust the stylish people.' She wiggled her perfectly shaped brows and Phoebe laughed.

'Okay,' she said with a nod. 'Show me.'

She stood still as the team worked their magic, and by the time they were done Phoebe had to admit she definitely looked the part. There was nothing more to do now but act it.

CHAPTER EIGHT

HER DRESS WAS PERFECT. She looked like an angel—and the cut of the fabric almost disguised her pregnancy. At her throat she wore the locket he'd sent with Xiomara, and on her face she had a perfect smile pinned. He knew it was just for show but no one else would, because Phoebe was a damned good actress. She looked serenely beautiful. She looked regal. He couldn't look away—he told himself he was also acting a part, but in that moment he wasn't acting. He was existing. He stared at her because he wanted to. She had been preceded by a collection of bridesmaids, none of them known to Phoebe, all of them from the aristocracy.

When Xiomara approached the front of the church, she winked at Octavio and he relaxed a little.

The ceremony itself seemed to go on for ever. There was so much to get through, so much custom and tradition, and Octavio was conscious of Phoebe beside him and how long she was standing, how much he wished he could put an arm around her waist for support. She wasn't heavily pregnant, and she was fit and young, but he still wanted her to be comfortable.

Finally, it ended, and they were invited to kiss one another.

Octavio's pulse ratcheted up about a thousand degrees.

He glanced at Phoebe and saw the same feeling in her face that was bombarding him. Worry.

Because when had they ever kissed and it had not overtaken them?

He leaned down, breathing her in, her fragrance so sweet and familiar that he almost groaned. He wanted her so much it was like a fire raging out of control. If he kissed her, he feared he wouldn't be able to stop. And so instead of giving in to temptation and drawing her against his body, tilting her head back so he had full rein of her mouth, he simply pressed his lips to hers for several seconds, allowing the cameras to snap the moment. She stiffened against him, as if she too was fighting something more, so he knew he'd made the right decision to keep this PG. Rapturous applause broke out and he pulled away, feeling as though he deserved a medal.

'Are you tired?'

Phoebe heard the question and tried not to think there was any concern for her in his tone. He was asking because of the pregnancy. 'Yes,' she answered honestly, smothering a yawn. Were queens allowed to yawn? She was glad she'd changed from her bridal gown and tiara into a simple cream suit—it would be much quicker and easier to strip out of, making it faster to get into bed. She was exhausted.

'Then we should go.'

'Oh, it's fine.' She shook her head once. 'The party's still going.'

'It will continue without us. It's after midnight. It's time.'

'After midnight? Already?'

'I'm glad to hear you've been enjoying yourself.'

She wouldn't exactly say that. The whole night, Phoebe had been in demand. Every dignitary, member of the aristocracy and anyone in between had wanted to speak with her. Her head was swimming with the sheer volume of conversation she'd entered into. From time to time, Xiomara had come to her rescue, and those had been high points of the night for Phoebe. Around Xiomara, she felt strangely relaxed.

Around Octavio, it was the opposite. She braced now as he put his hand in the small of her back and guided her towards a set of double doors across the ballroom.

Phoebe was still getting her bearings in the palace. She didn't think she'd used this access before. Sure enough, it brought them onto a small, terraced area, and beyond it, a car was waiting.

'What's this?'

'Our ride.'

She arched a brow. 'Ride? We live right here. I'm not too tired to walk the few hundred metres to your room.'

'We're not staying in the palace tonight.'

She blinked across at him. 'Why not?'

'Because it's our honeymoon.'

'Octavio,' she said, and her voice trembled a little, 'we don't need a honeymoon.'

He looked at her and the air between them seemed to pulse and hum, to swirl around her with a force that was mesmerising and magnetic. He moved closer and her breath caught in her throat, trapped there by an invisible force. 'It's the way it should be,' he said, his eyes scanning hers, probing them, as if looking for the answer to a question he hadn't posed.

'You mean it's what people will expect?'

His lips quirked in the hint of a frown. 'That, too. Let's go.'

They drove for so long that Phoebe became drowsy and her head fell onto Octavio's shoulder, but she was too tired to sit up again. At one point, half asleep, she murmured to him, 'Thank you for my necklace.'

She was barely conscious of his stiffening beneath her, and he was quiet for so long she thought he might not say anything. Then, he responded, 'It's tradition for Castilonian grooms to gift their brides something on the morning of their wedding. I thought you'd like it.'

Tradition. It probably wasn't even his idea. Octavio was hardly the kind of man to come up with such a thoughtful gift idea and do the legwork of finding a photo of Phoebe's mother, having it printed and set into the locket. And though it was still beautiful, the necklace lost some of its charm for Phoebe then. She'd loved it because of what it was, but also because he'd thought to give it to her. There was an odd heaviness on her chest that made her want to blot everything out.

She fell asleep and at some point woke up with Octavio's arms cradling her against his chest as he carried her from the car. She tried to wake up, to say something else, but she was exhausted in that way pregnancy led to, and it had been a huge day to boot. She surrendered to a wave of sleepiness, and the next thing she knew, she was waking up in an unfamiliar bedroom, staring right out at the beach.

She sat bolt upright, trying to make sense of where she was and with whom, and it all came rushing back to her. The wedding. The locket. The party. The dress. The people. The fact she was now married.

And a queen.

Octavio's wife.

Her heart raced as she looked down at her hand for confirmation and saw two bands there—the stunning engagement ring and a simpler platinum band with several small diamonds set into it.

She reached for her throat and felt the locket, opened

it and saw her mother's face and frowned, a maelstrom of feelings rolling through her.

She was alone in this room; she presumed Octavio was somewhere in this place though. It was, after all, their honeymoon.

She grimaced at the idea, because theirs was so far from a normal relationship, but she stood up, realising she was still in the pantsuit she'd been wearing last night. He hadn't even undressed her. Because he hadn't wanted to? Or because he hadn't felt that he had a right?

Whatever.

She was relieved, she told herself, moving from the bedroom and out into a corridor that was light and airy, the walls rendered white, the doorways carved and arched. She scanned the rooms and found him, not in the kitchen, where she'd been heading for her one and only coffee of the day, but rather on the balcony, shirt off, body ridiculously honed and tanned, staring out to sea.

Her mouth went dry.

Her insides squirmed.

And though she made no noise, somehow he must have detected her presence because he turned and looked right at her, so their eyes clashed and her whole body responded with a pulsing, aching need.

She glanced away quickly, her cheeks hot, the ground beneath her seeming trembly. She felt scared.

Scared to be here, alone with him. Scared of what it would mean for her and her ability to resist him. She'd spent a full week longing for him and managing to be strong, but how realistic was it to stick to that?

Would she really spend her whole life ignoring this desire?

Would he?

Did she want to?

Her legs moved of their own volition, across the floor towards the sliding doors and out onto the balcony. The air here was sweet, tinged with the fragrance of the Mediterranean Sea and the greenery that bounded it. There were white and pink Oleander trees forming a border and a heap of lavender scrambled beneath it, growing quite wild. Though not native to the Mediterranean, at some point a heap of palms had been planted around the beach and they gave the impression of being stranded on a tropical island rather than somewhere in Castilona.

'Where are we?' she asked, her voice a little raspy from disuse.

'It's a private beach, not far from Costa de las Estrellas,' he said. 'Do you know it?'

'I've never heard of it, but I love the sound of the name.'

'Coast of the Stars,' he said with a nod, but there was something in his eyes that gave her pause. 'It's a coastal town; an old fishermans' village, but over the years it's become synonymous with good food and wine and some of the best beaches in the world. As a result, it's an exclusive tourist destination. My family has had a holiday home here for a long time. This is our beach.'

'Our beach? You mean it's really private?'

He pointed down the sand in one direction and then the other. She noticed that the Oleander trees had been planted to follow the line of the coast, shielding the beach from view. On each side of the house, there was only vegetation.

'Completely private.'

She let out a low breath. 'So we're alone?'

'A housekeeper is available if we want one, but generally when I come here, it's because I am seeking my own counsel.'

She looked at him thoughtfully. 'Do you come here often?'

'I used to, before the coronation.'

She returned her attention to the beach. It was a warm day and the thought of swimming tugged at her.

'I grew up near the beach,' she found herself admitting. 'In the summer, you'd be hard-pressed to get me out of the water. I loved to surf.'

'That's something we have in common.'

Her hands gripped the railing, tightening around it.

'Where in New Zealand are you from?'

'Not far from Raglan. It's on the North Island.'

He nodded. 'Is that where you were planning to return to?'

She shook her head a little. 'After my mum died, I moved to Auckland. That's where I live now. Where I lived.' She frowned, remembering her old life with a shock. It almost felt like something that had happened to someone else. She thought of Christopher, recalled his text message, felt a hint of guilt for not returning it, but then anger that he'd thought he had any right to contact her.

'Where you met your ex-fiancé?'

Had he been reading her mind?

'Yes.'

'How did you meet him?'

She bit into her lip. 'I was a receptionist at a school, and he was a contractor brought in to run some professional development training for teaching staff. We got talking in the break room one day and…the rest is history.'

'Love at first sight?' he asked, and try as she might, she couldn't detect even a hint of mockery in his question.

She shook her head. 'I thought he was handsome, but I still wasn't over losing my mum. It had been a couple of years by then, but I took it hard. I was struggling. I wasn't ready to be involved with anyone.'

'So how did you get together?'

'He took it slow. He told me he understood. Bit by bit, he got me to open up. To trust him.' Her voice shook with anger. 'And then, to love him. Or to believe I loved him. Looking back, I don't know if it's possible to love someone who's using you like that.'

His finger brushed her shoulder lightly. She turned to face him, and something shifted deep in her soul. Christopher seemed like a thousand lifetimes ago.

'He hurt you.'

'He changed me,' she admitted, tilting her chin a little. 'At the time it hurt, but I'm stronger because of what I went through. I would never trust so easily again. Maybe I'll never trust anyone again,' she amended. 'But if I do, it would take a lot.'

'Not everyone is capable of that kind of deceit. In fact, most people aren't.'

'I don't know,' she said with a lift of one shoulder. 'I don't know if it's worth taking the risk. There were no markers with him. Everything seemed so normal. I had no reason to believe he was already married. What kind of psychopath proposes to another woman when he's married and expecting a baby, and then another, with his wife?'

'A psychopath, like you said,' Octavio agreed. 'You're better off without him.'

'I know that.' She nodded. 'I'm just glad I found out before we went through with some kind of sham marriage ceremony or something. I have no idea how far it would have gone if I hadn't learned the truth.'

'How did you find out?'

'I was out at lunch. Christopher just happened to be at the same restaurant, with his wife, their children and his parents. It was mortifying.'

'You hadn't met his parents?'

'No. He told me they were dead.' Her voice trembled a

little. 'I literally ran right into him when I was paying the bill. His wife was beside him, holding their children's hands. Our eyes met and I just knew by the look of mortification in his face, the look of worry and fear that I might out him, that I'd been the Other Woman. He couldn't act like he didn't know me—I'd said his name by then and asked what he was doing there. I hadn't realised until it was too late what was going on, so he had to come up with an elaborate lie about how we knew one another, and the penny finally dropped.'

'When was this?'

'About two months before I flew to Castilona.'

'That's not long ago.'

She shook her head. 'I came as quickly as I could pack up my life and get a passport sorted.'

'He's a bastard.'

'Yes.'

His hand moved to her chin, touching it lightly. He looked as though he was concentrating hard. 'You're—' His eyes dropped to her lips, lingered there, and though it was only a glance, it might as well have been a heady, intimate touch, for the way warmth spread through her.

'I'm...?' she prompted, but breathlessly, as though her lungs could hardly fill with air.

He closed his eyes then, the lashes forming thick, dark half moons against his tanned skin.

'Forget it.' His hand dropped away, and when he opened his eyes, determination was visible in their depths. 'I didn't bring you here to seduce you. You have boundaries and I intend to respect them. Let's go get something to eat.'

Phoebe's heart dropped to her toes even as it exploded in her chest.

'You have boundaries and I intend to respect them.'

Then kiss me! she wanted to shout. *Kiss me until my knees are weak and I forget I've ever, ever been hurt! Kiss me because when you kiss me everything makes a terrifying kind of sense, on a fundamental level. Kiss me now; kiss me and keep kissing me.*

But she said none of those things, and Octavio stepped backwards and then walked in off the deck, leaving Phoebe alone with the fragrant sea-breeze.

'There will be photographers,' he warned, as they approached a sleek black sports car parked out front of the beachy holiday cottage. 'Not specifically for us, yet, but because this town is the kind of place celebrities come. Don't be surprised if there's a lens pointed at you.'

She wrinkled her nose. 'Great. Sounds like fun.'

'You get used to it.'

'Really? Aren't we just going to get breakfast? That's not particularly newsworthy.'

'You'd be surprised.'

She sat in the front passenger seat and before she could do it herself, Octavio was reaching across Phoebe for the seat belt and sliding it into position. His hands brushed her belly and Phoebe's breath hissed between her teeth. She jerked her gaze to his, wondering if he'd felt it. The electric shock. The current of awareness.

'Do you mind if I...' He held one hand towards her stomach.

She shook her head. 'I don't mind. They're your babies, too.'

'But it's still your stomach.'

'Just a home right now,' she said with a shrug.

He pressed his palm to her side and one of the babies kicked immediately. Phoebe laughed, her eyes meeting Octavio's, who looked utterly shocked. 'Was that—a baby?'

'Yes.'

He swore under his breath. Another kick.

'That baby is active. I think they like your touch.'

She had meant it as a simple observation, but she heard the words and wondered how they'd sounded to Octavio. Like an invitation? Did they prove that she was every bit as needy as she actually was?

'Then I might have to touch more.'

'It could be your voice, too,' she murmured.

'Talk, touch. We are here for two more nights—let's experiment.'

Her heart raced. Two nights? It seemed like an eternity and nowhere near enough.

They had to drive through a heavily fortified security gate that was lined on either side by a fence at least four metres high, concealed by overgrown trees but nonetheless menacing and effective. Once through it, on the short road to town, Octavio spoke about the surroundings, the village, making conversation almost as if they were friends. It was so unexpected that when he pulled the car to a stop in the main street of a charming, ancient fishing port, she turned to him and blurted, 'Why are you being so nice to me?'

He frowned a little. 'I don't actually know. I keep reminding myself how mad I am with you, but then, when I'm with you, I find it hard to remember that. I suppose I find myself thinking about the future, and the fact we're having babies and wondering if we shouldn't try to let bygones be bygones, to some extent. If I think about you leaving the country, pregnant with my children, and never telling me the truth, I am furious. And yet, that didn't happen. Maybe it never would have happened; who knows? You're here, we're married, our babies will grow up as my children, my heirs. I have no interest in hating you for the sake of it.'

She let out a long, slow breath.

If only it were that easy.

Maybe it could be?

But when she looked at Octavio, it was impossible not to feel wary. Wary of how he'd hurt her, when he'd asked her to be his mistress. Making her feel as though that was all she'd ever be good for. Reminding her so clearly of how Christopher had made her feel. Breaking her all over again. Not her heart but something more than that—her belief in herself; her essence.

She didn't want to hate him either, but she was afraid to like him too much as well.

But so long as she remembered—remembered *everything*—like how easily Christopher had deceived her, how trusting she'd been. Like how Octavio hadn't been interested in her as a person—not in terms of wanting anything from her beyond sex—before he'd learned about the pregnancy. This was and always would be about the twins; so long as she didn't forget that, she'd be fine. Maybe she could even take a page out of his book and let bygones be bygones...

CHAPTER NINE

THEY SHARED BREAKFAST at an intimate café with views of the water and a small but excellent menu. Phoebe had woken starving and chose a magdalena as well as a frittata, washed down with a glass of orange juice. Afterwards, they walked the main street together. Phoebe glanced in shop windows at first, but as they walked, side by side without touching, she became more and more aware of the attention they were drawing. Not just the handful of photographers Octavio had suggested might be lurking but also regular tourists, all armed with their cell phones, taking photographs and videos and no doubt sharing them online.

It had been a beautiful start to the day, but Phoebe's patience quickly wore thin.

'Shall we get back to the villa?' he asked, as if reading her mind.

She glanced at him gratefully. 'Yeah. I'd like that.'

They drove most of the way in silence, Phoebe frowning a little as she lost herself in thought. After a while though, she turned to face him. 'Do you really get used to it?'

'For the most part.'

'Does that happen often?'

'Pretty much everywhere I go.'

She shook her head. 'It's just so invasive.'

'Mostly it comes from a good place. People are curious about my life.'

'Because you're a king?'

'And because my parents died when I was so young. I was orphaned. There was a lot of sympathy for me.'

She reached across, putting her hand on his knee in a gesture of comfort. She didn't say anything—she didn't need to. They'd discussed grief and loss; he knew how she felt. He knew she was sorry for anyone to suffer in that way.

As they approached, the gates swung open to allow his car to pass through them, and Phoebe expelled a sigh of relief. 'The town is beautiful but I like it here better.'

'I should have known. It's too soon.' He reached across, stroked her cheek as though he couldn't help himself. 'On the other hand, it will further sell our story as being legitimate.'

Phoebe's eyes widened. Was that what breakfast had been about? Had it all been for show? To display her around town, so the press could get images and feed the public's insatiable appetite for news on the royal couple?

She bit back a groan. Hadn't she just been telling herself that so long as she *remembered*, everything would be fine? And instead she'd been swept up in how decent he'd been behaving, treating her like a normal person. She'd forgotten that he was tactical, always thinking about his kingdom, his duties, treating her as anything but a whole, normal person that mattered.

She put her hand on the door the moment he parked, and opened it gratefully, stepping outside and breathing in, trying to anchor herself firmly to reality. But here, in this beautiful place, everything inside of her seemed to be shifting and changing, making it hard to know what she felt and wanted.

He walked closely behind her, and when they were inside he said, 'I'm going to catch up on some work. Take a look around—there's a well-stocked library, a media room with all the streaming services, a gym. Do whatever you want. Just—be careful.' His eyes dropped to her stomach. As if she needed any further reminders that this was all just about the babies!

He resisted the urge—but only just—to lock the door to his office. He'd come so close to reaching out and touching her stomach again, to touching *her*, to drawing her close to him and asking if he could kiss her. He'd wanted to drag her against his body all morning. In town, their hands had brushed as they'd walked. Such an innocent gesture, and yet it had been almost incendiary to Octavio, who felt as though he was burning up with desire for his wife.

But she'd made it obvious she didn't want that. Even when on one level she did, she was determined to avoid it—and him. And he had to respect that. So he buried his head in his work, surprised to find it was mid-afternoon before he looked up and wondered where Phoebe was.

He strode from the office, telling himself he was looking for a late lunch rather than his bride, but when he couldn't immediately see her in the house, worry began to curdle in his gut. He quickened his pace and stepped out onto the terrace, scanning the ocean. No Phoebe.

The property was completely secure; she couldn't be anywhere else. But knowing that didn't lead him to feel any calmer. He checked the house again and this time, found her. Asleep. No wonder she hadn't responded when he'd called her name. She'd drifted off on a sun lounger on the back deck, mercifully in the shade thrown by a nearby tree. She wore a singlet top and shorts, so her golden legs were on display, crossed at the ankle, and her breasts shifted with each gentle breath.

He stood staring at her, his nostrils flaring, his temperature rising, his hands balling into fists as he remembered
what it had been like to make love to her, to know her body
as intimately as he'd ever known anyone. He didn't make
a sound, and yet she shifted, sighed, pressing her hand to
her stomach, then blinking up at him. Her lips shaped into
a smile, full and generous and attributable only to the fact
she was still half dreaming.

'What time is it?' she asked, groggily, sitting up and
looking around.

'Just after three.'

She blinked. 'I've been asleep for hours.'

'Yesterday was a big day.'

She pulled a face. 'Yeah.'

He wondered at the pulling in the centre of his chest,
the slightly painful stitching sensation. 'Did you enjoy any
of it, Phoebe?'

Her eyes widened. 'It…wasn't about enjoyment. It's
something we had to do, right?'

He should have been glad to hear her speak so pragmatically. It was exactly what he wanted his bride to feel—and
to understand he felt. But Phoebe deserved more after everything she'd already been through.

'It was an experience I'll never forget,' she elaborated.
'That beautiful tiara—what an honour to have worn it.'

He moved to sit on the edge of the sun lounger. There
wasn't much space, so it brought them close together and
Phoebe's breath hitched in her throat.

'And the dress was really nice, too. That was amazing
how Marie was able to organise it so quickly. I had no idea
that could be done. And I loved meeting Xiomara. She's
lovely.'

Phoebe was babbling. In a very un-Phoebe manner.

Phoebe was nervous.

Because of him. Nervous good? Nervous bad? Nervous because she couldn't stop thinking about how much she wanted him?

'And the food was great. I loved it. My mum tried to make Castilonian food often, but she never quite got it right. It was—'

'Phoebe,' he interrupted, hearing the surrender in his tone and not caring. 'I want to kiss you.'

Phoebe's lips parted, her concentration visibly wavered, her gaze falling to his mouth. Everything inside of him tightened in anticipation. He'd vowed to wait until she asked, until she begged, but here he was, begging. Needing. Wanting so much it hurt.

He moved forward a little, his body flushed with heat. In the back of his mind, he heard the warning voice. The reminder that the more he wanted someone or something, the smarter it was to back away. It was how he'd lived his life—having had any affection withdrawn from him once his parents died, he'd naturally developed a coping mechanism that had him avoid relying on anyone. Needing anyone.

But sex was different. It was something his body felt and wanted, not his head nor heart. And Phoebe couldn't hurt his body.

Except, hadn't the last month and a half hurt him? Physically, at least? He'd barely slept that first month…

Don't do this.

The wise counsel in his mind should have been obeyed, but Octavio was too far gone to care. It wouldn't last. That was his sole consolation. At some point, the sexual infatuation would burn out, and everything would be normal again.

And it *was* an infatuation, the kind Octavio had never known. But he'd heard about it. He knew it wasn't rare or unusual. It was just a phase between two people who happened to have a certain chemistry.

He paused, close enough to her lips to kiss her, but doing no such thing. Not until she said something. Anything. He'd kissed her before without her issuing a verbal invitation, but this was different. He needed her to admit she wanted him as well. He was out on a limb and didn't want to be the only one. Perhaps he also wanted to demonstrate to himself that he was still in control. He wanted her but he wasn't lost to her.

Phoebe didn't say anything though. Instead, she closed the rest of the distance between them and claimed his mouth with her own, melding them in a way that made him—and her—moan in awareness and completion. It was the kiss he'd wanted to give her on their wedding day, the kiss that should have sealed their marriage ceremony. It was a kiss that lit every part of him on fire, igniting deep in his soul.

Her body was warm from the sun. He felt it as he pressed himself against her, the sweet roundness of her stomach, her beautiful breasts, he kissed her until she was writhing beneath him and the word *please* was flicking into his mouth like the tail-end of a whip, mesmerising him, calling to him, weakening any thoughts he'd had of restraint, any idea that this could just be a kiss.

It could never be just a kiss with them. That was their chemistry. He moved his body over hers, straddling her and kissing her, running his hands through her hair while he tasted her mouth, then removed her shirt, groaning at the sight of her braless body, her beautiful breasts. He remembered them, but they were different now. Fuller, the nipples a darker pink. He dropped his head to one, hungry to feel it in his mouth, needing to roll her nipple with his tongue and revelling in the way she arched her back and screamed his name when he did so.

This felt good. So bloody good. Control was still his; or if it wasn't, it was something neither of them had.

He ran his hand down to her stomach, pausing because emotions threatened to punch him in the gut and he didn't want to *feel* anything but the physical.

'It's fine.' Phoebe stroked his back. 'I asked the doctor at my last check-up.' He glanced up at her in time to see her cheeks flush pink. 'Just *in case* something like this happened. My pregnancy is low-risk, so far as twin pregnancies go. There's no medical reason for us not to—um—I mean, if that's where this is going.'

Her awkwardness and nervousness pulled at something dangerously close to his heart. He wasn't sure what he would say if he spoke, so he didn't say anything. He just went back to kissing her, longer, slower, more sensually, drawing this out to torment them both. And it was a torment. A torment to be so rock-hard against her sex but to have clothing separating them, a torment to have her naked breasts pressed to his chest through the fabric of his shirt. A torment to kiss her and not be inside of her. But he wanted to make this last, he wanted to maintain control.

Finally, it was too much for Octavio, and he stripped their clothes piece by piece, still making himself take his time, tracing her body with his tongue, flicking her breasts, her stomach, her hips, her sex, before finally he separated her legs.

'Would you prefer me to use a condom?'

She laughed. 'That horse has bolted, hasn't it?'

'I mean from a health point of view. I'm clean, but if you'd prefer me to take the precaution—'

'Oh, gosh, I hadn't even thought—' She shook her head. 'I am, too. I'm not exactly someone who does this often, and I've always used protection in the past. Always.'

He knew that, but for some reason in that moment, in that context, it made him feel powerful. Masculine. Special. He boxed those feelings away. All of them, especially the last one.

He wasn't special. Sure, he was King, but that was not the same thing as mattering to someone, and it had been a long time since he had.

Relief at not having to leave her to go in search of the condoms he had stashed somewhere in the villa was palpable. He positioned himself at her sex, looking down at her, realising he'd never done this with Phoebe. In the past when they'd been together, he'd entered her without looking at her face. Not intentionally, but simply because he'd been caught up in passion and had been at a fever pitch, desperate to lose himself in her. Now, as he pressed into her, he found his eyes were hooked to Phoebe's and wouldn't shift. He saw the way her pupils swelled and irises darkened, the way her skin flushed a darker shade of pink, the way she bit into her lip as if to stop from screaming out. He saw something shift inside of her gaze, something that pummelled him and threatened to break him, so finally he tore his eyes away, burying his head in the crook of her neck as he thrust into her completely and stayed there, buried deep. Her muscles tightened around his length and he was euphoric. It had been way too long and he'd wanted this way too much.

He surrendered completely.

He had lost himself to her, staring at her as she'd climaxed, marvelling at her beauty, her passion, at how alive she was. Marvelling at the fact she was his wife, that she would be the mother of his children. Marvelling at the fact she was his.

And was he hers, too?

He'd shut the thought down, even when he knew the answer. When it came to sex, yes. He was hers. Every inch of him was. She made him feel things he'd never known, and there was no point denying it. But even as his body had given up any pretence of self-protection, his mind refused to.

Sex was sex. That's all this was. He was capable of separating the physical from anything else. Beyond this, they were two people thrown together by circumstance. That was something else they had to navigate, but the fact they'd slept together shouldn't complicate it.

'God, I've missed that,' he said, afterwards, pulling away from her and stroking the side of her face. She went from sensually languid to confused to…different. Not languid at all.

'Me, too.' But her voice was a little strained. Why?

'You're okay?' Had he hurt her? He'd tried to be gentle but hell, it had been a long time…

'Oh, yes. I'm fine. It's fine.' She smiled, but was he imagining a tightness in her features?

'Are you hungry?'

'Um, yeah. I guess so.'

'Okay. I'll go reheat something.' He pulled away from her with regret, but consoled himself that things were different now. Having done that once, he knew it would happen again. Tonight? 'Take your time.'

She did take her time. She needed to. Something cool had slid into her veins and she needed to regroup, to make sure she didn't show him how she was feeling.

Which was what?

Ambivalent?

Uncertain?

Hurt?

But why?

I missed that. Not, *I missed you.*

It was semantics, she knew that, but it didn't change the

fact that he'd yet again made her feel as though sex was all he cared about. He'd missed sleeping with her. That wasn't the same as missing her.

Whereas she'd missed him?

She closed her eyes on a tremulous breath, moving towards the railing and looking out to sea. She'd pulled the same clothes back on, and her shirt was sun warmed from where he'd tossed it on the terrace.

Yes. She had missed him. She'd missed sex with him, too, but she'd missed more than that, and it was a terrifying thing to admit, because it was abundantly clear that Octavio viewed her exactly as Christopher had.

Sex.

Convenient, meaningless sex.

Extra convenient for Octavio, because he now had a queen and a couple of heirs on the way, and he hadn't needed to go through the rigmarole of a long royal engagement. Plus, they were great in bed together, which wasn't necessarily a foregone conclusion with the Princess he'd been intending to marry.

So all of Octavio's boxes were ticked. But what about Phoebe's?

Prior to meeting Octavio, she'd sworn off men. Her experience with Christopher had been more than enough. But once she'd found out she was pregnant, she'd been in a total panic. The thought of being a single mother had terrified her. She'd known she'd cope, but she also knew how difficult it would be, particularly given her lack of education.

'Phoebe?' His voice interrupted her thoughts, and she turned, still frowning contemplatively.

He'd dressed, too, in a pair of navy blue shorts and a crisp white shirt with the sleeves pushed up to his elbows. He looked good enough to eat. She looked away again.

'The food is ready.'

'Okay. Coming.'

And just when she thought she'd mostly got her head around where things stood between them, he reached down and caught her hand and lifted it to his lips, kissing the skin on her upturned palm. Goose bumps spread across her skin, and the ice in her veins began to thaw, just a little.

CHAPTER TEN

'MIND IF I ask you something?'

She looked at him, her mouth full of the saffron-infused rice he'd heated for their lunch, and nodded. They'd chosen to sit at the kitchen table, which was an informal yet beautiful space with views towards the front garden and cove. Phoebe thought she would never grow tired of this view. It was heartwarmingly beautiful. When she'd finished eating, she said, 'You're the King, aren't you? I'm pretty sure you don't have to ask my permission for anything.'

'With you, I'm just Octavio. Just like I said that first night we met.'

Her smile was wistful. Things had seemed so simple then. It had almost felt as though fate had thrown them together for that one night, because it knew he needed a comfort that only she could give and because she'd needed… what? To move on? To officially put an end to the chapter with Christopher by sleeping with someone else? Perhaps that had motivated her in part.

'Phoebe?'

She startled a little. 'Yes. I'm listening.'

He was too perceptive to have missed the fact she'd drifted off into her own thoughts. She focused on him now.

'Why did you choose to work at the *clínica*?'

Her brows knit together. 'What do you mean?'

'You were working as an administrator in a school. There must have been a lot of jobs you could have applied for.'

'Oh.' She nodded. 'Well, the pay was good, for one thing. And I guess...' She sighed a little. 'My mother worked as a cleaner at a hospital. When I saw the listing, I sort of felt... I don't know. It sounds so stupid, but I almost felt as if she was guiding me towards the job. Like maybe she was pulling strings.' Then, aware of how fanciful it sounded, she cleared her throat. 'Plus, the hours were flexible, and the notice period virtually non-existent. I wanted a job I could walk out of if—'

'If?'

'If I found my dad.'

Octavio's expression was sympathetic. 'Tell me what you know of him?'

'Not a lot. His name and the fact that mum was pretty sure he lived in the capital.'

'She didn't tell you anything else about him?'

'Nothing that would help me find him.' She sighed, pushing the paella around her plate. 'She said he loved music, that he played guitar as if taught by angels, that he sang beautifully and could swim like a fish. She told me he was kind and patient but that they both knew their fling would be brief. He left without giving her his number or email address or anything. She didn't even have a photograph.'

Octavio's frown deepened. 'That's it?'

She nodded. 'I've given all this to the investigator I hired.'

'And has the investigator turned up any information?'

'Not yet. I'm hopeful every day though.' She pleated her napkin. 'I know it's like looking for a needle in a haystack but I'd love to know who he is.'

'You have a lot of resources at your command, Phoebe. My security forces can help, you know.'

Her eyes widened. 'I hadn't thought of that.'

'When we get back, I'll arrange a meeting. You can go through everything with them. Maybe the palace will be able to find him.'

'Maybe.' Butterflies ignited in her stomach.

'And then he'll learn not only that he has a daughter, but also that she is Queen of his country.'

'That's a little overwhelming,' she said with a grimace. 'I'm not sure how he'll feel about that.'

'He'll be thrilled to know you, Phoebe. He'll think he's won the lottery.'

'Because I'm Queen?'

He reached out and put his hand on hers. 'Because you're you.'

Phoebe's heart turned over in her chest. She pulled her hand away quickly, rubbing it against her leg beneath the table.

Christopher had been charming, too. Christopher had said things that had made her feel so special and wonderful, as though he was the luckiest man on earth, and it had all been a lie.

'Don't say things like that.'

'Why not?'

'Because it's not…it's not what we are.'

'So I'm not allowed to compliment you?'

She shook her head. 'I don't need it. I don't want it. We barely know one another.'

He frowned at her characterisation but she refused to be swayed.

'If it hadn't been for the baby, we would never have seen one another again.'

'That was your choice, not mine.'

'There was no choice about it. You were offering something I could never have accepted.'

His frown deepened. 'More time with me?'

'As your mistress.' Her nostrils flared. 'Do you have any idea what that felt like?'

'I said *lover*, not *mistress*.'

'It's the same thing. You made it clear I wasn't suitable for anything but secret sex. What kind of woman, with a modicum of self-respect, would accept that?'

'I'm not your ex,' he said quietly. 'It's natural that you would conflate us in your mind, but I am not him. I was not intending to do the wrong thing by you. I was not intending to use you. I certainly didn't intend to lie to you.'

She bit into her lip. All that was true, but he'd still hurt her in the same way Christopher had. She'd still felt betrayed by his request. Offended, angry, hurt, hollowed out. Devalued and cheap.

'I thought that by laying my cards on the table, there would be no room for problems. I wanted to keep seeing you, but not to risk leading you on. Our chemistry is something that would be easy to mistake for...more. I didn't want to risk that in spending time together you might mistake our physical relationship for something like love. It happens, you know?'

She tilted her face away from him, staring out to sea, suddenly wishing she were far, far away from him and here, that she were out on the ocean, floating on her back in the shape of a star, limbs spread wide. Even there though, she suspected this feeling would follow her. She wasn't sure where she could go that would leave her safe.

'Has it happened to you?' She wasn't really interested, but she felt she needed to say something to buy some time. To enable herself to recover some equilibrium and seem something like normal.

'I'm always careful.'

Always. She turned to face him then, scanning his features. 'It can't have been easy for you to date.'

'No,' he agreed.

'You have lived your whole life in the spotlight.'

He dipped his head in agreement.

'So how did you do it?'

'The same way I did with you.'

Something panged in her chest. None of this was new for him. It was all the same.

'By being honest, ensuring discretion.'

'How did you know you could trust me?' she asked, pressing her chin into her palm, elbow resting on the tabletop.

His lips tugged downwards. 'I don't know.'

'I mean, I was working as a cleaner and selling sordid details of our night together could have earned me a lot of money…'

'I know.'

'So, wasn't that a risk for you to take?'

'I wasn't myself that night.'

'So ordinarily, you wouldn't have approached me?'

The silence stretched between them. She didn't know why it mattered so much. She was trying to get to grips with her own feelings but delving into his wasn't helping.

'I'd like to say no, but in all sincerity, there was something about you. I'd noticed you, even before I spoke to you.'

Phoebe's heart trembled dangerously. 'What had you noticed about me?'

'Your grace.' For some reason, she loved that he'd said something beyond the mere physical. It wasn't her hair or her eyes, but an expression of who she was. 'You walk as though you are listening to classical music. You walk as though you are dancing in your mind. I find it mesmerising.'

Her stomach swooped.

'I didn't realise.'

'I cannot be the first person to point that out to you?'

A memory hovered on the periphery of her mind. A

warm memory, that made her smile. 'My mother actually used to say that, too.'

'Did she?'

Phoebe nodded. 'She enrolled me in a couple of free "come and try" dance classes. I loved it. Ballet, particularly.'

'Did you continue to study?'

'No.'

'Why not?'

'She couldn't afford it. Nor could she get me to class reliably. She often worked two jobs, just to cover our bills.'

Sympathy softened his eyes but Phoebe tilted her chin. 'She was an incredible woman. I will always be proud of her for how hard she worked. She tried her best, every day. And it wasn't easy. She wanted better for me.' Phoebe pressed her palm to her stomach. 'So you can imagine how I felt when I realised I was going to be returning home to walk in her footsteps—a single mother, with a father who may or may not want anything to do with us.' She blinked quickly. 'At least, that's what I thought, when I found out I was pregnant.'

His voice was soft, but rumbly. Deep, as if drawn from the very depths of his chest. 'That would never have been your fate. From the moment I learned of the pregnancy, I have wanted to be here, to support you, to be a father.'

Tears threatened. She blinked again. 'I know that now.'

He expelled a breath and she had the sense he was holding something back, perhaps waiting until later. 'What did she want for you, Phoebe?'

Her mother. Phoebe pressed her fork into the paella thoughtfully. 'Just something better.' She tasted the rice, swallowed, then took a sip of her water. 'But then she got sick, and I had to leave school.'

More sympathy in Octavio's eyes. She focused on a point over his shoulder. His sympathy made her want to cry. Worse, it made her want to stand up and walk around the table, sit in his lap and let him put his arms around her. To hold her until his strength seeped into her and she felt whole again.

She'd been strong for so long. Strong on her own. It had been such a burden to carry, but she couldn't share that with Octavio. She couldn't ask it of him. That's not what they were. His words were burned into her brain, and she knew she'd need to hold them like a talisman in order to keep a cool head in all this.

'What kind of sick?'

'Cancer.' She toyed with her hair, pulling it over one shoulder. 'She only lived a year after her diagnosis. It was very aggressive.' Tears sparkled on Phoebe's lashes then. 'I was devastated.'

'You must have been. What happened to you, Phoebe? You were only seventeen and an orphan. Where did you live?'

She shrugged softly. 'I just didn't tell anybody. I kept paying rent until the lease ended, I kept going through the motions, but meanwhile, I was packing up Mum's stuff and working out what the hell to do with my life. I missed her so much it felt like I'd been shot.' She shook her head. 'I was just in a grief fog, I think.'

He nodded with genuine understanding.

'When did you get the job at the school?'

'That's what I was doing all along,' she clarified. 'When my mum got sick and I needed work. An old teacher of mine had moved there—she got the job for me. It was just basic admin work.'

He reached across then, finding the hand she'd withdrawn from him earlier, and weaving their fingers together, making it harder for her to pull away from him. Not that she wanted to.

'And eventually, you met Christopher.'

Her stomach dropped. She thought of Christopher, his steely blue eyes, dimpled cheeks, short blond hair. She thought of the way she used to look at him and believe him to be the most handsome, perfect man in the world. She thought of all the things she'd thought and how wrong she'd been, and it was a perfect reminder that she couldn't trust her instincts. She couldn't trust that what she felt was actually true. She'd been so wrong about him.

'Yes.'

'Tell me, *querida*, what was the age difference between the two of you?'

Her skin prickled with goose bumps at the easy way he slid the term of endearment into the question. It meant nothing though. He'd used the same phrase the first time they'd been together. It was just habit for Octavio, it didn't mean anything. None of this did.

Reluctance held her silent a moment. 'He was older.'

'How much older?'

She bit into her lip. 'About ten years.'

Octavio's eyes darkened. 'And did he know about your mother?'

'Yes,' she said quietly. 'One of the teachers said something. He'd remarked on me being very quiet, so she'd told him why.'

'I see.'

'What do you see?'

'A man who recognised a vulnerable, grieving young woman and turned that to his advantage.'

'The same could be said of you and me,' she pointed out. Then quickly added, lest he misunderstand her comparison, 'You were grieving. Did I take advantage of you?'

'We both know the opposite is true.'

'Oh, really? How did you take advantage of me?'

His thumb stroked the flesh on the back of her hand. 'Perhaps you were intimidated by me? I am the King. Maybe you felt you had to say yes to me?'

She gasped. 'Don't. Don't say that. Don't turn—what that night was—into that.'

He scanned her face. 'What was that night?'

Heat flushed through her. She felt dangerously close to a precipice she didn't even want to approach, let alone tip over. 'It was *not* that. I didn't care that you're a king. I never did. You asked me to call you Octavio and I did. You were… a man. And I was a woman. And what we shared that night had nothing to do with your position or power or pressure. It was about us wanting each other, wanting to comfort each other. It was a moment of shared madness, sure, but it wasn't a case of anyone being taken advantage of. You can't really think that?'

'No,' he admitted after a beat, and he smiled in a way that made her feel as though she were floating. 'But I'm relieved to hear you don't either.'

She squeezed his hand as a prelude to pulling away, but he held tight and she gave up quickly. It was a weakness, but she liked the way it felt to be intertwined like this.

'It's incredible to think that our babies were conceived that night, and we had no idea.'

'I used protection,' he said, rubbing his spare hand over his jaw.

'I know.'

'You're not on the pill?'

She shook her head. 'Christopher and I had discussed trying for a baby as soon as we were married.' Her voice cracked a little. She'd never get over how duplicitous he'd been, and how completely she'd fallen for his lies.

Octavio's eyes narrowed. 'When were you to marry?'

'About a month after I found out about his wife.'

He swore. 'That seems like a very lucky escape.'

'Yes.'

She looked away quickly. 'We were going to elope. Just the two of us. We were going to go to the South Island, choose somewhere remote and pristine and say our vows, just the two of us. I thought that was so romantic, but now I get it. He just wanted to make sure no one from his real world saw us. I have no idea how he was going to pull it off—I guess a fake minister to conduct the ceremony or something?' She shook her head, anger firing through her now where hurt and grief had once been. 'I can't believe I didn't see through it.'

'Being trusting is not a character flaw.'

'Yes, it is. I was trusting to a fault, and that's not a mistake I'll ever make again.'

'You can trust me,' he said, quietly, with intensity, squeezing her hand as if to reinforce that.

'No, I can't.' She pulled her hand away properly now, reinforcing the fact she was on her own. 'I know you're nothing like him, but I can't trust you; I can't trust *anyone*.' She sighed again. 'The thing is, I guess when it boils down to it, I don't trust myself. I went out with Christopher for years and was so in love with him I just didn't question anything.'

Octavio's features tightened visibly. 'His levels of deception were incredible.'

'But I didn't realise. I didn't suspect. I don't trust my instincts any more. I don't trust my perceptions of people.'

'Okay,' he conceded, rather than pushing a point she was stuck on. 'But let me say this—I will never lie to you. If I say something, it's the truth. That's who I am.'

She nodded, because she knew it was the only way to end the conversation. And she knew that he was probably being sincere. Phoebe also knew that regardless of his assurance, she would continue to protect herself by doubting, by believing him—and everyone—to be capable of the worst. If she'd done that with Christopher, she'd never have been hurt.

'He contacted me the other day, you know,' she volunteered spontaneously.

Octavio's whole bearing changed.

'Christopher?' His voice was sharp. Phoebe glanced at him, nodding once.

Octavio swore. 'He called you?'

'No, he sent a message through the app we used to use.'

'Did you reply?'

She shook her head. 'No. Why?'

'You can't speak to him.'

Phoebe narrowed her eyes. She hadn't been planning to, but the way he was telling her what to do rankled. 'It's really not any of your business.'

'I beg your pardon, but you are my wife.'

A shiver ran down her spine. Not a bad shiver, but a delicious, delightful shiver of warmth. Despite everything she'd just said, despite everything she knew to be true in her heart, hearing him call her his wife so possessively, so intently, set a fire in her bloodstream.

'I am also my own person.'

'Not any more you're not. You are Queen of Castilona and you are a target. People will be trying to sell stories about you for the rest of your life. This man cannot be trusted, Phoebe. If you engage with him again, he will betray you.'

Anger and something like crushing disappointment mingled in her belly, making her throat feel acidic. 'I know that,' she hissed, scraping back her chair and standing. 'He's ruined my life once already. Do you think I'd give him a chance to do it again?'

Octavio stared at her though, a muscle ticking in the

base of his jaw. 'It wasn't that long ago that you broke up. Do you still love him?'

'I hate him.'

'You can love someone and hate them at the same time.'

She pulled a face. 'No.' She was emphatic. 'I don't love him. He's nothing to me.'

'Then it should be easy to ignore his message.'

'Which is what I was planning to do. You don't need to tell me how to act, Octavio. I'm not stupid.'

'Except with him—'

'Don't say it.' She held up a hand, silencing the rest of that sentence. 'I already think the worst of myself for how I was with Christopher. I don't need you to reinforce that.'

He glared at her, the angry words they'd exchanged sparking in the air around them. Octavio controlled his temper first.

'I meant to protect you, not to undermine you. I know you understand what you should do, but when it comes to relationships, things get murkier.'

'I never want to see nor speak to him again.'

'Okay.' Octavio nodded slowly, but it was clear to Phoebe he didn't completely believe her. Maybe he'd learned the lesson she'd been preaching: trust no one. It was just safer that way.

Octavio watched her walk away, a sinking feeling taking over his body. He didn't like it.

He didn't like the way that conversation—argument— had made him feel. He didn't like anything about it. He didn't like her revelations about her ex, what the other man had done to Phoebe, how he'd lied to her and treated her. He didn't like to think how close she'd come to marrying the guy, how eager she'd been to have his baby. He didn't like to think that in an alternate reality, in which Phoebe hadn't discovered the truth, she *would* be married to him by now, perhaps still blissfully unaware of Christopher's duplicity.

But most of all, Octavio hadn't liked the way it had felt to learn that the other man still had a way of reaching out to Phoebe, of contacting her. Of trying to reignite their relationship?

Phoebe surely wouldn't be so stupid, after what he'd done, but the fact there'd been contact between them had flooded his body with ice and something else. Something foreign and unwelcome.

Anger.

The kind of anger Octavio had learned to steer well clear of, because it was counterproductive and clouded one's judgement. Courtesy of his uncle's cruelty, most of Octavio's life had been an exercise in control and restraint.

Only he hadn't felt restrained tonight.

He hadn't felt in control. He'd listened to Phoebe and had felt a violent rage towards Christopher. And then, when he'd learned about the text, he'd felt something else. Something that veered a lot towards jealousy.

He scraped his chair back, as if he could physically reject that feeling. *Jealousy?*

Impossible.

That's not what he and Phoebe were. So she had a past? Big deal. He was her present and her future, and in many ways, their relationship was exactly what he'd needed. She was providing him with the heirs he badly needed, but more than that, their chemistry was like a drug. He just had to be careful not to get hooked. And not to get confused. She was his wife, his lover, the future mother of his children, but they were not a couple, and that was just how Octavio intended for things to remain.

CHAPTER ELEVEN

THEY SLEPT IN the same bed and they made love as if it was the last chance they had to be together—with desperate, fervent passion—but in the morning, a sense of restraint was still between them. A tension that tugged at Phoebe and frustrated her. She didn't want to fight with Octavio. She didn't want to be here in this beautiful, beachside paradise and be at odds with the man she'd married. The man she was having twins with.

And so, as he pulled a fruit platter from the fridge and placed it on the counter, Phoebe took a seat on the stool opposite and rested her chin on her palm, doing everything she could to appear nonchalant even when her tummy was in knots.

'Tell me about your cousin Xiomara,' she started, her voice a little tremulous.

He glanced at her, offering a smile. A tight smile, but at least it was an attempt at civility. Her gut churned. Why should she care if he was annoyed at her? But why *would* he be annoyed at her? Because of their argument yesterday? Or because Christopher had messaged her? She wasn't in control of the latter, or even the former, when it came to it.

'What would you like to know?'

'I like her,' Phoebe said with a lift of her shoulder. 'She was so kind to me on our wedding day. She didn't have to be, but she really took me under her wing.'

'That's Xiomara.' He flicked on the coffee machine and slipped a mug beneath it. The kitchen filled with the aroma of caffeine as it whirred to life.

'You're friends with her?'

He hesitated almost imperceptibly, but Phoebe caught it. 'Yes.'

'Her father is Mauricio,' Phoebe prompted.

Octavio's eyes lifted to Phoebe's. 'Nobody's perfect.'

The joke tugged at Phoebe's lips, drawing a smile from her, and she felt the cracking of their tension, the easing of awkwardness with that one simple quip.

She breathed out.

'You don't like him.'

Octavio looked at her with a hint of bemusement. 'That's well established.'

'Why not?'

Octavio slid a coffee across to Phoebe, then set about making himself one. She lifted the drink to her nose and inhaled it. The doctor had assured her coffee—in strict moderation—was fine, and while she'd been happy to give up almost anything for the babies, this cup of half-strength coffee in the morning was one of life's greatest pleasures.

One of.

Her eyes lifted to Octavio reflexively, as her mind replayed the way they'd spent the small hours of the morning, and she flushed to the roots of her hair. 'Thank you,' she murmured.

His gaze was slightly teasing as it fixed on her, as though he'd read her thoughts.

She lifted the cup to her lips partly to conceal her face from him.

'My uncle is…' He hesitated, frowning, turning away to make his own coffee, so she realised he was doing his share of face hiding as well. 'He's nothing like my father,' Octavio said after a pause.

'Your father was oldest?' she asked, then realised how silly that question was, because of course Octavio's father, who'd been King before Octavio, had been the oldest. 'Never mind. Dumb question.'

'Not so dumb, actually,' Octavio said. 'My father was older, yes, but by only a few minutes.'

'They were twins,' she said on an exhalation, something prickling her spine—a sense of history repeating itself. She pressed a hand to her own stomach, as if she could communicate with the babies there.

Octavio nodded, turning back to face her, coffee cup clasped in one strong, tanned hand. 'All his life, Mauricio resented my father for something which he could not control. My father had been born first. By the law of the land, he was therefore the heir to the throne.'

She winced. 'That must have been hard, for everyone.'

'Yes and no. My father didn't have a resentful bone in his body. He was naturally very good at things. Sport, academics, he was well-liked, popular. Power came easy to him. Even without his title, his command was apparent.'

'Sounds like someone else I know,' she said, with sincerity.

Octavio's smile was automatic, almost dismissive. She wondered if he recognised the truth of her words.

'I think generally, twins are quite close. Almost codependent. The same could not be said for my father and Mauricio. For every accomplishment my father enjoyed, Mauricio seemed to act as though he was being robbed.'

'How do you know this?'

Octavio rubbed a hand over his jaw. 'Things I heard as a boy, things I've learned since, things I've read—quotes that Mauricio stupidly gave to journalists when he was in a fit of pique.'

'Why then would your parents nominate him to serve as your Regent?'

'They had no choice. It's enshrined in the constitution.'

'Right, I think I was taught that.'

Her mind had become hazy with all the lessons she'd consumed between getting engaged to Octavio and marrying him. 'Just the essentials,' her tutors had assured her. It hadn't felt at all essential to Phoebe to learn the obscure laws of Castilona, at least not in order to get married, but she'd sat there and paid attention. Mostly.

'Obviously they had no thought of dying. They were young, both in excellent health. Their deaths couldn't have been foreseen.'

'It was a car accident, wasn't it?'

He nodded, but slowly, like he was buried in deep thought. 'They were overseas, for work. Their trip took them to a remote village high on a mountain, where they intended to tour a school. Rain had been forecast, but it turned into a flash flood. Their car was caught in a deluge and pushed off the edge of the cliff.'

She shuddered. It was awful. Truly awful. 'Octavio.' She reached across for his hand, tears sparkling on her lashes. Pregnancy hormones regularly pulled at her emotions, but this was more than that.

'I know,' he said, and something morphed in her body— a sense that they understood one another's deepest thoughts and needs without words. It was a closeness she'd never felt before. But how ridiculous, a voice in her head chastised. They were *not* close. Not in any way but the physical. They were virtual strangers, still dancing around, getting to know one another gradually. Weren't they?

She'd *known* Christopher. Known him for years, but

never really understood him. She'd thought she could trust him with her life, and he'd betrayed her. Knowing someone was a fallacy.

She couldn't wrestle with the conundrum a moment longer because Octavio was talking again, almost as if the floodgates had been opened and he couldn't—or didn't want to—close them.

'I remember the day I heard so clearly. Everything about it is burned into my memory. Where I was, the light, the sound of Rodrigo's voice, when he came to tell me. He had been crying—which was unusual for him. He tried to hide it from me, but I could tell by the way his eyes were puffy and his voice raw. He sat me on his lap and held me close and explained to me that my parents were gone but that they would always love me. He told me that not only would my mother and I always have the stars, but she was now amongst them, so all I had to do was look up and see them sparkle and know that she was thinking of me.' He grimaced. 'I was nine—he was doing his best to be age-appropriate.'

'It sounds like he did a good job to me.' She dashed at her eyes, forestalling the tears that were threatening.

'From then, it was a whirlwind of change. Mauricio was quickly announced as Regent, ruling in my name until my twenty-eighth birthday.'

'Why so old? Why not eighteen or twenty-one, or even twenty-five?'

'Tradition. A tradition that had not, until me, been tested. It was an arbitrary number, decided upon several generations ago. I'm the first monarch to have been held powerless until that age because of the law.'

She sipped her coffee, a hand on her stomach on autopilot. 'You don't feel Mauricio did a good job?'

'I know he didn't,' Octavio said, his voice like steel. 'Everything Mauricio did was about consolidating his own power. I am still not convinced that he wasn't moving the pieces into place to stage a coup, closer to my coronation.'

She gasped.

'He installed loyal friends into the highest military positions, promoted his allies into important political roles. It will take years to gradually weed out troublemakers and ensure our government is working for the good of the people. For his entire regency, his focus was on how he might retain power, even after he was removed.'

'And has he?'

His eyes glittered. 'To some extent, yes.'

She blinked.

'It is one of the reasons I insisted on us sharing my apartment, in the palace.'

'Because the staff might leak to him?'

He hesitated a little. 'And because I needed to know you would be safe.' There was an uneasiness to his voice. Her heart fizzed and popped in her chest. His concern for her was like a firework, but she quickly understood it was not *her* he was worried about, but the babies she carried. That thought was confirmed a moment later when he added, 'Our children are a threat to him. If he could depose me, then he would be King. Once these babies are born...'

'You can't seriously think he means to fight you for the throne? Or that he would do anything to hurt our twins?'

His features, for a moment, seemed to tighten with sheer exhaustion. 'My parents were killed in an accident,' he said slowly, eyes raking her face, as if trying to understand something. 'But before they set off on that road trip, a report was issued from the village to the palace that flash flooding was expected. The report never made it to my parents' driver, nor their security detail.'

Phoebe gasped again, pressing her palm against her mouth. 'You think Mauricio did that?'

'I suspect, yes. It would be impossible to prove now. He's had too long to cover his tracks. But he was at the palace, and even then, he was currying favour in the hopes of gaining power in his own right.'

She bit into her lip. 'Oh, Octavio. I can't believe anyone would be so cruel.'

'Rodrigo suspected it. He was asking questions. And so, Mauricio had him exiled.'

She squeezed her eyes shut. It was damning, if circumstantial, evidence.

'He shut out his own brother, cut him off financially and, as it happened, effectively killed him. I appreciate it might seem far-fetched, but do you understand why I would not take risks with you?'

She nodded slowly.

'And why we had to marry quickly? Even a week seemed too long to wait, when I imagined what strings Mauricio might be pulling.'

'But you invited him to the wedding—'

'To not have done so would have drawn the kind of speculation I prefer to avoid. My intention is to remove Mauricio's thumbprints, his stranglehold, from the country, from government, and then I shall decide how to deal with him.'

Phoebe shivered. Octavio sounded so resolute, it was easy to believe he could achieve anything he wished.

'Won't that cause problems for you with Xiomara?'

He studied Phoebe a long while. 'I hope not.'

'But if it does?'

'I have to do what's right.' There was an uneasiness in the admission, and she felt the weight he carried, all on those broad shoulders of his. She stared at him and his eyes locked to hers, the air around them charging with voltage, so she struggled to look away, even as her cells were dancing with little electric shocks.

'Do you trust Xiomara?' she asked, trying to focus on their conversation.

'With my life.'

'Why, when she's his daughter?'

'She is nothing like him,' he said, as though it were so simple. 'Xiomara is loyal. She doesn't speak badly about him, but even as children, when Mauricio would delight in punishing me for no reason, by taking away things of value to me, she would sneak into my room with a treat and sit with me until I felt better.'

Indignation fired her blood. 'He did *what*?' Her voice was halfway to a screech.

Octavio shook his head. 'It was a long time ago.'

'So not only did he rule in your name, he was your legal guardian?'

'Only once Rodrigo was exiled,' Octavio said darkly. 'My parents had no control over who could rule the country in my name, but they did have a say over my guardianship. Rodrigo was appointed shortly after my birth.'

'And so that bastard sent him away.' She shook her head.

'With Rodrigo gone, every parental decision fell to Mauricio. He must have hated me, *querida*. For who I was, what I was destined to become, and most of all because I am so like my father.'

She blanched. 'He should have *loved* you for all those reasons.'

'Hatred is all he is capable of feeling.'

'That's his loss,' she said angrily. 'I don't know how I'll ever be able to be in the same room as this beast of a man again without giving him a piece of my mind.'

Octavio's laugh surprised her. Deep and throaty, it set fires in her pulse when she least expected it. 'While I appreciate the sentiment, I don't need you to protect me. I am more than capable of looking after myself.'

She stared at him and acknowledged that he was right. Octavio could look after himself, easily, *now*. He was smart and strong and powerful, and commanded as most men breathed. But what about the boy he'd been? What about the dear little nine-year-old who'd been shockingly orphaned and was cast adrift from the parents he'd loved, and then the uncle he was closest to, to be raised by a man who saw the throne as his stolen birthright?

'Yes, well, nonetheless, perhaps you might wish to keep Mauricio and me apart for a while. At least until the maelstrom of my pregnancy hormones has settled.'

He hadn't intended to confide any of that to Phoebe. Much of it was intensely private, thoughts he'd never shared with another soul. But as they'd spoken, and her big, intelligent eyes had stared back at him, her lovely face so expressive, he'd found the words drawn out of him, almost as if they were being magnetically tugged. And he didn't mind.

More than that, he realised she had a right—and a need—to know what he did.

Octavio had immediately installed his security chiefs to manage his own operations—men and women he knew he could trust implicitly. He knew because he'd been recruiting them for two years, silently, stealthily searching for the best of the best. Ex-military with the kind of code of honour that meant they would always turn to Octavio for leadership and would give their lives to protect the throne. He was not immediately worried about his personal safety, nor Phoebe's, so long as she was with him. But he worried about the palace and the deep tendrils Mauricio had been able to plant there, during his long reign. As much as possible, he'd ensured the staff waiting on Phoebe were newly hired by himself, but that wasn't always doable.

Mauricio had been a terrible legal guardian, except in one way. He had demonstrated to Octavio time and time again how futile it was to let feelings take control.

Mauricio had been cold when compassion had been required. Mauricio had been brutal in how he'd delighted in robbing Octavio of comfort and familiarity, in unsettling his life just as soon as he'd got comfortable. Mauricio held the puppet strings and he'd wanted Octavio to know it.

Octavio would never be like him, except for the fact he had learned to view things through a dispassionate lens. He could zoom out from almost any situation and see the facts calmly, make decisions with ice-cold certainty.

So he had laid out his plans for the marriage to Phoebe, knowing that was how it had to be. And if she wouldn't marry him, he would have kept their babies with him just to protect the children, because without that, the babies would always have been at risk.

And he'd told her the truth for the same reason now: to protect her. Knowing what she was up against and why trusting him was a necessity was the best thing for her and their baby.

He'd told her things he'd never told another soul—but not because he'd wanted to share with Phoebe, per se. This wasn't about them. It was about dispassionately acting in her best interests; it meant nothing.

CHAPTER TWELVE

BEING DRIVEN BACK to the palace was strange. They'd come here after the wedding and Phoebe had felt so estranged from Octavio. But after two nights in close confines, sharing a bed, making love, expressing their deepest thoughts and feelings, Phoebe felt a closeness to Octavio that the palace could very well threaten. Though they sat on opposite sides of the sumptuous back seat of the car, separated by the middle section, his presence seemed to wrap around her, making her skin flush and her heart race.

'You're quiet,' he murmured, as the car cut through the beautiful countryside, the city in the distance reminding her of the real world awaiting them.

'Am I?'

He bumped her knee with his. 'You know you are. Is everything okay?'

His concern warmed her further. 'Yeah,' she agreed. But she glanced at him and his sceptical expression made her smile. 'Okay, I'm not.'

'What is the matter?'

'I'm wondering about what happens next?'

'In what context?'

'When we go back to the palace.' She pulled at a piece of invisible lint on her trousers. It was an elegant suit, delivered with the rest of the clothes Marie had arranged for

Phoebe. She wasn't sure who had packed the bag for her honeymoon, but they'd chosen a selection Phoebe had found beautiful and flattering all at once.

'I'm still not understanding…'

Her cheeks flushed. 'With—this.' She gestured from her chest to his.

'Our marriage?'

'You're really going to make me spell this out, aren't you?' she muttered, glancing towards the driver, who was separated from them by a thick glass screen.

'It's soundproof. Unless you press that button, our conversation remains private.'

She bit into her lip. 'I just mean, we shared a bedroom back there. But in the palace…'

Octavio's eyes darkened. 'It was your decision not to share a bed at the palace before. On our honeymoon, it was your decision to change that. And when we get back, it will still be your decision.'

It was an answer that wasn't an answer, and it didn't tell her what he wanted. She looked towards the side window, watching as the countryside zipped past in a blur of brightly coloured fields and then shocks of green—the vines lush and overgrown as the summer sun did its work to fatten and sweeten the grapes this country was famous for—and in her stomach she felt a tightening knot of frustration.

She'd come to Castilona in a knee-jerk reaction to Christopher's betrayal. She'd come here because she'd always wondered about this place, because she'd felt alone and adrift. She'd come here seeking family and connection, wanting to learn about her father and to understand a part of who she was.

Instead, she'd met Octavio. There were times when they were together that made her feel as though none of that mattered. Nothing mattered that had come before—there was only them, a moment, a shared consciousness, almost. But then reality intruded, and she was reminded of all the reasons this would remain a carefully navigated partnership rather than a true relationship. The fact they were sleeping together couldn't be allowed to derail the fact that neither of them wanted the complications of anything more serious.

'If we were to share a room,' she said, turning back to face him, 'it wouldn't change anything, would it?'

The relief in his face was palpable. He reached across and took her hand. 'No. It couldn't.'

She felt something strong and sharp inside of her. She wanted to believe it was a sense of relief, but it didn't feel or taste like it. This was a bitter sensation, spreading through her and leaving emptiness in its wake.

But she was the one who wanted to be sure they were taking care. Sleeping with him didn't mean she trusted him; it didn't mean she would ever let her guard down with him. How could she, after what Christopher had done to her?

'Well, we can't really have the King sleeping on the sofa for the rest of his life,' she pointed out, as though it were simply a matter of logistics.

'There are other apartments we can move to. Bigger, with extra bedrooms…'

'We're going to need extra bedrooms,' she reminded him, gesturing to her stomach.

'A few extra,' he agreed.

Her insides felt all squishy. She might never risk her heart again, at least not in the romantic sense, but she would fiercely love and protect their children and give them absolutely everything in life. She would no longer be alone. She would no longer feel adrift.

'Yes, a few,' she agreed.

'But not one for me?'

Her eyes locked to his. It felt like an important question,

as though it required an important, thought-out answer, but in the end, it was simple. She shook her head, because there was not a single doubt in her mind that when it came to their marriage, the physical side of it was something she couldn't—and didn't want to—fight.

Octavio felt as though he could run ten marathons. He felt as though he could box with a wild bear and win. He felt as though he was a king not just of Castilona but of everyone everywhere. Power thrummed through his veins as he stared down at his wife's passion-ravaged face, her eyes huge, her cheeks flushed, and he had a primal, animalistic thrill because *he* had done that. He had caused her voice to grow hoarse from screaming his name, had caused her to run her nails down his back as though wanting to draw blood and reclaim her sanity.

And when his own pleasure had burst through him, it had been like a wildfire, totally untamed, all-encompassing, dangerously addictive.

Danger?

He pushed the word aside. There was no danger here.

Phoebe was his wife. She was his country's queen, the mother of the children they were expecting. She was his lover. She was many things to him, but none of them represented danger. Each aspect was separate, easily contained, kept distinct from the other, and he would never allow the lines to blur. It was the key to a successful marriage, he was sure of it.

He pulled away from her with regret, but only for a moment. He fell onto his back, the sheets crisp beneath him, and then drew her to his chest, enjoying the feeling of her soft skin against his, her breathing as she exhaled, her breasts crushed to his side. Even her stomach was sensual, growing with the lives he'd put there. Something like eupho-

ria burst through him. It had been a long time since Octavio
had felt that everything in his life was going to work out,
but with Phoebe at his side and the babies she was growing in his future, he felt a level of complacency he hadn't
known in a long time.

Since his parents had died and Rodrigo had been banished.

Since Mauricio had taken over his life.

He stroked her spine slowly, gently, wondering if she
would fall asleep? It was late, but he wasn't tired. In fact,
he was the opposite—energised after the return from their
honeymoon and this—their first night in the palace as a
married couple.

It had gone so well.

A shared dinner, during which she'd asked questions
about Castilona and its history, the palace and its importance, his goals for the country's future. Her eyes had zipped
with excitement, so he'd felt her shared love for this place,
despite the fact she'd only been here a matter of months.

What did that matter?

Castilonian blood ran through her veins and that side of
her was just waking up, stirring to life. She was Queen of
a country to which she belonged but had never known—
Octavio could certainly help fix the latter. They agreed that
dinner would be a time to strengthen her understanding of
Castilona. Though she had tutors, their lessons covered
the basics in an academic sense, whereas Octavio spoke
with passion and duty, with the loyalty and love of a man
raised to rule.

Phoebe had seemed completely swept up in his stories,
and he'd enjoyed that feeling, too.

Afterwards, she'd stood and held her hand out to him, inviting him with that simple gesture, but also with her eyes,
which seemed almost to plead with him…and he'd pleaded

right back, until they were riding a wave of ecstatic contentment together, bodies entwined, pleasure wrapping around them, through them, in a way they both needed.

'Octavio.' She tilted her face, so he felt her eyes on his features. His breathing was still rough, his chest moving with each inhalation. 'May I ask you something personal?'

He continued to stroke her back, ignoring the flicker of wariness in the pit of his gut. Why shouldn't she ask him whatever she wanted? They were married, he'd already shared things with Phoebe that he hadn't intended to and the world hadn't stopped spinning.

'Of course,' he said, his voice easy, hiding his initial reaction to her entreaty.

'After your uncle sent Rodrigo away, where did you live?'

It was the last thing he'd been expecting, and yet it shouldn't have surprised him. He'd glossed over his childhood, and yet someone as astute as Phoebe must have wondered.

Nonetheless, he tried to keep emotion out of his voice. 'I was moved to a smaller palace, in the south.'

'Why?'

His smile was a ghost of that expression, laced with the kind of bitterness even time couldn't dull. 'He said it was to shield me from the press, from my grief. But in removing me from this palace, he removed me from everything that was familiar, everything that reminded me of my parents. And he surrounded me with new people. New staff, new tutors. A nanny he'd hired.' The final sentence he spoke with undisguised resentment.

'You didn't like her?'

He tried to quell his feelings. To push them deep, deep down, just as he always did. He tried to contain the anger he felt when he reflected on that time in his life, remembered how vulnerable he'd been, how much he'd needed the adults responsible for him to do better. But it was there, whipping through him, like the building of a storm. 'No, *querida*. I didn't like her. I hated her.'

She stroked his chest, her fingers drawing invisible figures of eight. 'Because she wasn't your mother?'

'Because she was awful,' he corrected.

Her fingers stalled a little. 'Actually awful, or awful in a way that you would have felt about anyone who was charged with your care at that time.'

'Her name was Benita,' he said, slowly, and even now, so many years later, a shudder ran through him. 'And when I misbehaved, which according to her was very often, she would lock me in a room no bigger than a wardrobe, with no light except for the tiny sliver that came under the door.'

Phoebe gasped. Her fingers pressed flat, so her palm was against his chest, as if she could reach through time and draw him out of that dark space.

'She said young princes needed to learn to be tough. That she was hard on me for my own good. When I cried—and remember, I was nine, and my parents had just died—she smacked me until I stopped.'

Another gasp, this time more of a half-sob. 'How dare she?' Phoebe pushed up onto her elbow so she could see him better, keeping her body pressed to his side, and he was glad for the physical comfort of her nearness.

'One day, a servant saw her smack me and reported it to palace security. Enough people had been made aware that she was removed. Someone else was sent.'

'Someone better?' she asked hopefully, but with a frown around her eyes that showed she was beginning to understand.

'Someone who didn't use physical violence to punish me,' he said, holding her gaze for a moment and then looking away. 'Marta was the second nanny—'

'The second of how many?' she asked indignantly.

'There were many. I stopped learning their names as I grew older.'

She closed her eyes, her delicate features showing pain and outrage. 'What was Marta like?'

'She also believed I had to be tough. I suppose Mauricio explained this to each of them, because no matter which nanny I mention, they all shared a common trait of cruelty, which was supposed to be for my ultimate benefit.'

Phoebe's eyes sparkled with tears. He felt her indignation. She stroked his side again, her fingers shaking a little.

'Marta would promise things and then withhold them for no reason. A phone call with Rodrigo that was then taken away because I'd made spelling errors, or the promise of a run after dinner that was removed because I'd slept late. Within a few months, I realised that the more I wanted something, the more she delighted in denying it to me. I learned a lot from her, and I don't mean in the academic sense.'

A tear slid down Phoebe's cheek. 'And after Marta?'

'Marta I had for several years. She retired and then there was Ines. She employed a combination of techniques to toughen me up, notably taking me into the bush surrounding my palace and leaving me there, telling me to find my own way home.'

Phoebe gasped. 'You were a *prince*,' she pointed out. 'How dare she? What if something had happened to you?'

'Mauricio would have been delighted.'

Phoebe ground her teeth. 'Did you ever see him?'

'Twice a year I would come back to this palace.'

'He must have wanted to see you a little, then?'

'On the contrary, it was written into my parents' wills.'

Her cheeks flushed with anger. 'Do you think they knew what he would be like?'

'No. I don't think they could have imagined what a cruel and power-hungry man he was. They pitied him, I believe, for his resentment. It made him so small and bitter, and they were both far too kind to be able to understand the things he was capable of.'

'What was it like when you came here?'

'More of the same. I was assigned to a room far away from where I had once lived, far away from all the rooms that were familiar to me. Mauricio delighted in telling me things about my parents that I know to be false. He would hint that both my father and mother had cheated, that they'd never been one hundred per cent sure I wasn't a bastard, that he couldn't see any of my father in me. This, at least, is provably false.'

'You look so like him,' Phoebe murmured, scanning his eyes.

'Yes, and not only that, I have done a DNA test. I didn't trust Mauricio not to go to the papers with the story. If he did, I wanted to have a counter-argument ready to go.'

Another tear rolled down Phoebe's cheek. He wiped it with the pad of his thumb.

'The only good thing about being in the palace was Xiomara.'

Phoebe placed her chin on his chest, eyes still locked to his face.

'She was here, and she would come to find me, work out how to sneak me away from my nanny. We would run and play and she would bring me food from the kitchen—treats, like I'd enjoyed when my parents were alive. With her, the sun started to shine again. I always paid for it, afterwards, but it was worth it.'

'Did she get in trouble?'

'She had her mother to protect her. While her father ruled the kingdom in my name, and also my life for a time, in their family, Mira—my aunt—was in charge, at least of Xiomara. And for Mira, Xiomara could do no wrong,' he added with an affectionate smile.

'Then what about you? Surely Mira could have intervened on your behalf? Surely Xiomara told her how miserable you were?'

'I don't know if she ever understood the extent of it. My nannies did an excellent job of teaching me to be tough, to rely on no one. To trust no one. Besides, my time with Xiomara was too precious to ruin with complaints.' He sighed. 'Also, she was the one person who still treated me like she had before the accident. She'd always looked up to me, seen me as the strong, older cousin. I didn't want that to change by breaking down to her.'

'Oh, Octavio,' she sighed, dropping a kiss to his chest. 'How absolutely awful.'

'Yes. It was. But it's all ancient history now. I am King, and Mauricio will have to live with that.'

She pressed another kiss to his chest; he felt a tear splash down beside where she'd placed her sweet, full lips. 'Despite all his efforts, you are a good man, Octavio. He must hate that.'

'He hates everything about me.'

'Then that's his mistake, and it's his loss.' She looked up at him, and he saw now her cheeks were completely wet with tears.

That was the last thing he'd wanted. He used both palms to wipe them dry.

'Please, don't cry, Phoebe. This is all in the past—none of it matters any more.'

Her smile was twisty, a haunted reflection as she studied him intently. 'Doesn't it?'

Her words haunted him as he fell into a sleep that was fractured by memories of an upbringing he wished to forget.

CHAPTER THIRTEEN

'*THIS IS ALL in the past—none of it matters any more.*'

Phoebe replayed those words through her mind over and over again in the days that followed. Days that turned into nights and bled into days, which all took on a predictable, comfortable pattern. Days separated from Octavio—often he was gone by the time she woke up, but that was fine, she'd come to expect it. Even when she craved him and wanted to see him, she refused to feel disappointed, because this was the schedule they'd tacitly agreed to stick to.

Besides, in the evenings, she received her compensation. They shared dinner each night, and then they shared a bed, and it was in bed that she felt as though pieces of her were slotting into place—pieces she hadn't even realised were missing. It was there that she felt as though all their barriers slipped away and they were just two people communicating in the most basic and essential way. Neither sought to protect themselves, they were both totally open to and subjugated by the passion they shared. It commanded and controlled them; it *was* them.

It was in bed, a week after their troubling conversation on the matter of his upbringing, that Phoebe lay with her head pressed against Octavio's chest, listening to his heart, and she felt her own heart beating in perfect unison. As though they had been designed to run at the same time, to the same beat. As though they had their own beat, and her heart had somehow managed to find his.

It was a thought that came totally out of nowhere and almost took her breath away with how fully formed and strong it was. But also, how *wrong* it was.

There was no such thing as a silent matching of hearts. How fanciful.

Besides, her heart had nothing to do with Octavio and their marriage. Her heart had nothing to do with anything—Christopher had made sure of that.

But the next night, curled around him, naked and covered in a slight sheen from their lovemaking, her body stretching with the new life they'd created, she felt it again. This time, a physical tug in the region of her heart, as though her body were trying to force her to reach out and grab him. Not just grab him, but to take his broken heart in her own and make it better.

She fell asleep with a small frown on her lips and the undeniable sense that things were morphing beyond her control, in a way she was entirely uncomfortable with.

And then, she had the dream.

The dream that had perhaps been forming on the periphery of her mind for some time. A dream that was born of all the experiences she'd had recently. Her feelings on becoming a mother, her missing her own mother, Octavio's admissions about his treatment at the hands of his uncle.

'All I want is for him to be loved,' a woman's voice whispered through her mind.

Phoebe was standing beyond the palace, looking through a locked glass window at Octavio. He sat in a chair in the middle of an empty room, staring straight ahead, not seeing her. Phoebe went to knock on the glass, but her hand couldn't quite reach it.

'As a mother, it's what you want most for your child,

Phoebe. To know that someone sees them as they are and loves them for that person—flaws, dreams, ambitions, all of it. My Tavi deserves to be loved.'

All Phoebe wanted was to make Octavio see her. She tried for the glass again, but it was as though an invisible barrier was holding her just far enough away that she couldn't break through.

And then, in that way dreams had, everything changed, and suddenly Octavio was fading before her eyes, slowly losing colour and becoming invisible.

'I could accept dying but for one thing. Leaving my child behind, knowing that he would be alone and how he would miss us. I hoped someone would love him, would hug and hold him and make the hurt better. But no one did. He hurt so much, for so long.'

She could only see his eyes now...jet-black, staring straight ahead. The rest of his body had faded into nothing, leaving the most haunting, awful sense that churned Phoebe's insides.

Then even his eyes disappeared, and Octavio was completely gone...

She woke, screaming, so Octavio woke, too, reaching for her instantly, looking around to ascertain if there was a danger.

'Phoebe?'

'It's—'

Her heart was racing, her body was covered in sweat. She stared at him, reaching for him, sobbed when her fingers connected with warm flesh. There was no barrier here. Octavio was in their bed, close enough to touch. She wrapped her arms around him and hugged him, listening to his heart again—racing now at the shock of being woken by a scream, as her own was racing from the shock of watching him disappear.

'Are you okay?'

She nodded, her throat thick. She wasn't sure she could speak.

'It was a dream. A terrible dream.'

She felt him stroking her back, seeking to reassure her. All she could think about was the way he'd disappeared before her eyes. And a voice, his mother's voice, though Phoebe had never heard it, pleading with her to love him.

Her throat felt thick. She was caught between the dream and reality, between who they were and what the dream had seemed to push her towards.

Sadness clawed at her insides.

It was a construct of her own pregnancy. An amalgam of her hopes for their babies and a reflection on the things Octavio had endured.

'Would you like to talk about it?'

She instinctively shied away from that. How could she talk about it when she barely understood it? How could she talk about it to Octavio, of all people?

She forced a smile but the effort physically hurt. 'That's okay.' Her voice was hoarse. She cleared her throat. 'It was just a dream.'

Except, it wasn't just a dream. It was a tangible force that prevented her from sleeping, so for once she was awake when Octavio stirred and stepped from their bed a while later. Naked, glorious, but broken. Broken in a way she hadn't fully understood before now. Broken in a way she saw and wanted to fix.

But why?

Why should she?

Would he even want that?

'My nannies taught me to be tough. To rely on no one.'

Was it a lesson that could be unlearned? Would he come to understand that she could be trusted?

Phoebe stared at his back, rigid and strong, and her insides swirled. More importantly, could she trust him? What she'd been through with Christopher had been devastating, but Phoebe had been a grown woman who'd known herself to have been loved by her mother for her most formative years. Octavio had had the rug pulled from under him at a vital age and had then been raised by a man who—from the outside—seemed determined to destroy the young Prince.

'Octavio?' she said his name into the room, as the dawn light softened their surrounds and made everything seem almost coated in gold. He turned, frowning.

'You're awake?'

She nodded.

'Because of the nightmare?'

'In part.' She hesitated. 'Do you need to go straight away?'

His frown was infinitesimal. 'Do you want me to stay?' he asked as he moved back to the bed and sat next to her.

Her stomach was a tumble of nerves. She did. She wanted him to stay desperately, but she was terrified of this conversation. Just as she was about to tell him she was fine, that he could leave, she heard his mother's voice; she saw Octavio disappearing from her and she sat up straighter, reaching for the sheet and folding it under her arms.

'Just for a bit. I need to speak with you.'

But why had the dream devastated her so much? Why had the thought of losing Octavio flooded her with so much pain it had been like a visceral, gaping wound? What could she say to him now? Was she really going to tell him that a version of his mother's ghost had come to her in a dream? It sounded ridiculous. She shook her head. This wasn't about the dream; it was about what he'd told her.

'Octavio.' She put her hand on his thigh. His strong, powerful thigh. All of him was strong, his power was absolute. And yet he'd been emotionally stripped raw as a boy by an adult who'd been trusted to care for him. Her outrage overtook anything else. 'What happened to you, after your parents died...it wasn't okay.'

A muscle jerked in his jaw. 'I've made my peace with it.'

'But have you? Have you really?'

'It was a long time ago, as I said.'

'But isn't it still affecting you?'

His nostrils flared. 'My uncle has no ability to affect me any more.'

'I can see why that's important to you to feel, but he was the one person who could have loved you and shielded you and really cared for you, and instead—'

'Instead he did everything he could to make me miserable. For as long as I was his ward. Yes, I am aware of this. But I came of age more than ten years ago. I dealt with my feelings then. Now all I care about is retaining the power that is my birthright and erasing his damage from my parents' legacy.'

Her heart panged and it was impossible to miss the feeling, nor to misunderstand it.

She didn't want that to be all he cared about.

She wanted him to care about her, too. Not just as the mother of his children, but as a woman. As the woman he'd married, the woman he wanted. She wanted him to more than care for her; she wanted him to love her. If Octavio loved her, would she trust herself to love him back? Would she be willing to risk getting hurt all over again, but so much worse than it had been with Christopher?

Was it even an option?

It wasn't about trusting herself to love. Somewhere along the way, she'd fallen in love. Actual love—the all-consuming, heart-stopping, world-shaking love. She couldn't pinpoint the moment it had happened, but when she looked back, she wondered if even that first night, in the hospital, when she'd stayed with him instead of doing the smart thing and leaving, if there hadn't been a part of her that had somehow been destined to be with him. To love him and to help him accept that love was safe after all. At least, it was with the right person.

Her tongue darted out and licked her lower lip. She stared across at him, her heart in her throat, her whole body on tenterhooks.

'Is that all you wanted to talk about?'

She stared at him, terrified. She loved him. She loved this man who'd told her again and again that their relationship would never be real. She loved a man who was so emotionally closed off because of what he'd endured that she had no idea if she'd ever get through to him, but she knew she had to try.

'No.' The word was almost a groan. She closed her eyes on a wave of nausea. 'Octavio, in my dream, you were in the palace and I couldn't get to you. You were there, staring straight ahead, but you couldn't see me. I kept trying to knock on the glass but I couldn't quite reach it. There was something invisible holding me back. And then you started to disappear in front of my eyes, fading away from me, and I couldn't stop it. I lost you, and it was the worst feeling in the world.'

He frowned, as though he couldn't comprehend what she was saying. 'But I'm right here. It was just a dream.'

'You're missing the point. I thought it was a bad dream, and it was, but maybe it was actually the dream I needed to have to wake me up and make me see with my own eyes what my heart has been telling me all along.'

He was suddenly very still, his features locked in a mask of disciplined coldness. 'And what's that?'

She wanted to bury herself under the sheet; she wanted

to run away. But she couldn't. Not after starting this. 'I love you.' Three small words, so simple, but so life-changing, whether they were returned or not. 'I love you,' she repeated. 'I love everything about you. I know what we both agreed this marriage would be, but it's so much more than that. We're going to be parents, a family, and I want to start that with total honesty. Mostly, I want you to know that you are so loved. By me. I love you,' she said, again, when he was silent.

He closed his eyes, his face paling before her eyes. As though it was the worst thing she could have said. As though he had hated hearing it. 'I see.'

'I don't think you do,' she contradicted fiercely. 'I *love you*. All of you. I love who you are, who you've been, what you've done, what you're working towards. I love that you're going to be the father to my children. I love you.'

He stood then, dislodging the hand she'd placed on his thigh. 'With respect, you do not.'

Her heart twisted but she stayed the course. 'I think I know how I feel.'

'You're misinterpreting it. You're seeing sex and reading love. They're not the same thing. I warned you about that.'

'They're not the same thing, but nor are they mutually exclusive. I love you. I love having sex with you. Both things can be true at once.'

'But they're not. This is just about the sex. And maybe a bit about your pregnancy hormones making you feel things—or want things—that would turn this sham of a marriage into something more desirable. You want to believe we're living some kind of fairy tale but that's not what this is. We got trapped by a stupid one-night stand and we've made the best of it.'

She sucked in a sharp breath at his awful, hurtful words. How dare he say that?

'I'm not saying I'm not pleased. I need an heir, and you being pregnant means I will have not one but two, and quickly. This is very good news for me. But I have been clear all along about what you mean to me, what our marriage is to me. This is a means to an end, nothing more.' His nostrils flared. 'You *do not* love me.'

She swallowed hard but her mouth was dry and her tongue would hardly cooperate. He turned towards the wardrobe, disappearing inside of it and returning only moments later dressed in an impeccable suit, looking regal and untouchable. She shivered.

'Don't think about this any more. It's a silly child's fantasy, and you and I both know better than to hope for that.'

He began to walk towards the bedroom door, and she was so angry she would have pitched something after him if there were an object to hand.

'You can say that a million times, it won't change the way I feel, Octavio. I love you!' She shouted the last words, as if by raising the volume of her voice they would permeate his stupid, stubborn head and find their way to his heart.

He slammed the door when he left the suite, and Phoebe fell back against the pillows, tears forming on her lashes.

He felt like a caged predator, a wild beast that had suddenly been locked away, as he went through the day's meetings, scheduled back-to-back, just as he usually liked it. But today, he would have killed for an ounce of breathing room. Just a little freedom to think clearly about Phoebe and her dream, her words, particularly three little words she'd said again and again. Only the moment he allowed his mind to turn to her, to recollect her face as she'd said those words, everything in his body had come to a catastrophic stall. It was as if his blood ceased pumping, his heart ceased working, his lungs stopped inflating, his cells froze. Every part of him rejected every part of what she'd said. He couldn't let her do this to him. He couldn't let her make him think and feel…feel anything.

It just wasn't what they were, and it sure as hell wasn't what he wanted.

But was that the truth?

Hadn't there been a small part of him, a part that Octavio had immediately tamped down, that had heard her words as one might see a perfect ray of light piercing thick, grey clouds? Hadn't there been a part of him—the part that his childhood had all but destroyed—that had wanted to revive and delight in what she was offering him?

He dropped his head forward on a rush of disbelief and determination. There was no way he would be so stupid as to let that part of him grow, however. Octavio knew what he wanted in life, he knew how to get it, and most importantly, he knew what Phoebe and his marriage were. This wasn't about love.

It wasn't about anything personal.

But what if it is? That niggling voice pushed, harder and with more determination. What if, despite all his efforts, something about Phoebe had got under his skin, too?

He tried to follow that thought through to its conclusion, imagined the impact that would have on their marriage and the way their relationship would change. He imagined the power she would have over him, the destructive ability to *hurt* him, and he knew it just wasn't possible. To love someone was to trust them in a way that Octavio had learned never to trust. It would make him vulnerable, and Octavio had to be strong—for himself and the sake of his country.

Phoebe didn't love him. She couldn't. She had been caught up in a fantasy, because of their marriage and the pregnancy, but she'd see and accept the limitations of what they were again soon. Wouldn't she?

Thoughts like this chased themselves around and around his head all day, and as the day drew on, the thought of returning to his apartment, and to Phoebe, kept having the same impact on him. He didn't want to see her; he didn't want to risk having more of the conversation she'd started that morning. He couldn't hear her say those words again, knowing that he'd never return them. Even if he wanted to. Which he didn't.

He was gripped by a need for space and time, by a need to run away. And though it was a childish urge to surrender to, as the afternoon fell, he called for his private secretary. 'I'm going to the embassy in Spain for a night or two.' He took a deep breath, imagined how Phoebe would feel when she realised that he was hiding from her.

Coward, his inner voice growled. *Be man enough to face her.*

But then he saw Phoebe's face in his mind, and everything inside him began to twist with panic. He had to get away. 'There's something I want to work on there. Would you have someone let Her Majesty know?'

With a curt nod, the aide was dismissed and Octavio was able to breathe a little more clearly.

She caught him as he was on his way to the helipad and her temper was such that she clearly didn't notice the guards standing watch just across from them.

'You're running away? Are you kidding me?'

His eyes narrowed, a muscle jerking in his jaw. He hadn't wanted to see her again; he hadn't been prepared for this. Clearly his message had reached her prematurely; he'd planned to be in the air before it was delivered. 'I beg your pardon?'

'You can beg all you bloody want. You won't get it. I never had you pegged as a coward, Octavio.'

He glared back at her, his nostrils flaring. 'You have no right to speak to me like that.'

She flinched. 'Don't talk to me like I'm a stranger.'

'You are acting like one. What the hell has got into you?'

'You're running away.' She jabbed a finger against his chest. 'Because you're scared to finish the conversation we started this morning.'

He turned towards the guards and dismissed them with a gesture. Alone in the corridor, just a flight of stairs from the rooftop, he turned back to her. 'That conversation is already finished as far as I'm concerned.'

'You think?' She folded her arms with a huff of something like disdain. 'You think you can just walk out on a woman who's baring her soul to you?'

'You are letting your hormones control you. This will pass.'

'Don't you dare do that. Don't gaslight me. I know what I feel and I know what I want.'

He drew himself to his full height, his expression ominous. 'Unfortunately, so do I.'

'And it's not me?'

'It's this marriage, with you, and it's these babies, but it is not love, it is none of the things you spoke of this morning.'

'Wow.' She blinked quickly, her body trembling slightly. With anger? 'So you're saying you don't love me?'

He stared at her for several long beats. 'We've discussed this.'

'I need to hear it. Say the words.'

But it was a bridge too far. Octavio knew what was in his heart, he was pretty sure he knew what was in hers, too. This wasn't love, for either of them. He wasn't a complete bastard though. He had no interest in saying things that were bound to hurt her.

'I've said how I feel.'

'No, you haven't. Not directly. So say it,' she challenged, shoulders squared.

He focused hard on her face, willing her to see into his soul, to understand that he would never love anyone. It just wasn't a part of his capabilities any more. It was no deficiency of hers; it was just how Octavio was. As he'd been bred to be, after his parents' death. 'I have no wish to hurt you.'

She flinched.

'I have always been clear about that.'

'Yes, you have. Calculatedly so.'

'You say that as if it's a bad thing.'

Her lips trembled a little. He felt the bones in his body grow tight and painful. He looked away, dragging a hand through his hair. 'I'm not running away,' he said quietly. 'But we both need some space from this. In a few days, you'll realise how stupid it all is.'

She flinched again. 'Loving someone isn't stupid.'

'Did you love Christopher?'

Her face paled. 'Don't bring him into this.'

'Why not? You were wrong about him. How do you know you're not wrong about me?'

'Because you're a completely different person. Don't you think I've thought of that? Don't you think I've been fighting with myself about that—you, him, my flawed judgement—this whole time? But you are *not* him, just like you've said. You are his exact opposite in every way. Loving you is not a mistake, and it's not based on a lie.'

'Maybe it is. Maybe I've been lying to you without realising it. Because if you're standing there expecting me to be able to say that I love you, then you've totally misunderstood who I am and what I want in life. And how can you be in love with me, if that's the case? How can you love someone you don't know?' He felt as though he'd landed the winning shot. His words made so much sense, all the sense in the world, so he breathed out, relieved that he'd offered an argument that would surely sway her.

He took a step backwards, preparing to escape, but as he turned his back, she said, sadly, softly, 'Or what if I know you better than you know yourself? What if I can see what you're not capable of seeing? What if I love you so much that I understand how hard it is for you to admit you love me back, but I'm willing to wait? What about that, Tavi?'

He didn't want to hear that. He didn't want to hear it and take it on board, and so he kept walking, shoulders squared, face set in a mould of determination. It was only as the helicopter took off that he dropped his head forward and admitted to himself that he had the strangest sense his world was crumbling down around him again, in almost the same way it had when his parents had died.

CHAPTER FOURTEEN

THE HELICOPTER LIFTED and the palace began to look small. Tiny, really. A place that held so many memories for Octavio, so many memories of his life. His time with his parents and Rodrigo, times of happiness and care, of love and warmth. Times that he hated to think back to, despite their warmth, because of how badly they contrasted with what came next.

The loss, the grief, the despair. The feeling of being completely uprooted from everything and everyone he'd ever known. The conclusion he'd reached at that point, that there were no guarantees in life. That the only thing he would ever be able to control was himself, his interactions with people and who he let near him.

And so he'd been careful.

He'd been careful in terms of who he surrounded himself with, he was careful with his time, attention, focus, relationships. His boundaries and rules. He was careful *all the time*. And it was exhausting. But what was exhaustion when the alternative was allowing someone else to hold the controls to your life and happiness?

So he was still careful, even with Phoebe, which was precisely how he knew he didn't love her. He didn't *need* her. He'd be fine without her. The whole idea of her loving him was a construct, some kind of romantic notion dreamed up because of the pregnancy. Just like he'd said to her. She was hormonal. Fanciful. Just plain wrong.

He dropped his head forward as the air whooshed out of his lungs.

Had he actually said that to her?

The morning's conversation came rushing back to him, the conversation he'd been avoiding remembering all day. He could see now how hurtful he'd been. He'd chosen words almost as if deliberately aiming to wound her, to insult her intelligence and—what had she called it?—gaslight her. He'd been so afraid of what she was saying, of the picture she was painting, of even the merest possibility that he might not have been able to maintain the control he fought so hard for, that he'd responded to her brave confession by shutting it down in the most direct way possible. Because he hadn't wanted to hear it.

He'd panicked.

The city was now a blanket of lights, and yet he could still pick out the landmarks, the layout, the streets and parks he knew so well and was now in command of.

He loved this place. He loved his people. He loved the honour that had been bestowed upon him, to be King of this ancient Mediterranean country. There he was able to love without restraint, because countries could not hurt people. Countries could not wound.

Was he so afraid of Phoebe hurting him?

No.

It wasn't that. It was a deeper fear: that he might lose her. That he might lose not just her, but one day, her love. That she might turn away from him? That he didn't deserve her. Just as all those nannies and his uncle Mauricio had made him feel, all his life.

He was afraid. Terrified.

And hadn't he known that all along? From his first meeting with Phoebe, hadn't he sensed something within her that was different and unusual, something that threatened not just his equilibrium but the very safe, very ordered lines he lived within? The intensity of his need for her—not just physically, he conceded now, but in every way—had overtaken his senses from that first meeting. When he hadn't been with her, he'd craved her. He had fought that, tooth and nail, pretending that he was only proposing because of her pregnancy, pretending that their marriage was the last thing he personally wanted, when wasn't the opposite true? He'd wanted *Phoebe*. Not as the mother to his heirs, but for herself. Her wonderful, beautiful self.

But he'd run from that. He'd been running from it for as long as he'd known her, fighting himself and what she was coming to mean to him, because of the survival skills he'd developed to cope with the emotional abuse he'd endured every day since his parents' death, until finally, as an adult, he could liberate himself from that oppression.

He sat up a little straighter, a strange heady rush of adrenaline pumping through him.

He knew his upbringing had been wrong and cruel. He knew that he'd been deliberately worn down, and he thought that had made him strong. Despite their attempts, he'd grown up and shown them all: no one could break him.

No one could hurt him.

But what if they were hurting him still? What if their efforts to whittle away his joy had long, snaking tendrils, creeping into his life still, stopping him from seeing what was right in front of him? What could be in front of him for all time, if he played his cards right and was very, very lucky? It was a risk—but wasn't everything? Wasn't getting in this helicopter a risk? A plane?

He was almost breathless when he reached for his headset and slipped it in place, allowing him to communicate directly with the pilot. 'Take us back to the palace. Immediately.'

Phoebe had stayed in the corridor until the sound of the rotor blades had disappeared and then she'd begun to walk away. Slowly. Each step felt like she was wading through mud, and that had nothing to do with her growing stomach.

It hurt.

Everything hurt.

The last thing she'd called after him was that she was willing to wait for him to wake up and realise how he felt about her. But was she really? Could she do that? Could she live this life, by his side, raising his babies, knowing he might never love her back?

Or worse—that he might love her but have no idea how to admit it?

She groaned, pressing her fingers to her forehead. She was lost, wandering aimlessly through the palace, staring at ancient art, flowers, guards' faces, seeing nothing, because her whole heart and mind were taken up thinking about Octavio and how much she wanted him to see what they were. She wanted him to trust this, but he wouldn't. She knew how stubbornly he wanted to hold to his habits of not letting anyone in, and she could understand why. Hearing about the way he'd been treated after his parents' death only hardened her resolve to be brave: to admit she loved him and put herself on the line again. Just like with Christopher.

But nothing like it, at the same time.

She had never loved Christopher. She could see that now. She'd needed him in the sense of the time they'd met—even years after her mother's death she had still been floundering and miserable. He'd filled a void for her and distracted her from the worst of her grief. She'd become used to him and had liked spending time with him. Theirs had been a relationship of natural progression, at least for Phoebe. She'd liked him, therefore she'd thought it logical that after a certain amount of time she might love him. And a little time after that, she'd realised that the sensible thing to do was to get married and start a family. It had all been a series of steps, a path she'd started on and just kept following because…why not?

It wasn't like that with Octavio.

She needed him because of who he was. She hadn't been able to get him out of her head from the very beginning because he'd started to exist in her blood. Meeting him had been the striking of a match and the next minute, she'd been in the middle of a full-blown wildfire. The heat was scorching, her love for him would not end. She stopped walking and closed her eyes.

When she opened them, she glanced around, a little lost. Where was she? This part of the palace was no longer familiar. She pushed through a door, nodding once at the guard outside, finding herself in a room that was very old, very formal and very beautiful. If somewhat intimidating.

She took a seat by the unlit fireplace and stared at it, wondering when the aching in her heart would stop.

He had no idea why she'd ended up in the cigar room, of all places, but according to his guards, that's where his wife had gone after he'd left. His wife. The words took on a whole new significance now. Octavio jogged through the corridors, thinking with a small smile of what his mother would have said. She had scolded him when he'd run like this as a child, delighting in the never-ending expanses of corridors, perfect to treat like a sports stadium when he was bored. She'd scolded him but always with a slight smile in place, as though she understood that a fire was in his soul, and this was the only way to put it out.

He ran faster, until his lungs hurt, and as he rounded the corner of the corridor that housed the cigar room, a guard, who had perhaps been feeling the effects of a long day at his post and was almost asleep on his feet, reacted with a look of shock to see the King come sprinting past him.

'Your Majesty,' the guard said in surprise.

Octavio didn't stop.

Only when he approached the door he wanted did he slow down to allow air to fill his lungs so that he would be capable of speech. The guard at the door gave him a quizzical look and then nodded once.

'Her Majesty has not left.'

'Excellent. See that we are not disturbed.'

'Yes, sir.'

Octavio hesitated at the door a moment, but he'd come this far and wasn't going to let a little something like last-minute nerves get in the way. He knocked on the door perfunctorily and then pushed it open, his gut twisting at the sight of Phoebe. His wife. His pregnant wife. His beautiful, kind, selfless, pregnant wife, who had also suffered so much in her life and deserved better than to ever feel like this. For the woman in the chair across the room was a study in grief and despair, and he had done that to her.

He closed the door and crossed the room, startling her out of her reverie just as he had the guard.

'Octavio!' Her eyes widened, her pinched features did their best to rearrange themselves and hide the sadness she was feeling. 'What are you doing here?' She wiped her hands over her skirt. 'I thought you were flying somewhere or other.'

'I was,' he admitted. 'I got up there and looked down at

the palace and thought of you and realised that this, here, is exactly where I want to be. So I came back. I came home.'

Home. Yes. That's what Phoebe made him feel—that he had a home. And it wasn't about the palace, but rather wherever she was. It had been so long since he'd felt anything like that. It was a revelation to Octavio, but the revelations kept coming.

'Oh.' But she was uncertain and unsure. Could he blame her? She'd put herself out on a limb for him, not once but twice. He thought of how brave she'd been to admit her feelings even to herself, but then to confess them to him that morning and chase him down this afternoon. She had been brave where he'd been determined to fight and hide.

'I'm sorry,' he said, because it felt important to admit that. He'd messed up. He knew it, he wanted her to know it, too.

'It's fine. You were right. You were honest with me from the beginning. I let my own wishes get in the way of reality. I wanted this to be a real marriage. I wanted us to love each other and to be having a baby out of love. Maybe that's because I never saw that with my parents and always craved the ideal of a happy family. For whatever reason, I imagined something that wasn't there. You don't have to apologise for not being as stupid as I am.'

'You're not stupid,' he responded indignantly. But his gears were churning, his mind spinning. 'Are you saying you were wrong about your feelings?' And did that matter? Having realised how he felt, wasn't it his job to be brave and admit that he loved her, even if she took back what she'd said earlier?

'I'm saying I shouldn't have brought any of this up. I wanted you to know how loved you are, but you don't need that. You don't want it. I was being selfish, saying what I wanted to say without respecting that it's the last thing you wanted to hear.'

'That's just not the case, Phoebe. You are never selfish, and it's certainly not selfish to tell someone you love them.'

'With you, it is. So I'm the one who's sorry.'

'Stop. Don't do that.' His voice was raw and he realised then how much she was hurting him—without realising it. He pressed a finger to her lips, needing her to stop winding back everything she'd said. He couldn't bear it. 'Listen to me. I don't know what you're saying and what it means. Perhaps you don't feel as you thought you did, or you have changed your mind. Regardless, I need to tell you what I realised, as the helicopter lifted up and took me in the opposite direction of you.'

She blinked across at him, her eyes so lovely and bewitching. 'What?' The word was whispered against his finger, her breath warm. He closed his eyes on a predictable wave of desire. This was not the time to let their chemistry run the show.

'You're where I want to be.' It sounded so simple, and maybe it was. 'You are my home,' he said, because that was the best way to describe it. 'And you have my heart.'

Her own heart was racing so hard she could barely hear him over the gushing in her ears. She heard his words and she was sure she understood them, but what if she was wrong? She needed to be very, very clear before she reacted, because so much was riding on this conversation. The nature of their marriage hung in the balance—because she knew one thing for sure. She couldn't keep living with him, sleeping with him, when she loved and he did not reciprocate those feelings.

'You are my wife,' he said, but in a way that imbued the word with an almost mythical quality. 'The only wife I would ever choose or want. You are the wife I want to live with and love for the rest of my days, to have by my side at all times—good and bad. You are the person I want to raise a family with, hold hands with as the sun sets, share meals with, talk to until our voices are raspy, wake up next to, reach out for in the middle of the night. You are everything I have ever wanted and thought so far out of my reach.'

She gasped, her heart trembling now.

'I realised, as I flew away from you, how conditioned I had been to believe I didn't deserve this. That no one would ever love me. That's why I fought you this morning, and again just now. How could anyone love me? But particularly, how could *you*? You are so perfect—an angel, here amongst men—there was no way I could believe you were actually saying these things. No way I could trust your love to be true.'

'It is true,' she said emphatically, sharply, furious at what those awful nannies had done to him, at the behavioural programming his uncle had employed. 'I love you and you are so, so worthy of that love, my darling Tavi. My husband.' And when she said the word, it was just as imbued with meaning as Octavio had made the word *wife* seem—so much more than a title or a statement of fact. It was everything. A statement of the truth in her heart and the gift she wanted to make of it for him. She caught his face with her hands, holding him steady so she could look at him—but more importantly, so that he could look at her and really see her.

'In the dream I had, you couldn't see me. I was calling to you, and I just couldn't reach you, couldn't make you see me nor hear me. It was a nightmare.'

'I see you now. I see what I have, what I have been blessed with.'

'What *I* have been blessed with,' she said with a shake of

her head. 'You don't understand—I came to Castilona looking for my father. Needing family and connection, after my
mum and after Christopher. I didn't want to feel like this
piece of meaningless flotsam any more, uprooted and disconnected. I didn't want to be alone any more, even when
I was also terrified of making the same mistakes all over
again. But I had no idea that in coming here I would meet
you, my other half, and that we would on that very first
night conceive two babies who would bind us for ever.' A
tear ran down her cheek. He lifted a hand and gently wiped
it away.

'You came to Castilona looking for family, and you found
it,' he said, dropping his forehead to hers. 'And we will still
try to find your father, *querida*, to complete the puzzle for
you. But in the meantime, you are here, and you are mine,
as I am yours.'

She nodded, with a levity in her heart because she knew,
without a shadow of doubt, that he spoke the absolute truth.
This was their destiny, and their fate, and they'd found their
way to it despite everything they'd been through. Or perhaps
because of it. Despite their determined efforts to avoid anything like love, perhaps their experiences had made them
both recognise how special their connection was even before they were ready to admit it. Phoebe couldn't analyse it
more deeply than that, in the moment, but she was aware,
as their lips brushed and held, that something almost magical had happened between them, and she would never stop
feeling grateful and glad.

Except, as time passed and Phoebe fully stepped into a life
with King Octavio—a life in which each knew how loved
and valued they were and what a true partnership they'd
formed—she found her mind turning to the key points of
their relationship, analysing it, and her sense of wonderment

only grew and grew. So much so, that one night, when they were standing on a private terrace of the palace, Octavio's arm wrapped around Phoebe as they stared up at the starlit sky, Phoebe admitted something that she hadn't fully comprehended herself yet.

'That night we met,' she started slowly. 'Do you ever think it seemed almost beyond our control?'

He glanced down at her, frowning a little.

'That sounds vague,' she admitted, laughing softly. 'It's just…' She searched for the right words. 'I told you that my mother was a cleaner in a hospital, and that's part of the reason I took the job at the *clínica*, but lately I've been feeling like it was more than that. Like maybe somehow, on some level, she was pushing me there. Towards you.'

He didn't dismiss it. Instead, he nodded, thoughtfully. 'The night I met you, I was thinking of my own mother. She would say to me, whenever she travelled, *"We'll always have the stars."* It was her way of reminding me that no matter where we were, if we were separated, we could both look out at the sky and see the stars and know we were thinking of each other. But that night, there were no stars. When I needed her most, in my grief, I felt only her absence. I felt alone. And then, there you were, right when I needed you.'

Phoebe's smile was wobbly. 'There's one more thing I haven't told you.'

He waited for her to speak.

'That dream I had.' She shuddered even now, remembering it. 'Your mother was in it. Well, not your mother, but her voice, telling me that her deepest hope was that you would be loved. That you would understand you were worthy of love.'

In response to that he closed his eyes as though his feelings were too deep.

'It made me realise my feelings—and how selfish I was,

in not being honest with you. Your mother was right—you are so worthy of love, and as soon as I understood how much I loved you, I knew that my own fear of making a mistake like I had with Christopher wasn't a good enough reason not to tell you how I felt.' She shook her head. 'It was a terrible dream, but I'm so glad I had it.'

'A terrible dream with a happy ending,' he agreed, placing a hand on her stomach. The babies kicked and they both smiled. The stars shone down on them and Phoebe felt a warm, perfect sense of completion. She knew, without a shadow of a doubt, that she was right where she was meant to be.

EPILOGUE

IN THE END, they learned the truth of Phoebe's father quite by accident. Or perhaps it was yet another example of the hand of fate exerting itself over their lives, driving them towards a future that was truly and utterly complete.

Some years after they'd reached out and grabbed their happiness with both hands, Octavio was meeting with a group of advisors and politicians. He had worked tirelessly to restore the country to a state of good government, and these men were amongst his most trusted team members. Some of them had even served in his parents' government and parliament.

One in particular, he found he relied on quite heavily, in terms of counsel and advice, a man whose wisdom always seemed to be just what he needed to hear in the moment. But there was something else about the man that held Octavio's attention, something familiar that he just couldn't place. It was at the end of the meeting, when Rafael Herrera was packing up to leave, and Octavio couldn't help but notice a certain efficiency to the man's movement that was almost graceful. He felt a frisson of something spark in his belly.

'Would you stay a moment?' he asked, his voice slightly hoarse, his heart racing with the possibility…but surely it was extremely unlikely. The name was not the same, and he'd known this man for years. But perhaps Rafael might have a relation, a brother, who shared the same name as Phoebe's father? Or perhaps he was being fanciful; seeing ghosts out of a desperate need to help his wife. Though she was happier than he'd ever known another human to be, at times, he caught her looking into space and frowning and he'd understood where her thoughts had taken her.

'Of course, Your Majesty.'

'Please, call me Octavio,' he invited, because this was going to be a very personal conversation. 'I wanted to ask you something—something quite unusual.'

'Anything, of course.'

He was not going to just come out and say it though. 'Have you ever been to New Zealand, Rafael?'

The other man looked a little taken aback. 'Is there a reason you ask, sir?'

'You know my wife is from there.'

'Yes, naturally.'

Octavio frowned. Rafael Herrera knew the Queen was from New Zealand and he had undoubtedly seen pictures of her. If there was a similarity between them, wouldn't he have noticed it himself? Then again, according to Phoebe, her father had never known she'd even been conceived. It was a stretch to think he might have been able to make the connection without knowing one existed.

'For some time, she has been looking for her biological father. All she had was his name and the fact that he was from Castilona. Once, we thought we were close—a man was found matching the physical description, name and approximate age, but he had never been to New Zealand.'

Rafael was standing very still, and Octavio's skin lifted in goose bumps all over.

'What is her father's name?' he asked with urgency.

'Carlos Guttierez.'

'I need—I'm—' Rafael looked around, quite helpless.

Octavio moved quickly, grabbing a seat and placing it behind the older man.

'Sit,' he urged.

He collapsed into the chair, dropping his face into his hands.

'And her mother's name?'

'Jennifer James.'

'Jenny,' he whispered, groaning. 'Dear God, Jenny.' He looked up at Octavio, his eyes huge. 'I didn't know.'

'Why don't you start at the beginning, and if it checks out, I will bring this to my wife.'

He found her in the rose garden, a picture of serenity, surrounded by their children, books and blocks, and his heart tightened. Silently he signalled for the nanny to take over— a nanny they had screened and found to be a paragon of love and kindness, just the sort of person one would wish to care for their children when busy with official engagements.

'*Querida?* We need to speak.' He drew her to a private part of the garden and they sat together on a white timber bench.

'Back then,' Octavio explained carefully, after the initial shocking announcement had been made, 'your father did not work as a diplomat—he was a spy, involved in some very dangerous missions. He was holidaying in New Zealand and when he travelled, he always did so under a different identity. His work was very dangerous, and it didn't enter his mind that it would cause a problem for your mother. He says they were careful—she was on the pill, they used protection, he had no reason to think there was even the slightest chance you had been conceived.'

Tears filled her eyes. 'I cannot believe this. And you say you *know* him?'

'I've worked with him for years,' Octavio admitted. 'My parents knew him, *querida*.'

Phoebe gasped.

'A couple of years after returning from New Zealand, he stopped his work as an operative and joined the parliament. He quit once my parents died and Mauricio became King and then returned shortly before my coronation. He is on a committee of advisors I meet with regularly, and I have no doubt, my darling love, that he is your father.'

Tears ran down her cheeks.

'He is very upset,' Octavio admitted. 'He intentionally left no way for your mother to contact him, though he asked me to tell you that, had his life been different, he might have left everything behind to be with her. He says that though their affair was brief, he's never forgotten her.' Octavio hesitated. 'He is married now, though, and has children from that marriage.'

Phoebe blanched, and then squealed. 'You mean I have *siblings*?'

Octavio's relief was immense. He wasn't sure what he'd expected, but her delight in this was more than he'd hoped. 'Yes, darling. Two sisters and a brother, and though Rafael and I agree you must decide how you'd like to proceed, he asked me to let you know that he couldn't wait to meet you, and that he knows his wife and children will feel the same way.'

'I can't believe it, Octavio. We have *family*. Extended family. And a family who can tell us about my mother and about your parents. Can you believe we are really this blessed?'

He stood then, wrapping his arms around her. 'I can, my darling. I really, really can.'

And they were blessed, and a great blessing indeed to the country of Castilona. Before this happy, happy conclusion to their story though, there was a hardship for the royal couple, one that they navigated, side by side, and with the help of cousin Xiomara. Like all expectant parents, every prenatal appointment was a time of deeply mixed emotion. Happiness and excitement, mixed with fear and adrenaline, because it was so easy to believe that something might go wrong.

Phoebe though had become somewhat complacent. After all, these babies were so 'meant to be,' they'd been conceived almost as if willed into existence by fate and angels.

So when she lay on the bed for her twenty-week ultrasound, her stomach covered in goo, the last thing she expected was to see lines of concern on the obstetrician's face, and the announcement that he would need to consult with a colleague.

The director of the *clínica*, Lola Garcia, attempted to distract them, but it was an impossible task. All Phoebe could think about was the unmistakable signs of worry on the doctor's features, and her whole stomach had turned into a tangle of knots.

After receiving the news that parents dread, that indeed, there were medical complications with their pregnancy, Octavio's first call was to Xiomara. His cousin was his closest ally, aside from his wife, the one person he could rely on, always, to have his back.

'Help me, Xiomara. Help me. I'll do whatever it takes...'

'And so will I, Tavi. Leave it with me. Everything's going to be okay. I promise.'

And Xiomara left Castilona with that promise heavy in her mind. Everything would be okay, because she'd damn well make sure of it...

* * * * *

MILLS & BOON®

Coming next month

THE HEIR AFFAIR
Heidi Rice

'Poppy,' he shouted.

The girl's head whipped around, responding to her name. Joy exploded in Xander's chest, as the need shocked him. Those eyes, that face. It was her. But as she turned toward him, depositing the tray back on the bar with a clash of glasses, his greedy gaze swept down her figure.

His steps faltered. And he blinked, exhilaration turning to shock, then confusion, then another blast of hunger. A compact bulge distended her apron where he had once been able to span her flat, narrow waist with a single hand.

He reached her at last, but it felt as if he were walking through waist-high water now as he tried to make sense of all the warring reactions going off inside his head.

But then his gaze snagged on her belly again—and the only question that mattered broke from his dry lips.

'Is it mine?' he demanded.

Flags of color slashed across her cheeks, but all he heard in her tone was the sting of regret when she whispered, 'Yes.'

Continue reading

THE HEIR AFFAIR
Heidi Rice

Available next month
millsandboon.co.uk

COMING SOON!

We really hope you enjoyed reading this book.
If you're looking for more romance
be sure to head to the shops when
new books are available on

Thursday 28th August

MILLS & BOON

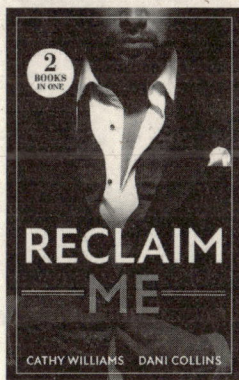

afterglow BOOKS

Afterglow Books is a trend-led, trope-filled list of books with diverse, authentic and relatable characters, a wide array of voices and representations, plus real world trials and tribulations. Featuring all the tropes you could possibly want (think small-town settings, fake relationships, grumpy vs sunshine, enemies to lovers) and all with a generous dose of spice in every story.

For all the latest book news, exclusive content and giveaways scan the QR code below to sign up to the Afterglow newsletter:

SCAN ME

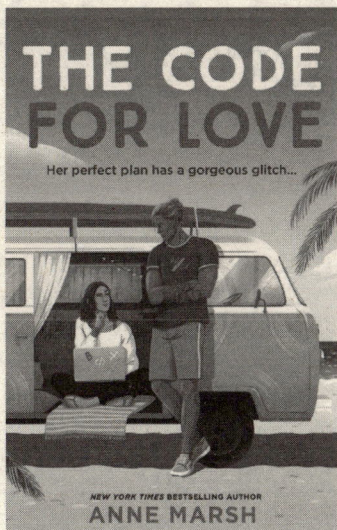

LET'S TALK
Romance

For exclusive extracts, competitions and special offers, find us online:

f MillsandBoon

X @MillsandBoon

O @MillsandBoonUK

♪ @MillsandBoonUK

Get in touch on 01413 063 232

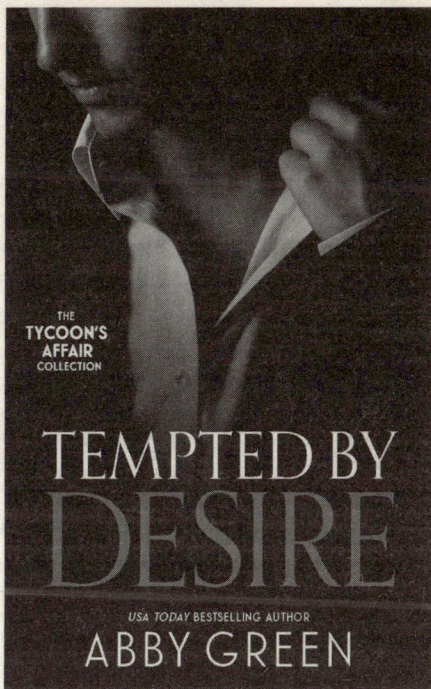

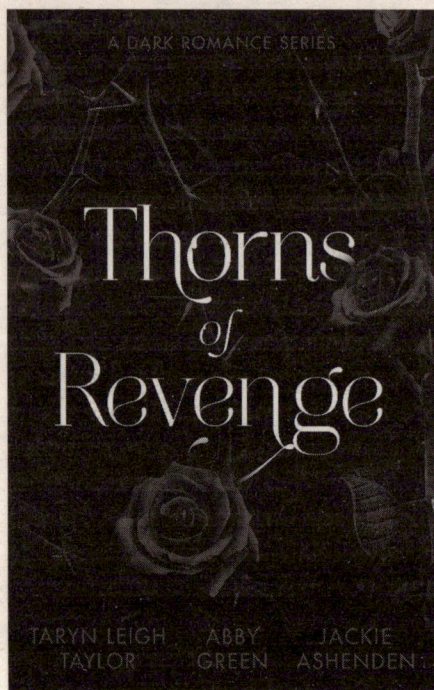